WARLOCK HOLMES

My Grave Ritual

Also by G.S. Denning and available from Titan Books

WARLOCK HOLMES

A Study in Brimstone
The Hell-hound of the Baskervilles
The Sign of Nine (April 2019)
The Finality Problem (April 2020)

G.S. DENNING

WARLOCK HOLMES

My Grave Ritual

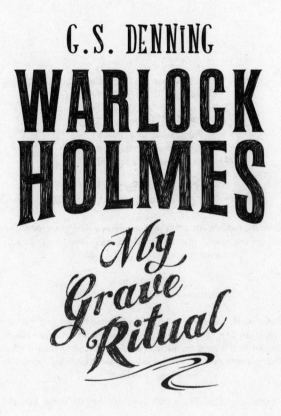

TITAN BOOKS

Warlock Holmes: My Grave Ritual
Print edition ISBN: 9781783299751
E-book edition ISBN: 9781783299768

Published by Titan Books
A division of Titan Publishing Group Ltd
144 Southwark Street, London SE1 0UP

First edition: May 2018
10 9 8 7 6 5 4 3 2 1

Names, places and incidents are either products of the author's imagination or used fictitiously. Any resemblance to actual persons, living or dead (except for satirical purposes), is entirely coincidental.

A CIP catalogue record for this title is available from the British Library.

Printed and bound in Great Britain by CPI Group (UK) Ltd, Croydon CR0 4YY

To the healthy expansion of Geek Culture.
When I was a child, Geekdom was mostly white, mostly
male, mostly straight, marginalized and rather lonely.
Now, as our culture overtakes the mainstream* we at last
begin to realize that geek is not a color. It is not a gender.
It is not a preference (well... not that kind of preference)
and it's more fun for all of us when everybody gets to play.

* Can anyone think of a sports movie that out-earned Avengers?

CONTENTS

The Adventure of the Navel-Starer   9

The Adventure of the Blue Gob-Runkle   61

The Adventure of the Disgusting Stain   103

The Adventure of My Grave Ritual   155

The Adventure of the Copper's Screeches   199

The Adventure of the Red Heads' League   263

The Adventure of the Three Apprentices   315

A Scandal in Boh-grah-grah-grah   355

THE ADVENTURE OF THE NAVEL-STARER

DEAR READER, I BELIEVE I PROMISED YOU AN apocalypse, did I not?

Yes, I recall it distinctly. Two volumes ago, I began this narrative to describe the events of humanity's ruin—and don't think I've forgotten. Yet the fact remains that our downfall was a long, quiet process—a carefully crafted masterpiece of betrayal by a criminal mind beyond compare: James Moriarty. This volume does not contain the final strokes he dealt to our reality, but rather the first ones following his long absence. Though it would take Holmes and me some time to realize he had returned, I shall commence this tale on the very morning he first brought adventure to our door.

An utterly wretched morning, if I'm honest.

In fact, it had been a pretty rotten month and a half since the Battle of Baskerville Hall. Though that adventure ended in victory, my good friend Warlock Holmes had suffered sufficient injuries to knock out eight or nine battle elephants. By mid-December, the danger to his life had passed. Yet, a new danger soon emerged.

11

He was bored.

As less than two months had passed since he'd been impaled through both legs by six-foot wooden spikes, Holmes found himself feeling... less than nimble. Being confined to bed-rest is trying for any man, but Holmes had a particular distaste for inaction. He also had a notable ability to cause trouble with only the power of his will. Recalling the permanent damage he'd wrought to the fabric of reality the last time he'd been incapacitated (see "Silver Blaze: Murder Horse"), I felt it was nothing less than my duty to mankind to ensure that Holmes remained occupied.

But, how to fill the time? His hundreds of books were no distraction—he'd read them over and over. He gained some satisfaction honking away with his concertina and singing boisterous songs, yet this pursuit could not distract him for more than two or three hours of the day (much to the relief of the neighbors, I should think). He loved to doodle. At first I despaired of it, for he tended to scrawl all over his walls, his blanket, his books and whatever else came within reach. His drawings were simple outlines. Crowns and coins, swords and hearts decked every surface he could reach. He liked to draw the same stick-figure family over and over—two parents holding a celebrating child on their shoulders. He'd frequently do little men fighting—one with a huge armored fist, the other with an oversized instrument that might have been a cross or a large hammer. Also featured prominently in his scribblings was a machine of dubious purpose. I asked him what it was, one day.

"Thumbscrews!" he declared, happily.

Strangest of all was a cluster of parallel lines. I'd have thought nothing of it if this grouping appeared only once or twice, but he repeated it constantly. "What is this?" I asked.

"Oh… hard to say, Watson. A bundle of sticks, I should think."

"And why have you seen fit to cover your walls with drawings of bundles of sticks? Look, you've drawn them all up your right arm!"

"Because they are so very easy to do. One can have a satisfying bundle with only a few moments of the slightest effort. You should try it, Watson."

I didn't. Instead, I spent my hours shuttling him sheaf after sheaf of paper and bottles of fresh ink. Better he should cover every inch of 221B in silly little doodles than he should find himself unoccupied. As the days wore on, it became ever more difficult to distract him and I think I came to view myself as nothing more than an overworked baby-minder. So deep was my self-pity that I ignored the terrible clues staring me right in the face. Gods, when I think of it now!

Don't you see?

Why was Holmes constantly drawing the *same nine shapes*? The Crown. The Coin. The Sword. The Heart. The Family. The Gauntlet. The Hieroform. The Cruciator. The Fasces.

Whatever was wrong with me? I suppose I was undergoing a small crisis of self—a moment of fading identity. All of my personal business—and it sometimes seemed, most of my person—had been subsumed by Warlock Holmes.

Until that fateful morning. Until I got the letter.

To Dr. John Watson 221B Baker Street, London, said the front of the envelope, in loopy, purposely important-looking script. The ink was deep violet, the paper so heavy that this single envelope probably cost more than an average meal. I was stunned. I hardly remembered that I *could* receive letters, so long had I dwelt in Warlock's shadow. It was exactly the kind of thing that was needed to reverse my boredom, mend my mood, and make this miserable December Monday worthwhile. Or at least, that's what I thought, until I turned it over.

"Oh God, it's from Percy Phelps."

"Eh?" said Holmes, leaning out from the doorway of his room. "Who is that?"

"A fellow I knew at school. Ugh." I sighed and flipped the letter back onto our table.

"I must say, Watson, you don't seemed pleased to renew the acquaintance."

"No."

"Why ever not?"

"Because he's exactly the sort of mewling little snot you'd expect to be named *Percy Phelps*."

"He can't be all that bad," said Holmes.

"Oh no? Here's a test: I'll just open this letter and read it aloud, shall I? I don't know what he's got to say to me, but I'll bet you a pound of your favorite tobacco that you can't make it to the end without detesting the man."

"What fun! Read on, Watson!"

I tore the envelope open, withdrew the delicate slip of pink paper that lay within and read, "'Watson! Oh, sweet, sweet Watson, do you remember me? Do you recall humble little "Tadpole" Phelps who was in the fifth form, when you were in the third? What fun we used to have—oh, the larkish larks of imperturbable youth! How you would weep, I think, to hear the misfortunes that have befallen your childhood friend!'"

Here I paused to growl, "Friend? He was never my friend. He was my victim, on more than one occasion…"

"Victim?" said Holmes. "But you're not the sort of man who has many victims, are you, John?"

"Generally speaking, I am not. But there was just something about Percy… I don't know what it was, Holmes, but I could never stop myself from bullying him. Perhaps it was just that, no matter how badly I treated him, he kept coming back for more. Perhaps it was only the novelty of thrashing a fellow two years my senior. I don't know. I'm not proud of my behavior. Still, if he'd delivered the letter in person, I'm not sure I could stop myself from punching his froggy little face!"

"*Watson!*"

"Well, I'm sorry, but there is the truth of it. He continues: 'Woe, that the travails of Job should finally have been superseded! And woe again that the helpless recipient of the Almighty's fury would be me—blameless Percy! I had thought that no help might come to me—

mortal or divine—until our mutual acquaintance, Michael Stamford, mentioned that you had fallen into the habit of unwinding mysteries the like of which perplexes me now.'"

Here, again, I paused to mumble, "Mike Stamford, I'm going to punch you too."

The letter continued, "'I will not speak of what befell me. I cannot. My poor constitution could not bear it. Nine days I have been sunk in brain fever, after the event that ruined me. And though it was only by the narrowest margin that I cheated death, I knew I must write to you, sweet Watson. Won't you come to me? Won't you test whether your skills are sufficient to save the dearest friend you ever had?'

"Dearest? What? How dare he?" I howled, crunching the letter in my fist. "Weedy little squid! I wish he were here so I could show him how *dear* he is to me! Argh! I haven't seen him for years—haven't even thought of him—and now, three minutes after he's reintroduced himself, I find myself wishing I could knock him about a bit."

I raged about the sitting room while Holmes leaned out from his doorway, looking bemused. I was about to shout something ungenerous at him, about finding mirth in my misfortunes, when—at last—I realized the most important development of the morning. Such had been my eagerness to receive the letter, then such my disappointment with the contents, that I'd ignored the very news I'd hoped for, for more than a month.

"Wait! Holmes! You're... you're standing! This is amazing!"

"Oh… er… yep. It's really… really good news, I suppose. Yes."

"How has this happened? What a sudden reversal! I must examine you."

"What? No! Or, I mean: there's no need. Everything's fine. You know what, I think I'll just go lie down for a bit. Good night."

He turned to flee back to his bed, but gave the most horrific wobble. It seemed as if he would tumble out into the hall, but he yanked himself back upright in a motion that was absolutely alien to human locomotion. His eyes were full of fear, but not of falling. He wore the exact expression of a five-year-old lad who fears all his shenanigans are about to come to light. With a final, unsteady lunge, he disappeared into the confines of his room.

But not quickly enough. I had already set my jaw and begun a headlong charge towards the hall, to see what it was my friend was hiding from me. In that half a heartbeat between Holmes jumping back onto his mattress and him managing to get the blankets back over himself, I cleared the doorway and beheld his mischief.

His legs…

They were grotesque. His knees were twisted backwards, like a deer, or goat. He had that curious setup, common amongst four-legged herbivores, wherein the legs jut first forward, then back, then forward again, in the manner of a limb which cannot fathom what its own function must be or lacks the decisiveness to pick a direction and stick with it. No wonder he'd been so unsteady. The

His legs… They were grotesque!

transformation seemed more experimental than complete. He still did not possess actual cloven hooves. Or, I assume he didn't. If he did, he'd managed to get his bedroom slippers on over them.

"Wait, Watson! Before you get angry—"

"No. Too late."

"But hear me out: this is really more your doing than mine, you know."

"Is it, Holmes? *Is it?* Did I come in here, surgically reverse your legs, then go to sleep and forget I'd done it?"

"Well... no..." The poor fellow wrung his hands together for a moment. "But you did tell me about how my legs did this after the fight at Baskerville Hall."

"In the presence of an immense magic, which threatened to destroy our world, I think."

"Yes. But *why* did they do it, eh? Don't you see? Perhaps this is their natural state!"

"Natural state?"

"Just so. And perhaps—by returning them to their more natural position—I might ameliorate some of the damage they've taken."

"Holmes, that is preposterous."

"But Watson, *I can walk.*"

"Except that you can't, because I forbid it."

"*What?*"

"As your doctor, as your friend, as a man who does not wish to be burned at the stake as an accessory to witchcraft, I absolutely forbid you to go trotting about on goat legs."

19

He looked at me as if I had struck him, but I refused to relent.

"Put them back," I said, nodding at his legs.

"But, Watson, it hurts."

"That is to be expected, Holmes. Most fellows who have had both legs impaled report a certain level of discomfort. But it is survivable. We'll get you through it. You're going to walk again."

"I already ca—"

"*Normally*. Now, put them back."

He gave me the grimmest of looks, then shut his eyes and began concentrating. With revolting alacrity, the bones of his legs shifted about beneath his skin. The crunching and popping noises they emanated were... well... I'm sure that only the fact that I was a medical professional kept me from vomiting. When it was finished, he stared at me with eyes rimmed with the promise of tears. Not only born of pain, but also disappointment. It was clear: Holmes was ready to sulk.

"There. Are you satisfied? I am an invalid once more. Never to walk again, I shouldn't wonder."

"Holmes..."

"Well done, *Doctor*."

"I'm sorry, Holmes. You know I am. We shall put you back to rights, I promise, but it must be all the way back to rights. We must accept no demonic shortcuts."

He rolled away from me, to face the wall.

* * *

The second letter from Percy Phelps arrived just three hours after the first. It was written on pale green stationery of astonishing quality. Or, no, not quality. *Cost*. It was one of those things which one held in one's hand wondering whether it was more monstrously hideous or monstrously expensive—a carefully crafted affront to good taste. Such was my wonder at who would create such a thing that I later tracked down the particular manufacturer. I can state with confidence that Percy's second letter was written on a paper called "Hopes of Easter's Grace".

The third one was on "Vermillion Effete" and arrived just before sunset.

I railed at both of them, to Holmes, for as long as he would listen. Which, since he was bed-bound and had nothing else for entertainment, was quite some time. Holmes, to my dismay, was rather taken with Percy's flowery bloviations.

"He has the soul of a poet, Watson," Holmes declared.

"No. He has the soul of that wretched little bastard in your prep school who *thinks* he's a poet. The sort of fellow who spends four hours a day staring into his own navel and concocting cut-rate verses about all the universal truths he finds therein. He's sure all the girls ignore him because they don't understand him, when—in fact—they ignore him because they *do* understand him."

"He is suffering."

"Yes. On purpose. Ever since I met him."

* * *

My repeated attempts to get Holmes up and walking were met with staunch resistance. This is not to belittle his ordeal. His pain was real and of no small account, I am certain. Still, he put forth very little effort in healing himself.

That is… until he thought I was asleep. Half an hour after I'd closed my chamber door, Holmes wrenched his legs around backwards again and traipsed off to the pantry to get himself toast and soup. I had been upon the threshold of sleep, but the grinding, popping noises woke me. I poked my head out to find Holmes halfway between the pantry and his toasting racks, looking merry as a satyr dancing in a bacchanalian garden.

And exactly the same shape.

I yelled.

He pouted.

My lack of progress continued until almost noon the next day. Until Percy Phelps's fifth letter. Until Holmes made me the devil's deal.

The fourth letter (Ebullient Salmon) had been waiting, when I awoke. The fifth (The Love and Joy of Man's Orange-ish-ness) was brought up, just as I'd begun to hope that one more cup of tea might induce me to forget the annoyance of the fourth. As I stood in Holmes's doorway, loudly protesting my correspondence-based mistreatment, he interrupted me to say, "Watson. You must help him."

"What? No!"

"But why not?"

"Because I do not care for the man. I do not care for

myself when I'm near him. And besides, he's given us no indication of what it is that's bothered him. You don't know him like I do, Holmes. You have to realize that if he's dropped his biscuit and his butler's not there to pick it up for him, that would absolutely warrant five letters."

Holmes thoughtfully tapped at the first letter (which I had lent him, so that he might enjoy Percy Phelps's "mastery" of our tongue). He regarded the envelope for a moment, lingering over the return address, and said, "Briarbrae House...

"...Briarbrae House..." he said again. "I feel I might be induced to walk there."

"To Woking?" I asked, somewhat archly.

"Of course not, Watson. But... from here to a hired cab. From the cab to a train. From the train to another cab and thence to Briarbrae... Yes, I think I might be induced."

I stared at him levelly. He met my gaze with challenge in his eyes.

"Normally," I clarified. "With human legs?"

His expression faltered, momentarily, as he reflected on the amount of physical discomfort he was promising to undergo.

"Of course, Watson," he said, then added, "I suppose it is about the only place I might be induced to walk to any time soon."

I hung my head and sighed. "I'll just wire ahead and let them know we're coming, shall I?"

* * *

Briarbrae House was a thing of beauty—the worthy seat of an illustrious family. True, December had lessened the beauty of its gardens, yet the smell of winter fir trees went a great way towards compensating for this. The air was just cold enough to be bracing, with another five degrees to go before it became miserable. The bell was answered by an austere old butler, who looked as if he ought to be named Perkins, or Bixby or something. (It later turned out to be Pixby, so I'd been quite close.)

"Dr. Watson. Mr. Holmes," he intoned. "We are so pleased you could come. The staff is perfectly distraught. We dearly hope you can shut the young master up."

Then he caught himself and stammered, "I mean: ease the young master's pain."

"Yes. I think I know *just* what you mean," I said. "I only wonder if we might have a moment to rest, first? The journey has been difficult for my friend."

Holmes was in a state. I'd been cursing myself ever since the train arrived in Woking that I'd let myself be bullied into taking him. A few gentle steps would have been ideal. A trip to a stranger's house, miles away, was the prescription of a doctor working more from frustration than reason. Holmes was pale and shaking.

"Please do not tarry long," Pixby urged. "The young master is insufferable. Oh! No! The young master is *suffering*."

"Well do I know it," I assured him.

As Holmes enjoyed a few moments' much-needed rest, a robust, imp-faced man in his early thirties descended from the upper story to meet us. An I'm-a-bad-lad-up-to-no-good smirk seemed to have conquered his face some decades ago and held the territory against all challengers.

"You two must be Holmes and Watson, eh?" he said. "Glad you made it. Poor Percy's at his wits' end. I'm not sure anything can help my brother, but he seems to pin all hopes to you, and—for my part—I hope he's right."

"I was unaware that Percy had a brother," I said. "In fact, I am unaware of any only child who has a brother."

"Yes, yes, well, he hasn't got one *yet*. My name's Joseph Harrison. No familial relation. But, as Percy's marrying my sister…" His words trailed off, but his satisfied smirk essentially continued the thought: …*I'm about to be tremendously wealthy.*

Perfect.

Yes, just what this trip was missing. Not only was I about to be re-burdened with Percy Phelps, but it appeared I would also be in the company of a transparent gold-digger and her disreputable brother. Wonderful.

"Wonderful!" cried Holmes. "Ah, is there anything sweeter than two young hearts intertwining? Noble Percy: was ever there a soul more worthy to be loved?"

Joseph and I both turned to Holmes, to stare incredulously.

Mr. Harrison pointed one finger at Holmes and wondered, "Is he…?"

"No, he is entirely earnest," I said. "Of course, he has yet to meet Percy."

"Oh, that explains it," said Harrison. "Come on, won't

you? I know Percy will want to see you as soon as possible. Go easy with Annie, though, eh? My sister's not convinced Percy's ready for company yet."

With an air of familiarity that bordered on ownership, Joseph Harrison led us down the hall to the closest bedroom door. He knocked once and called, "Good news! Visitors from London."

"Hush, Joe!" hissed a woman's voice from within. "I've told you before: Percy's nerves!"

Harrison rolled his eyes and swept open the door. There on the bed lay Percy Phelps. He was pale. Shaking. Eyes bagged with exhaustion of body and of character. He seemed aged beyond his years and on the very cusp of collapse.

So, pretty much the same as ever. Slightly more so.

Sitting in a chair by the side of the bed, clutching Percy's hand with rapturous protectionism, sat Annie Harrison.

Immediately, I realized I'd been wrong about her. I had expected one of two scenarios. Possibly, she would be a smoldering temptress, parlaying her natural gifts into a life of comfort. If not that, then a clever-eyed con-woman, undermining Percy's will and insinuating herself into a social stratum far beyond her right. But no. The instant I laid eyes on her, I realized this was a love match.

I suppose we've all met girls like her. Girls who are everyone's hovering mother by the time they're seventeen. Girls who know exactly which hat everyone needs to wear if they go out this evening, or else they shall catch their death. Girls who won't let you eat the shellfish, because they don't like the look of it and you'll thank them later, when you haven't caught typhoid and died. Yes, Percy Phelps was precious to Annie Harrison, but not because of his station. Not because of his wealth.

Because of his weakness of character.

Here was the blanching hypochondriac she'd always wanted: the man who would need her and heed her from the moment they met, until death should part them. She glared at Holmes and me in open challenge. If our intrusion should upset Percy, her gaze promised, she would kill us both. Then, after the funerals, she'd dig up our corpses, kill them, burn them, and kill the ashes.

A perfect match.

"Watson? Is that Watson, come at last?" Percy wailed. He tried to sit up but faltered as soon as his head left the pillow. His eyes darted this way and that, in a paroxysm of suffering, staring all about the room in search of something to anchor him—something to stop his inevitable descent back to the pillow from whence he'd risen. Alas! Too late! With a terrible (theatrical?) shudder, Percy lost his will and sagged back down upon his sickbed. Annie lunged forward to cushion his three-inch plummet as best she could manage, then turned to glare at me with fierce, how-dare-you-you-wicked-man-ish fervor.

Holmes gave a cry of sympathy and staggered to the side of Percy's bed to clutch his hand and assuage his suffering, however he might. I gave a sigh and answered, "Yes. It's me. Now what do you want, Percy? You've written five letters and still haven't said."

"Five?" he wondered. "Have my last three letters not reached you yet? Is there no help from the British postal system in my hour of need?"

"What do you want?"

He didn't say. Instead, he fainted. Then we had to go and wait outside while Annie revived him. Then he was in no shape for visitors. Then we all had dinner, in the company of Percy's long-suffering parents. Then Percy awoke to find himself possessed of a fresh resolve (Annie promised us that he had a boundless reservoir of strength) and felt that he might at last be able to speak about that evening that had so upset him, provided only I was in the room. To speak of his failure in front of Annie was more than his heart could bear, we were all assured.

"Come on, Holmes," I muttered. "Let's get this over with."

If Percy realized his injunction of solitude had been broken, he didn't mind it. He hardly even glanced at Holmes as my friend took Annie's chair by the side of the bed and held Percy's hand as he began his tale.

"As you no doubt know, about ten weeks ago I accepted a position as clerk in the Foreign Office."

"How would I have known that?"

"It was in all the papers."

"What, because the government hired an entry-level clerk?"

"No, because they hired *me*."

Much as I hated to admit it, Percy Phelps had a point.

The illustriousness of his family was such that one of them getting a case of the sneezes might garner the front page of *The Times*. All I could do was mutter, "I can't imagine what motivated them to do it."

"One night, my superior—and uncle—Lord Holdhurst…"

"Ah. That's why."

"…My uncle called me into his office for a special assignment. He gave me a communication from a potent foreign power, and told me to copy it. It was early evening; the rest of the office had gone home, yet he bade me stay and copy the communication, no matter how long it should take. He was most insistent. We were in his office—totally unobserved, I am sure. He gave me a little metal attaché case and bid me examine the contents and prepare a… well… not even a copy, really. I suppose a *synopsis* would be the proper term. He wanted me to glean the meaning—the thrust—of the thing, then put it into my own words, so he could alert the prime minister without surrendering the original. He then left the office."

"And you were totally alone in the Foreign Office?" I asked.

"Nearly. There is a commissionaire—Mr. Tangey—who stays all night, in an office at the foot of the stairs. He shall be important, as you shall see. Well, I began my task, but could make no headway with it. The document—shall I call it a document?—was altogether strange to me. I know not the language it was in, nor could I describe the contents of its message."

"So… difficult to copy, then?"

"Exceedingly. I thought a cup of coffee might do some good, so I rang for the commissionaire I mentioned earlier. Imagine my surprise when a woman came to answer the summons. I did not know her. She explained that she was the commissionaire's wife, that she was our charwoman, and that she would happily have her husband prepare some coffee. She left and I went back to my task. I made little headway. Discerning the meaning of the message was difficult, especially because—it seemed to me—it was constantly changing."

"Changing?" I said. Holmes and I exchanged a loaded glance.

"And vexing me, mightily," Percy confirmed. "I soon realized it had been over an hour. I was desperate to finish my task and go, for my beloved Annie's brother was in town. I'd hoped to meet him and accompany him back to Woking, but I knew my time was short. And I *still* hadn't got my coffee. Well, I stamped downstairs to see what could be keeping that wretched man from bringing my drink and you'll never guess what I found! Go ahead! Try and guess!"

This was exactly the type of challenge Holmes lived for, so he cried out, "An assassin! A minotaur! Pixies?"

"Er… well… no," said Phelps. "He'd fallen asleep. There was my coffee, bubbling away behind the man while he snored on his desk."

"That's nearly as good as pixies," said Holmes, encouragingly.

"What was I to do?" Phelps demanded.

"Pour yourself a cup of coffee and go back upstairs?" I hazarded.

"I woke the man up and began shouting at him!"

"Ah, yes… I'd forgotten your difference in station, I suppose."

"I think he had just begun to realize the seriousness of his transgression, when the bell rang again and the commissionaire's face went as white as a sheet. He tried to interrupt me a few times—oh, the cheek!—and finally, when I asked if he understood why he must be punished, he asked me how I'd rung the bell. I told him I hadn't. Someone else in some other room must have. But he said there was nobody in the building but us, and that the bell was the one for my own office. I began to get a bit worried at that point, so I ran back up to my office, and what do you think I found?"

"Probably *not* the secret document," Holmes reasoned, "or you wouldn't have fainted for nine days and written Watson all those sad letters."

"I say, Holmes, well done! Your powers of deduction are improving every day!"

"Thank you, Watson."

Percy gave a sad wail and threw himself down on his pillows, crying, "He's right! It was gone! *Gone!* And with it all my hopes! From that moment forward, I had nothing left! Nothing but shame, professional dishonor—"

"And several manor houses," I reminded him. "And pots of money. And armies of servants. And the basic surety that you will live a long, luxurious life that would put most of Europe's kings to shame."

I don't think he even heard me. He wrung his hands and complained, "I knew my uncle would be furious. I struck the commissionaire, then summoned the police and made him take me to his house to confront his wife. He said she'd left after asking him to make the coffee. Ha! A likely story! I demanded she be arrested and tortured. But the police found nothing! They've been following and interrogating them ever since and still nothing! Or so they tell me. I'm afraid I missed most of it. I was stricken with brain fever that very night!"

"Brain fever?" As a medical doctor I was familiar with the affliction—it being one of the most epidemic of Britain's made-up illnesses. Whenever one of the last generation of English doctors could not be bothered to diagnose their patient, they would simply declare a case of brain fever, prescribe rest and present a bill.

"Yes, I get it quite often," Percy explained. "We called Dr. Ferrier, who said I was slightly overwrought, but I set him straight. I said this was a clear case of brain fever, if ever there was one—"

There wasn't.

"—and that I must be returned home. Well, they whisked me here and set me up in this very room! They wanted to bring me to my own room, but there were stairs in the way! *Stairs!* So I made them kick Joseph out and put me in here. He didn't mind. He's a solid fellow. And here I have languished, in and out of consciousness. My uncle blames me for the loss of his message! He's furious with me! He's threatened me, several times!"

My eyebrows went up. This didn't sound like the Lord Holdhurst I knew. The man was an arch-conservative politician, but famous for his even temper and courtesy. His political reputation was for upholding basically indefensible beliefs by remaining calm and genial until his opponent's patience ran out, he yelled, and by the laws of British propriety therefore forfeited the debate.

"Do you think you might help me, sweet, sweet Watson?"

"Do you think us to have hearts of stone?" Holmes cried. "Of course we'll help!"

I sighed my exasperation, but was forced to admit, "There are elements of this case that seem to fall under Holmes's special purview. Most especially, that note you were tasked with copying. You say it is not quite a letter, not quite a document, that its meaning is changing? It sounds most irregular. Can you describe the thing?"

"No!" Percy howled. "I dare not! Lord Holdhurst was most clear! I can tell you whatever you like about the case it was kept in, but to describe the… item… to anyone is as good as death to me. Oh, when I think of what he would do to me… It's… no, it's too much! Oh! Oh! Brain fever!"

He threw the back of one pale hand across his brow, moaned, sank back amongst his pillows, and was still.

Finally.

"What do you make of it?" Holmes asked.

"There are certainly some features of interest. What is this strange document? What kind of thief rings a service bell in the midst of their crime? And…" I stared down at the helpless form of Percy Phelps. "…is it wrong to punch someone in their sleep?"

"I should think so," said Holmes.

"Yes. Yes, of course it is," I said, wiping my brow with the back of my sleeve. "I just… I needed to hear it said out loud. Thank you, Holmes."

No sooner had I opened the door to leave than we were accosted by Joseph Harrison. He'd plainly been hovering outside the whole time.

"Did he tell you about it? Do you think you can help?" Harrison asked.

"He told us most of his troubles," I said, "but the case is murky and ten days cold. I'm not confident."

"Well, did you at least cheer him up enough so I can have my room back? He chased me out so fast, I never even got all my belongings."

"Ha! I can well believe it. But surely, he wouldn't mind if you came in to reclaim your things."

"My sister would," Joseph growled, "and she never leaves his side unless his mother sends three nurses to watch over him while she sleeps."

"Well, she's not in there now," I pointed out, but was instantly made a liar.

At that moment, Annie Harrison turned the corner, saw Phelps collapsed across his bed and screamed, "Percy! What have those beasts done to you?" She jammed her left elbow into my belly, her right into her brother's and exploited the resulting gap to force her way into the room, to the side of her fallen love.

Joseph rubbed his stomach and told me, "Just let me know if there's anything I can do to help you get me my room back, eh?"

He turned and trundled off down the hall. As soon as he'd gone, bleary-eyed Mr. Pixby approached and said, in a discreet undertone, "The master and missus are most distraught. If you are able to bring this matter to a satisfactory conclusion—that is, to repair the young master's reputation and constitution to the point where he can rejoin civic life, be married and installed in his own home, far from here—Mr. Phelps would be happy to pay you... well... practically *anything*."

"I'll bet," I harrumphed.

"Will sirs be staying for supper? Shall I prepare chambers for the night?" Pixby wondered.

"No," I said. I stared guiltily at Holmes. To ask him to travel further was cruel. And yet, it was only an hour by train back to Waterloo... "We've already spoken to Percy—the only man in this house who was present at the scene of the crime. There's nothing more for us here. I think we need to visit the Foreign Office and perhaps seek an audience with Lord Holdhurst. Are you up for a journey, Holmes?"

"Always."

* * *

We returned to Baker Street that night, to get Holmes some much-needed rest. The morning found him in better health than I expected. Perhaps his repeated magical restructuring of his legs had helped put them back to rights. Or maybe—and this suspicion had been growing in my mind for some time—Holmes was only ever as wounded as he *remembered* to be. Distracting Holmes seemed always to be a strangely efficacious method of healing him.

When we arrived at the Foreign Office we were met by Detective Inspector Forbes, who had charge of the case. He'd been given instructions to be forthcoming and helpful, yet even the illustrious Mr. Phelps had no power to command him to enjoy our company. To Forbes, we were nothing more than the latest in a long line of ridiculous demands from the Phelpses—hampering a case he had long ago deemed hopeless.

And who could blame him? Eleven days of regular use had quite obliterated every clue the Foreign Office might once have offered. Forbes introduced us to Mr. Tangey, the much-abused commissionaire. In the absence of evidence against him, he'd been allowed to continue in his position, but it was clear that the close attention of Scotland Yard had weighed heavily on him. Forbes confided in us that the investigation against the Tangeys had utterly bogged down. Their inquiries had done nothing but waste the Yard's time and afford the actual perpetrator ample time to pursue his agenda unharried.

We saw the hallway that ran past Percy's office and

examined the exits from the building. The only information they yielded was this: they were exits. Anyone who had left by either of those doors eleven days ago by any means fair or foul might by now be anywhere in London. Nearly anywhere in Europe. We could learn nothing.

Forbes informed us that Percy's office had not been used since the night of the crime. Imagine my surprise when I entered only to find it had been positively ravaged. Papers lay strewn everywhere. Every lock on Percy's desk had been forced, every drawer bottom pried off in search of hidden compartments.

"Is this the result of the investigation?" I asked Forbes.

He bristled at that. "Not *my* investigation. Lord Holdhurst saw fit to mount his own. Now and again, when he's in his cups, he comes down here and mounts another one."

Though it looked as if the room had been thoroughly combed, I nevertheless climbed up on a chair and examined the conduit through which the bell-pull entered the room. Oh, how I had hoped to come down off that chair waving the missing communication and tell Forbes, "Ha! Did you not think to look in there? Did you not realize the criminal stashed his loot before making good his escape? That is why the bell rang when Percy was berating the commissionaire! It was not bravado, not coincidence, but the natural result of a desperate man hiding treasure up against the bell-pull!"

But no. If ever the criminal had engaged in that particular obfuscation, he'd had days to return and claim his prize, and there was nothing to be found but dust and spiderwebs.

"Any luck, Watson?" asked Holmes.

"I fear not. Perhaps we'll learn something from Lord Holdhurst."

"Ugh. Politicians…" said Holmes. "Never liked them. All responsible and grown-up and huffy. But they do tend to be busy, at least. Maybe he won't have time to see us. Wouldn't that be nice?"

Forbes grunted out a laugh. "Oh, I imagine he'll make time. If he thinks there's a chance you know anything of his missing secret, I promise you'll not make it off these premises without seeing him. Go ahead: try and make a run for the door. See how far you get."

Forbes was quite correct. As we exited Percy's office, we were met in the hallway by a sallow-faced clerk who wondered how our inquiry was progressing and whether we might be prepared to report our progress to his superior. Two minutes later, we stood before the massive doors of Lord Holdhurst's office, awaiting our summons. Though there were many petitioners waiting when we arrived, we were ushered straight past them and made to stand before the doors for exactly eight seconds while the clerk went inside to see if his Lordship was ready to receive us. A muffled, yet rough and husky voice from beyond the door shouted, "Yes, damn it! Of course!"

Lord Holdhurst's office was not much better off than Percy Phelps's. Again we saw papers in disarray, furniture out of place and drawers turned out. A surprising amount of clothing was discarded about the room and no small collection of dishes. No sooner had our names cleared the clerk's lips than he turned and fled the room.

From behind his desk, Lord Holdhurst fixed us with a hungry gaze. The man looked practically feral. His hair was mussed, his clothing wrinkled into a most disreputable state. His shoulders heaved as if he'd just been running and his eyes bespoke total exhaustion. Though I'd never met him personally, I knew his reputation well and let me say that if I had not seen several pictures of him in the papers, I'd have never believed this could be Lord Holdhurst. Was this the bastion of traditional English propriety and decorum? He looked like a man ruined by anger.

"Have you found it?" he demanded.

I hesitated, overcome by surprise. Thus, it was Holmes who made our answer. "I don't think so," he said. "Then again, we don't know exactly what *it* is."

"No!" Lord Holdhurst roared. "We won't be speaking of it! Don't ask! It is a secret of the highest import! I'll tell you the same thing I told that fool Scotsman, MacGuffin: it doesn't matter what it is, only that we're seeking it! You'll know it if you see it! You... you haven't seen it?"

"The only thing we've seen is your nephew, Percy Phelps," said Holmes. "He's suffering; did you know?"

"Not suffering enough! He lost it! He ruined everything! My sister won't let me see the little squid! And it's a good thing, too, for I know what I'd do! I'd kill him! I'd kill him with my own hands!"

Lord Holdhurst brandished those hands at us. They were soft and—until recently—well maintained. They were the hands of an upper-class, indoor worker: unused to wielding anything heavier than a pen and utterly devoid of strength, but for that which desperation lent them.

Something was very wrong with Britain's foreign minister. Even Holmes recognized it, for he gave me a sideways glance, raised his eyebrows and cocked one thumb at our host, as if to say, "Would you look at this?"

I gave a nod of agreement and said, "Yes… well… we have nothing to report, so… perhaps we'd best go look for it, eh?"

"Good idea, Watson," said Holmes, beginning to edge back towards the door. "No time to waste, is there?"

"Not a minute," I concurred, beginning my own subtle retreat. "We'll let you know if we find it, of course."

"You bring it right here!" Lord Holdhurst bellowed.

"Oh. Of course. Right here," Holmes agreed.

"Don't look at it!"

"Why would we?"

"Don't open the case! I'll know if it's been opened!"

"Of course you would," said Holmes. "Well… that's all, then. Goodbye. Good luck to us. And… er… we are dismissed."

With that, he reached back and whisked open the door. The two of us leapt through, slammed it shut and leaned back against it.

"That's a fairly intense statesman, Watson."

"Agreed, Holmes. He seems quite unhinged. Probably

lying, as well. Did you hear him say he'd know if the case had been opened? Yet he gave it to Percy and ordered him to open it. Has he seen it since he gave it to Percy?"

"How?" Holmes wondered. "Why?"

"Well, he was one of only two people to know Percy had the thing. And he clearly values it. I'd been wondering if Lord Holdhurst himself might be the thief."

Holmes gave me a doubtful glance.

"I know… it seems unlikely. Yesterday I began to think: suppose Lord Holdhurst found himself in possession of a secret he wished might be lost, yet did not want to be the fellow to lose it. Might he not have given it to Percy then arranged for it to be stolen, just to have a scapegoat in place?"

Holmes gave me an incredulous eye-roll and said, "A fine theory, Watson, and one I might congratulate you on if I had not just seen Lord Holdhurst. Let me tell you something I suspect you know: that man *wants* something. Whatever it is that's missing, he yearns to have it back. He has lost control of himself and the thing that's got control now is called desire."

"I am forced to agree. And didn't it seem… still fresh? He seemed acutely desperate. I cannot imagine how much energy it would take to maintain that level of anxiety for eleven days."

A polite cough caused me to look up. The entire roomful of petitioners was staring at Holmes and me.

"Yes… well… perhaps we had best continue this discussion at Baker Street, eh, Holmes?"

"I think I'd rather continue it in Antarctica than right here. Let's go."

Waiting for us at Baker Street were the three undelivered letters Percy had complained of the day before. In addition, there were three more he'd written that morning. I would have ignored them all were it not for the fact that his father had written one as well. I cut the envelope, folded it open and in no time, gave a cry of alarm.

"What is it?" wondered Holmes.

"There has been an attempt on Percy's life! Last night, as he slept!"

Holmes gave me a queer look, stern and searching at the same time.

"What is it, Holmes?"

"Watson… where were *you* last night?"

"I was here, with you!"

"The whole time? It's not as if I had you in view all night long."

"Holmes! You don't suppose I—"

He leaned in and redoubled the intensity of his doubtful stare.

"I wouldn't kill Percy Phelps, Holmes."

If he leaned any further, he was sure to tumble over.

"No! Look… I may have chucked him in the duck pond once or twice… filled his cap up with figgy pudding… but I would never… *Stop looking at me like that!* See here, Holmes, if my word is not enough for you, check the train

42

schedules! There is simply no way I could have made it all the way out to Briarbrae House, made an attempt on Phelps and returned here before you missed me at breakfast!"

"Bah! Very well!" Holmes cried. "Then your name is cleared by a happy technicality, and yet your guilt is plain to any who care to behold your face!"

"Good Lord, Holmes, you're beginning to sound exactly like Scotland Yard. Anyway, I suppose we've got work to do. Heavy though it makes my heart, it seems we must hurry back to the bedside of 'Tadpole' Phelps and see if we can figure out who's tried to bump the little blighter off."

We returned to find Briarbrae House transformed to Briarbrae Fortress. It seems the old home had served as the regional arsenal some centuries ago. Thus every groom, every stable boy, every cook and scullery maid had been outfitted with ancient helmets and bracers, armed and sent into the field. The grounds were patrolled by gangs of bitter-looking chambermaids armed with sixteenth-century harquebuses, which were certain to be instantly fatal to anyone so foolish as to try to fire one. As we approached, Pixby burst from the front door, armed with a pike and clad in a droopy white surcoat with a red cross. The thing was worn so sere as to be nearly translucent and seemed as if it was old enough to have been used in the First Crusa—

Wait…

No.

No, it's not possible…

Is it?

"Who goes there?" Pixby demanded. Yet, since we were standing right in front of him and he'd met us only the day before, he was in the perfect position to recognize exactly who went there. He therefore demurred, lowered his pike and said, "Ah! Dr. Watson. Mr. Holmes. So pleased to see you once more. The young master is intolerable. No! Ah! He's in *danger*. Terrible danger. That is what I meant to convey."

"Of course it is. Come on, Holmes."

If the household staff of Briarbrae House had been pressed into service as an impromptu army, I might have guessed their general. Annie Harrison had properly fortified Percy Phelps's temporary infirmary. She'd drawn a heavy wooden table across the doorway and stood behind it, ready to challenge any who approached. She'd placed a second table between the room's two windows. Both were lined with a collection of England's finest Brown Bess muskets. Unlike the weaponry on display outside, each of these had been seen to by Annie herself and lay cleaned, loaded, cocked and gleaming. It seems Miss Harrison had no patience for reloading but had piled ready weapons in such numbers that she could simply discharge one, cast it aside and grab the next with such alacrity as to murder an entire cavalry regiment if one should be so foolish as to try to charge her position.

She glared at me. Behind her, her brother leaned

on the second gun table looking apologetic and glum. His eyes were baggy with… not just fatigue, clearly, but actual lack of sleep. I tried to remain calm and calming as I heaved aside the table and squeezed into Percy's sick room/fortress keep.

"All right, Phelps?" I asked.

"Watson? Sweet Watson, is it you? Oh, you won't believe it! As I slept, last night! A murderer! Horror! Confusion!"

"Holmes, would you be so kind as to lower Percy back down upon his pillows and stroke his fevered brow? If you don't I'm sure he's going to faint again and we'll be stuck up here forever. Now tell me about this murderer of yours, Tadpole."

"Well, as I lay, not quite sleeping, composing an ode on the subject of the unknowability of God's plan and how it is unfairly stacked against England's aristocracy…"

It actually was a good sign. As a doctor, hearing that Percy was turning his efforts back to the faux-artistic navel-staring of old was a sure indicator of recovery.

"…I thought I heard a noise! Just there, at the window! I pulled the covers up around my nose and waited. Sure enough, in only a moment more a dark figure lunged at my window from outside and smote it open with a sword!"

"No! A sword?" Holmes exclaimed, eyes alight with happiness. "Horror! Confusion!"

I rolled my eyes at the two of them and stepped to the window Percy indicated. Clearly, the thing had never been sword-smitten, yet I did find a few scratches near

45

the latch. So, by "sword" Phelps was likely to have meant "some flat instrument, slid through the crack to lift the window latch". A screwdriver, perhaps? No, it wouldn't fit through such a narrow gap…

In the course of my investigation, I opened the window and looked down. Practically every flower in the bed below had been trampled and the earth that held them was crisscrossed with footprints. Whatever else, there seemed to have been a fairly impressive quantity of lurking done here, in the past few days.

I closed the window and turned back to Percy. "What happened next?"

"The fellow came straight at me, to that corner over there!" said Phelps, pointing to a dressing table on the far side of the room.

"Hmm… So, in an attempt to murder you with a sword, the attacker steps over here…" I muttered, walking away from the bed to the place he indicated. Next to the dressing table were a few water pipes, which had been poorly fitted when the ancient house gained running water. "What happened then?"

"Well, I knew I was cornered," said Phelps. "What could I do? I knew I must stand and fight!"

"You?" I asked, archly. "*Stood?*"

"No, I didn't actually have to. For, you see, I gave a mighty battle cry. Hearing that he wouldn't have it all his way, my attacker's courage broke. He flung aside his sword and fled through the window."

"You have his sword, then?"

Joseph Harrison gave me a glance as if I were a complete fool and said, "No. We didn't find a sword. Percy had a nightmare, that's what I think."

Harrison seemed to be at the end of his patience with the whole affair. I turned back to Percy and asked, "Did you get a good look at the fellow?"

"No. He wore a dark cloak, pulled up around his face."

"Hmm… And what happened next?"

"Well, my mighty battle cry alerted the household. Annie, Pixby and one of the nurses were in here in a flash!"

"Wait now… There was nobody in the room with you? Joseph told me that either Annie or a flock of nurses were constantly at your side."

Percy colored a bit and mumbled, "Well, yes. Until last night I was never unattended. But you gave me such hope, sweet Watson! I thought… with you on the case… perhaps I was well enough to be on my own."

"So, the 'murderer' struck on the very first night you were alone? That is telling. Now, Annie, when you arrived, was the window open?"

She clenched her musket in both hands and gave me a grim nod which not only let me know that the window had been open, but also that if she ever found out who had opened it, she would gun him down that very instant.

"Unlikely to have been a nightmare, then," I noted. "Unless it was one that could open a window."

"Oh, there are plenty of those, Watson," Holmes assured me.

"Nevertheless…"

I turned my attention back to the far corner of the room and was rewarded, in short order, by the gleam of silver from behind the water pipes. Leaning down, I extricated the culprit, held it up for all to see and asked, "Percy, is this your butter knife?"

"Yes. But I have no idea what it's doing back there."

"I think I might," I said, with a smile. I looked about the room, carefully gathering my thoughts and vetting my theories. Yes… the case was coming together.

"What shall we do, Watson? How shall we protect Percy?" Annie demanded.

I gazed out the window at the failing light. December days are short and darkness, I knew, would soon hold sway. "This is what I suggest…"

The Briarbrae Militia was disbanded. As this was accomplished without any of the grooms blowing their fingers off, I consider it an unqualified success.

Percy was moved to his own quarters—a task more difficult than dissolving any militia you care to name. There were stairs in the way, you see. I gather he was no great enthusiast for them, even when he was well. A great team of grooms, gardeners, stablehands and—I made sure—Joseph Harrison were led from one sick room to another by the indefatigable Pixby. Tadpole Phelps mewled the whole way.

I'm sure Annie Harrison wished to be ever by his side, but I could not allow it. I had other uses for her. I let her wrap Percy up in a cocoon of soft blankets and mop his brow, but as the litter-bearers scooped him up, I blocked Miss Harrison's way. "Madam," I told her, "I am afraid you must remain here."

I was pleased she wasn't carrying one of her muskets at that moment, or those would likely have been my last words.

"What are you talking about, sir? By what right do you pretend—"

"Has anybody told her my occupation?" I wondered aloud.

Straining beneath the weight of Percy Phelps (and a few hundred blankets), Joseph grunted, "Listen to him, Annie. He's a doctor."

Miss Harrison's eyes went wide. I could barely contain my smile. We doctors enjoy a number of social allowances that should never have been extended to us. Lenders are unshakably certain that a doctor will be able to pay his debts, no matter how crushing. Constables seem to be willing to let us get away with a bit more than the average gentleman, but their tolerance is nothing compared to what judges allow us. Nevertheless, there is no facet of society that grants us greater stature than these: hypochondriacs and worrywarts. To them, we are next unto God.

Annie faltered. I spoke. "It is of utmost importance that Percy be given time to recover his own internal strength. He must have no outside assistance. Like a baby bird which cannot flourish unless he bursts his own shell, Percy must either take heart and grow strong, or he will be coddled and begin his final decline. You might think it a kindness to offer Percy your hand in his hour of need but I tell you this: if you go to attend him tonight, Percy will *die*."

Did I say next unto God? To those who thrive on over-concern, any doctor who is willing to foretell doom far outranks the Almighty. Annie Harrison steeled her features and asked, "What must I do?"

"Stay right here. Should the murderer decide to finish his deed, he will no doubt return to the place where he believes Percy to be resting. Look: darkness is gathering. He may come at any time. Hold this room, Miss Harrison. Do not leave it for anything, or it may be the end of Percy. If you need food, ring the bell. If you need to use the lavatory... er... look, there is a flower pot. Do you understand the severity of this responsibility? Will you do your best to preserve Percy?"

Of course she would.

Poor Miss Harrison missed quite the dinner that night. To the Phelps family and the staff at Briarbrae, any tiny move towards normalcy was an occasion for raucous celebration. Sherries were called for and quaffed with great abandon by any who cared to partake. Then brandies. Then a surprising quantity of Scotch whisky. I was a bally hero, too. Though I was constantly seized by the shoulder, shaken, congratulated, and offered libation, I did my best to abstain. So did Holmes, though I always knew I could count on it. Due to brandy's complete failure to be either toast or soup, Holmes had no interest in it. After an hour or so of such treatment, I began to make our excuses.

"No, no, no. Holmes and I have urgent business in London."

"But won't you—"

"We shall return tomorrow to check in, but I expect every success."

"Are you sure you won't—"

"I'm afraid we cannot. Come along, Holmes."

On the way out, I stopped at Percy's former sick room to make one important modification to my defenses. "Miss Harrison, may I have a word? I fear I may have made a mistake placing you *within* this room. What if the killer should spy you through the window? You might scare him off. Or he might be armed with a pistol, you see? No, I think it would be better if we placed you in the hallway, just outside the room. That way you are in no danger and yet positioned to make sure the killer cannot make his way further into the house."

Miss Harrison heartily agreed, dragged her table full of muskets to the other side of the doorway and fortified herself in the hall. At last, I was free to leave.

As Holmes and I stepped out into the cold December air, my friend mentioned, "You know, Watson, it's a pretty inconvenient hour to try and get back to London."

"We're not going to London," I told him. "We are going to the next flower bed down from Percy's sick room."

"Are we? To what purpose?"

"To finally solve this thing and extricate Tadpole Phelps from my twice-damned life. Now, come on. We've got to go a way along the road so it looks like we've left, then double back and get in position."

The flower beds did not offer sufficient concealment, but Holmes found a little stand of trees that would suffice. It had a good view of the windows to Percy's old room and yet enough concealment that we might easily go unnoticed. Even the moon did its part, hiding behind the clouds and shedding very little light across the lawn. Holmes moved with complete normalcy, his wounds seemingly forgotten, along with his strange desire to sport goat legs. Indeed his chief complaint was, "It's cold, Watson. Are you sure this is going to work?"

"I think so, Holmes. I have a narrative that suits the clues and can think of no other. It begins with the question: 'Why would a thief ring a bell in the middle of his crime?'"

"I can think of a dozen reasons."

"Of course you can, Holmes, for you possess more creativity than sense. But try this one on for size: because he did not intend to *be* a thief! Let us recall that Percy expected to meet someone in London that night."

"Oh! Joseph Harrison?"

"Just so. Let us suppose Harrison tired of waiting for Percy and went to call on him at the office. He finds Percy gone, rings for the commissionaire to see what has become of him, then his eye lights on… well… whatever it was that Percy and Lord Holdhurst seem so eager to hide. Does it have a clear monetary value? If so, Harrison might easily have seized it and made good his escape while Percy harried the commissionaire downstairs."

"And then he came back here?"

"Yes. And—here's the important bit—he hid his ill-gotten find in his room."

"Why is that important?"

"Because he got chased out of that room as soon as Percy returned. Remember, he complained that he was turned out without even the chance to 'reclaim all his belongings'. Since that time, Percy, Annie and the army of nurses have ensured he had no chance to remove his treasure."

"Until last night," Holmes reasoned.

"Exactly! And how would a thief or murderer know Percy was alone in that room, unless he was somebody who spent his days inside that house? If that's not enough, consider that the intruder lifted the window latch with one of the Phelps's own butter knives. And did you see how tired Harrison looked? There was a man who'd lost a good portion of sleep last night, I'll wager."

"And the sword?"

"There was never a sword! Percy saw the butter knife and panicked."

"Oh, so that's why the murderer didn't approach the bed."

"Yes. He never wished Percy any harm. Or... no more than the rest of us do. He simply moved to recover his stolen goods—"

"Until Percy gave his battle cry!"

"'Squealed like a piglet' is what I think you mean. But yes, Harrison was foiled. Likewise, he had no chance to recover his treasure with the entire staff armed and marching the grounds. Nor could he get it once I'd fooled his sister into guarding the room all day."

"But she's gone now."

"No, she is in the hallway, just outside. Otherwise, he might simply walk into the room and make good his theft. With Annie Harrison blocking the internal door, Joseph Harrison has no way into that room except…"

"One of those windows, right there!" Holmes crowed.

"Correct! But hush! I see a shadow—here he comes!"

"Er… rather a *small* shadow, don't you think, Watson?"

"Is it?"

"That would be the cat, I think," said Holmes, giving my shoulder a comforting pat. "I don't know if anybody's told you, Watson, but you have a tendency to get a bit worked up in moments such as this."

Indeed, we had to wait over an hour before our man made his move. I huddled in my coat, struggling against the two drinks I'd been unable to refuse, which filled my blood with a warm glow and made every effort to persuade my body that this would be a fine spot for a nap. At last a sound came to our ears: the none-too-stealthy shutting of the servants' door. Soon a shadowy figure crept along the side of the house, and—I had to admit—he did appear notably less feline than my initial suspect. He wore a dark cloak and covered his face with a mask, but I was fairly sure, from his weight and bearing, that I had guessed right. It was Joseph Harrison. We saw the gleam of silver as he lifted the window latch with another of the Phelps's butter knives.

"All right," said Holmes. "Let's get him."

"Wait! Give him a moment to get inside and retrieve his treasure."

"Why?" Holmes wondered.

"Er… because it's late and it's cold and I'm too tired to look for it?"

"Fair enough."

Thus, Holmes and I gave Harrison a few seconds' head start before we worked our way across the lawn to the window. We could hear him in there, puttering about behind the water pipes. It seemed I'd overlooked a little maintenance hatch, built to allow water shutoff in case of leaks. By the time Holmes and I peeped in, Harrison had already retrieved his ill-gotten treasure and was turning back towards us.

"You there!" I bellowed, as I struggled through the window. "Halt!"

Joseph Harrison gave a little squeal of surprise and turned to unleash the only weapon he had to hand. The butter knife whizzed over my shoulder and struck Holmes dead in the center of his forehead.

But… you know… handle first.

"Ow!" said Holmes, as the discarded utensil plopped down into the flower bed at his feet. "I say! That was uncalled for!"

I had one leg through the window. Harrison would have done best to attack me while I was off balance, yet he did not. He was more a man of mischief than of action, I deemed. Across his chest, he clutched the oddest little case. It was styled as a diplomat's attaché, yet it was just slightly too small and made not of leather, but of a dull gray metal. The lazy gleam and obvious weight of the thing proclaimed this was most likely lead. Joseph Harrison cradled it like a precious thing. His eyes turned from me, to the inner door, to his only other means of escape.

"Holmes!" I cried. "The other window!"

"Very well." Still rubbing his reddened brow with one hand, Holmes pointed the other at the second window. A purple streak of hellfire shot forth and blasted it right out of the wall.

"Holmes! What have you done?"

"Seen to the other window, just as you asked."

"That wasn't what I wanted!"

"Well then, you should have clarified, shouldn't you?"

"How could *that* be what I wanted?"

Yet, the sudden blast of hellfire was enough to convince Harrison he wanted nothing to do with that particular means of egress. He turned back towards the door, threw it open and tried to escape down the hall.

Which he should not have done.

There in the doorway stood Annie with a Brown Bess under each arm and an expression of vengeful resolve on her face. She pointed both weapons at the masked intruder's chest and yanked back the triggers. Annie Harrison must have had some martial knowledge, for— judging that range and accuracy would be of limited use in such close confines—she had double-loaded both muskets. Four balls slammed into Joseph's chest, utterly ruining his heart, his aortic arch, both lungs, one pulmonary artery and… well… fairly hollowing the poor fellow out. Even as he fell, my trained eye could see there was no point in trying to save him. Then again, some effort might be well spent trying to save myself. No sooner had the twin gouts of smoke mushroomed off Joseph Harrison's shattered chest than Annie threw down both muskets and reached for a second pair.

"No! Miss Harrison, it's me! It's Dr. Watson!" I cried, raising my hands and nearly falling back out of the window.

"Hello, Annie!" said Holmes, waving jovially through the smoking hole he'd made in the wall.

She leveled the second pair of muskets at me and asked, "What are you doing here?"

"Chasing the criminal. He'd stashed Percy's missing case in this very room on the night of the theft. We let him retrieve it, then came in to get it from him, but… Oh, Annie… I'm so sorry… It was your brother. That's Joseph."

She glanced down at the still-twitching body, gave a derisive little sniff and grumbled, "Well, he shouldn't have stolen from my Percy, should he? I warned him his scheming would get him in trouble someday. I told him and told him. But did he ever listen to me?"

Apparently not.

Annie's eyes traveled the fallen form of her brother and came to rest on the case he still clutched in his left arm. "Is that it? That's what my little Tadpole lost?"

I hesitated, stunned that even Annie called Phelps "Tadpole".

"Er… yes."

Annie dropped one of the muskets and reached down for it.

"Wait! Miss Harrison, Holmes and I must examine that."

"No."

"Please, Miss Harrison—"

"No! Lord Holdhurst was very clear: Percy's only hope is in returning this, with its secrets intact. You'll not endanger my Percy!" She pointed the remaining musket straight at my heart.

I had little doubt she'd use it. All I could do was hiss, "Holmes! Stop her!"

"You know, Watson, in light of recent events I feel I should clarify: do you mean you wish me to kill her with demon-fire?"

"*No!*"

"Well, there. You see? I'm glad I clarified. What would you like me to do?"

"Stop her; get that case back."

"With or without resorting to magic?"

"Without!"

"How do you propose I do that?"

It was too late, anyway. Awakened by the sudden burst of musket-fire, Pixby and a few other ready braves burst into the hallway behind Annie. "What is it?" Pixby cried. "What has happened?"

"The intruder is dead," Annie said, evenly. "I'm afraid it was my own brother, Joseph. Misguided soul… On a happier note, Percy's treasure is recovered and his future restored. Out of my way, please, I am bringing this straight to my little Tadpole."

"But, Miss Harrison, we have to—"

"*Straight to Percy!*" Annie insisted, pointing the musket at Pixby's dour little moustache.

It should surprise nobody that Annie Harrison got her way. Percy was ecstatic. He fainted with joy. Three times. Word was sent to London that very night. Lord Holdhurst appeared the next morning and—though he did not explicitly forgive Percy Phelps—he disappeared back down the lane clutching his precious case and laughing like a maniac.

Lord and Lady Phelps were oddly pleased by the turn of events. There is a certain reticence whenever a lowborn, less wealthy young lady marries into a family such as theirs—there is always the question of her motives and her loyalty. It turns out that gunning down one's own brother in defense of one's fiancé is a fine way to prove exactly whose side one is on. Her iron-clad loyalty to Percy confirmed, Annie was welcomed into the family. Everyone was so delighted, they barely even cared about the grand new hole in their wall.

Holmes and I returned to Baker Street feeling somewhat defeated. Yes, we'd solved the mystery. Yes, Percy had been restored, which also meant he had no reason to pester me further. The turmoil that had so disturbed our Foreign Office was ameliorated and life was free to return to normal. Yet, Holmes and I never got to look into that attaché case. Even that day, it rankled us to have come so close to an arcane mystery and not encountered it. At first it seemed merely an annoyance. In less than two weeks, I'd find out how dire that setback had truly been.

THE ADVENTURE OF THE BLUE GOB-RUNKLE

AH, LONDON AT CHRISTMASTIME! IT IS THE VERY heart of our empire and—one may well be forgiven for feeling, at times such as these—the center of the world. And if it should snow? What a strange phenomenon it is to see London's millions put aside their daily rush and look up in happy expectation. The white flakes descend, blanketing all with purity. Each eave and chimney finds itself ennobled by a crust of white. Each pane, kissed by delicate traces of frost. How wonderful to see it. How blessed is the man who lives in London, in the season of Christmas, in the rule of Victoria, in the legacy of Dickens, in the snow. All the bustle of the great city ceases as each man and woman reflects on the great gift it is to live here and now.

For… I should say… about five minutes.

Then commerce resumes, but with more shouting about what the snow is doing to traffic. And now the street urchins' feet are cold, so they wail a bit louder. Horse and man, beast and boy answer the duties of nature and void their filth into the snow. The chemical plant and belching smokestack take up the less biological equivalent, blanketing the white drifts in soot. Millions of feet, wheels and hooves churn any surviving traces of purity to blackened piles of slush, which lie about everywhere, sometimes until February.

This was the state of mixed blessing and blight when I opened the door on Christmas Day 1882 to behold the vampire detective, Vladislav Lestrade, lurking in the hallway. His normal expression of displeasure was gone, replaced by something resembling embarrassment. He refused to meet my gaze. He had an unfamiliar hat on his head and a huge goose in his hand. Though it was still alive and almost half as large as its captor, the poor beast had little chance of escape. Its wings were tied against its sides. Its legs were secured with twine. Its beak was strapped shut as well, and Lestrade had handcuffed the bird's neck to his right wrist. The gigantic bird stared at me with unexpected hatred. In that gaze I found not only intelligence, but familiarity, as if he knew me personally and wished me to die, writhing, at my earliest convenience.

"Um… good morning," I said.

Lestrade shuffled his feet, gazed down at the toes of his shoes and said, "Dr. Watson, I have captured this goose." He brandished it at me.

"So I see."

"I thought I would… well… I thought I would pull its head off and drink all its blood out through the neck. You know… for Christmas."

"How festive."

He shrugged at me and shuffled his feet again. Since he seemed to have naught to add and nothing better to do than stand about at my door holding a doomed goose, I continued, "I suppose I should have expected you'd be up to something of the sort. I confess, it would not bother me at all if it were not for one small but worrying detail: you came here. I hope you did not intend to enact this little yuletide murder at my home."

"I… rather did…"

"Lestrade—"

"No! Wait! I only want the blood, you see. The body is no good to me. So I thought… if you and Holmes had no plans for Christmas…"

I recoiled from the open door and stammered, "Did you just… Did you invite us to Christmas dinner?" Not only were such gestures of camaraderie foreign to Vladislav Lestrade, I had thought such an offer impossible. Honestly, I hadn't even realized vampires *observed* Christmas. Perhaps it was my upbringing; the superstitious Scottish side of my family would have no trouble accepting the existence of vampires, but I'm sure that, to a man, they'd insist that any vampire who dared to utter the word "Christ" or "Christmas" would burst into guilty flame instantly.

"A partial invitation!" Lestrade insisted. "You can't come to my house; it is not suited for company."

Indeed not. In fact, to call any of Vladislav Lestrade's haunts "houses" was to abuse the definition beyond all bearing. The diminutive inspector lodged not in any

"I have captured this goose."

recognized form of dwelling, but in little dugouts and crawlspaces he'd constructed for himself under a few of the city's busier abattoirs. They had the advantages of anonymity and solitude as well as providing him with the constant supply of blood he required to keep the unpleasantness he called life from ending. Yet, they came with no small assortment of disadvantages, as well. They were not ideal for entertaining.

Lord only knows how he kept his clothes clean.

"So we'll have to do it here," insisted Lestrade. "We can't use Torg's because he won't tolerate the mess. But we must invite him. He gets lonely around Christmas. You probably hadn't realized, Doctor, but he drinks."

This was enough to cause me to recoil a second time. Not from surprise, but from abject fear. Lestrade's fellow inspector, Torg Grogsson, was a literal ogre, so far as I could tell. He had five traits for which he was truly remarkable: his size, his strength, his vocabulary, his physical resilience and his ability to self-govern. Three of these were so great as to beggar belief. The other two were somewhat sub-par. I'll leave it to the wit of the reader to guess which was which.

And that's when he was *sober*. The amount of damage an overindulged Grogsson could do to an unprepared London suburb must be great indeed.

"By Jove," I reflected. "How much liquor would it take to get Grogsson drunk?"

"It's probably why he doesn't do it more often," said Lestrade, nodding. "The sheer expense dictates we are safe for most of the year. Yet, every Christmas Eve he buys a barrel of Scotch from the publican down on Little Turnbridge Street. Every Boxing Day, he returns the empty barrel."

"Egad! We've got to stop him!"

"So you'll do it, then? You'll have dinner with me?"

"Well… I… er…"

I was rescued—or at least interrupted—by Holmes, who called out from the confines of his room, "I say, Watson, who is that you're speaking to?"

"It's Lestrade. He wants to murder a goose all over our sitting room, drink the blood out of it and use the rest to throw a friendly feast for you and me, Grogsson and himself."

"That sounds capital!"

"Does it?"

"Most of it. Do come in, Lestrade! Compliments of the season to you!"

"Thank you, Holmes. Merry Christmas to you as well," said Lestrade, failing to burst into flame.

Holmes went to the window, threw it open, took in a deep breath of refreshing December air and used it to shout, "Oi! Wiggles!"

An instant later a little brown rat scurried onto the curb below and looked expectantly up at him. I never knew exactly what to expect when Holmes called for his lycanthropic friend, but on this particular occasion, I should have guessed. Being a shape-shifter, Wiggles might choose to appear either as one of London's innumerable street urchins or one of London's innumerable rats. Then again, we'd just had snow. One of Wiggles's forms wore tattered rags and worn-out shoes, stuffed with newspapers to keep out the cold. The other came with a nice fur coat.

"We've got a Christmas turkey," Holmes called down. "Go and fetch Grogsson, won't you? He may be a bit tipsy already, but if you can get him here we'll give you… oh, I don't know… the intestines, or something. Oh! And all the feathers to make a warm little nest for yourself. Won't that be nice? Off you trot."

As Holmes negotiated with the local rodentia, Lestrade plunked the unhappy goose down on our table. He removed the handcuff from his wrist and clasped it shut around the table leg. From the bird's foot, he removed a battered gift tag, which read: *To Mrs. Henry Baker*. It was crudely emblazoned with the logo: *Alpha Inn Goose Club*.

"Can't trust this bird," said Lestrade. "I tell you, he's almost got the better of me four or five times."

Holmes closed the window, gave a happy little sigh and said, "What a fine idea, Lestrade! It'll be a delightful evening for all. Well… except this poor little fellow. I must confess, I get rather sad about turkeys at Christmas. Hardly fair on them, is it?"

He looked with sympathy at our intended dinner. The bird turned haughtily towards him and fixed him in a cold, merciless gaze. Until that moment, I had no idea geese could sneer. He seemed particularly fascinated with Holmes—in his beady little eye, one could almost read the thought, "Ah! It's you! My great enemy! You may have the advantage of me, sir, but I am the better man. Take it from me, this is your final hour."

There was something just *deeply* wrong with him. I boggled for a few moments, watching the goose examine Holmes from head to toe, carefully cataloguing his weaknesses, then turn his eyes slowly all about the room, noting each potential avenue of escape.

"Er… where did you say you'd bought this goose, Lestrade?" I asked.

"I didn't. I captured him."

"Out in the wild, you mean? Or from some sort of evil poultry farm?"

"It's a queer story," said Lestrade, with a toothy smile. "I suppose we've time for it, while we wait for Torg."

"I love a good Christmas story!" Holmes enthused. "Do tell all!"

"Just this morning, I was proceeding down Tottenham Court Road, having just received testimony from a terrible liar who—I strongly suspect—killed his business partner. As I turned the corner down near the bakery, I spotted a man coming the other way, carrying this bird. He was a shabby sort of fellow who looked as if he were trying to appear the gentleman on a pauper's budget. He'd hardly made it halfway down the street when another man lunged out of a shadowy alley, crying, 'He's mine! The white one with the black-barred tail! Give him to me!' Well, the first fellow tried to defend himself. He raised his walking stick and harried his attacker around the head and shoulders. Little good it did him! The ruffian didn't pay any heed to it. In fact, the only solid blow the old man landed was on this goose! He fairly knocked it senseless."

I leaned in to examine the goose, but the creature yanked his head away and snorted as if to say, "Unhand me! If I require medical aid, I shall call for it! If I do, I certainly hope for a more qualified practitioner than yourself! Tell me about your current practice, *Doctor*, and I'll tell you a tale of hard-earned skills wasted by disuse!"

He was, on the whole, a highly suspicious bird.

"Go on, Lestrade," Holmes insisted. "I do love a two-old-men-fighting-over-a-turkey-with-sticks-on-Christmas story!"

"It's a goose, Holmes," I said, but he had no mind for me, only Lestrade's tale.

"I ran forward, waved my badge and shouted for them to stop fighting. So… both men… well, they ran away."

"Why?" Holmes asked.

"I was shouting, you see," said Lestrade, with a guilty blush. "I *may* have let my mouth open a little farther than I should have."

"Ah!" I laughed. "So the two of them had their fight interrupted by a slavering fang-beast from hell."

"I wasn't slavering."

"Well, eye of the beholder, eh, Lestrade?"

"I wasn't! Anyhow, both men made away in opposite directions and I was left with the spoils of battle. The shabby fellow had dropped this goose—which was too stunned to get away—and his hat as well. That's it, over there."

As I made for the hat, Holmes gave a laugh. "And thank you for this second gift, Lestrade. If Watson doesn't get to do his little deduction trick every few days, he gets quite testy."

I turned and gave my friend an acidic look, but he stared defiantly back at me and said, "Well? What do you make of it, Watson?"

I had just one chance to put the hat back on its hook and prove that I didn't *need* to do my little deduction trick every few days, but... Argh! I just couldn't! I carried the thing back to the table, set it next to the evil goose and its recently removed leg tag and regarded it carefully. It was shabby, even by Lestrade's none-too-demanding standards. It had been tallow-stained again and again, but the spots had been inexpertly masked with ink. At first I thought the ink was black, but as the light of our fire fell across it, it gave a distinctive violet gleam. The inside of the hat was lined in faded red silk and the initials H.B. were just visible.

"Hmmm... I think I feel very sorry for Mr. Henry Baker," I said. "I've the sudden desire to return this hat and goose to him, as I suppose it is most unlikely he will be able to afford a replacement for either of them. He's newly poor, but accustomed to better times. He still has a strained sense of self-respect, but it's difficult for him to maintain even that, as his marriage is on the rocks, his apartment has no gas, and I suspect him to be a massive drunkard. It's likely he made his living as a poet—but can't anymore because he's just awful—and that his wife is toying with the idea of murdering him."

The look of shock both my companions gave me was… well… perhaps I'll just go ahead and admit that Holmes was right and I rather did enjoy the odd bit of deduction, answered by the acclaim of my fellows. It was indeed a welcome gift Lestrade had brought me, that Christmas.

"You got all that from the *hat*?" Lestrade exclaimed.

"Didn't you? It is perfectly apparent. Look here: this hat is of a sort very popular three years ago. It's well-made, monogrammed, silk-lined and of no small cost. Three years ago he was well in funds. Yet, look at the amount of wear on this poor hat! If he still had any money, he would surely have replaced it."

"Well done, Watson," said Holmes. "Tell me, how do you read of his embattled self-respect?"

"He's tried to cover the stains over with ink. It's not working, as you can see, but time and again he strives to keep up appearances."

"But… the gas in his apartment?" asked Lestrade.

"All five of these stains are tallow. He spends a great deal of time around candles."

Holmes leaned in, wondering, "How do you know he is a poet?"

"I don't, with certainty. Yet I have only ever known three men who employed ink such as this. All were poetic and all insufferable—the kind of fellow who not only enjoys purple prose, but who feels it needs to be written in *actual purple*. Percy Phelps used ink like this, if you'll recall."

"But how can you be sure the man is married?" Holmes wondered.

Lestrade jumped in with an answer, just to prove he was still a detective, after all. "The initials in the hat are H.B. The tag on the goose is addressed to Mrs. Henry Baker."

"And the state of his marriage?" prompted Holmes.

"Three years ago, his wife was married to a prosperous man. Now, her apartment has no gas. Trust me, the marriage is troubled."

"Even to the point where she considers murder?"

"Wouldn't you? Imagine standing behind this man, ironing one of his shirts in your cold, dark, gasless apartment, watching him hunched over his little desk fretting over every word of some wretched sonnet you know has no hope of restoring your fortunes. How could you do that every day without reflecting what a relief it would be to step up behind him with that iron and just bash and bash and bash him, until he moved no more? Poor fellow... The goose was a peace offering, I shouldn't wonder. He's been saving up for it. Look: it's from a local inn's goose club. He's probably been putting his pennies in all year, waiting for his Christmas goose. Now, see what's come of it..."

"Ah!" cried Lestrade. "And you naturally assume that any fellow with fortunes so low would resort to drink!"

"No," I told him. "It was the hat again. Any man who's managed five tallow spills in three years has the unsteady hand of a man who may possibly drink. Any man who's managed five spills *up onto his hat*... well..."

"Oh, I see."

"Imagine what his shoes must look like."

My attention was arrested, somewhat, by the extraordinary behavior of Mr. Henry Baker's lost goose. It seemed to have momentarily lost its appetite for revenge and was staring absentmindedly at our ceiling, as if nothing very interesting were going on at all. Such was its conviction that it took me some time to notice the disturbing regularity of the movements of its wings and legs.

"Wait a moment!" I cried. "Look at the goose! It's trying to work its ropes loose!"

"Wouldn't you, Watson?" said Holmes with a shrug.

"Not if I was a goose! That bird is ten times smarter than it ought to be!"

The goose ceased its struggles and shot me a savage look.

"Twenty?"

It arched an eyebrow at me, as if to say, "Oh a great deal more than that, as you are about to learn. At no small cost, I should think. At no small cost."

Yet my attention was caught once more, this time by the arrival of Grogsson and Wiggles. As Wiggles had chosen to wear his human form, they were both able to issue raucous shouts of Christmas cheer, which drew thumps of protest from Mrs. Hudson in the rooms below. Grogsson had elected to bring his "Christmas feast" and share it with all his boon companions. That is to say, he had four humongous puddings and a half-empty barrel of Scotch whisky strapped to his back. In his right hand he gripped a magnificent wooden tankard, which he'd obviously been quaffing from during the walk. He'd several times encouraged Wiggles to join him. Wiggles had dutifully protested that he was too young for such things. But he hadn't protested *very* hard and the two of them were fairly well on.

Greetings were exchanged and Lestrade was encouraged to once again relate the tale of his fortuitous goose-capture. What a jolly holiday it might have been if not for two notable occurrences during the second telling that had been absent from the first.

This time, Lestrade described the gentleman who'd attacked Henry Baker. "Oh, he was a piece of work," said Lestrade, who was quite enjoying the attention, in spite of himself. "He looked like an aristocrat gone feral. Like a man with plenty of money, accustomed to every comfort who one day forgot he had all that and went to live in the street, hunting rats to survive. Ah... Present company excepted, of course."

"Course," said Wiggles, sneaking yet another sip of Grogsson's brew.

"You know the funniest thing: I could even name the aristocrat he looked like," snorted Lestrade. "Bless me, but he looked just like the rough-and-ready twin of Lord Holdhurst!"

I gave a cry of alarm and jumped to my feet. Even Holmes recognized the severity of that statement, for he got all wide-eyed and muttered, "Uh-oh. Are we in trouble, Watson? Because it feels like we're in trouble."

Holmes and I had yet to tell our Scotland Yard friends about our previous misadventure with Lord Holdhurst. We began it with some earnestness. Yet, in our excitement we failed to pay as much attention as we might have to our surroundings, which occasioned an opportunity for the second notable occurrence.

While we were distracted by the tale, the goose worked one leg loose from its twine. Silently, carefully, it reached up with one webby little toe and pried the strap off its beak. Next, mindful of every metallic clink, it inched its neck back through the handcuff. Thus, nearly freed, it turned its attention to the final and most important element of its bondage—its wings. Try as it might, the frustrated fowl could not pull free. The loops around each wing played against the other and could not be made loose, even with the wings stretched back as far as they could go.

At least…

Not with them stretched as far back as they could *naturally* go. It lowered its left wing to the table top and stepped down on it.

"Ha!" said Holmes, pointing. "Look what the turkey is doing. Silly little fello—"

The goose wrenched its body to the right, yanking as hard as it could until its left shoulder slid out of joint with a horrible "pop".

"*Oh!*" cried Wiggles, Holmes and I.

Our feathery prisoner slipped its right wing out of the

loop, then let himself fall sideways onto the table. There was an audible crunch as its left wing reseated in its socket.

"*Agh!*" said the same three.

Grogsson raised his tankard in admiration. "Dat bird's well hard!"

With a grim determination in his eye and a gritted beak (yes, it turns out beaks can be gritted) the goose struggled to its feet, shook the loose rope off its left wing, and lunged straight towards me. Yet, at the last moment, a sideways glance over my shoulder gave me to realize I was not his intended target. The window! He *wanted* me to duck out of the way. It was all part of the goose's plan. I threw myself into his intended path. He collided with my face, honking his frustration.

"Grab him!" I cried. "He's going for the window."

The goose rewarded me for making his plans public by lashing at my left eye with his beak. I managed to turn away, but it nevertheless drew blood and set my eye to throbbing. As I collapsed backwards, already reflecting how lucky I was not to be half blind, he kicked me in the throat and reversed direction.

"The door!" shouted Lestrade.

Grogsson lunged between the goose and his second avenue of escape and barked, "No! You stay!"

Again, the foul fowl turned aside. Though his wing was badly injured, he flapped clumsily to our mantelpiece.

"He seems to be going for your gun, Watson," Holmes noted.

And do you know something strange: he was. I'd

been cleaning the thing earlier and had left the case open, atop the mantel. I had only a moment to wonder how a Christmas goose proposed to make use of a large-caliber pistol, before his head pecked down into the open case and re-emerged with something shiny in its beak.

"He's got a bullet!" shouted Lestrade.

With a gleam of triumphant malice in its eye, the goose flipped the bullet down into the fire.

"What the 'ell?" demanded Wiggles, as we all dived for cover. "Why's 'e so smart?"

"Why's he so mean?" I shouted back from my hiding place behind the sofa.

An instant later, the cartridge discharged. The bullet spanged off the lamp by the table and rebounded towards the door, blowing a nice hole in our elephant's foot umbrella stand. The spent casing spun out of the fire, dropping embers across the floor and bouncing off the back of Grogsson's head. Grogsson gave a roar of rage and Holmes admitted, "You know, Watson, I'm beginning to come around to your assessment of our turkey."

"It's a goose, Holmes."

"Well, whatever it is, it seems to be unusually gifted."

"The window, again!" I cried, for our gifted goose had let none of the advantage gained by its distraction be wasted. Even at the instant the bullet discharged, it began a wounded, sideways flap towards the one open window. At last, Lestrade joined the fray. Moving with the preternatural speed of his kind, he leapt into the goose's path. One hand closed around the unfortunate bird's head, the second around its neck.

"Raaaaaaaaaar!" Lestrade screamed, and yanked with all his might. With a visceral squelch, the goose's head came away from its body.

"Rhaaaaaaaaaaaaaa!" cried Lestrade again, and upended the headless bird above him. One of the peculiarities of Lestrade's physiology is how very far he can open his mouth. Now he dropped his head back until his eyes were staring out the window behind him and the entire top of his head was naught but a fang-lined maw. Above this, he suspended the still-twitching goose, whose lifeblood sloshed down from its severed arteries into the waiting gullet below.

Well... if I'm honest, a great deal of it wound up on Lestrade's shirt and my floor, but...

"Rhaaaaaaaaaaaaaaaaaahr!"

At last the crimson gush diminished to a few odd drips. Lestrade lowered the hapless corpse to his side, re-hinged his head into its regular approximation of human form and realized just how many of his friends were staring at him, aghast.

"Wait! No!" he said, pointing a remonstrating finger at all of us. "I warned you I was going to do that! It was always part of the deal!"

Wiggles and I stood agape. Holmes wiped a little glob of goose neck off his sleeve, kicked an ember back into the fireplace and said, "No, no. It's fair play. He did warn us." He then reached for the bell and gave a ring. In a moment the door opened to reveal a suspicious Mrs. Hudson.

"It seems we are to have turkey for dinner. I wonder if you'd mind cooking it up for us."

"Not your housekeeper," Mrs. Hudson growled.

"No, but I thought—"

"Not your friend."

"I thought you might join us for dinner."

For just a moment, her expression of hatred faltered. She eyed us each in turn, finally letting her gaze rest on the headless goose. "I get to pick the bits I want," she grunted.

"A few parts have already been promised," said Holmes. "Wiggles is to have the feathers and the viscera. Lestrade is to have... do you know what? I think Lestrade has been covered. Other than that, if you would be so kind as to fix it up, I think it only fair that you should get your pick."

"Drumstick," said Mrs. Hudson.

"Well that's a relief," said Holmes. "I thought you'd pick something far more inappropriate."

"Both drumsticks," said Mrs. Hudson, visibly irked that she'd made such a reasonable first offer.

"Let's not get greedy," said Holmes.

"No, it's all right," I told him. "I would suggest that if the Alpha Inn is filling the streets of London with evil geese, which are being hunted by the mind-ruined waste of Lord Holdhurst, we have larger concerns than who gets the drumsticks. It takes hours to cook a goose. I would suggest that the time might be well spent in determining the origin of this bird, of his strange nature, and exactly how he knows the head of our Foreign Office."

"And of course, in restoring the fortunes of Mr. Henry Baker," Holmes insisted.

"Holmes…" I gave him a stern look, urging him with my eye to focus on matters that… mattered.

"Watson, it's Christmas."

Lestrade gave a derisive snort. "Holmes, you are *riddled* with demons. Do you expect us to believe that Christmas is special to you?"

Holmes rounded on him. "It is a time for friends and families to gather. To share stories and a loving cup. To exalt in happiness and fellowship. It is everything I have been denied and everything I fight to preserve. Of course it is special to me, and if you think I intend to mark the occasion by leaving Henry Baker and his wife to suffer, then perhaps you do not know me as well as you thought. Get your coats, everyone."

How strangely masterful Holmes could be at times. As we prepared to go out, Lestrade walked over to Mrs. Hudson and handed her the remains of our most recent enemy.

"There's something wrong with its neck," he told her.

We all turned to stare at him. "Do you mean that someone has torn its head off?" I suggested.

"No. Did you see how slowly the blood came out? There's something in its windpipe, pushing against the arteries," said Lestrade, with a wounded sniff.

"Prob'ly a gob-runkle," Grogsson suggested.

"A what?"

Anyone with as few words as Grogsson is naturally

uncomfortable when called on to explain himself. He shifted on his feet a moment and then mumbled, "Well... yeh've got yer gob, right?" He indicated his mouth. "So if anyfing ever gets runkled down in 'ere and stops fings up... dat's a gob-runkle."

This explanation was generally accepted. Just as we turned to leave, Grogsson shook his empty tankard at us and said, "Hey! It's cold out dere..." Thus, bundled from head to toe and fortified with Grogsson's brew, we made our way out among the filthy drifts of snow. To my dismay, Grogsson slipped the whisky barrel's makeshift straps over his shoulders and brought it with him.

"Where are we to go first?" asked Holmes. "To see if London is besieged by evil geese, or to save Henry Baker's Christmas?"

"We can't help Henry," Lestrade muttered. "It's very nearly the most common Englishman's name. There are like to be a quarter of a million Henrys in London. Probably half as many Bakers and hundreds—really, hundreds—of Henry Bakers. We'll never find him."

I rolled my eyes. Much as I would like to have focused on the more pressing elements of the day, I found his intellectual laziness disgusting. "Of course we will. Our Henry Baker is a poor man, Lestrade—he's unlikely to spend much on cab fares, is he? Indeed, the time you saw him, he was afoot. The Alpha Inn is likely to be very near his house, as is Tottenham Court Road, where you saw him. It wouldn't surprise me if he was walking home when you met him. Not many folks go about their daily errands carrying a live goose, do they?

When we get to the Alpha, we shall inquire about the goose *and* the man who bought him. Once we are in the right neighborhood, you can describe him to the first constable we see. We are not helpless children, Lestrade. Of course we can track Henry Baker."

Fortunately for us, the Alpha Inn was a lowly enough establishment to be open on Christmas Day. It was one of those places where the working-class lonely came to forget they had nobody. And indeed, when they were there, they had each other. As we neared, the clink of cups and the sound of laughter filled our ears. The proprietor was an honest-looking, heavy-browed man who welcomed us inside with a friendly wave. He had his hands full with the Christmas crowd, but he made his way over to us in short order and asked, "What may I do for you gents?"

"You ran a goose club this year," I said. "We have reason to believe you provided a goose to Mr. Henry Baker, is that right?"

"Yeah, I got a bird for Henry," the barman said, letting his gaze wander over our strange group of friends. "Er… he's all right, ain't he?"

"Why do you ask?" I said, levelly. "It's not because you realize you sold him a highly dangerous killer goose, is it?"

"Look here!" the barman roared. "Someone had to take it! And Henry din't have all his pennies in. By all rights, he shoulda had no goose at all. Instead, he got the biggest of the lot, so what's his complaint, eh?"

"Merely that he's been killed by a demon goose, on Christmas."

The bartender staggered back in guilt-struck horror.

"No, no, my good man," I told him. "Henry is all right. I only needed to know if you were an unknowing participant or the proprietor of some sort of wicked-livestock distribution center. Am I right in assuming not all of the geese you sent out this year were possessed by evil?"

"Just the one. Gawd, he was a right piece of work. Always coughing, like he'd had somethin' runkled right down his gob. Still, he was smart as you like and none too kind. I never been afraid of a bird before, but…"

"Where did you get him?"

"From Breckinridge—one of the goose-dealers at Covent Garden. See if I ever go back there again. Say, you're sure Henry's all right, right?"

"We did want to check on him. Do you know where he lives?"

"Some way down near Goodge Street, but I don't know it exact."

"We'll find it!" said Holmes, raising a glass of Scotch he had no intention of drinking.

"We will, but not right now. There is some chance that this Breckinridge has stayed open to sell some last-minute geese, but that chance decreases with each passing hour. We must make haste to Covent Garden."

"Oh, very well."

We made a Christmassy sort of haste. I went by the straightest path, but my companions—overcome by the spirit of the day and the spirit Grogsson brought—made it an occasion for raucous caroling. Though I had not realized it, misfit policemen and lycanthropic urchins each had their own particular brand of carols and took a queer pride in teaching them to one another. Most popular were "I Arrest You, Merry Gentleman" and "Baby Jesus, Stop Your Noise".

We were *exceedingly* lucky to find our man that day. Covent Garden Market was not actually open for business and the entire area was almost deserted. The only people we saw were a few beggars, some young friends out walking and one vicious-looking goose vendor. Breckinridge was a large, burly man with hairy arms and an eyepatch. Despite the snow, he stood in nothing but an apron and shirt, with the sleeves rolled to the elbows. He wore the sort of expression designed to communicate that he'd punch you if you didn't buy a goose, kick you if you tried to haggle the price, and beat you within an inch of your misbegotten life if you attempted to point out the market was closed and he probably ought to just go home.

"Rough-looking fellow," Holmes muttered.

"Never mind that," said I. "Watch as I cleverly manipulate him into telling all we wish to hear."

I strode up to the man and said, "Breckinridge?"

"I am."

"Got any geese left?"

"Think I'd be standin' round here in the cold if I didn't?"

"I'm looking for one as good as those you gave the Alpha Inn. Do you happen to have any of that batch left?"

His good eye narrowed. "Here now! What's everybody so worried about that particular batch of birds for, eh? Everyone comin' round askin' for 'em! You and that crazy politician, too! Where'd I get 'em? How long have I kept 'em? Where'd I sell 'em to? Well look here: they was good birds. I gave good money for 'em, I took good money for 'em and that's an end to it. That's commerce and we can do without all the questions!"

I decided to bait the man. "Meaning you do not know the answers," I scoffed.

"Oh, don't I? Bring the book, Jim!"

A shabby-looking lad of nine or ten stumbled up with a gigantic hard-backed tome and pushed it onto the counter next to Breckinridge.

"In this book, I've got complete records of every bird that comes through this shop. I've got each bird's name, see, and a little picture. Above 'em I write where they comes from, and when. Below, I write where they goes to, and when."

"Wait, wait, wait," I spluttered. "Names? *Pictures?*"

"Sketches, yeah. Maybe I'm tormented by guilt, eh? Maybe I've come to reflect on the inequity of my career. Like… how come my one life is maintained by the sacrifice of so many hundred smaller, more innocent ones? So maybe I make little sketches of every single bird with big, sad eyes. Maybe it's a record of each and every goose so accurate as to strain credulity. Maybe there's little bits of poetry in there, too. Maybe. But you'll never know it, 'cause this is personal. Now, bugger off!"

And my inquiry might have ended there, but for a happy chance. As Breckinridge leaned forward and scooped up a cleaver to brandish at me, his apron came away from the front of his shirt. There, protruding from the front pocket, I could see the stub end of a betting slip. Breckinridge was a gambling man.

I smiled.

"Well if you won't be helpful, I'll just have to start with what I know and go from there. At least I know it was a country-bred bird."

"Shows what you know," Breckinridge scoffed, "for that bird were town-bred!"

"Oh, I know a bit too much about geese to fall for that," I replied, waving a finger at him.

From behind me came a heavy drunken sigh and a gruff, "Argh. Hurry up!"

"Torg, hush!" said Holmes. "Watson's being very clever and we mustn't rush him."

Grogsson gave a grunt of annoyance. Undaunted, I continued. "Now look here, my good man. I've bet a fiver that that bird was country-bred and I don't intend to lose—not on some scabby tradesman's half-remembered word!"

"Well, you've lost your fiver, for it's town-bred!"

"Ha! I've another sovereign to lay to it! Look here, I'll bet you a pound you can't prove it's town-bred!"

"Oh? You think you just wave a sovereign around and I show you my private goose diary? Well I told yeh—"

With a final sigh of vexation, Grogsson stepped past

me. He stretched his right hand down near his left hip, then brought it violently up and across, fetching Breckinridge a monstrous backhanded slap to the side of his face. The blow lifted Breckinridge up and sent him collapsing sideways, down onto his counter and from there to the cobblestones below, utterly senseless. His boy, Jim, stared up at Grogsson with incredulity and horror. Grogsson looked down at him with a perfectly blank expression. At last, he suggested, "Take da day off." Little Jim nodded once, turned on his heel, and sped off down the street. Grogsson reached down, turned the book to face us, flipped it open to the last few entries, grunted with concentration as he read them over, then announced: "Mrs. Oakshott. 117 Brixton Road. We go."

By the time we reached Mrs. Oakshott's home, the day was well along. Darkness had not yet fallen, but it threatened at the edges of the eastern sky, the western tinged with pink. Our goose must soon be ready and our adventure at an end. Though my comrades happily discussed the idea of returning home to a hot bird and further caroling, I found myself growing anxious. I had no desire to leave the matter unsolved. Was it indeed Lord Holdhurst who had attacked Henry Baker? If so, what was the cause of his extraordinary behavior? And, speaking of extraordinary behavior, what the devil had been wrong with our goose? There was a story of intrigue here, one we stood ignorant of.

I knocked upon Mrs. Oakshott's humble door. From within came the sound of surprised but merry voices. A moment later the door swung open. Mrs. Oakshott was a gruff but friendly woman in her fifties, with a tight bun of graying hair. From the sounds within, it seemed she had a good company of friends and family over and her expression made it clear she'd like to get back to them.

"'Ello?" she asked. "What can I do for you?"

"Mrs. Oakshott?"

"Yes."

"Ohhhhhhhhhhhhhhhhh," sang Holmes, gesturing to the others to join him. "I arrest you, merry gentleman, that's not your bag of loot! Now come along all quiet or I'll punch you in the snoot! You stole that from the gov-er-nor, you stole that from the nurse—"

"*Holmes!*" I shouted. "Mrs. Oakshott, I'm sorry to bother you, but we came to ask about a batch of geese you sold to Breckinridge, of Covent Garden."

Her eyes narrowed with suspicion, just as Breckinridge's had. "All the geese," she asked, "or just *that one*."

"Ah! So you recognized it too!"

"How could I not? But I've done nothing wrong. I told Breckinridge one of the birds weren't right. Warned him never to untie it, not even for an instant. Gave him a discount, I did, so I fail to see what more was wanted. Now, if you don't mind—"

But before she could shut the door, Holmes sprang forward and said, "Please, Mrs. Oakshott, please. We're not trying to get anybody in trouble. We're not looking for anyone to blame. We're just trying to remedy a bit of misfortune that started with a wicked turkey—"

"It was a goose, Holmes."

"Won't you tell us what you know? Please. It's Christmas."

Mrs. Oakshott gave a sigh, glanced over us all appraisingly and finally shrugged. "All right. I had twenty-six birds this year. Two dozen for Breckinridge, one for us and one for the Foreign Office."

"The Foreign Office?"

"Yeah, they had a party on yesterday, from what I gather. Well, three mornings ago, I hear a bit of a scuffle outside and I realize someone's at me birds. So I takes up me husband's old shotgun—God rest him—and I goes out to make an inquiry. Sure enough, there's a rough-lookin' gentleman and he's got one of me birds and he's runklin' somefin' down its gob, as hard as he can! And yeah, the fellow looks pretty rough, but he also looks like a gentleman, so it's hard to know what to think. So I lets one barrel off, up into the air to get his attention, and I points the second barrel at his chest and asks what he thinks he's doin'. An' he says—get this—that he needs to hide the master!"

"Did you happen to recognize the gentleman?" I asked.

"Yeah. It were Lord Holdhurst, no less."

"Damn," I muttered.

"Put me in a bit of a spot, it did, for one of the birds was marked down for the Foreign Office and… since he's the man what runs it… He asks me what I'm owed for the bird and I says six shillin's which—God help me—is a bit of a lie. I always hopes to get six and sometimes I do, but two's the price to a wholesaler and three or four to the open market. Lord Holdhurst asks if I've change for a sovereign and I say I don't and he says that's all right, I can just keep it and suddenly I realize I don't mind all that much if he does take the bird now. So I shows him the one we had set aside for him—biggest of the lot, it were—but he says he don't want it. He wants the one he was wrestlin' with before I scared him with the shotgun—the white one with the black-barred tail. 'Well, take the one you want and Merry Christmas to yer,' I told him. He grabbed his bird and laughed like a man who's lost his wits, and off he goes, over me fence. Only, here's the thing…"

I slapped my forehead down into my head and uttered, "There were *two* white ones with black-barred tails."

"And I never could tell 'em apart," Mrs. Oakshott confirmed. "When Lord Holdhurst left, I found the other bar-tail stretched out behind the coop, chokin' and gaspin'. Never was the same after that. Couldn't trust 'im. Used to be a sweet bird, but not no more. Fairly took Breckinridge's eye out, from what I hear. Wears a patch now. But I warned him."

"Thank you, Mrs. Oakshott. Merry Christmas to you."

Our story now in place, we set off to help Henry Baker—starting our search at the intersection of Goodge Street and Tottenham Court Road. My company was merry, but my mind distracted. What was this strange object that had affected Lord Holdhurst so profoundly? Was it the same item he'd lost when it was stolen from Percy Phelps?

If so, why had he seen fit to force his reclaimed treasure down the throat of a goose? Was it possible he'd simply gone mad? Yet there were aspects of the story that strongly suggested a supernatural element. Percy had described a message, constantly changing. And what could account for the extraordinary behavior of our goose?

Lestrade had the answer for us—or was convinced he had—and was willing to defend it against all better sense. "It was really quite ingenious," he said. "Lord Holdhurst had a small and valuable item—he did not wish to be caught with the item in his custody. He knew of the goose that was owed to his office. He also knew that geese have crops—a strange little organ at the base of their throats that serves as a sort of food-storage area past the mouth but before the stomach. He may have feared his person would be searched, but would anybody think to search inside the goose he carried? He forced the item into the goose's crop and knew it was safe from discovery."

"An astute theory, Lestrade," I said. "I can think of only one flaw: geese do not have crops."

"But… they do!"

"Some birds do. Geese do not."

"He's right, Lestrade," said Holmes. "Only some birds. For example: the South German crop sparrow."

"What? That's not a—"

"But perhaps Lord Holdhurst labored under the same misinformation as Lestrade," Holmes continued. "Whether or not geese have a crop, if he *thought* they did, might he not try to take advantage of it?"

93

"He might," I admitted. "But I cannot yet construct a tale which describes all the phenomena we have observed. There's something we are yet missing. Still, there's nothing for it at the moment. Here we are, the intersection of the street where Lestrade encountered Henry Baker and the street where the innkeeper thought he lived. Inspector Lestrade, kindly blow your police whistle for me."

Two or three minutes later, a breathless, red-cheeked constable ran up and asked, "What is the matter?"

"Nothing pressing, officer, and I apologize for having made you run. We're looking for Henry Baker; we believe he lives hereabouts."

The constable did know him—Henry Baker being a well-loved neighborhood character. In no time at all, we were at his door. The poor fellow had been less than two streets from home when Lord Holdhurst caught him. At our knock, the door was opened by a bristle-whiskered fellow in his mid-fifties. He had an air of abused scholarship with a chaser of cheap gin.

"Mr. Henry Baker?" I asked.

"I am."

Holmes leapt forward and, with the help of our fellows, belted forth, "Ohhhhhhhhh, Baby Jesus, stop your noise, it's really not that cold out. We gave you the best manger, the lambs have all been rolled out!"

This time I stood aside to let my companions finish their carol. Two minutes later, they stood with that breathless pride only drunken troubadours know. Henry Baker clapped and said, "Well sung! Merry Christmas, sirs!"

"Merry Christmas!" they all yelled back.

"I fear I have no tokens of the season to dispense to you," said Baker, "but I want you to know the gesture is well appreciated, none the less."

"Oh, no, no," said Holmes. "We've come to bring seasonal tokens to *you*. We heard about the misfortune with the goose, you see, and we wanted to bring you a feast! It's been... um... *cleverly delivered* to your rooms, while my friends and I distracted you."

From within Henry Baker's apartment came a muffled boom and the sound of a woman screaming.

"Damn it, Holmes," I growled under my breath. "No magic! There is a perfectly conventional way to restore Mr. Baker's fortunes!"

"Is there?" said Holmes and Baker together, the latter with some eagerness.

"I believe so. Observe Mr. Baker's fingers. Note the purple ink stains? Sir, are you a poet?"

"More than that! I am the scholar who perfected English poetry! And still, they dissolved my professorship."

"You... *perfected* poetry?" I asked, doubtfully.

"It wasn't hard. There are only two improvements necessary to bring us to the zenith of artistic expression. First: poetry must always take the time to explain what it means. Second: we must take full advantage of the fact that any two words that end in 'y' rhyme. Especially if it is pronounced 'eye'. Take, for example, William Blake's classic."

At this, Henry Baker thrust his chest as far forward as

he could without permanently crippling his back, threw a hand to his heart and thundered:

> "Tyger! Tyger! burning bright
> In the forests of the night,
> What immortal hand or eye
> Could frame thy fearful sym-eh-treye?

"Ah! Was ever a more perfect verse put to paper by the hand of man? Of course, he should have gone on to explain he was only writing it because he loved God for making lambs and babies, but he was a little upset because he'd just realized God must have made tigers and Gatling guns and leprosy, too. Oh, and probably the devil. Oh! Ah! And he should have added a simple quatrain to explain that the tiger wasn't actually *burning*, just—you know—shiny."

Holmes leaned close to me and whispered, "The more this man speaks, the more I think perhaps he should give up on poetry."

"The more he speaks, the more I think everybody should," I replied, then raised my voice and said, "Mr. Baker, I wonder: have you ever put your hand to prose? Perhaps you ought to try producing a ha'penny pamphlet and selling it down on the street corner, next Sunday. I'll give you a topic: do you happen to know who it was who tried to steal your Christmas goose?"

"Well… no."

"None other than Lord Holdhurst, of the Foreign Office.

I'm sure some sport could be made of that by a talented fabulist. You'll sell hundreds. Better still, pop round to the Foreign Office with a rough draft and ask to interview one or two of the clerks to finish your story. I think you'll find yourself the recipient of a fairly generous offer to not sell any at all. Good day, sir. Merry Christmas to you. Lestrade, do return this good man's hat, won't you?"

"Merry Christmas!" crowed Baker, and one could at last believe that it was, for him.

Darkness had fallen by the time we returned to 221B. The first flakes of a new flurry had just begun to fall, to blanket their blackened brothers in a fresh coat of white. The air was crisp and sweet. We turned our red and ruddy faces to a warm hearth, a good meal and the not-so-unwelcome-as-usual company of Mrs. Hudson.

To the reader who loves our world and wishes to believe it will continue, let me say:

Stop.

Stop, right now.

Close this book, set it aside and never read anything else I write.

There. We're well rid of those folk now, aren't we? To you who can at least face your oncoming doom with open eyes, I will tell the rest.

We settled in to our meal in high spirits. Mrs.

Hudson—better than her word—had also raided our supplies for whatever fresh vegetables we had on hand and prepared secondary dishes with them. These, combined with Grogsson's much-abused puddings and Scotch made for a full-enough board. As we labored to find space for all the people and all the food within our crowded rooms, the first Christmas debt was paid: Wiggles was given his prize. Though, not without caveat.

"No! Wiggles, no!" I cried. "I am willing—in the spirit of the season—to let you sit in the corner gnawing on goose intestines. You've earned as much, I'll admit. Yet, I'm afraid I must insist on this point: you need to be a *rat*. I'm not going to sit here watching a young urchin slurping down guts. Change. Right now."

"Awww… Whatever…"

I let Holmes carve the goose. It was only fair. I knew he would not be eating any of it—at least not until it had been rendered to broth—but should he not enjoy the ritual? He smiled. He cut the twine Mrs. Hudson had bound the drumsticks together with. He touched the knife to the goose's breast.

It got up and slapped him.

The instant the knife touched its flesh, our well-cooked goose leapt to its feet and raked its crispy wing across Holmes's face. The blow could not have been very forceful, but it filled Holmes's eyes with delicious drippings, and he fell back, howling. Next to receive rough treatment was Mrs. Hudson, who sprang forward to grab the wayward dinner. She got a swift drumstick-kick, right in her rotted teeth. The bird spun away from her and bolted to the window. It was closed, but a determined main course might possibly have put its shoulder to the glass and broken through.

We'll never know. Howling his battle cry, Grogsson stood to block the way. He drew back one massive fist and plunged it forward, catching the hapless bird full in the chest. The measure of well-cooked poultry is how easily the meat will flake away from the bone. Let me tell you, Mrs. Hudson had done an admirable job. So had Grogsson.

There was a luscious meat-splosion.

The left wing and drumstick tore free and bounced off the Baker Street wall. The entire right half of the bird was reduced to delicious shrapnel. Tempting morsels spattered our floor, walls and ceiling with the gentle pitter-pat of flying meat. Clearly, the carving knife would be unnecessary. The goose's headless neck stretched out against the blow, straining across the top of Grogsson's fist as if it still yearned for the window beyond—still thought it might be free. Then, in that instant of stillness between its forward momentum ceasing and the beginning of its floorward descent, something slid free of that outstretched neck.

The mysterious gob-runkle slipped forth.

I'm sure Holmes did not see it, being freshly wing-slapped. Grogsson most likely missed it as well, seeing as he had just coated his own face in shredded breast meat. Wiggles, Lestrade and Mrs. Hudson were all somewhere in the process of flinging up their arms to shield their eyes, or diving for cover.

But I saw it.

I saw the tiny streak of blue flame. The sigil. The rune. Even in that instant of time it took to fly from the goose wreckage to the wall, I saw its shape change, like an ambiguous word shifting from one meaning to the next. Like nuance. I felt again that strange conviction I knew when I saw the rune the first time—nearly one year before, as it lay trapped in Holmes's chest—that idea that it must be a word, in some language I did not know. A name. Yet, on this occasion I felt a dread our first meeting could never have engendered. For this time, I knew whose name it was.

Moriarty.

I was certain of it.

The flickering sigil hit the wall, yet even as I sprang forward to grab it, I saw this would be impossible. It didn't stop. The little blue flame went right through. It left no hole, no scorch upon the wallpaper, only passed through as if the front of our house were a non-existent thing. I ran to the window and watched the tiny fire arc across Baker Street, illuminating the flakes that fell past it with a bright, malicious blue.

From the shadows on the opposite side of the street, a human figure emerged shouting with joy and waving his grasping hands skyward. To this day, I do not know if he followed Lestrade after their first encounter, shadowed our joyful band as we returned home, or was simply drawn by his master's call. But there stood Lord Holdhurst, hunched and dirty, half ruined by cold and hunger, yet laughing into the sky with the pure abandon of a witless child.

As the little flame disappeared over the housetops, Lord Holdhurst turned to follow, clattering down an alleyway, begging his precious master to wait for him. When they had disappeared from sight, I turned back to the room and stammered, "Holmes! Our goose! It was Moriarty!"

"What?" he said, rising and wiping goose juice from his eyes. "I mean... I will grant I have seen a few things this day which most fellows might find hard to credit, but... *what*?"

"No, it was! Moriarty is back! We had him in our power, but we didn't know it and now he's free!"

Holmes stood, regarding me, weighing his trust in me, and my obvious earnestness, against the preposterous nature of my claim. After a moment, he said, "It may be as you say, Watson. If it is, it means that dark days lie ahead of us. Still, it is a problem for another time. We must focus our efforts on present issues. Here is what I propose: everyone grab a fork and just wander about the room, eating whatever you find. If you come across a drumstick, it must be surrendered to Mrs. Hudson. Come along now, Watson, there's work to be done. Here's your fork. Oh, and...

"Merry Christmas, one and all."

THE ADVENTURE OF THE
DISGUSTING STAIN

NO NEWS, THEY SAY, IS GOOD NEWS. THIS CAN HAVE two meanings, both of them cynical. Perhaps it means that no single piece of news has ever been favorable—that all new information bodes ill. In my darker moments, I sometimes find myself in agreement with this view.

Fairly often, now that I come to think of it.

A related but subtly distinct reading would be that the optimum life is one of comfortable equilibrium—that once a man has established himself in a pleasing situation, his highest hope should be that nothing occurs which might change it. In other words that the best news one can have is that nothing is occurring to disturb one's domestic tranquility. The reader may well be forgiven for supposing this to be my natural leaning.

And yet... that particular morning, the absence of news rankled me. I stared angrily at my copy of the *Daily Telegraph* and gave it a little shake, as if throttling the thing would dislodge one or two more facts it had been hiding. Perhaps a few extra words would fall out upon my table and let me know what had become of Lord Holdhurst.

The very toffiest of toffs

He was missing. *Still*. The paper gave that fact and vexingly little more. I'm sure I wouldn't have minded, if not for the fact that the last time I'd seen him, he was chasing the disembodied spirit of James Moriarty as it flew across London. I found the government's official explanation—that he was probably off in the South of France or something—utterly insufficient. Hence my current opinion: that no news was bad news. I had the distinct impression that great wheels of misfortune were turning—powerful machines that might emerge from the mists of ignorance and crush me to death. I feared that my own destiny was being decided by powerful forces or individuals whose actions I knew nothing of.

Which turned out to be the case.

Even as I sat, dreading the unknown danger, the heralds of misfortune let go their cloak of obfuscation and knocked upon my very door.

Well…

Very nearly.

In fact, it was a fit of angry kicking that suddenly exploded forth upon the far side of my chamber door, accompanied by Mrs. Hudson's shrill little voice, screeching, "Oi! Couple o' toffs to see Warlock Holmes."

I threw down the paper, rose with an exasperated sigh, marched to the door and opened it, saying, "Mrs. Hudson, I will thank you not to refer to my guests as—"

But they *were* toffs.

The very toffiest of toffs. Before me stood none other than Lord Bellinger—the current prime minister of

Britain. With him was another, younger gentleman whom I did not recognize, but his dress, his complexion and the callouses on the side of his right hand and where his pen touched his fingers proclaimed him to be a high-placed, well-to-do government official. Both of them hovered at the door with the droopy-eyed impotence of those who are just beginning to waken from a deep, dreaming sleep. They teetered on their heels. Their mouths hung slightly open. When they saw me, Lord Bellinger mumbled, "Warlock Holmes..."

"He isn't dead," his companion noted.

"Just as the master said. He must aid us."

"Then we must capture him."

"We shall take him unawares," said Bellinger, with a dim-witted smile.

My eyes sought Mrs. Hudson's, on the (admittedly overambitious) hope that she could explain the state of the visitors she had brought. She offered me nothing, apart from the observation, "All your friends is weird." She then turned and stomped off down the stairs.

"Aid us, Mr. Holmes," the younger man urged.

"Then be captured," added Bellinger.

"Hm... Well, much as I'd like to be of service," I said, "I am not Warlock Holmes. My name is—"

"Where is Hooooooooooooolmmmmmmmmmmmmes?" Lord Bellinger shrieked with such passion that I feared his voice might shatter my teacups.

"Er... I'll just get him for you, shall I? Yes? Good. Do come in, gentlemen, and make yourself comfortable here, on the sofa. There. I'll just nip off and fetch him."

As soon as the two statesmen had sat down, I ran for Holmes's sanctum.

"Holmes!" I hissed, knocking upon his bedroom door. "Holmes, there is something very strange going on!"

From within came a harrumph of annoyance and a brief scuttling. At last, the door opened. Holmes had a look of indignant fury on his face. One of his arms had transformed into a snake and the other into some form of badger. He must have had some command of them, for he'd got the snake to curl twice around his doorknob so he could pull the thing open. Yet the beasts must have had some level of mastery over their own actions, for they continually hissed and nipped at each other as he spoke to me. "Strange? Perhaps to some. Yet I never trouble you over the normalcy—or lack of normalcy—of the actions which occur behind your closed door and I will thank you to extend the same courtesy to me!"

"No… er… I mean, strange things are occurring *out here*. The prime minister is in our sitting room, Holmes. There's something very wrong with him and he seems to be bent on your capture!"

"Oh? How pleasantly outré!" Holmes declared. In a blink, his animal companions were gone, replaced by his regular arms. Such was the speed and silence of their departure that I might have thought the entire thing an illusion—were it not for the fresh badger claw marks upon the doorframe. "Let us go forth and examine this splendid new adventure, shall we?"

"Perhaps you ought to put some trousers on first, Holmes."

"Ah… yes… I shall be with you presently."

A few moments later, I marched my friend into the sitting room and announced him, "Mr. Warlock Holmes."

"Yes. Hello, gentlemen. I am Warlock Holmes; how may I be of service?"

"Holmes," said Bellinger.

"Alive," his companion said. "Just as the master promised."

"Aid us," said Bellinger. "Then we capture you and take you to the master."

"Hm… An unusual request…" said Holmes. "I can hardly remember the last time I was captured and dragged before a master, of any sort. Yet—since I do not like to dwell upon the prospect of my impending doom—we might be best served by turning our attention to the other matter. How can I be of service to you?"

For the first time, true emotion crossed the brows of both our guests. Sadness, guilt, worry.

"We have… lost something," Lord Bellinger said.

"Loss," sighed his companion. "Loss."

"I see. And exactly what is it you have lost?" asked Holmes.

This question seemed to cause some consternation for our visitors. They shifted about uncomfortably for a few moments, then the younger one said, "A communication."

"A letter," Bellinger volunteered.

"Powerful."

"Beautiful."

The two of them became nostalgic and wispy-eyed as they sat on our couch reflecting on the power and beauty of… whatever the damn thing was. I traded glances with Holmes.

"They've been mesmerized," he said, then looked at them for a moment and added, "Just *astoundingly* mesmerized. I don't know who or what might be responsible for their current state, but I can tell you this: something has crushed their power of reason, even as a fat schoolboy might crush the spine of an ancient, osteoporotic pony."

I blinked at him.

"I've seen it happen," he explained. "Quite sad."

"That's all very well, Holmes… or I don't know, maybe it's all very tragic, but it still leaves us uncertain as to why the highest powers in this land wish for your aid, followed by your capture. Or what this strange communication might be. Or whom it might be from." I leaned towards our visitors and asked, "Can you describe the message to me?"

"Wonderful."

"Powerful."

"Yes, yes, but what sort of paper was it on?"

"No paper."

Holmes and I drew our brows into furrowed lines.

"No paper? What was it written on?" I asked.

"Nothing. It was just a single letter. Writ on nothing, in a hand of fire."

"A word, I think."

"A name."

I recoiled in horror. I knew the object of which they spoke. Holmes might be unwilling to let himself believe it, but I was certain the disembodied spirit of Moriarty now haunted London. Apparently he'd been visiting the highest circles of London society.

"It was trying to show us something," Bellinger said. "To teach us what to do."

"Capture Holmes," the younger man reminded him, "and destroy… something…"

"Couldn't tell what it was called."

"Something like: Wosson…"

My breath caught in my throat. Me? The disembodied personality of Moriarty had just ordered Britain's prime minister to kill me? I realized it in an instant. Holmes, of course, did not.

"Most peculiar," Holmes observed, scratching at his chin. "You know, there was a Swedish warship called the *Wasa*. Perhaps that is your target. Oh, but it's already sunk, I think. Hmmm… I think I would have better luck understanding what it is you've lost, if only we could work out what it wanted you to destroy."

He put his hands up to his lips to ponder, but I was already on my feet, shouting, "Conference! Conference, Holmes! I'd like to speak with you in the bathroom, I think!"

"By Jove, I do believe he's worked it out!" Holmes laughed. "And no surprise. He's a clever man, my good friend Wat—"

But I clapped a hand over his mouth just in time and

dragged him backwards. I did not release him until I had the two of us crowded into the bathroom. Though it was rough treatment, Holmes did not protest. Rather, as soon as I released my grip, he declared, "I say, Watson, you seem quite worked up! What is it? Don't leave me in suspense; what are they trying to destroy?"

"Me!"

"Eh? Why would they do that?"

"Because he's angry at me."

"He? He who?"

"Moriarty!"

"But that doesn't make any sense, Watson. Moriarty is gone. He's dead."

"You always say that, Holmes. You've been telling me that almost since the day we met. But you're wrong! I've seen the thing they describe. I told you about it, remember?"

"The thing that came out of our turkey?"

"Goose, Holmes."

"It may be as you say, Watson, but... do you think you might be acting a bit like a paranoiac? Is it not equally likely that some magical trickster enchanted our Christmas turkey—"

"Goose."

"—and that Moriarty is truly dead? Perhaps you finally killed him."

"No! Holmes! Stop saying that! You're always wrong!"

"Watson, you're being dramatic."

"No. I'm not. Look: something has addled the minds

of our highest government officials. We agree on that, don't we? Something has ordered them to capture you and destroy me."

"Or perhaps the Swedish warship, *Wasa*."

"Holmes! Damn it! We have a major problem. That man in there can order the army about. He commands Scotland Yard. He's got diplomatic ties the world over. If he unleashes the might of Britain against you and me… Well, the sun never sets on the British Empire, but the empire might set on us, rather hard."

"Hmm… You have a point, Watson," Holmes conceded. "Even if it is not Moriarty—"

"Which it absolutely is."

"—even if it isn't, we do have a challenge before us. Exposure to the established power structure had always been my chief fear. It seems to have come to pass."

"Yes," I agreed. "The only thing going for us right now is that the two of them seem somewhat… er…"

"…stupid?" Holmes volunteered.

"Well, one doesn't like to use such terms when describing a sitting prime minister."

"But look at them, Watson."

Peeping around the doorframe, I beheld the two gentlemen, slouched forwards, leaning on each other so as not to collapse, staring with happy, vacant expressions at the far wall, drooling all over my coffee table.

"Yes, all right. Stupid. Here is what I propose: agree to help them. If they've got any useful information, I'd like to have it. Then we get rid of them. We keep our heads down, stay out of the way of police and soldiers, and we figure out what has happened and how to fix it, before they capture you and destroy me."

"Or the ill-fated Swedish warship—"

"*Holmes!*"

"Oh, very well, Watson. Let's finish interviewing our clients, shall we?"

"Yes. Thank you. But you mustn't call me by name."

"Of course, Watson. I shan't."

"But you just did."

"Well, I won't do it again, Watson. Never fear."

"But you just did. Again."

"Well, not in front of anybody. Really, you must learn to trust me, Watson."

"Oh, God…"

I have seldom been more affrighted than I was when we walked back into the sitting room to confront the mesmerized remains of Britain's prime minister. Holmes was the very picture of calm. He strode back in, smiled warmly and said, "Well, I think my partner Wat— um… Wat… whatever his name is and I are prepared to take your case."

"Yes. Aid us."

"I shall."

"Then we will capture you."

"Oh, I don't doubt it, gentlemen," Holmes assured them. "But before you do, can you tell us anything more about the mysterious letter?"

"It was beautif—"

"Yes, but where was it kept?"

"He had it," Lord Bellinger said, indicating his companion with no small amount of blame creeping into his stuporous monotone.

"Capital. And he is…?"

"Trelawney Hope," the man introduced himself.

Holmes looked just as lost as before, so I told him, "Mr. Hope is the Secretary for European Affairs, Holmes. He's quite the rising statesman. Or… he was…"

"And exactly where did you keep it, Mr. Hope?" Warlock asked.

"In my home, Whitehall Terrace," he said. "In my bedroom. In my dispatch box, where I keep all my important papers."

"I see. So, you took a piece of *fire* and put it with all your important *papers*," Holmes said, then turned to me and mused, "Well, I suppose he may not have been all that intelligent, even before he was mesmerized, eh, Wat— er… whatever your name is, eh?"

"Perhaps not," I agreed.

"So, you put the fire in with your papers, and then what happened?" asked Holmes. Yet, if the Moriarty Rune did set fire to any government documents, Trelawney Hope seemed to have no regard for it.

"Lord Bellinger…" Hope said. "I called him in to see if he could tell me what it was."

"Ah. I see," said Holmes. "And I have to suppose that's when it started in with the whole mesmerism thing, yes?"

"We used to stare at it for hours," Hope said.

"Admire it," said Bellinger with a sad, wistful look in his eye.

"So beautiful."

"So powerful."

"Capture Holmes."

"Destroy the doctor."

I gave Holmes a rather pointed look. To his credit, he recoiled, shocked and dismayed. The prospect of his own capture had caused him no concern, but the idea that I was in danger rocked him to the core. "What?" he spluttered. "No, no! Don't do that!"

Yet Holmes's admonitions were nothing against "the master's" repeated brain-washings. Bellinger leaned in with renewed vigor and insisted, "Destroy the doctor!"

"Destroy!" Hope agreed, in high-pitched, strident tones.

"Destroy! Destroy! *Destroy!*"

"I said no!" Holmes insisted, leaping to his feet. He cast his eyes about the room, as if searching for a weapon.

Eager that my friend not murder the prime minister in our sitting room, I suggested, "Perhaps we'd best concentrate on the present dilemma, gentlemen. We must recover your lost item. Can you tell us where you got it?"

"Lord Holdhurst," said Hope.

I nearly fell over backwards. "Do you know where he is?" I blurted.

"He had to *go*," said Bellinger with a malicious smile.

"Um… er… to the South of France," Hope added, unconvincingly.

"I got a hammer," said Bellinger, "and sent him to the South of France."

"No!" Hope insisted. "My axe and my letter opener! We sent him to the South of France!"

Though I was quite taken aback, at least some of the mysteries of the last week were taking shape in my mind. I cleared my throat and asked, "So, when did you last see the master?"

"Yesterday evening."

"We were looking at it."

"Admiring."

"Trying… trying to hear what it was telling us."

"So frustrating."

"So beautiful."

"Very well," I said. "One presumes this occurred at Mr. Hope's house?"

"Yes," Bellinger said.

"Whitehall Terrace," added Hope.

"At what hour did you see it last?"

This question demanded the act of recalling one's actions—a particular challenge for our guests, it seemed. They grunted and strained for a few minutes, until Bellinger finally decided, "Two, I should think. Two in the morning."

I nodded. "And when did you discover it was missing?"

"We awoke this morning at seven," said Bellinger, "to admire it."

"So beautif—"

"Yes, yes, yes! And powerful, I know," I interrupted.

"And that's when you discovered it was gone?"

"Gone!"

"Lost!"

"What do you think happened to it, Wat— er... Person-Who-Lives-With-Me?" Holmes wondered. "Did somebody take it?"

"I don't know," I said, then turned to our guests to ask, "Who else knew you were in possession of this message?"

This idea drew a howl of rage from Bellinger. "No! No one! The master must be kept safe!"

"Secret!"

"Secret from everybody!"

I drew a sigh and asked, "Mr. Hope, is that a wedding band on your finger?"

"Yes."

"And is your wife in residence at Whitehall Terrace?"

"Yessssssssss."

"And do you suppose she failed to notice that you spent the better part of the week holed up in your room, staying up until all hours, with the *prime minister of Great Britain*?"

The thought sunk slowly through the layers of fog that obscured the minds of our two visitors. They sat in silence. I had no idea how long it would take to register and had begun to doubt they would comprehend it at all when Bellinger suddenly screamed, "Destroy the wife!"

To my horror, Hope also screamed out, "Destroy!"

"Destroy!"

"Destroy!"

The two of them began to struggle up off the couch, but I leapt up before them and urged, "Gentlemen! Calm yourselves!"

"Do not calm! Destroy!"

"But wait! Wait… Don't you want Holmes's aid, first?" I reminded them.

"Aid us." Hope's tone was pleading. The rage dropped away from him in the merest heartbeat, replaced by an expression of haggard helplessness. I'd always supposed mesmerism and hypnotism to be relaxing endeavors, but here was proof that the last few days had been emotionally exhausting, even for these robust politicians. Poor fellows…

"Yes. Yes, that's right," I said, patting his arm. "Holmes will aid you. And until such time as he is finished, there is to be no capturing and no destroying *of anybody*, is that clear?"

"But… capture Holmes…"

"Well, if you capture him, how can he aid you?" I asked.

"But… destroy the wife…" Hope muttered.

"No, you mustn't." I tried to keep my voice stern, but fair.

"Destroy the doctor," Bellinger volunteered.

"No! You must especially not do that," I urged. "What if the person you destroyed was the only person who knew where your lost message was?"

The idea filled them with pure horror, but after a moment of fretting, Bellinger asked, "Then… what do we do?"

"One hesitates to presume," I said, "but if you will entertain a humble suggestion: attend to affairs of state."

"But... destroy!"

"No! Bad!" I yelled, shaking my finger at them both. "Attend to affairs of state! Say it!"

Bellinger slumped like a chastened dog and mumbled, "Attend to affairs of state."

"Attend."

"Attend."

"Good. Well, now that is settled, we must bid you gentlemen good day. Holmes and I will conduct the investigation and then call on you at Whitehall Terrace or 10 Downing Street."

They both nodded.

"Good. Now, get out of here. Attend to affairs of state."

"Attend," said Hope as I pushed him towards the door.

"Attend," came Bellinger's voice from the stairs as he stumbled towards the street.

I turned back to our sitting room and heaved a sigh. Even Warlock was forced to admit, "A curious case, indeed."

"And I think a very dangerous one," I said. "Help me understand something, Holmes: if Moriarty escaped your body after I shot you, what would he do?"

"Ha! He'd be frantic," Holmes laughed. "He's hardly anything, right now. Merely a disembodied personality. Something like... the *idea* of Moriarty. And an idea that is not in anybody's mind—an opinion held by nobody—what is that? He's managed to find a way to make his personality

121

long survive his physical form, but the accomplishment has not come without a cost. He'd immediately need a host to live in, or at least somebody to be transfixed by the idea of him, or else he'd simply fade away."

"Let us suppose that he found Lord Holdhurst."

"Which makes sense," Holmes admitted. "If he couldn't find a powerful magical entity to possess, he'd at least want a thrall with either great wealth or political power."

"So he hypnotizes Lord Holdhurst, who runs the Foreign Office," I surmised, pacing the room as I followed the tread of my own imagination. "Trelawney Hope is Secretary for European Affairs, so of course he works with Lord Holdhurst a great deal. He notices the change in Lord Holdhurst, coaxes news of the source from him and begins to feel that the prime minister ought to hear of this strange 'communication'. Of course, Lord Holdhurst does not wish to lose his new treasure."

"Oh!" cried Holmes. "That's why he wished Percy Phelps to copy it! So he could pass the copy along without surrendering the actual rune."

"An impossible assignment, probably. Then again, it didn't matter, since Joseph Harrison stole the rune before Percy could fail."

"Then we got it back for Lord Holdhurst, without knowing what it was," said Holmes.

"At which point Lord Bellinger—who was no doubt a bit tired of Lord Holdhurst's extraordinary behavior—tried to confiscate it."

"So Lord Holdhurst stuck it up a turkey!"

"Goose, Holmes. And yes. We have gone far into the realm of speculation, but it seems that shortly after Lord Holdhurst got the rune back from Phelps, he elected to hide it in a goose. Perhaps he needed a host to keep it alive. Perhaps it was merely an expedient way to get across town without being searched. Bellinger's cronies would surely check his pockets, but would they think to look inside a goose?"

"They didn't have to, once we ate it for Christmas dinner. They must have gotten their hands on it some time after Grogsson… er… set it free," Holmes reasoned. "After all, they're both spectacularly mesmerized by it and it sounds as if they've done something rather rash to Lord Holdhurst."

"What would you expect a Moriarty-enthralled Bellinger to do, if Lord Holdhurst tried to reclaim the rune from him?"

"Oh, he'd murder him on the spot! Or, to use the parlance of the day: extend an immediate invitation to the South of France."

"Which, it seems, they have," I said. "With an axe and a hammer."

"Don't forget the letter opener," Holmes reminded me. "Some of them are quite savage. Do you know the kind I mean? The kind that's supposed to be for envelopes but looks like it's for throats?"

A sudden commotion on the street outside broke my concentration and summoned me to the window. The source of the outcry was harmless enough: our pair of mesmerized politicians had failed to negotiate their way even to the end of the street. They'd wandered into traffic, it seems, nearly been killed by a hackney carriage and caused a bit of a traffic jam. Raised voices and shaking fists predominated. Yet of all the people who stopped to stare at our recent guests, one in particular commanded my attention. A woman in a white cloak watched them from the partial concealment of a street-vendor's stand. When the two statesmen finally staggered out of sight, she made directly for our door.

"It seems as if we are to have another visitor, Holmes."

"Oh? Who?"

"I can't be sure, but her youth, the richness of her dress, and the fact that only an idiot could look at Mr. Trelawney Hope without realizing something was dreadfully wrong with him leads me to surmise that it may be *Mrs.* Trelawney Hope."

"Well, if it is, let us hope she isn't intercepted and destroyed before we can find out what she wants," Holmes said.

We hadn't long to wait, for at that very moment came the sound of Mrs. Hudson answering the front door. Soon there was a rap on our own door. When I answered it, Mrs. Hudson jerked a thumb towards our cloaked lady and announced, "Posh bit o' crumpet to see you."

"Mrs. Hudson, really! I will thank you *never* to describe my visitors in such terms!"

"Yeah, but she is, though."

"Immaterial!"

Our guest waved impatient hands at Mrs. Hudson and

insisted, "It is of no account." She cocked her head to one side and stared at me expectantly.

"Oh… yes, of course. Won't you come in, madam?"

She stepped over our threshold, turned to Mrs. Hudson, said, "Thank you for showing me up; that will be all," and gently but unapologetically shut the door in my landlady's face.

I liked her.

This, I think, must have been the common reaction, for my guest was one of those people who is perfect in every respect. She was beautiful in the extreme, fair-haired, with white skin and a graceful, swan-like neck. Her nose was aquiline; her green eyes shone with vigor and intelligence. And it got even better.

"Mrs. Hope, I presume?"

"Lady Hilda Trelawney Hope, pleased to make your acquaintance."

"Lady? Forgive me, I was unaware that the position of Secretary for European Affairs conferred title upon—"

"No, no, no. Daddy is Duke of Belminster."

So: rich, beautiful, smart, well-mannered, kind, and daughter to a bloody duke, no less. She gave me an apologetic smile, which, I realized, she was forced to do with everybody she ever met. It was merely a quick little grimace to say, "Yes, I am aware that my very existence is unfair; that the gifts of nature are distributed with grotesque inequity. I'm sorry, but there's nothing I can do about it."

"Well, Lady Hilda, I am honored to meet you. I am Dr. John Watson."

At my name, she gave a little gasp and cried out, "Yes! That's it! That's the name my husband has been trying to work out for the last several days. You are in danger, sir!"

"As are we all, I fear. Allow me to present my colleague, Mr. Warlock Holmes."

"A pleasure to know you," he said, stepping toward Lady Hilda and bowing his head. "You are indeed a very posh bit of crumpet."

"*Holmes!*"

"What? She is."

"Immaterial!"

"Gentlemen, I've little time to waste," Lady Hilda interjected. "I need your help with an… ahem… *purely theoretical* problem."

"Theoretical?" I asked.

"Purely. Yes, you see, I'm… well, let us say I am writing a book."

"Oh! I love books," Holmes enthused. "Is there magic in it? Is there kissing?"

"Well… perhaps. You see, the heroine of this book is a lady who is married to a rising politician. She tries to do her best by her husband and the realm, but she has been injudicious in her youth and certain indiscretions have come to the attention of one Eduardo Lucas—a wretched foreign spy who lives at 16 Godolphin Street. Did you note the address? 16 Godolphin Street!"

"I believe I have it," I assured her.

"It seems he's come into possession of a rather compromising letter she once wrote to her tennis instructor, who had buttocks so taut you'd swear you could forge a sword on them. The awful spy says he'll make the letter public, unless our heroine steals a certain document of her husband's and delivers it to…?"

"16 Godolphin Street?" I hazarded.

"Just so. Now, our heroine is glad to have that particular 'document' leave the house anyway, for it seems to be having an effect on her husband's wit. So, night falls, the item is duly stolen, brought to 16 Godolphin Street and traded for her injudicious letter. Our heroine returns home, has a sit–down, swallows three glasses of sherry, spends an hour in fond remembrance of the back half of her tennis instructor and chucks the letter into the fire. All would seem to be well, wouldn't it?"

"It would," I agreed, "unless her husband discovers the loss and goes somewhat crazy over it."

"Oh, my God! *Somewhat?* There's every danger that the army and navy shall be called out at any instant. What should our entirely fictional heroine do?"

"She should seek help, I would think."

"Very wise, Dr. Watson. Ah! Perhaps she has heard of someone who might help. Perhaps word has come to her of a powerful sorcerer and his rather mundane keeper—a set of fellows with a penchant for unraveling such problems. Do you think they might help her?"

"I'm sure they would not fail," I replied. "Though I might suggest 'finest of the mainstream' in place of 'rather mundane'."

"Well," she said, granting me a smile with just a touch

too much mischief in it, "you may be right. Oops! I seem to have dropped a piece of paper on which someone has written the address of the hotel I'm staying at and the assumed name I'm using. Perhaps it's for the best. After all, if anyone knew of further developments for that book I'm writing, they could most likely reach me there."

"I think I might have some material contribution, soon," I told her.

"Good. Any missing story elements you recover should be brought directly to me. To attempt to return them to my husband, the prime minister or Whitehall Terrace would be foolhardy in the extreme. Well, good day, gentlemen. I suppose I had better get back to my 'writing'. Who will see me out?"

"Watson, most probably," Holmes said. "He always seems desperate to spend time in women's company, and I haven't got my slippers on."

"Watson it is, then," Lady Hope said, extending her arm to me.

As I escorted her down the stairs she pressed against me. It may have only been the narrowness of the passageway that was to blame, but… No, she was *entirely* too familiar. I blushed to think what might be supposed if anyone happened to observe us. What would occur if her husband saw how she hung on my arm as we descended the steps? Well… I suppose he was bent on my destruction anyway. I began to perspire. The chaotic slew of emotion she caused in me was either a strange accident or devised by a master of stagecraft. Her touch was unexpected, terrifying, embarrassing and yet… not unwelcome. On the last step, she paused. She stepped just slightly back from me and stared up at my face with strange earnestness. After a moment's scrutiny, she asked, "Dr. Watson, if I needed any little thing… or if I wished someone to talk to… would I be welcome in your home?"

"What? Well, I should think… that is to say… of course you would."

"Whenever I wish?"

"Whenever you wish."

"Thank you, John. It's just what I wanted." She leaned up, gave me a little kiss on the cheek, opened the door to Baker Street and stepped out into the light. As she left, she spared me a little smile of… what shall I say? *Ownership*, nearly. Then she set off up the street.

I tottered on my heels for a moment, then turned and stumbled up the stairs. What had just happened? I'll admit I was not a worldly fellow. Not experienced. Too much a child of propriety, perhaps. I knew there must be a thousand required steps of protocol between the act of first greeting an unknown lady and the act of… you know… generating a child. I'll also confess to a certain frustrated ignorance as to what those thousand steps might be. Yet that day, as I returned to 221B, I had the distinct feeling I'd just been shown three or four of them.

I returned to find Holmes poking at a loaf of bread with a long knife. It was part of his daily ritual. Hovering. Probing. Deciding whether it would be best to carve off a slice of that loaf and toast it, or whether discretion was the order of the day. I knew the answer perfectly well. *Toast* was the order of the day. Every day. I never saw him enjoy any discretion. Yet, at that particular moment, I gave him no time to complete his ritual.

"Holmes, get your coat."

"Why?"

"We have to go. 16 Godolphin Street."

"Because it is in some aristocrat's unfinished novel? Really, Watson, I think you attach too much importance to the literary aspirations of Britain's idle rich. What do you think, would it be wise of me to have a slice of toast or not?"

"But we have to go! 16 Godolphin Street! Eduardo Lucas—"

"Is an entirely fictional individual. Lady Hope said as much."

"She had to! Don't you see, Holmes? The things she was admitting to are more than domestic indiscretion— they are tantamount to treason. I, for one, have not sat here agonizing about my lack of information only to ignore both a new mystery and the mystery's solution when they are conveniently dumped in my lap! Now, get your coat."

A look of worry crossed his brow. "I don't know, Watson, if it's as you say…"

"It is."

"…If this is some cleverly veiled confession…"

"None too cleverly, I would think."

"…Then doesn't it seem just a trifle *too* convenient?

It dropped in your lap, just as you say. One visitor delivers the exact mystery you've been looking for. Five minutes later, a second drops the answer and you rush out, unprepared, to deal with it? It all seems a bit too much of a coincidence. Not only that, Watson, but... the more I think of her story... the more certain aspects of it make no sense."

Whatever my opinion of Holmes's intelligence, I was forced to admit he enjoyed a vast superiority of experience compared to my own. Likewise, it was true that my intellect could be somewhat compromised by the touch of a pretty lady—a flaw precluded by Holmes's dispassionate aloofness. Though the notion was repellant to me, it was entirely possible he had captured some detail that had eluded me. I paused. "Really?" I asked. "What was the matter with her story?"

"'Injudicious'," Holmes replied, tapping his lips thoughtfully with the edge of his knife. "Yes... Yes, the more I think on it, the more certain I become: 'injudicious' is not a real word."

"Holmes," I said, carefully swallowing a sudden urge to strike him in the side of the head, "firstly, it is a real word. Secondly, if it were not, it would not matter. Here is a secret of the English language you appear to be ignorant of: any improper word spoken by the daughter of a duke as wonderful and as beautiful as that *becomes* a proper word the second she utters it. Now, get your coat. We're going."

* * *

The instant our cab turned onto Godolphin Street, I could tell something was amiss. The gigantic knot of policemen standing about outside Number 16 was a clue, but not the main one. No, the true herald of misfortune was the terrible reek that overhung the entire area. Even in London—not known for the freshness of her breezes—the smell was shocking and aberrant. So severe was it that the cab horse snorted and shied back. His master appeared to agree, for the cabman pulled up and declared, "Here we are, gentlemen."

"Is this Number 16?" Holmes inquired.

"It's close enough! Out you get!"

Still, I can't complain of the treatment, for as I reached up to pay with one hand (covering my nose with the other) the cabman disregarded me. He whisked the cab around in a half-circle and set off at an unnecessary gallop. Much to the horse's relief, I suspect. As Holmes and I turned to walk the rest of the way to Number 16, we were surprised to find Lestrade standing on the walk before us. He wore the same dour expression as he always did—a particular disadvantage of his character. When disaster struck, poor Lestrade had no facial method of communicating it, since he walked about at all hours of all days wearing a look most people reserved for the death of a dozen saintly orphans.

"I'm glad you've come," he said. He didn't look glad.

"What has happened, Lestrade?" Holmes asked. "Has something unfortunate occurred at Number 16?"

Lestrade stared at him a moment, then replied, "Warlock, I invite you to take a deep breath in, through the nose, and then tell me if you think what you smell could possibly be the result of very good fortune. Come with me."

The group of policemen outside Number 16 clustered as far from the door as they could get without abandoning their duty entirely. One unfortunate young constable had been assigned to guard the door, beside which he had vomited multiple times. As we stepped past him, it took all my courage and fortitude to enter that den of unbearable stench. Even Lestrade had to grit his terrible teeth.

16 Godolphin Street was a well-appointed Westminster home (excepting the smell, of course). It was decorated in a style that spoke of adventure, with curios from the orient prominently displayed on every wall. Lestrade turned right and headed into the first room, which must have been a study of some sort. Grogsson was there; he offered us no greeting but turned and stared at us with rage. It seemed his natural desire to punch something to death weighed even more heavily on his mind that particular morning. Yet, I detected a subtle undertone of desperation to his unfocused fury, as if what he really wished to say was, "This smell is hurting my tummy. Help me."

The center of the study's floor was bare. There had been a desk, but it was smashed. So smashed, in fact, that it took me a moment to realize I was looking at a bookcase, also. The two had been driven together with such force that their wreckage had become one and the plaster of the wall against which the bookcase stood had been shattered. The display cases on the walls had suffered as well. They seemed to have held a variety of exotic armaments from far-flung reaches, so the clutter at the edges of the room must have represented ten or twelve interesting and unusual ways to kill a man. Still, none of them explained the body of Eduardo Lucas.

His face was easy to explain, for it was the face of a dead man. He wore a look of utter fear—as one might well understand. His feet and lower legs were easy to explain too, for they were merely the lower extremity of a dead man. Yet everything between his mid-thigh and the base of his neck defied reason. He'd sort of... melted. The hollow frame of his ribcage was visible through his torn shirt, but all the flesh within the middle span of his body was gone. He lay in a puddle of horrific brown slop, which—one assumed—was the remnant of his torso. Greasy strands of it still clung to the bones, giving the impression that this puddle was not what had killed the man, but rather the earthly remains of the man himself. Thankfully, it had dried somewhat—to the consistency of spilled beef stew, left in the sun for a few days.

Except, not as appetizing.

"I think my colleagues are unlikely to believe this was a pistol wound," Lestrade complained. "Even worse, I would think this particular murder has a sufficient level of sensationalism to command the front pages. We had best solve it."

"Very well," I said, "but I think my medical expertise will not suffice to determine cause of death. The closest thing I've seen is the unknown toxin from Grimesby

Roylott's syringes, but its mechanisms remain a mystery to me. Holmes, do you think you can work out what did this?"

"Well," said Warlock, stepping forward and withdrawing his magnifying glass from his pocket, "let us see what I can see…"

He crouched over the unfortunate form of Eduardo Lucas, peeping first at this bit, then the next, then back to the first again. In less than a minute, he stood, straightened his sleeves and delivered his expert opinion.

"Magic."

"Thank you, Holmes," I muttered.

Lestrade went a step further. He fixed Holmes with a look of cold fury, set his hands on his hips and demanded, "That is all? *Magic?* You were more useful in the past. Remember? You always used to have a prophecy when we needed one."

"Yes, but that was when Moriarty was trapped within him," I reminded the stunted Romanian. "Holmes has not issued any prophecy since Moriarty left."

"What? Yes I have!" Holmes insisted.

"No you haven't," said Lestrade, Grogsson and I.

"How dare you? Prophecy is a gift of mine! Never of Moriarty!"

"No. Moriarty," we all said.

Grogsson added, "You a liar."

"Oh? *Oh?* I'll show you! Show you all! Then you'll be sorry!" Holmes pouted. He threw himself into the nearest corner and began intoning, "Ohhhhhmmmmmmm!

Ohhhhhhmmmmmm! Secrets–are–coming–to–meeeeeeee! Seeeeeeeeecretssssssssss…"

Turning from Holmes, I suggested, "Perhaps we should examine the room for clues." There were plenty of them. The un–gooed portion of the rug upon which the body lay showed a positive flurry of footprints, made with force and haste.

"Unless Eduardo Lucas died of over–dancing, I'd say there was a bit of a scuffle here," I said.

"Ooooooommmmmm… uhmmmmmmm… soon–I'll–know–everything…"

"Shut up, Holmes," Lestrade suggested, leaning in to examine the scene. His skill at reading footprints was infinitely superior to mine. In only a moment he cried, "Look! This second print: the foot is small. And see this blocky imprint here? That was made by a hard, separated heel."

"A woman?" I asked.

"Just so, Doctor."

"Yes… a woman…" said a thin, spectral voice. Grogsson gave a sudden cry of alarm and leapt sideways, as if someone had unexpectedly pinched his bottom. There stood Holmes with his arms splayed to either side, elbows bent and palms down in that unrealistic pose marionettes often adopt. His head was cocked backwards and to one side. His eyes drifted back and forth across the ceiling, as if scanning for hidden knowledge. As he spoke, a strange vapor drifted up from his mouth.

"Wait, is he…? Did he actually do it?" Lestrade wondered aloud.

"I know her," Holmes mused in a willowy, unearthly tone. His head flopped to the other side and he continued, "And she knows me. She knows him and him…"

Holmes indicated first myself, then Lucas.

"…but not him or him…"

Grogsson and Lestrade.

"She wanted something so much, she killed this man to take it. She *still* wants it… She is looking…" Holmes's feet began to move as if of their own accord. His head jerked this way and that as his body was yanked first one way, then another, by his wayward legs. Holmes the puppet danced his macabre minuet, reciting, "She has minions… unwitting minions who search for it… searching at her behest…"

I'd never seen him in such a state and—my own suspicions of supernatural phenomena notwithstanding—I thrilled to see it. He seemed to be on the right track. The footprints did indicate a woman had been here, yet beyond that there seemed to be no mundane clue as to her identity. Perhaps Holmes could serve the deficiency. "Who is it, Holmes? Who is this woman?"

"It is *the Woman*."

"All right. Yes. But that might describe half the world's population. I don't suppose you could narrow it down a bit, eh? Oh! Holmes! Careful! Don't step in…"

But it was too late. Holmes's ethereal wandering took him directly across the crime scene. With a horrible crunch and squelch, Holmes's foot sank through the ribcage of Eduardo Lucas and down into the muck beneath.

"Eeeeeeeeeeeeeahughah!" screamed Holmes. My shoulders sank—it was clear Holmes's trance was broken.

"Damn it, Warlock," Lestrade complained, "you were just about to become useful."

"Augh! No! By the gods! My shoe! Look at my shoe! Get it off me!"

"Gwarrr-har-har!"

"Help! Get it off! Grogsson, help me!"

"No! Hey! You stay back from me!"

Holmes ran to each of us in turn, seeking aid, tracking horrid drops of Eduardo Lucas sauce all over the crime scene. We drew back. At last, he settled onto the crushed desk and peeled his shoe off with a bit of smashed wood.

"By Jove, look what it's done to my sock!"

I couldn't help but give a little grunt of laughter at Holmes's plight. Yet something he said kept crossing my mind.

She wanted something.

And I thought I knew what. If Lady Hilda's story was true, Lucas may well have spirited the Moriarty Rune to this very room, last night. Was he interrupted and murdered here? Murdered by some woman who had been seeking the rune? The room certainly seemed to reinforce that idea. The desk, the bookshelf and every display cabinet upon the walls had been smashed. Clearly, somebody had been looking for something. Somebody whose behavior showed as much penchant for force as distaste for patience.

She still wants it.

So she hadn't found it. The mysterious woman had

come here sure she'd find her treasure, murdered Lucas, and then failed to find what she'd been looking for. Was that because it had never been concealed in this room? Or had she simply overlooked it? Was it still here? I cast my gaze about, looking for a place the murderess had not checked. Every piece of furniture had been smashed and rifled. I could even make out a line of dust upon the floor and a corresponding change in the fade of the floorboards to show me the rug had been moved. It seemed she had checked everywhere. I circulated the room, searching, while the others saw to Holmes.

"Grogsson! Help! It's on my trousers!"

"Gwarr-har-har!"

"Get my trousers off!"

"No!"

"Well then, bring me something to wipe it up with, won't you?"

With a shrug, Grogsson stepped to the middle of the room and grabbed a clean corner of the rug on which the corpse lay. He picked it up, clearly intending to drag it over to Holmes and use the corner to mop up some of the slop. As he lifted the rug, I saw a stain upon the floorboards. The Lucas-goop had seeped through the rug, leaving a second stain that exactly corresponded with the first.

"No! Put that down, you great fool," Lestrade cried. "We must not disturb the scene!"

A bit late for that, I thought, looking over Warlock's gooey footprints and discarded clothing. Suddenly a thought struck me.

"Wait! Grogsson! The rug! We must move it! Help me shift it, won't you?"

"Do not encourage him, Doctor," Lestrade complained. "I've been trying to break him of this habit for some time now."

"But see here," I said. "Holmes says the murderess is still looking for the thing she sought in this room, yes?"

"So?" asked Lestrade.

"The rug has been moved!"

"At the risk of repeating myself," said Lestrade, "so?"

"The faded square on the floorboards does not match the current position of the rug, but the stain underneath *does*! Don't you see? If she had moved the rug while searching, the stain would be different. It would at least be larger than the stain upon the rug. Smudged. But it isn't. The rug was moved *before* Lucas met his death."

Holmes, Lestrade and Grogsson turned to look at me, searchingly, then with one voice they all said, "So?"

"So, if our mystery woman did not move it after killing Lucas, someone moved it before! Who? We know the murderess believed the rune to be hidden somewhere in this room, otherwise why would she have searched it so rigorously? But what if Lucas had a few moments in the room, before she got here? *He* moved the rug! Just before he was slain, he hid something under that rug!"

Lestrade gave a sigh of consternation, but eventually nodded. Apparently, my previous help had earned me just enough cachet to allow the shifting of one crime-scene rug.

"All right, you big oaf," he hissed at Grogsson. "Lend

a hand. We'll put it over by the fireplace."

The three of us picked up the rug and carried the mortal remains of Eduardo Lucas to one side of the room. As soon as it was disturbed, the brown sauce proved to be only semi-solidified. Though the top had dried, the lower layer was still liquid—a liquid that seemed overjoyed to spill from the carpet and slop all over the floor. It was difficult not to gag.

Having moved the body clear, we all returned to examine the floor at the center of the room and eagerly beheld...

Nothing.

Search as we might, no trace could be found of the Moriarty Rune. It had not been simply thrust under the rug. Nor was it stuck to the bottom. I checked—an act that nearly cost me my breakfast and the better part of my stomach lining. Where the rug had been, we found no trace of any hatch or compartment.

"Well," said Lestrade, gazing around the slop-sloshed ruins of his crime scene, "I suppose we will have some explaining to do to the commissioner. A pity Dr. Watson's instincts have failed him, this time."

But Holmes said, "No..."

He stood by the wreckage of the desk. He had only one shoe on, and one sock. He had borrowed Grogsson's straight razor to clumsily hack away at the befouled leg; his trousers were in ruins. On his face was a dreamy look— just a hint of the trancelike state he'd been in earlier.

"...I think Watson may be right."

His left hand drifted up from his side. He held it open and stared down at his palm, as if curious. Suddenly, he snapped it shut and, with a wrenching squeal, all the floorboards in the center of the room withered and bent. Grogsson roared his approval. Lestrade cried out, "Oh, come now! How am I to explain *that*?"

"But wait!" I said. "What is this?"

In the center of the wreckage lay a small section of floor that had not succumbed to Holmes's spell. It was irregular, its shape defined only by where a few of the smaller boards began and ended. Wading through the twisted wooden waste, I grasped this section and drew it up. Beneath was a small compartment, hardly a foot deep, two feet long and some few inches across. Within lay nearly a dozen documents (which proved to contain government secrets of a most salacious nature) and, much to my delight, the same battered attaché case Annie Harrison had taken from her fallen brother. Drawing the case out of its sanctum, I learned that my earlier suspicions had indeed been correct. Its sides were constructed not of leather, but of dull and dented lead. Yet, despite its weight, I could just feel the soft flutter of something moving within. Something alive.

"Holmes," I whispered, "I think it's him! Moriarty!"

"Well, open it up. Let's have a look."

"But… won't he get out?"

"You may be right, Watson. Just the corner, then."

We all drew close. Flipping one of the catches, I drew the strap loose and bent up the corner of one side of the flap. Through the crack we could make out the irregular flickering of the tiny blue flame of the Moriarty Rune.

"Ha!" Holmes exclaimed. "We've got him! My great enemy! Not so scary now, are you, Jimmy?"

"You unner arrest," said Grogsson, pointing at the case.

"I don't know how much good that would do, Torg," said Lestrade. "The courts are not in the habit of trying little bits of fire."

"Then what should we do with him?" I asked.

"He must be destroyed," said Holmes.

"How?"

"Well, that's the trick, isn't it? For now, Watson, I think we'd best get him safely back to 221B."

"I don't think we'll be going anywhere," said Lestrade. "There are a dozen constables outside and the commissioner is on his way. When they see what we have done to the crime scene, well... Holmes, Lestrade and Grogsson all in one room, with the suspicion of guilt upon them? It's all Scotland Yard has been hoping for. I should think we'll be arrested for the murder of Eduardo Lucas. The judge will find a way to make himself believe it. Then we'll be hanged. It's no more than we deserve."

"Lestrade, you ought to adopt a puppy. Quickly, before you become just insufferable," I told him. "As it so happens, I once had to use a lie against Mrs. Hudson which will, I think, prove itself serviceable again."

Three minutes later, I found myself standing on the doorstep of 16 Godolphin Street, chiding a dozen constables and the recently arrived police commissioner.

"Gentlemen, you say this is a case of murder? Why would you think so? Is there a pistol wound? The mark of a knife? Inspector Lestrade, at least, has had the wisdom to consider other possibilities. He has summoned me—Dr. John Watson, of Baker Street—to perform the Heinzwald–Gershwitzerbarden test."

"Oh, I've heard of that test," said Holmes, exactly as we had coached him. "Isn't it rather destructive to the surroundings where it is conducted?"

"It is," I faux-admitted. "Yet the results are conclusive. Gentlemen, I can confidently state that Mr. Eduardo Lucas was not felled by murder, as you are all too willing to believe, but that he instead succumbed to that dread disease, Indo-Brazilian super-gonorrhea! If you love your country, gentlemen, if you value the peace, you will cease conjuring imagined murders and devote your efforts to combating the real threat. The wolf is at your door! Disaster looms! Stay vigilant! Be particularly on your guard against French chorus girls! That is all. Good day. Goodbye. No questions, please."

The local lawmen being suitably impressed, we made our way down the street—Holmes in his bare feet with one trouser leg hacked away, Grogsson with the little leaden case tucked into the inner pocket of his overcoat. All seemed right until we arrived at Baker Street. Even as we prepared to mount the steps to our home, we were met by Mrs. Hudson as she escorted a pair of disappointed visitors out.

"Lady Hilda Trelawney Hope, to see Mr. Holmes," Mrs. Hudson announced.

It was clear, concise and polite—by far her finest introduction of the day—yet I could not stop myself spluttering, "No it isn't."

The lady upon the steps had no resemblance to our earlier guest. True, she was well dressed, but she was older, plainer, more severe, and utterly devoid of the oh-save-me-I-am-a-thrilling-rich-attractive-woman-who-needs-your-help aspect of character that had so charmed me earlier that morning. She was accompanied by a pinch-faced butler, so austere and haughty that even I was taken aback by his extreme Britishness.

"Excuse me, but I certainly am Lady Hilda Trelawney Hope!" she said huffily. Her aristocratic aspect of superiority had suffered somewhat from the shock of having Grogsson wedged into the staircase right in front of her, but it was nevertheless unmistakable. "I have come to discuss a matter of utmost import and delicacy."

"We may know something of it already," I muttered.

This second version of Lady Hilda stiffened even more and declared, "My words are for the ears of Mr. Holmes only! Oh, and maybe that hanger-on lad I hear he employs. Word has it, he is occasionally useful."

"I strive to serve," said I, then turned back to my party and suggested, "Lestrade, Grogsson, perhaps we had best catch up with you later. Torg, I don't suppose you'd mind lending me your coat and its… contents?"

He scowled at me and grumbled, "No. Torg will stay and talk with pretty lady."

"By God, you shall not! Give me that coat, this instant!

Now, get out! Off with you! Lestrade, get him clear, won't you? Holmes and I will find you later."

As soon as I had the Moriarty Rune and was relatively sure that Grogsson was not going to come bashing into our sitting room and propose marriage to Lady Hilda, Holmes and I settled in with the morning's second damsel in distress to hear almost exactly the same story. This woman claimed the same identity as our first guest, told of the same blackmail threat by the same Eduardo Lucas, worried of the same exposure of her same treasonous misdeed, expressed the same admiration of the posterior aspect of the same tennis instructor and enjoined us to eradicate all the consequences of her poor personal decisions, just as our earlier guest had.

When she and her awful butler at last departed, I sank wearily back into my chair and let my mind parse the whirlwind morning. My wit flittered between the mesmerized minister; the beautiful, wonderful Lady Hilda; the not-so-beautiful-or-wonderful Lady Hilda; Moriarty; the threat to my own person; and the horrible sauce-murder of Eduardo Lucas. All was shrouded and uncertain; there was only one thing I knew for sure.

"The second one. That was the real Lady Hilda."

"Indubitably," said Holmes.

"Did you see how angry she was? How improprietous she found it that such things should happen to a person of her station? That's the real duke's daughter, if ever there was one."

Holmes nodded sagely. "And when I noted that she,

too, was a posh bit of crumpet, her butler slapped me."

"As well he should, Holmes. As well he should."

"It's a pity," Warlock sighed. "I much preferred the first lady, you know. I wish she was the real one."

"Precisely! It's as if she knew just what we'd want Lady Hilda to be and then she became that person, to deceive us. She's played her game like a true master, Holmes. She fooled us before she'd even met us. But why? And how? How did she know so much about the rune? About Lady Hilda's indiscretion and Lucas's involvement? Why did she come to us at all? What does she want? Is she after the rune, or sabotaging the prime minister, or the real Lady Hilda or—"

"And why did she shoot Milverton?" Holmes interjected.

"Exactly! Why did she... Eh? What are you talking about, Holmes?"

"Remember? About a year ago, when she dressed up as an Irish servant girl and murdered Charles Augustus Milverton while we were hiding behind the curtains? Why did she do that?"

Realization can take many forms. Some say it is a flash—the touch of divinity in the mortal mind. Some say it is like beholding a thousand scattered puzzle pieces and knowing, in your heart, the picture they will make as they unite.

Personally, I just got a headache. Knowledge and cranial pain flooded over me at the same instant; the onset was so sudden and so severe, I swear I lost the vision in my right eye. I roared with rage, though whether I was angry at her for tricking me, Holmes for holding his tongue until then, or myself for being such a dupe, I could not say.

"Holmes! Why didn't you…? When did you know?"

"Oh, I just thought of it. Just now. It was her eyes, I think."

Yes. It was. I should have seen it myself. There had been a few other clues—her size, the slope of her jaw—but the real clue was those piercing green eyes. Gone was the splatter of freckles she'd had that first night, the dizzying blast of red hair and the scared, subservient manner, but the eyes were the same. They'd been five feet from my own, looking right at me. If only I'd looked back. If only I'd paid attention to the truth of those eyes, instead of the lure of her story, they would surely have betrayed her to me.

"She's a formidable person," Holmes continued. "I'm a little bit afraid of her, Watson, and I don't mind admitting it. She's pretty good at fooling people. And pretty good at killing them, too. She shot Milverton. Almost shot you, by your own account. Killed Lucas too, I shouldn't wonder."

"But why? How? It doesn't make any…"

But it did make sense. Perfect sense. After all, how many people had even known about the Moriarty Rune? Milverton had seen it, perhaps, but he'd died a moment later. Holmes had surely seen it, but had been stricken insensible. I'd seen it. The murderess had, too. Somehow, the rune seemed to have gotten out of Holmes and made the acquaintance of Holdhurst, Bellinger, Hope and Lucas. Now two of them were reduced to helpless imbecility and the other two were *ahem* in the South of France. Thus, outside that sitting room at 221B Baker Street, I could name only one capable person who surely knew of the Moriarty Rune. Well... I suppose I could not *name* her. Merely label her.

The Woman.

What a foe! I had let the Moriarty Rune slip away from me as Holmes lay nearly dead, one room over. She had found it. When? Only as Lucas blackmailed Lady Hope for it? When it spellbound Hope and Bellinger? Or even Lord Holdhurst? Whenever she had rejoined its adventure, she'd done it in rather bold style. According to Holmes's prophecy, she'd killed Lucas for it. Imagine her dismay when she couldn't find the thing. And yet, I could not help but admire her creativity and adaptability. Only a few hours later, she'd come and put Holmes and myself onto the track she'd lost. A white cloak, a sob story and a kiss on my cheek had been all she'd needed to set the world's most powerful sorcerer running errands for her. Ye gods, in his prophecy, Holmes had even said: *She has minions... unwitting minions who search for it...*

He might have mentioned he meant *us*.

"What are we to do?" Holmes asked.

I thought about that for a few moments, turning the card the Woman had left us over and over in my hand. Finally, I smiled. "We have the advantage of her, Holmes. She has no way of knowing we've discovered her deception."

"Unless she was following us," Holmes reasoned. "She is a master of disguise, so she could have passed herself off as anybody and observed us—"

"Yes, yes! But *most likely*, she is unaware. She expects us to march blithely into her hotel and present our findings to her. I propose we do exactly that!"

"But I think we should keep Moriarty," Holmes whined.

"Oh, we will. And more than that, we'll be capturing the Woman, as well."

"Oooooh, I just don't know if I'm comfortable with that, Watson. I don't like the idea of helping you start a girl collection—I've long feared the day your lonely mind snapped and did exactly that. Besides which, she's smarter than we are. We are outmatched."

"Holmes! The game is afoot! The wheels are turning! Do you propose we should let others determine our fate while we sit idly by?"

"Please? Just this once?"

"Get your coat, Holmes."

Much to my chagrin, the false Lady Hope had selected a hotel nearly all the way across town. As the day was wearing on, London's famous traffic had reached full swing. The journey took longer than I'd have liked, especially as we had to stop twice along the way to pick up a small attaché case and some cheap gray paint to disguise it. Yes, the original case was safe at 221B, but I had a fairly good facsimile under my arm when we at last alighted outside the Crooked Crumpet.

It was not as I'd expected. From the outside, it looked just like any other disreputable East End hovel. One step through the door, however, and the visitor was met with the perfect cross between his familiar neighborhood tavern and Emperor Caligula's debauched boudoir. The dimly lit room was hung with scarlet bunting and shone in the flickering light of a dozen perfumed-oil lamps. The place seemed to be composed entirely of dark corners. Several men lounged at tables and on piles of cushions, drinking liquor from tiny crystal goblets and smoking strange cigars. From behind a gilded and gaudy bar lined with dozens of bright glass bottles, a perfectly working-class bartender asked, "Help you, gentlemen?"

"I certainly hope so. I am looking for… er…" I glanced down at the card and read, "Bang Cleopatra."

The bartender shrugged and scratched an eyebrow. "Won't be cheap. Especially for two of yeh. Oi! Bang-bang!"

A muted clamor ran through the clientele. All eyes turned to the top of the stairs. Momentarily, there appeared a muscular young man in his twenties. He wore a long Egyptian gown, dark eye-makeup and a clinking beaded wig. He glided gracefully to the banister then, with sudden violence, thrust both hands down to point directly at a suspicious bulge halfway down his dress which gave the astute observer reason to believe he was probably *not a lady*.

"Bang!" he yelled, then raised both hands above his head and spread his fingers as the boughs of a breeze-kissed fig tree and breathily whispered, "Clee-oh-pa-ta-rahhhhhhhhh!"

"I know I called our foe a master of disguise," Holmes reflected. "Still, I cannot help but suspect: that isn't her."

"Damn!" I cried. "Damn it all! Back to Baker Street!"

We were too late. The first thing that greeted us as we rushed in was the prostrate form of Mrs. Hudson. For a moment, I feared the worst. (Best?) Yet, as I leaned in to check her pulse, she stuporously muttered, "Lady came to see you gents. Nice lady. Gave me the sweetest little kiss…"

At the top of the stairs, the door to our rooms lay open. When Holmes saw it, his eyes went wide with terror.

"No! Impossible! Nobody can get in there!"

"I hate to correct you, Holmes, but with Mrs. Hudson out of the way there was nothing to stop her. I don't recall that we even locked the door."

"*Locked the door?* How long have you known me, Watson? Do you assume a mere door latch to be the extent of my defenses? Have you ever—*ever*—seen anybody enter my home unbidden?"

"I have."

"No! Never!"

"But I have," I told him, thinking carefully back. "James Munro did it, the day he brought us the Adventure of the Yellow Bastard."

"He *re*-entered 221B," said Holmes, "having first been

invited in by Mrs. Hudson in our absence. Remember, she is the owner of this house and ownership is dashed important in magical matters."

"Well then, what about Grimesby Roylott? He smashed our door right in, if you recall."

"He was a powerful practitioner of magic, Watson. More to the point, he was in current possession of this domicile's ancient mystic guardian."

"Mrs. Hudson?" I gasped. "I remember that she was dangling off his leg, but am I supposed to believe she is an ancient mystic guardian?"

"You must at least concede she is ancient," said Holmes. "Come on, let's go and see what's happened up there."

Little had changed. Some papers had been shuffled about on our mantel. There was a kiss-mark left on my pillow in bright red lip-rouge. I was fairly sure it wasn't one of mine. Yet, our main loss was apparent and the lack of damage to 221B must have corresponded with the obvious placement of our invader's target. The battered attaché case was gone from our dining-room table. Moriarty was once more beyond our power.

"No!" cried Holmes. "How? Nobody can come here uninvited!"

"Oh… er… about that, Holmes…" I spluttered. "I *may* have invited our first Lady Hope to visit us again. Erm… whenever she wished."

"What? Why would you do that?"

"Why not? I rather liked her, at the time. Besides which,

how was I supposed to know about your little invitation trick? You never told me."

"And you never guessed? Damn it, Watson! I must say, your famous powers of deduction have failed you. You have been most… most…"

"Injudicious?" I volunteered.

"*Injudicious!*"

Holmes flung himself into his favorite chair and fretted for the rest of the evening, occasionally pulling at his hair and uttering prognostications of unavoidable doom. I made him some toast and soup, but he ignored it.

For my part, I felt strangely invigorated. Yes, it was impossible to call the Adventure of the Disgusting Stain anything but a defeat. Yet still… So many threads from our earlier adventures were beginning to weave themselves into a cohesive whole. Moriarty was back and making trouble. And this new antagonist of ours, so wonderful and deadly—I think, even in those early hours, I'd become fascinated with her. I fancied that if Moriarty was Holmes's great nemesis, the Woman was mine. Yet I managed to disregard the most important thing I knew about her: the perfect truth of Holmes's warning.

She was smarter than us.

We were outmatched.

THE ADVENTURE OF
MY GRAVE RITUAL

RUMINATION WANTS TOBACCO.

How else is the well-bred gentleman to communicate to the world that he is deep in thought? If he cannot furrow his brow, lean the leather-patched elbow of his thinking jacket down upon the table in front of him, chew thoughtfully at the stem of his pipe, taking occasional, reflective puffs and staring off into the middle-distance—how is he to make it clear he's engaged in deep cogitation? Why, he might just be sitting there, doing nothing at all!

In other words, it was a damned inconvenient day to be out of tobacco, for I had much to ponder. I elected to do what any gentleman would. No, not put on my boots and walk a block to the tobacconist's. To steal some of my companion's, of course. Holmes had tobacco. I knew it, because of the rather strange storage method he'd worked out. A few days previous I'd woken to find my friend had nailed an old Persian slipper to our mantel, hanging toe downwards. To my continued surprise, I found it stuffed with tobacco. I'm sure I meant to howl at him for it, but I'd forgotten. What was one more domestic peculiarity, in the face of my present woes?

I had this problem with the Woman, you see. I had this problem with Moriarty.

I stole a pipeful of Holmes's shag and sat down to worry. Clearly, the game was afoot once more. I knew my opponents, but not their goals. In point of fact, I didn't even know the Woman's *name*. (Though there was every indication it wasn't Bang Cleopatra.) I puffed and pondered. I had to assume the Woman's plan continued to move forward to some nefarious purpose, hidden from my sight. What was my counter-move? I needed to make one, didn't I? Surely I should not just sit about, smoking, while the game moved on without me!

Speaking of which...

I got up and helped myself to a second pipeful of Holmes's stash and sat back down.

At least my two problems had become one. The Woman—so far as we knew—was in current possession of the Moriarty Rune. But was she working with him or against him? Whatever the case, I realized I must think of Moriarty as nothing but an accessory to my true, current nemesis. Yes, my current focus must be upon the Woman and my first moves must be designed to gather information. I had almost decided to get up and actually do something, when the door opened and removed my chance.

"Hullo, Watson!" Warlock piped up, hanging his coat on its hook by the door. "How goes the brooding?"

"Fairly well, I suppose. Oh, I hope you don't mind, but I helped myself to a bit of your tobacco."

"Think nothing of it," said Holmes, and started jauntily back towards his room. Just as he swung open his door, he stopped. It seems some unpleasant remembrance had suddenly arisen to trouble him. His lips pinched together in thought for a moment, then he slowly said, "Except… I am currently *out* of tobacco."

"No you're not; you've got a whole slipper full of it, hanging just over there."

"Ah! What have you done?" shouted Holmes. He recoiled, staring back and forth between myself and the slipper, then demanded, "Who are you?"

"Me? I am John Watson. Your friend."

"Are you? I do not address the flesh only, but the will that commands it! Name yourself!"

"Um… still John…"

"I invoke the name of Xantharaxes the Undying! If he is present, he must declare himself!"

"I'm John. I'm Watson. Same as always."

"Oh?" said Holmes, brightening. "Well that's lucky, isn't it?" He marched over to me, took my pipe, stared thoughtfully into the bowl for a few moments and gave the ash a poke. "Hmmm…" he said, then went to the mantel and gave a few thoughtful finger-jabs down into the slipper. "So, this can be *smoked*? I wouldn't have thought it."

"Of course tobacco can be smoked. That's what it's for."

"I know perfectly well what tobacco is for," said Holmes, rolling his eyes at me. "What I do not understand is why you'd assume this to be tobacco."

"Well… because it looks and smells like it."

"Really?" He gave a few more pokes down into the slipper, then gave it a reluctant, inquisitive sniff. "I suppose it does, rather."

"Holmes?"

"Yes, Watson?"

"Are you telling me that's *not* tobacco?"

"What? Oh… er… you know what, let's not worry about that, eh?"

"Holmes, what is in that slipper?"

"I'm not sure you want to know, Watson."

"Well, now I really do."

"You promise you won't be angry?"

"No. I don't promise that at all."

Holmes gave a little sigh and asked, "Have you heard of Darius I?"

"The Achaemenid Persian king?"

"That's the fellow. He wasn't born to that throne; he took it by force. He had a whole story set up, where the reigning king wasn't really who he claimed to be, but an impostor who needed to be murdered. Which Darius did, with the help of six rich friends, three thieves, two tricksters and one rather impressive sorcerer: Xantharaxes the Undying. But once he had the throne, he had a problem: those twelve people knew for certain that he wasn't the legitimate king. The rich friends got to stay, but it wasn't long before he decided the thieves, tricksters and sorcerers needed to go. Of course he worried—not without reason—that the murder of Xantharaxes the *Undying* might be a bit of a difficult egg to poach. Xantharaxes had made the claim that the pieces of his mortal remains, no matter how damaged, would mend and regain life after his death. Darius, it seems, had reason to believe it. Thus, immediately following the execution, Xantharaxes was mummified, shredded, wrapped in some of his old clothes and scattered across the length and breadth of the Persian Empire. It was thought that this might prevent his resurrection—if not forever, then for a very great while."

"I just smoked part of a mummy?" I cried, clutching my throat.

"Nobody's fault but your own, Watson."

"But… why is it even here?" I asked.

"I stole it from Moriarty, years ago," said Holmes. "He had a fascination with immortality. It was his main pursuit, while he lived."

"And why did you decide to nail it to our mantelpiece?"

"I caught it trying to walk out of here a few nights ago. Nailed the thing to the fireplace to keep it from wandering off."

"I see," I said. "So, in fact, the contents of your old Persian slipper are not tobacco, but…"

"An old Persian," said Holmes. "And if I'm honest, Watson, it seems like a much more apt thing to keep there, don't you think? Why, if someone came up to me and said, 'Guess what I've got in this old Persian slipper?' I think, 'An old Persian,' would cross my mind long before, 'Some delicious pipe-weed, which you have chosen to nail to the furniture.' Really, Watson, that famous intellect of yours seems to have failed you. Not your finest hour, I fear."

I could not bring myself to disagree. Holmes kept peering into the slipper, giving its contents the occasional, exploratory poke. "Who would have thought?" he mused. "It's a poor sort of immortality that can be overcome by a trusty old briar pipe and a match, eh? Oh! Say, Watson, I don't suppose you'd consider doing the world a favor and finishing the old fellow off, would you? Just think: a weekend with a good book, a snifter of brandy and as many pipefuls of the old Xantharaxes as a fellow could ask for!"

"Er... well... now that I know the nature of the stuff, I'll confess I'm a bit less keen. Holmes, am I going to be all right?"

"I should think so. You haven't infused yourself with all of Xantharaxes, you know, just a tiny part of him. And he was known for nothing but immortality and prophecy, in any case. Nothing dangerous. I should think you'll notice nothing but a few minor effects along those lines."

"What do you mean?"

"Oh, you know, minor invulnerability. If you nick yourself with your razor this week, you might not bleed. You might stub a toe and not care. Oh, and some lesser powers of prophecy. Might be a good week to purchase a lottery ticket or invest in stocks. And some prophetic dreaming, I would think. Yes, that's practically a given."

"Prophetic dreaming?"

"Absolutely."

* * *

That night, as I lay dreaming, I beheld eight haunted dolls.

Tap. Tap. Tap. Upon my window glass. I rolled over. At first, all I could see was the porcelain hand—tiny fingers outstretched but partly curved, perfectly white and fused together into a dainty little scoop. *Tap. Tap. Tap* went the little hand, then a white face and blonde curls sprang up behind it.

"Aiaghughugh! What the devil?"

Tap. Tap. Tap.

Apparently, she wanted in. As I hesitated, terrified, clutching the covers up to my chin, she tilted her head to one side and asked, *"Whose is it?"*

"I… What now? I'm not sure I understand your question, madam."

If she possessed the power to clarify, she did not employ it. Instead, she directed her gaze over my shoulder. I was about to ask if there was something in my room she wanted when I heard two more questions, from behind me.

"Whose must it be?"

"What was the month?"

I whipped my head around and beheld two more of the darling little homunculi, advancing across my floor towards me. I had no chance to even gasp before I heard, *"Where was the sun?"* from the pillow just beside my ear.

I hope the reader will believe me when I claim that I had not brought a dolly to bed with me that night. Yet, when I flipped over to behold the source of the noise, there she lay—her delicate cheek resting just beside my own.

I'll not try to print the sound I made. English spelling

conventions fail me. You'll have to imagine it. I'll give you a clue: it was loud and unmanly.

I sprang from my bed to run. Or maybe to fight, if you credit my character with such. In any case we shall never know, for I neglected to properly remove my bedclothes first. I wound up on the floor with a bloodied nose and a tangle of sheets around my ankles. From beneath the bed, a fifth doll emerged, wondering, *"Where was the shadow?"*

Dolls 2 and 3 continued to march forward, while Doll 4 opened my window for Doll 1 who looked—in as much as a person with a rigid porcelain face can—as if she was a bit wounded that I hadn't opened it myself. My wardrobe door opened with an ominous creak. Doll 6 was all tangled up in a pair of my trousers, but still desirous to know, *"How was it stepped?"*

From the moment Holmes had mentioned it, I had the distinct feeling that prophetic dreaming and I would be a disastrous mismatch. Now I was certain. My medical bag sprang open and a seventh little white face popped out to inquire, *"What shall he give for it?"*

"Careful in there! Those medicine bottles are fragile, you know!"

"Why is it given him?" asked an eighth, struggling out of the water jug on my bedside stand.

"How did you get in there? Look at you: you're soaked right through!"

Slowly, daintily, they closed on me—a circle of toys, tightening on a cowering adult. They paused, looked up at my face, drew a collective non-breath and asked together, *"Whose is it?"*

From behind me came a deep rumbling voice. "Today, the diadem! Tomorrow, the thief!"

Whirling about, I beheld Holmes. If I failed to hear his footsteps, I think I can be forgiven. He hung in the air, his toes just brushing against the floor. His head was cocked to one side so his ear nearly rested against one shoulder. His green eyes burned. His arms hung to his sides, but bent up at the elbow, then down at the wrist, in exactly the pose that sub-par puppeteers the world over feel is the natural human stance. Eight doll heads turned worshipfully towards him, as if to say, "Yay! The father of all haunted marionettes is here! We missed you, Creepy-Daddy!"

"Whose must it be?" they all asked him.

"The doctor. The soldier. Governor. Dupe." The green flames that masked his eyes reflected in the dead glass orbs of my visitors.

"Er... I don't suppose we might have a different dream?" I asked, hopefully.

"What was the month?"

"A fresh birth in winter," Holmes boomed.

"It's just... I'm a bit uncomfortable," I said. "Really, this is my first prophetic one and I do feel you could have started me off with something a bit more accessible, don't you think?"

But the dolls paid me no heed.

"Where the sun?"

"Over the oak."

"Where the shadow?"

"Under the elm."

"Right," I harrumphed. "It seems you have no intention of stopping. Well, I just want it noted that I protest."

"How was it stepped?"

"North by ten and by ten, east by five and by five, south by two and by two, west by one and by one, and so under," said Holmes.

"Could we not have a nice dream about unattached debutantes bathing, or something?"

"What shall he give for it?"

"All."

"Why is it given him?"

"Faith. Fidelity. Sacrifice. Reward."

At last, the strange assembly fell silent. I heaved a sigh of relief. I did not know what should come next and was just beginning to construct a socially acceptable way of asking unbidden dolls to leave one's bedchamber when they started up again.

"Whose is it?"

"Today, the diadem. Tomorrow, the thief."

"Oh, good. We're doing it again, are we?"

"Whose must it be?"

"The doctor. The soldier. Governor. Dupe."

"And you know what I've just realized? My feet are cold. I am not asleep, am I?"

I was not. Xantharaxes's powers of prophecy must have been greater than Holmes had imagined. He and the dolls repeated their strange chant five more times, before they at last fell silent and dispersed to their respective chambers and waiting six-year-old owners. Happily, I had the presence of mind to fetch pen and ink and put their chant to paper, ere I forgot it.

Whose is it?
Today, the diadem. Tomorrow, the thief.
Whose must it be?
The doctor. The soldier. Governor. Dupe.
What was the month?
A fresh birth in winter.
Where the sun?
Over the oak.
Where the shadow?
Under the elm.
How was it stepped?
North by ten and by ten, east by five and by five, south by two and by two, west by one and by one, and so under.
What shall he give for it?
All.
Why is it given him?
Faith. Fidelity. Sacrifice. Reward.

The next morning, I confronted Holmes. He remembered nothing at all, but did complain that his elbows seemed stiff. I showed him the list of questions and answers and asked him what he thought.

"I think that's what you get for smoking ancient wizards. Honestly, Watson, if that's the worst that happens I think you must consider yourself lightly dealt with."

"I can't help but think it means something, Holmes."

"Of course it does. All prophecies do. Else they wouldn't be prophetic, would they? The question is, do they mean anything *worthwhile*. Ninety-nine times out of a hundred, they simply foretell that the next salad you order is going to be a bit disappointing. Really, Watson, disregard it."

"But... but..."

"No, let that be an end to it," Holmes declared. He turned to march away, but stopped suddenly, tilted his head and asked, "Hold on a moment, did you say 'a fresh birth in winter'?"

"I did."

"I've heard that somewhere before."

"It's the only part I've been able to figure out, Holmes. It's the answer to 'What was the month?' so it must refer to January—the birth of the new year."

"It's January now, Watson."

"Yes. I'd worked that out, too."

"But where have I heard that phrase, I wonder?"

Try as he might, he could not call it to mind. I wasn't overly surprised. But I was exhausted. Given my late start at slumber and the significant interruption I'd suffered, I was bleary all morning. I elected to take a midday nap.

"Musgrave," said a voice in my ear.

"Er... *Now* am I having a prophetic dream? Am I asleep?" I wondered.

"I hope not," said Holmes, from where he'd leaned in over my bed. "It makes you much harder to speak to. I've remembered where I heard that bit, before. Musgrave. Reginald Musgrave."

"Who is that?"

"An old friend of mine, from my school days. Curious lad. His family had this hereditary chant they all had to memorize. The Musgrave Ritual, they called it—none too creatively, I thought."

"Does he know what it means?" I asked.

Holmes shrugged. "We might drive round and ask him, I suppose."

I was half awake as Holmes bundled me into a cab. I fell asleep for the drive, forcing Holmes to wake me again as he shuffled me onto a train. I slept for half the train ride, too. I think we were nearly at Sussex before my eyes suddenly popped open and I blurted, "Wait a minute! An old school chum?"

"Yes. Reginald Musgrave."

"Holmes, you are over two hundred and fifty years old! Exactly when did you go to school?"

"It must have been some time after Moriarty abandoned me upon the moor. Nobody wanted to take in an odd-mannered orphan with no family to pay his tuition. Then again, when rumor got about that I'd accidentally turned one or two metal items to gold, a few of England's more forward-thinking schoolmasters began to feel that an exception might be made."

"He's dead, Holmes. Reginald Musgrave is surely dead."

"Well, he wasn't the last time I saw him."

"And when was that?"

"Oh… er… let's see… I'm afraid I cannot recall the date, but I remember everybody was quite upset because some round-headed fellow had dissolved a mint."

"Eh?" I had to take a few minutes to sleepily parse his meaning. Round-headed? The Roundheads? "Holmes, do you mean Oliver Cromwell dissolving Parliament?"

"Just so, Watson! You've touched it on the nose!"

"1653. Dead. He's dead. Someone turn the train around. I want to go home."

"Well, I don't mean to be indelicate, Watson, but… so what if he is? It was a hereditary ritual, after all. His ancestral home, Hurlstone Manor, is one of the oldest houses in Britain. They love that old-tradition sort of stuff. Believe me, somebody there will know about the ritual."

I was forced to concede that my friend had a point. At the station, we hired a carriage to drive us out to the track of underachieving hills or slightly bumpy meadows known as Hurlstone Downs. Upon beholding the house, I was ever more sure that Holmes was correct: here was a place where history mattered. Indeed, where history still existed. Though a portion of the home was modern, this was clearly a recent addition that had been cobbled to an existing section, which must have been built one or two centuries before. This, in turn, was an obvious addition to another section, which had been constructed a century or so before that. And so on. And so on. Hurlstone Manor must have been practically a quarter-mile long, beginning in contemporary comfort and ending in a jumble of rock-and-timber ruins that may well have been pre-Druidic. The central portion of the house gave every impression that it had begun service as a motte-and-bailey keep. Indeed, one could still spot the remains of a catapult atop its jagged parapets, which could have had no other purpose than to hurl stones down all over Hurlstone Downs, if ever the owner felt sufficiently threatened.

Alighting from the carriage, Holmes marched up to the main door and gave the bell-pull a jaunty tug. At first it seemed as if our call would go unanswered, but just as Holmes was about to give a second ring, we heard a bustling behind the door and it swung open. A gentleman in his early forties stood before us, wearing a dressing gown and house slippers. I hardly had time to process my shock at how poorly country butlers were allowed to present themselves, before Holmes crowed, "Why, Reginald Musgrave! As I live and breathe, how long has it been? My, my, look how gray you've gotten."

"Do I know you, sir?" the gentleman asked.

"Probably not," I said, stepping forward to introduce myself. "I am Dr. John Watson; this is my friend, Mr. Warlock Holmes. Some time ago, he was familiar with a Reginald Musgrave, but I would think your youth precludes the possibility it might be you. I would suppose it might be another member of your family with the same first name."

"Quite possibly. Ours is an ancient family, ruled by many traditions. The males of this house have only two names: Reginald and Spotsgrave."

"Spotsgrave Musgrave?"

"I'm afraid so," said Reginald, with respectful gravity. "I consider myself fortunate indeed to have inherited the tolerable name. Every Reginald Musgrave does. But then comes the day he has a son and the wretched duty falls to him to curse his newborn babe with the name Spotsgrave Musgrave. Mine is a mixed blessing."

"Er... and what if you should have more than one son?" I wondered.

"A frequent problem, but easily handled. In fact, if they were not away at the moment, I could introduce you to Spotsgrave A, Spotsgrave B and my daughter, Karen. But Mr. Holmes here has some business with my grandfather?"

"Or his. Or maybe his," said Holmes, cheerily. "Anyway, one of them asked me to look into that family chant of yours—the Musgrave Ritual—and I never got round to it."

Our host gave a cry of disbelief and spluttered, "What? The ritual? Again? Why, it's hardly to be believed! The damned thing's been all but forgotten for generations, then suddenly it's cost me a butler and a housemaid, and brought strangers to my door, all in the same week! Well, you'd better come in then. I'll have Brunton… oh… well I suppose *I'll* make us some tea. This way, gentlemen. Step this way."

Reginald Musgrave shuffled off towards his kitchen with Holmes and me in tow. The modern section of the house proved to be quite small—hardly more than a façade and a sitting room. Three steps in, we were back in the Tudor age and by the time we'd reached the kitchen, the earlier Plantagenet style was all around.

"What a singular home," I remarked.

"Hrmph. *Singular*. It is that," Reginald grunted. "To be born a Musgrave is to be born the curator of an eclectic museum. Now, where did I lay that damned kettle? Ah! Here we are… People seem to think it's an impressive thing to be the scion of one of Britain's oldest houses, but I can't fathom why. The first son of every Musgrave generation knows he will live, cradle to grave, surrounded by curios and relics. Ancient. Bizarre. Meaningless. All we do is live off the proceeds of hereditary investments and try to keep the house from falling in on itself. We're not very impressive people, really."

He gave an apologetic shrug and gestured to his paunchy, dressing-gown-clad self. His wrinkled clothing and unshaved cheek proclaimed the truth of his words. Yet, there was a charm to Reginald Musgrave—an easygoing friendliness that made me like him. Musgrave filled a perfectly modern tea-strainer, then dropped it into an old clay pot that looked like something Alfred the Great might have lying around the house. He swatted a bit of loose tea off his sleeve and said, "Now Brunton—that's my missing butler—*there's* an impressive fellow! Spoke twelve languages. Played almost any instrument you cared to hand him and played it so sweet you'd cry. Handsome devil, too. That chin! That hair! I'd say he was the terror of the ladies, except they always seemed more excited than afraid. He practically had a queue. Know what his name was? Richard. Isn't that nice? Isn't that normal? Richard Brunton—a forceful name, but accessible. Let me tell you, there never was a Spotsgrave Musgrave who could speak that name without envy. Oh, I do hope nothing too terrible has happened to him."

"I hope so, too," said Holmes.

"When did he go missing?" I asked.

"Wednesday last, I awoke and rang for him and… well… there he wasn't. We found his bed unslept in. All his clothes are still here. All his possessions. Even his money, so it's hard to think he left on purpose. I've got the whole staff searching the house for him, to see if he got stuck somewhere. We've made it back to the Norman invasion, but beyond that the house gets a bit spotty."

"And you think his disappearance has something to do with the Musgrave Ritual?" I asked.

"I'm afraid so."

"Tell us about it," Holmes encouraged him. "Watson and I are specialists in mysteries, especially when ancient and mystic secrets are involved. I'm a bit ancient and mystic myself."

Musgrave thought it over for a few minutes, as he rifled

his kitchen for cups that didn't look as if they had dried-up witches' brew in the bottom. "Well... I don't know you gentlemen at all. But then again, there's no call for secrecy, is there? And, if it might help Brunton... All right."

So we sat about, drinking cup after cup of tea and speaking of mystery.

"I think it all began when my father, Spotsgrave Musgrave XXIB, passed away last year. I was called to his bedside and made to recite the Musgrave Ritual. Such is our tradition whenever a new Musgrave inherits the house. The dying man asks the questions and the inheritor answers. Where was the sun? Where was the shadow? All that nonsense. It's a sad thing we Musgraves do. Whenever anybody gets old enough and sick enough, there comes a day where someone says, 'Well, I suppose we'd better dig out that old manuscript and set to memorizing.' Everyone gathers around and the words are said. Usually, everyone's sniffling and mourning in advance, but Brunton seemed rather excited by the whole thing. He became utterly fascinated by the ritual, I'm afraid. A few weeks later, I became peckish in the night and went down to get a biscuit. Know what I found? Brunton had got a screwdriver, prized open the bureau we kept the ritual in and he was sitting there, reading it by candlelight! It's not the sort of thing a gentleman is supposed to allow. There are rules about such things. So I told him, 'This is a liberty, Brunton! A damned liberty! Why, it is not to be tolerated! Tradition demands of me that I demand of you that you leave my service!'

"'This very night?' he said to me.

"'Egad, no! Take a fortnight to get your affairs in order. At least. Take a year, if you need it. Or more. There's really no limit to how long we could stretch it, as long as we don't speak of this to anybody. Let's not speak of it.'

"I gave the man every chance to weasel out of it. I hinted again and again that if he just apologized, dismissal would be unnecessary. 'You know, Brunton,' I said one night, 'I've been thinking: perhaps I was only dreaming when I thought I saw you—'

"'No, sir, you were awake and I was rifling your possessions. It is right and good that you should eject me from your home. I shall be ready to leave in a week or so.'

"'Oh come on, Brunton, don't be like that!'

"But he wouldn't relent! The next time I got hungry for a biscuit, what should I find on my way to the kitchen, but Brunton, at it again! This time he had pen and ink and was copying the damn thing. I had to pretend I was sleepwalking and shuffle past with my eyes half-closed."

"Maybe you should have asked him why he found it so fascinating," I suggested.

"You know, I was on the point of doing exactly that when he disappeared. I was nearly ready to throw aside my family's ancient pride and just ask him if I could help with whatever he was trying to figure out. I don't think anybody in my family had ever managed to make head or tail of the thing, but Brunton was cleverer. I caught him a few times surveying the grounds or holding midnight meetings with linguists and experts on parchment, trying to determine the age of the original manuscript."

"It sounds as if Brunton was sparing no effort," I said.

"No, indeed," Musgrave agreed. "I confess I was rather eager to see what he uncovered. But then things went all strange with Rachel Howells and he disappeared. I don't know if the disappearance has something to do with the ritual, or something to do with Rachel, or… well… I don't know what's behind it, but I worry for him and I've got this strange guilty feeling that I ought to have taken better care of the matter."

"Perhaps you'd better tell us about Rachel," I suggested.

"Oh, well her name is Rachel Howells, but we call her Rachel Howls, because she does."

"She howls?"

"More than we'd like. Now don't get me wrong, she's a good girl. A pure heart, has Rachel. But she is a bit… Welsh."

Holmes and I made faces at each other. "Aren't rather a lot of people Welsh?"

"Yes, but Rachel is full-blooded. Or at least that's how she was explained to us when she entered my service. Between you and me, she doesn't seem entirely… normal. But she's a good heart, as I said. She used to work in the barn. She's got a way with animals. They all love her, even though she had the roughest jobs with them. She was very good at gelding. Didn't even need tools. But we began to feel she was a bit too savage, you know? We began to worry about her future. So we invited her in to be our second housemaid and made her get used to wearing finer clothes and keeping them clean and saying 'yes, marm' and 'no, marm'. I thought she was doing quite well, but then things all went wrong with her and Brunton.

"You see, Brunton had been seeing Janet Tregellis— the gamekeeper's daughter—but they broke it off. Rachel had noticed that most of the local girls had been involved with him at one time or another and she wanted to know when it was her turn. She asked me if she might have him. I was rather tired of his ways and thought maybe she'd be the girl to settle him down so I said she was welcome to make her suit to him. She marched right up to him, told him he was her boyfriend, and dragged him off into the woods."

"Oh dear," said Holmes.

"Indeed," Musgrave agreed. "We're fairly sure she had her way with him, then and there. We're not certain, of course, but... well... not to be indelicate, but Rachel had a habit of singing about her thoughts. She composed a little song called 'Happy Fanny' so... we're all rather certain. We had a devil of a time trying to get her not to sing it when company came around."

"Bah!" said Holmes with a dismissive wave. "What value has propriety when compared to love?"

"Well *she* was in love, but Brunton rather wasn't. At first we tried to make it work. 'No, no!' we'd tell her. 'You mustn't throw Brunton! We must be kind to Brunton. Go throw a goat, if you must throw someone.'"

"She threw goats?" I asked, scandalized.

"On her bad days. Well… even on good ones if she was trying to amuse our peculiar goat. He seems to like it. I've no idea what's wrong with the animal. Yet the main point is that Brunton wanted out. He came and asked me to intercede for him—said he and Janet had reconciled and he was worried what Rachel might do. This was just after I'd caught him reading the ritual, so he seemed to feel a bit strange asking for my help. Still, I couldn't see him courted against his will, so we called Rachel in and made things clear to her."

"How did she take it?" Holmes asked, with a sympathetic sigh.

"Not well. Tears all the time and no shortage of bruised goats. She wanted to go back and work in the barn. We tried to keep her here, but it was clear she was unraveling. Then, the day before Brunton disappeared, she suddenly seemed happy again. From her inappropriate songs, it was clear Brunton was the source of the change. I asked Janet if things had come to an end again, but it was all news to her. Then came that horrible, Brunton-less morning. Rachel was beside herself with grief. She took to her bed with a fever and would not come out. We could all hear her in there—howling even more than usual—and then the next afternoon she said she wouldn't stay here another day. Smashed through her window and ran out into the woods—that's the last any of us have seen of her."

"You've no idea where she's gone?" I asked.

Musgrave made a sly little face. "I've some idea she might be sleeping in the barn. We never see her there, by day. Yet in the chaos following Brunton's disappearance, we forgot to assign someone to feed the animals. Rachel had been doing it, in addition to her indoor duties, and it was quite three days before I remembered the poor beasts. Well, I went out to the barn, fearing what I might find. All the animals had been fed and seen to. Now, the barn is well away from the house, but it isn't that far from the edge of the wood. I've had the maid leaving meals out there, trying to lure Rachel back. The food is always gone in the morning and the cutlery stacked just as we'd shown Rachel to do it, but she still has not come to speak with any of us. And that's where the matter rests, gentlemen. One missing, one run off into the forest—and I fear the worst."

Holmes went to Musgrave, laid a hand on his shoulder and said, "You are king of a strange little world, sir."

"If I am, I've made a right hash of it. Can't say much for the happiness or the safety of my subjects, can you? Well, that's the entire history of my problem. What do you gentlemen think?"

"I think…" I said, tapping thoughtfully at my lips with one finger, "I think I'd like to go Rachel-hunting."

The Hurlstone estate was huge. The main barn was well away from the house, past two fallow fields, along a muddy lane. I'd half expected it to mirror the manor—modern at the front, descending to Celtic chaos at the rear. But no, here was a perfectly ordered world. Well kept, well loved.

Each animal had its place and seemed happy in it. It was a warm respite from the January cold—a musty, hay-scented haven. Musgrave showed us the loft and pointed out the magnificent hollow where he suspected Rachel spent her evenings. Indeed, there was a saddle blanket up there folded and laid alongside a filthy pillow. The depression in the straw was immense. I think three of me could have slept there comfortably.

"Remember: she's Welsh," said Musgrave, when he saw my astonishment.

Yet my reverie was interrupted by Holmes, who drew up to my elbow and hissed, "Watson! Listen!"

Sure enough, the sound of rustling came to my ears, along with the occasional worried grunt. It sounded as if a bear were loitering in the woods, just behind the barn.

"The back door," I said. "Quick!"

We leapt down from the loft, threw the door wide and stepped out into the cold air. Sure enough, the undergrowth just before us gave a rustle and a voice shouted, "Who's there?"

"It's me, Rachel: Reginald Musgrave," our host declared.

"Who else?"

But Musgrave ignored the question and said, "We've been worried for you, Rachel. Are you all right?"

"Lonely fanny…"

"*Rachel!* Is that any way to speak? We have guests!"

"Don't care."

"Rachel, please," Musgrave pleaded, "we've been

beside ourselves. What happened to you? What happened to Brunton?"

Rachel Howls proved her name. From behind the scrub came a sound saturated in loss and grief. Just as I feared my eardrums might burst, she laid off and blurted, "He found the secret place. But there was a bad hat. And it made him say bad things. And Rachel did bad things. Go 'way!"

Musgrave stepped back with a shrug, as if to say, "Well, that's the end of it."

Yet I would not be dissuaded. Stepping forth towards the edge of the wood, I said, "Rachel Howells, come out this instant!"

"No!"

"It is clear you know something of the disappearance of Richard Brunton. You may be innocent in the matter, or perhaps you are not. Either way, the best you can do is step out and make a clean breast of it."

"Er, Watson…" said Holmes, peeping at me from around the edge of the barn's back door, "are you sure you should…"

"She may be a murderess, Holmes!"

"All the more reason for caution, don't you think?"

"No, Holmes! I shall not be so easily cowed! Rachel Howells, surrender yourself!"

"Mehh–eh–eh–eh–eh!"

"Egad! She's got a goat! Scatter!" Reginald Musgrave cried.

"Mehh–eh–eh–eh–eh!"

"Mehh–eh–eh–eh–eh!"

The first of the furry projectiles slammed into the barn door just behind me, drawing a yelp of alarm from Holmes. It staggered to its feet, shook the cobwebs from its head and gave me a resentful stare, as if to say, "There. Now she's upset. Are you pleased with yourself?"

The second plunked into a hay bale beside Musgrave and the third stuck me square in the face. It bowled me off my feet and sent me crashing backwards through the open door. No sooner had I slid to a halt than the goat rose to its feet, gave me a look of triumph and bounded off into the woods to offer itself as a projectile a second time.

He must have been the peculiar one.

Yet his services would not be required. The bombardment was over. Through the open door, I caught a glimpse of my antagonist. Rachel Howells stood up from her hiding spot and ran into the woods, crying. She was clearly not human. Though not much taller than I, she must have been two or three times broader in the shoulder, with long, muscular arms, which she used to help her run. Her hair was so mussed it had served as camouflage. Have you ever seen pictures of the Polynesians? Of those grass skirts they wear? Well, if someone left two or three of them out to dry to scratchy brown tufts, then mussed them up and stuck them atop someone's head, the result would exactly reproduce Rachel's hair. I just caught the flash of her much-abused maid's uniform as she disappeared amongst the trees, followed by her loyal goats.

I struggled up, but nearly fell again. Confused and goat-dazed, I ran to Holmes, pulled at his sleeve and shouted, "Hurry, she's getting away!"

"Hmm… Perhaps we ought to let her."

"But she knows what happened to Brunton! There's every indication she killed him!"

"If she did, she seems rather broken up about it, don't you think?"

"So?"

Holmes fixed me with a strange look, both pitying and annoyed. "She *throws* those goats, Watson, and yet they choose her side over ours. What does that tell you?"

"That the world we inhabit is broken and insane?"

"No. Well… I suppose… *yes*, if I'm honest. But it shows us a great deal more than that. I have always trusted those who are loved by children and animals, Watson. Nobody else can rival their ability to tell a good soul from a bad one. Rachel Howells is likely a better target for our sympathy than our vengeance."

"But…"

"Besides, I doubt she'll move very far from this barn. And if we ever need to take her into custody, I know just the fellow to hunt her."

I stared at Holmes a moment, confused and incredulous, before spluttering, "What do you mean? Grogsson?"

"I think they might get along rather well," said Holmes. "In any case, the light is failing us and I have better things to do with my evening than spend it chasing a heartbroken goat-flinger through the woods. Shall we retire?"

At this point, Reginald Musgrave rejoined us, scuttling from behind the watering trough where he'd been hiding. "What about Brunton? We still don't know what's become of him!"

"No," said Holmes, "but we know this much: he was clever enough to solve the Musgrave Ritual. Well, as fortune would have it, I've brought a clever fellow of my own. Watson here ought to be able to manage it.

"Or," he added under his breath, "I could always ask the nearest demon what became of him."

"Don't you dare," I whispered back.

"It's settled, then. Watson and I shall return on the morrow, prepared to solve the Musgrave Ritual."

"Why don't you stay the night here?" Musgrave offered. "I so rarely have company."

"We wouldn't be a bother?" Holmes asked.

"What style room would you like?" Musgrave asked, cheerily. "Queen Anne? Restoration? Anglo-Saxon?"

In the morning, I began my search. Freshly filled with eggs and bacon, armed with a borrowed compass, I led Holmes and Musgrave out into the grounds of Hurlstone Manor. My starting point had not needed much consideration—I'd noticed it the moment we first drove up. As we walked, I explained, "Four of the eight questions of the ritual describe whatever mysterious object lies at the end of our search. They speak of whose it is, whose it will be and what that person must pay for it, yet they give no clue as to its location. The other four do. And one of them has an obvious answer: January—which is of some importance. Two of the other clues seem to speak of shadows and trees. *Where was the sun? Over the oak. Where the shadow? Under the elm.* Yet, is there any hope they may be of use? Hundreds of years have passed. Even if the trees referred to yet live, we can expect they must have grown considerably, changing the length of their shadows. We have no way of knowing exactly when the ritual was penned. Even if we did, we would be hard-pressed to determine the exact height of the tree at that date."

"Then what are we left with?" Musgrave asked.

"That."

I pointed to the oak. Certainly the forest about Hurlstone Manor might contain several hundred—nay—several thousand of that species, but to any who beheld Hurlstone Manor, there could be only one object worthy of the title "the Oak". It stood some distance from the house, completely dominating the field. Its thousand bent and knotty limbs held themselves to the sky, in defiance of the ages. Within those branches was soil. Doubtless the tree's own leaves, caught within the smaller branches and held from ever reaching the ground, had degraded into fertile loam from which now hundreds of lesser plants had sprouted. It might take a man five minutes to pace around the base of the trunk. Truly, I had never seen its equal.

"Yes, I've always supposed it must mean that one," Musgrave agreed. "Yet here is where the ritual breaks down."

He gestured to the open downs on every side of us and pointed out, "No elm."

"Indeed," I said. "And no clear idea where we should even look for it. The elm must have grown wherever this tree's shadow ended in January, some centuries before. But what time of day? In the morning, when the sun was over the oak? In the evening as it set on the other side? At noon? The puzzle was preposterous, even on the day it was written. All I can say for certain is this: that as we are in the northern hemisphere in a winter month, the sun traverses on the southward side and the elm in question must have been in a northward arch. Start searching the grounds. We are looking for any trace of an ancient elm."

We found more than a few eligible stumps, but most were too small, I thought, to be the tree in question. The ones that still bore bark were mostly poplar and yew. At last we came upon the remains of a stump both ancient and broad. Its bark and wood had suffered too long in the elements to tell us what type of tree it might have been, but as we drew close, Musgrave gave a cry of triumph. A tiny red flag fluttered from its far side. I smiled. It seemed Brunton must have felt this was the right one. Who else could have marked the tree?

"Holmes, stand here, won't you?" I said, pointing towards the stump. I then ran back to the oak, pulled forth Musgrave's compass and took careful note of the bearing 296 degrees. Roughly west-north-west. The ritual must have meant the rising sun, in the eastern sky over the oak. I rejoined Holmes, who wondered, "What now?"

"Now we pace it, Holmes."

"North by ten and by ten, east by five and by five, south by two and by two, west by one and by one, and so under," Musgrave recited.

"Yes," I agreed. "Or we might just go sixteen steps north, and eight steps east, since the latter two directions do nothing but cancel out part of the earlier two. Really, whoever wrote this thing… just an idiot…"

No matter if we walked the ritual as written—in a decreasing spiral—or as I figured it, the destination was the same. A featureless patch of ground.

"Er… what now?" Holmes wondered.

"Wait! 'And so under'!" Reginald crowed. "The ritual says 'and so under'! Should we dig?"

"I think not," I said. "Rachel said that Brunton found 'the secret place'. Certainly, he did not find it here or there would be a gaping hole already. No, I suspect there is a piece still missing from our understanding of the ritual— and I think I know what it is. A second shadow."

"Eh?" Holmes wondered. "But there's only one sun, Watson. So, the oak would have only one shadow, wouldn't it?"

"Yes, but what about the shadow of the elm? The ritual does not say where to begin pacing. It could mean the base of the elm, but then why mention the oak and the direction of the sun and shadows in the first place? More likely, the ritual means us to begin pacing from wherever the shadow of the elm ended at the exact time of day and year when the oak's shadow fell at the base of the elm."

"Oh, blast," muttered Holmes, "more maths."

"Yes, but you needn't fret. After all, it's impossible maths. Even if the elm were still there, we'd have no way of knowing its height the day the ritual was penned. Really, whoever wrote this was no great philosopher."

"So, we can't solve the ritual?" Musgrave asked, with sagging shoulders.

"No, no. We can. I took the bearing between the oak and the elm stump, remember? We may not know the length of the elm's shadow, but we know its direction. We have already paced the steps outlined in the ritual, therefore if we travel in a straight line from this spot, upon the proper bearing, we shall find what we seek."

And it would have been no harder than that, if what we were seeking was an old stone wall. Not five feet along our path, we ran smack into the side of Hurlstone Manor. Holmes and Musgrave traded shrugs.

"So much for that plan, eh?" laughed Musgrave.

"No. The plan is sound," I said. "Look, the house is only one story, here. How tall was the elm? It is very possible its shadow used to fall on the far side of the house."

"Or even on the roof," said Holmes.

"Oh God, let's hope not. Now, what we need is some sort of very tall marker, which we can place here, so that when we get to the other side of the house, we can see where to start from."

A fine plan it was, too, until we got to the other side. We found ourselves mired in the most labyrinthine section of the sprawling wreckage of Hurlstone Manor. What had possessed the previous occupants to favor so many damned add-ons, I will never know. But there they were, in their dozens, radiating from the main section in broken splendor. It seems this had at one time or another been the optimal spot to add guest rooms. Or servants' quarters. Or pantries, stables, barns, dungeons… who could tell? Some sections were more or less intact, but some were naught but ruined, knee-high walls of stone. Even worse, there had been a fair amount of subterranean building too, and many of these chambers had since fallen in. Given that the entire area was overgrown with ivy, brambles and scrub, it was very easy to take a wrong step and find yourself up to your hip through the roof of a collapsing medieval cellar.

We searched until lunchtime, took a break, ate, despaired, returned and stumbled about the wreckage for a few hours more. We were in real danger of losing our daylight by the time we stumbled across the door. The thing was so overhung with ivy that I think we'd been past it two or three times before it caught Holmes's eye. He gave a cry of discovery and summoned Musgrave and me at once. To my joy, I could back-trace an increasing spiral around that particular section of ruin that exactly matched the steps of the ritual.

Yet, that was academic.

More to the point: someone had been there in the last few days. Two someones. Brushing the ivy back from the ancient doorway, we beheld a passageway down a mostly intact section of the house. Though the floor tiles were still visible, the wretched condition of the roof above them ensured that they were covered in a deep filth—the slick of ages. In this, we could clearly see the print of a man's shoe and what could only be the mark of the most preposterously large maid's footwear you'd ever seen. I stared, agog.

"Yes, I know," Musgrave said. "We have to get them made, special."

"So that's Rachel, clearly," said Holmes. "And… *Brunton*, we assume?"

"I would think so," I said. "And look at how many prints there are. It seems he came and went a number of times. But see how there are fewer of Rachel's prints? One set in and one set out."

"So… Brunton found something and wanted to show Rachel what it was?" Holmes wondered aloud.

"Possibly," I agreed. "I don't suppose we'll know for sure until we discover what it is he found. The last part of the clue is 'and so under'. That must be our 'and so under', right there."

A dozen feet in from the overgrown doorway, an ancient flight of stairs led down beneath the ground. The cellar it brought us to was larger than I'd imagined, and in fairly decent repair. One wall had partially collapsed, but the majority of the room was clear. In the dead center of the room lay one suspiciously large flagstone. It must have been eight foot by six and I can hardly imagine the weight. Next to this lay two crowbars and a magnificent oaken beam whose side was marked and scored from propping that stone up—or so I supposed.

"Looks like the ritual should have ended 'and so under, and under'," Holmes remarked.

"One more imperfection to add to the silliest ritual I think I've ever heard," I said. "I think we've solved it, gentlemen. See where the edge of the stone is chipped? Here's where Brunton attempted to pry up the stone. And it's easy to see why he suddenly felt the need to engage the aid of Rachel Howls. This must weigh half a ton! Here, Holmes, grab that crowbar there and we'll see if we can't—"

As I spoke, the huge flagstone popped up over the lip of the stones beside, wiggled itself free and slid over to the neighboring wall.

"Damn it, Holmes!"

"Well, I'm tired, Watson! You've had me tracking back and forth across a ruined castle all day, searching hither and yon for who-knows-what, just because a gang of magical dolls told you to. I'm all worn out and I want some soup."

"Be that as it may, Holmes, there's something you've forgotten." I jerked a thumb back at Reginald Musgrave, who stood at the doorway with his eyes wide and his mouth hanging open.

"Oh! Right," said Holmes. "Well... er... doubtless there was some clever mechanical hoist system, built into the floor. Yes. That's it, I shouldn't wonder."

"Are you prepared to believe that, Mr. Musgrave?" I asked.

Our host shook his head back and forth.

"What explanation would suit you?"

"It's like magic!" he spluttered. "Sorcery!"

"Yes! Fine! All right! It was!" Holmes complained. "Please don't tell anybody. Now, do you two want to see what it is we've discovered, or don't you?"

I already knew the first thing we'd find. French gourmands have an expression to explain how the presentation of a meal is just as important to its enjoyment as its taste. The first bite, they say, is with the eye. With food, that is likely true. However, in forensic matters, the first bite is most often with the nose.

And it's rarely pleasant.

I think if I were a French gourmand, I'd have to call the atmosphere of our little chamber *L'air du Brunton, mort*.

He hadn't been down there long enough to really go off, yet. Still, one could hardly describe him as spring-fresh. Peeping over the lip into the chamber below, we beheld the discolored remains of Musgrave's missing butler. He lay curled in a little ball at the foot of a white marble sarcophagus. In his arms, he cradled an ancient iron crown. The three of us all cried out, but for different reasons.

Musgrave, on behalf of Brunton. Holmes, because he saw the crown. I because...

Well...

I was *home*.

As I stared at that sarcophagus, a feeling of belonging swept over me—perfect and powerful belonging. Can you imagine what Livingstone felt, returning from that first adventure along the Zambezi? So long away, in a land so strange, with his fate uncertain. There must have been a moment, when he first came home. When he opened his own half-forgotten front door and breathed in the smell of his own pantry, his own couch and rug, his waiting bed. When he heard the voices of those who missed and loved him, with so much longing to hear of his adventures and so much to share of what had passed in their own lives. That is what I felt, when I beheld my home—my final home. This little underground tomb was for me. The ritual was clear.

Whose is it?

Today, the diadem. Tomorrow, the thief. So, the iron crown must have been placed there before the ritual was written. Brunton's misdeed and subsequent fate seem to have been foretold.

Whose must it be?

The doctor. The soldier. Governor. Dupe. I was a doctor. I'd been a soldier. How was I spending my days, if not as Holmes's governor? Dupe? I liked to think not, but my recent defeats at the hands of the Woman left it difficult for me to mount any compelling rebuttal.

What shall he give for it?

All. Yes, of course. That's what one gives, for a tomb.

Why is it given him?

Faith. Fidelity. Sacrifice. Reward. My breath caught in my throat. Tears came to my eyes. Both gratitude and humbling doubt struggled for control of my mind. Faith? I had next to none. Fidelity? Was mine worth anything? What sacrifice had I made? Honestly, almost everything

I did, I did for my own sake. How could I have earned such a reward? It was remarkably well crafted. Masons long forgotten had laid it here and chiseled wreaths and bevels that endured, unspoiled. Upon the front relief, maidens wept for the body that would one day lie within that empty vessel. Carved kings and priests raised grateful hands towards the honored dead, still absent. What was it about this failed doctor, this fallen soldier, this petty and unremarkable man that generations past had seen worthy to venerate?

Holmes was pulling on my arm. He wanted me to look at the crown. See how black and ill-seeming it was? See how the iron was free of rust, despite all those years in an underground cell? Did I feel how magical it was? Even Musgrave said he could, though all I could feel was love for that little white box.

Holmes waved the crown at me—said it was a thing of powerful evil. Insisted it was whispering to him. Commanding him. Giving him thoughts. Now, Holmes was certainly strong enough to resist its influence, but what of Brunton? What had it made him say? What foolish thing had crossed his lips in his moment of triumph? That he did not love Rachel? That he had used her to a purpose and she'd been fool enough to let him? Couldn't I see that Brunton was far too smart to make such a mistake when he stood in so vulnerable a position? And Rachel—kind Rachel—so used to absorbing the derision of her peers. Were we to believe that it was the natural action of her heart to drop the stone back into place over the man she loved? No, no, no! It was all the fault of this wicked crown, couldn't I see?

I didn't care.

Musgrave wanted to know about Brunton. Had he suffered? Was it slow suffocation that had done him in? Or had he starved? Or had the stone hit him and dashed him senseless?

I made no answer.

In fact, for the remainder of my time at Hurlstone Manor, I was dazed and useless. Holmes and Musgrave put everything to rights themselves. The crown was left beside the sarcophagus. Holmes didn't want it at Baker Street and the vault had kept it safe this long, hadn't it? Rachel was forgiven and invited back to work in the house. Holmes was adamant on that point. In the presence of such powerful and evil influence, nobody was answerable for their actions. As for explaining the death, that was easy. The fact that Brunton had been exploring the house was common knowledge amongst the staff. That he might have been injured and trapped in a disused area and subsequently perished was a well-understood hazard. Still, our later correspondence with Musgrave made it clear that Rachel never forgave herself. She never forgot that moment of anger and hurt—that horrible instant when Brunton yelled up at her, out of the pit and she let herself drop that stone.

Holmes wanted to talk about it on the train back to London. Yet my thoughts and, it seems, my words kept veering back to the little tomb. Holmes's vexation was plain.

"Look here, Watson. It's more than a little disturbing how attached you are to the place. Aren't men supposed to be horrified by the idea of their own mortality?"

"I suppose. But I'm not your average man, Holmes. I was a soldier in a losing fight. More than that: I'm a doctor. Of course I understand I'm going to die. I just... Well, it never occurred to me I might die for a *reason*. That I might accomplish something worthy of that kind of remembrance. Oh, I hope it's true! Can't you understand?"

"Even if I can, that doesn't mean I have to like it," Holmes complained. "You're not allowed to die, Watson!"

My feelings towards that perfect white sarcophagus were in no way morbid. In the story of my own life, nothing—*nothing*—had ever been more welcome. Even now, as I sit to write this, as the final reckoning nears and the world of man begins to crumble, I reflect that I have yet to deserve such thanks. Perhaps I have one card left to play—one deed left in me that will at last earn that final reward. Even now, it gives me hope.

In fact, it's the only thing that can.

THE ADVENTURE OF THE
COPPER'S SCREECHES

FATE IS A FUNNY THING. OUR NEXT TWO ADVENTURES were unrelated, except in one aspect: hair. The next six months of my life would be spent either in action, or in bed with shattered health and broken bones, all for the sake of *other people's hair*.

One Tuesday, I returned to our Baker Street rooms just before lunchtime, in some vexation. I'd been investigating a man who had supposedly served as potion-maker to Moriarty. Sadly, he'd been naught but a charlatan. His primary claim to magical brilliance was that he'd concocted an elixir to regrow hair and combat ague. My analysis revealed it to be nothing but Yorkshire ditchwater, morphine, vanilla and just a pinch of cinnamon. Needless to say, the man was in high demand. Lines of sufferers flocked to his little stand by day and night, because really: vanilla? *And* cinnamon? Any of the thousand cures available in London's druggists might feature ditchwater and they all featured morphine, but had anybody thought to make them palatable?

Genius hides in plain sight, they say.

I was just preparing to vent my failure to Holmes when he said, "Watson, we have a guest."

"Eh? A guest? Who is it?"

"She says her name is Violet," said Holmes, indicating, with some trepidation, the dark corner we'd set aside to store our food. Sure enough, a young girl bustled back and forth, straightening this and rearranging that. She had an air of propriety about her. Not the haughty propriety of one who practices it to prove their superiority to the lower classes, but the I-know-my-place-and-could-teach-your-children-how-completely-they-outrank-me propriety that had become so important in our modern economy. At first glance, I could discern it. Our guest was a governess; she could be nothing else.

Which was a pity. There was something about her...

She was very small. She had a head of vibrant copper locks and a smattering of freckles to match. These were present in such numbers that an ungenerous observer might label them grotesque, but to me it just seemed as if nature had looked upon her face and deemed that it was worthy to be decorated. She had soft blue eyes, which bespoke not only intelligence and liveliness, but a depth of consideration utterly wasted in a life of domestic servitude. She *was* a governess. She *might have been*... well... who knows? In a world unlike our own—not governed so rigidly by societal rules and expectations—who can say what she might accomplish, or how far she might rise?

Oh, and speaking of societal expectations...

"Holmes! Why have you set our 'guest' to cleaning?"

"I didn't! She did it! She made me!"

"Oh, did she now?"

"I did, actually," she said. "I am Miss Violet Hunter, at your service, sir. You must be Dr. Watson?"

"I am. And I'm pleased to make your acquaintance, Miss Hunter. Won't you come join us in the sitting room?"

"No. Very sorry, sir, but I'm entering Mr. Holmes's service."

"She's what?" I turned to my friend and demanded, "Have you advertised for a maid?"

"No! I didn't! I wouldn't! She just barged in here, Watson, and started straightening up—going on about becoming a wizard's thrall and earning my protection and such. I don't know what she's on about. Look! She's touching my toast racks! Make her stop!"

"Miss Hunter," I said, "please, won't you have a cup of tea and tell us exactly what brought you here?"

"No. Not until this one takes me into his service."

"Watson! Toast racks!"

"I'm sorry," said Miss Hunter with an apologetic shrug, "but I need Mr. Holmes's protection."

"Aaaaaagh! My soup pot!"

"No! Stop! Everybody, stop!" I shouted. "Holmes, Miss Hunter, I appeal for calm."

Ten minutes later, we found ourselves seated in the room named for that purpose, holding steaming cups. This alone was enough to quiet me. There was a certain comfort in that simple act—a feeling that everything was in its right place. Where were we? A sitting room. What were we doing? Sitting. So, we couldn't be that far off the mark, could we?

Once we were settled, Miss Hunter began her tale. "Gentlemen, I am an out-of-work governess with no family. I don't know if I can impress upon you what a terribly precarious position that is. There are few prospects for a girl like me and—though a fall from so low a height may seem to be of little consequence to many—I assure you I have no interest at all in living the life that might be afforded to me if I cannot maintain my position. Perhaps my youth and minor attractions might be sufficient to engage the attentions of some dockside brute to keep my frustration numbed with alcohol until the day that either it or he might prove to be the end of me. As I said: I've no interest in it."

"But… you are so poised!" I protested. "So very well spoken!"

She shrugged. "It is no great trick to seem better than I am. Yet the moment my standing is tested—either by need of money, of influence, of people who support me… well… it all crumbles in that instant.

"For the last two weeks, I have been living in rented rooms at Holden Court, watching my funds dwindle and hoping that Miss Stoper—who runs Westaway's agency— might secure me a new position. You can imagine my relief, then, when yesterday morning a messenger knocked at my door and asked if I might report to Westaway's and present myself to a client whose needs I seemed to match exactly. When I arrived I found a small army of hopefuls present.

Half had been interviewed and disappointed, the rest awaited the moment they might be adjudged. Nevertheless, Miss Stoper's clerk knew I had been summoned and escorted me past the line to her door. When the next lady marched dejectedly out, I was called in immediately.

"As I entered, Miss Stoper announced, 'Mr. Jephro Rucastle, this is Miss Violet Hunter.'

"The moment he saw me, Mr. Rucastle jumped up and exclaimed, 'Yes! She is the one! Precisely what I need!'

"What a strange appearance he presented, gentlemen! I think you will hardly believe me if I describe him."

Holmes and I shared a glance.

"Oh," Holmes sighed, "we might."

"He looks like... well... rather an awful lot like... a *turkey*," Miss Hunter said, glancing around to see if anybody had seen her slight her potential employer. "He is tremendously fat, but he carries it all down low, you see. His shoulders are narrow, his neck rather long. And he has this... wattle... I mean, of course it is only normal human flesh, but the placement of it... the way it shakes... almost exactly like a turkey's wattle. And he has a laugh to match it! It sounds as if he's gobbling, I would swear. Now, in spite of this, he is charming. I know it sounds strange but I think he knows he looks funny and so he chooses to *be* funny. He's rather disarming. Such a friendly man, so ready to laugh—"

"A perfect villain!" Holmes declared.

I gave him a sideways look.

"No, really, Watson, I am in earnest. Nothing hides

maleficence so well as a smile. Nothing lures like a word of kindness. The man shall prove a villain: rely upon it!"

"If he does, he'll be the second evil bird-like creature in as many months," I muttered. "I am considering a moratorium. Miss Hunter, pray, continue your tale."

"Well, I was rather shocked that a man who had turned away so many hopefuls would wish to hire me the very second he laid eyes upon me, without knowing my history or qualifications at all. I said, 'Mr. Rucastle, are you not being a bit hasty?'

"But he said, 'Oh, tut, tut! You mustn't call me Mr. Rucastle! Nobody calls me that! I'm simply the Copper, my dear. I came by that name because of the color of my hair—copper, just like yours. Or it was, in my youth. But those days are gone, hey? Gone with a song and a smile and a loving cup!'

"'Very well, Mr.... Copper,' I said. 'I can teach reading, writing and arithmetic, of course. Music. A little German—'

"But he scoffed at me. 'Bah!' he said. 'That's well and good, as far as it goes, but when you are being considered for a position such as this—raising a child who may one day figure prominently in the future of our realm—there is one question and one question only: have you the deportment of a lady?'

"Here he paused, leaned in expectantly at me, then threw his arms up and delivered the verdict, 'You have! So that's all settled, then. You must come up and join us at the Copper Beeches. That's the name of my house. It's not on the coast, I'm afraid. We're in Hampshire, near Winchester. No proper beaches. It's named for beech trees, you see! We have beech *trees*! Ha! I hope you won't be too disappointed. Now, how much did you earn in your last position?'

"I told him, 'I had four pounds a month.'

"He sprang back and shouted, '*Four?* Per *month?*' Now, I knew my last salary had been a bit better than the average governess might command, but not so lofty as to cause such indignation. I feared Mr. Rucastle was about to come forth with a scanty offer indeed. But the very opposite was true. 'Four a month? That is sweating! That is slavery! Why, if I had that criminal here, I would... I would... I don't know *what* I'd do! How could anybody...? No, no, no! Your salary, madam, will commence at one hundred pounds per year.'

"'Very generous, sir,' I told him. 'And what would be my duties?'

"'Why, you must take care of my boy, little Barghest!' Mr. Rucastle laugh-gobbled. 'Oh, you'll love him. Cutest little nipper, but he thinks he's the fiercest thing alive! Ha! You should see him killing spiders! Zap! Smack! Zap! Three, gone in a second with whatever he's got to hand. His shoe, his hands, his teeth, it doesn't matter. Ha!'

"'Only the one child?' I asked. 'That will be the extent of my duties?'

"'Oh, well... not the full extent,' he said. 'I'm sure you wouldn't mind indulging my wife's little fancies, eh? Always providing they were such commands as a lady might, with propriety, obey. We might like you to sit here, or sit there. Or wear a certain electric blue dress. Oh, and your hair… My wife is very particular upon that point. It must be cut very short. I trust such things would not inconvenience you, eh?'

"I must have visibly blanched, for Miss Stoper gave me a very severe look. I didn't mean to quail, gentlemen, for I desperately needed a position, but… well, I've never had much. Never any money. Not many luxuries, not many possessions of any kind. Very nearly nothing to set me apart from my crowd of fellow unfortunates… except… my hair. It's always what I've been known for, don't you see? I know it probably sounds foolish to you two, but—"

"It doesn't," said Holmes, gravely. "There is a great power in hair. One must always be cautious with it."

"Really?" Miss Hunter wondered.

"That has long been my colleague's professional opinion," I told her. "Yet, you may wish to reserve judgment of its wisdom until you hear which form of hair most concerns him."

Miss Hunter turned to Holmes expectantly.

"Ear hair," he opined. "*Especially* ear hair."

In the interest of truthfulness and completeness, I must report: Violet Hunter made a bit of a face.

"And is that the only part of Miss Hunter's tale that concerns you, Holmes?" I asked. I was still in the process of encouraging him to learn observation, inference and deduction.

"Not at all," my friend replied. "Thinking back to our Adventure of the Solitary Tricyclist: is she not the second woman to come to us, lured into the service of a disreputable gentleman for unknown, nefarious purposes, for exactly the salary of a hundred per year?"

"She is," I confirmed. "In point of fact, the second woman *named Violet*."

"Some sort of conspiracy, do you think?"

"I'm not sure, but I am considering another moratorium. Miss Hunter, pray, continue your tale."

"Mr. Rucastle must have noticed my hesitation, for he reached into his coat, produced his wallet and withdrew a fifty-pound note. 'Perhaps I did not mention… it is always my custom to provide half of my staff's wages in advance,' he said. 'Yes, you see, that way you can procure whatever little necessaries you might require for the trip. Here you are. I do hope we can expect you at the Copper Beeches tomorrow or the next day, eh?'

"But the offer—far from tempting me—repelled me to my core. Whatever misgivings I had been forming, here was proof that the situation was not to be trusted. I stood and said, 'I am sorry, Mr. Rucastle. Thank you for the generous offer, but I could not possibly sacrifice my hair. I'm sure you shall find any number of suitable candidates waiting outside.'

"Miss Stoper rose to see me out. She pinched my elbow with some vehemence as she led me to the door and said, 'Miss Hunter, your name will be removed from our lists. I really cannot see the point of including it when you turn down offers of such *extraordinary* generosity! Good day to you, Miss Hunter.'

"The door slammed shut behind me and I walked back home. When I found two fresh bills waiting there for me and little enough left in my account to answer them… well… I began to think I had been rather hasty. What fate would I rather? To be a shorn governess, or a well-coiffed flower girl?"

"Oh, I don't think I've ever seen one of those," said Holmes.

"No, indeed," Miss Hunter agreed. "I agonized about it all last night. But this morning I had this."

She placed an open letter on the coffee table. This is what it said:

To the estimable Miss Violet Hunter,

Oh, how I regret the terms on which we parted yesterday. When I think of what an ideal governess you'd make for young Barghest, I am brought practically to tears. Will you not reconsider? I have told my wife of your suitability and she is very eager that you should come. She has urged me to increase the offer to £120 per year. I do regret that she is inflexible on the subject of your hair, but that is her fancy and it will not be denied. Perhaps the extra remuneration might compensate you for its loss? Do reply and let us know if we might expect you.

Yours in hopefulness,
Jephro "The Copper" Rucastle

"Well," said Holmes, frowning down at the letter, "that's a trap."

"No question," I agreed.

"That much was clear to me," Miss Hunter said. "Nevertheless, I have accepted."

"You did *what*?" I cried. "Why? Why would you do that?"

She gave me a sad look, but to answer me, she turned to Holmes. "My brother was Nicholaus Hunter. Do you remember the name?"

"I cannot say I do."

"He used to do work for Clifford McCloe—a lieutenant of Moriarty. He ran afoul of you and Inspector Grogsson outside a jewelry shop, about four years ago."

"Ah! I recall it!" Holmes said. "Yes! Brave lad. He shouted for his confederates to run, then turned to cover their retreat. Did quite well for himself, if I remember. Put a bullet through my favorite hat, shot Grogsson in the leg."

"What became of him?" I asked.

"Well… he shot Grogsson, so…"

"As I believe I mentioned: I have no family," Miss Hunter said, with a sad smile.

"*Ah.*"

"I do not blame you for it, Mr. Holmes," said Violet. "Or even Grogsson. Poor lads who turn to crime often conclude their tales bleeding in the street. Either that or twitching at the end of a rope. Nevertheless, my brother was my keeper, for a time. And when he brought home his blood money, he brought tales as well: tales of ancient secrets, of magic and wonder. He walked in that world, gentlemen, albeit in a reprehensible capacity. Now, he is gone and I am faced with a choice. Either I can follow him—I can see the wonderful, dangerous majesty of this world, though it may mean my doom—or I can turn away and let the sad grayness of London digest me. His end was not so bad. He suffered only a moment. The demise that awaits me in the alleyway would take longer, torture me to my soul and be unworthy of remembrance. That is why I accepted the Copper's offer, gentlemen, and it is why I came here. I am going to walk out of the subtle trap that awaits me here and into the stranger one presented in this letter. Yet, before I go… My brother also told me of how men could serve Moriarty in return for his protection."

"Ugh, that's true," Holmes reflected. "His patronage was enough to ensure that even Scotland Yard must fear the humblest safe-cracker."

"Moriarty is gone," Miss Hunter said. "Not that I would place my troth in him, in any case. But my brother told me about *you*, Mr. Holmes. I know what you are. You are a sorcerer without equal and if Moriarty can take people under his protection, you can do the same. That is why I need to enter your service, sir. Then I shall go to the barber, sacrifice my hair, and face my fate."

Holmes sat in silent consideration a moment, then shook his head and muttered, "I'm sure Moriarty knew more than I of such things. Likely there was a contract, or some exchange of favors and tokens. Blood, probably.

Or—somewhat ironically—hair. It's true that I look after my friends, but I've never had an actual thrall, per se..."

"How can I earn your help, Mr. Holmes?" Violet urged.

"Well, I think the main idea of the thing is: you must do something for me. You must accomplish a task that is to my benefit, which I have no power to effect myself."

"Such as what, Mr. Holmes?"

"Well I don't know! That's the problem! I can do *anything*!" Holmes's eyes swept across the room, looking for something he could task Miss Hunter with.

"Pretty sure it's got nothing to do with my toast racks," he muttered.

Finally, his eyes came to rest on me. He gave a sudden start and gasped, "Wait, now! Watson... Watson has lately become fascinated with a new foe of ours..."

"Because she presents mortal danger to us, Holmes. Because she bests us totally whenever our paths cross."

"Is that why?" said Holmes. "You keep saying so, but each time you do I am less and less inclined to believe you. Every time you think of her, I can see a little more doom in your future. And let's not forget the recent fascination you have gained with your own grave. You might be unafraid to die, but then what should become of me? No, something must be done!"

Holmes turned to our guest with a malicious grin and said, "Miss Hunter, you must kiss Watson."

"*What?*" said the two of us together.

"Yes. See if you can't kiss some of that doom off him."

"Holmes!" I protested. "This is most irregular! Miss

Hunter has never met me before this day and—even if she had—you cannot force a lady's affections in this manner!"

Yet as I protested, Violet Hunter rose, gave a little smile and took a step in my direction. "The attitude does you credit," she said, "and yet I need to perform some service that Mr. Holmes cannot…"

As Miss Hunter walked up to the side of my chair, I spluttered, "Holmes, look here! This is highly—"

But she very calmly asked, "Dr. Watson, you would not send me to the Copper Beeches devoid of protection, would you?"

"Of course not, but—"

"Well then…"

She leaned down and placed her hands on either side of my face. I recall that my shapeless panic was given a sudden focus: how well had I shaved? Coolly as she handled it, I could tell the impropriety of the situation was not lost on her. The shadow of a blush lit the skin beneath her freckles and the smile she gave me was both embarrassed and sympathetic. She leaned in towards me and…

Argh!

I am sure I would not be confessing this to you, reader, if there were not a world-ending cataclysm looming, but…

It was my first kiss.

Well, I mean, discounting mothers and aunts and such. Oh, and Beryl Stapleton had kissed my cheek once—which very nearly made me wander off into a bog and die. The Woman had done the same, just after I ruined Holmes's magical defense against her. But as far as *proper* kisses go, this was the first.

And it was everything I hoped it would be.

Violet Hunter was a funny little thing, with her tiny frame and her bobbing copper bun. Yet it hadn't taken me long to come to admire her—her intelligence, her resolve and her bravery. She was a worthy person and the moment our lips touched, I was flooded with the feeling that she—how shall I say it?—that she deemed me worthy, too. That there was nothing separating us, now. There she was: soft, warm and alive—choosing *me*. Me, out of all the others who would be lucky to have her. For the first time, I understood what it was to be truly with another person.

And then it was over.

I've no idea how long it took. I hadn't the foresight to look at the clock, either before or after. It might have been the barest moment. Or perhaps some minutes. All I know is that as she drew back from me, her cheeks were properly, *scorchingly* red and her breathing was quick. I stared up at her with—oh, how I dread to report it—my mouth hanging open like an utter idiot. She smiled down at me.

"Thank you, Dr. Watson. Such… such a funny little thing, isn't it? I mean… to keep myself safe… what a peculiar method of… don't you think?"

Holmes stepped up behind her and said, "Thank you, Miss Hunter. I believe that will suffice. You may go with my thanks and the knowledge that, when you need my help, you shall not despair of it. Watson's too, I'll bet."

"Oh. Yes, of course," she spluttered. "Well… thank you both and I'll just be off, shall I?"

"Do try to take care of yourself, won't you?" Holmes asked.

"I'd like to," she said with a shrug, "but I'm afraid I intend just the opposite."

That wretched little blighter Holmes did it just to distract me—of that much, I am certain. And do you know what?

It worked.

Over the next several days I continued my clumsy investigations of Moriarty's criminal empire and the mysterious woman who so endangered Holmes and myself. But… oh, I don't know—my heart just wasn't in it.

Look, it's not as if my distraction was without reason! Violet Hunter was in very real and significant danger. True to her word, she marched straight out of 221B to the local barber, sacrificed her hair, sent a telegram to Jephro Rucastle and reported to the Copper Beeches the very next day—she sent a letter that told us as much. After that: nothing. Frustrating, terrifying silence.

So yes, I spent my days chasing after snippets of information on Moriarty and the Woman. Yet I found myself hastening back to Baker Street whenever I could to check the post. To see if we'd had any telegrams. Of course, there was the possibility that no danger at all loomed over Violet Hunter. Perhaps her new employer was simply an eccentric. If such was the case, would Violet feel any need to send word?

Then again, dead people don't send a lot of telegrams, either.

At last, on a drizzly Wednesday, Mrs. Hudson brought up a telegram.

```
I shall be at the Black Swan Hotel in
Winchester at noon on Saturday. Can you
come? HUNTER
```

Though the telegram was devoid of any real news, though it failed to say whether Violet's fortunes had been fair or foul, I nevertheless rejoiced to have any sign of her. Even Holmes seemed relieved.

Though he also made fun of me.

Look here, I needed to get my best suit cleaned—it was long overdue. Oh, and pressed. And then tailored. And then re-pressed, because it had been tailored. And I needed a haircut. And some cologne. All of these errands were things I should have done anyway, but their proximity to Violet's visit—and the rabid enthusiasm with which I pursued them—caused Holmes no end of merriment. I had it all done by Friday morning, which left me precious little to do for the next twenty-four hours but just walk about 221B, glancing at the clock; then I'd pace, then check the clock again, then I'd pick up something that belonged to Holmes or me and just *shake it and shake it and shake it*! Then I'd check the clock again.

At last, Saturday morning arrived. I dragged Holmes to Waterloo Station. Thence, to Winchester. Thence, to the Black Swan. There, on a couch by the window, we found Violet Hunter. As soon as we came in she rose and said, "Gentlemen, I'm glad you came! Things have been so strange, I simply... er... Dr. Watson, have you... have you *curled* your hair?"

"Ah, yes. It's the fashion, nowadays."

"Is it?" Miss Hunter wondered.

"We told him it was," Holmes said, exploding into fits of laughter.

I went red with rage. Holmes bent double and laughed so hard he nearly toppled over.

"Very nice. It suits you," Miss Hunter said.

"Thank you," I replied, and made a mental note to KILL EVERYONE I KNEW!

"I'm sorry, Watson. I'm sorry," Holmes giggled, breathless and teary. "I only thought Miss Hunter might feel better if she had a partner in hair misfortune."

Now it was Miss Hunter's turn to blush. She raised a hand to where her copper locks weren't and gave a sad little smile. With her diminutive frame, her profusion of freckles and that chopped hair, she rather looked as if one of the London street lads had put on a dress. Nevertheless, her resolve and self-confidence remained undimmed.

As did my respect for her.

We adjourned to the lunch room. As we settled in to dine, Violet leaned in and began her tale.

"On the day I arrived, Mr. Rucastle picked me up at Winchester Station in the dogcart. He was in high spirits and seemed greatly relieved I had come. As we drove he joked—on several occasions—pointing at the horse who drew us and explaining that he was sorry, but the actual dog had the day off. I laughed politely, but... well... the size of the traces... the oddly shaped harness... The rig was poorly suited to a horse or pony and I rather wondered if the thing *had* been designed for a dog, though it would have to be of monstrous stature.

"When we arrived at the Copper Beeches, it was just awful! Sure enough, there were two copper-colored beech trees, flanking the door. *Bright* copper. Painted so, by no expert hand. Inside, the home is just as bad. There are six or seven rooms still in service, but the bulk of the house is shut up, dusty, and dark. There is practically no staff. Only Mrs. Toller—who does all the cooking and cleaning—and her husband. Mr. Rucastle describes Mr. Toller's duties as 'fixing this, fixing that and seeing to the animals' but it would seem that a better description might be 'emptying every bottle from here to Manchester'. Mr. Toller is grim, gristled and, I think, never entirely sober. Oh, and Mrs. Rucastle! Her behavior is most unsettling. She's a sad, colorless, smile-less sort of person. She wears an expression of constant worry and oppression. Yet the moment she saw me, she burst from the front door, crying, 'She's perfect! Oh, just perfect!' and threw her arms around my neck, weeping.

"There are, I think, at least two secret residents. I frequently hear noises coming from the sealed portion of the house. I have seen Mr. Toller bearing food there. He has a key attached to his watch-fob. On my second day, as

Mr. Rucastle showed me about, he said we must go to the kennel. He led me into the forest, at the back of the house, to one of the outbuildings. His usual joviality dimmed somewhat as we approached it, and I can see why: the thing is a massive stone structure. This kennel looks large enough to service probably twenty dogs, but only one lives there. I have not seen it, but I heard it, for as we approached it threw itself at the door, barking and snarling. Though the door is constructed of four-inch timbers, I still feared it might break through, such was its ferocity. Mr. Rucastle told me, 'We don't have to stay, my dear. I just wanted to bring you here and let you know: this beast will be loosed onto the grounds, some nights. He's enough to dissuade any thief, you know, but he's a rough one. Why, even I do not feel safe around him. Toller's the only one he'll pay any heed to. So, I wanted you to know that it is best to stay inside of an evening, eh? A moonlight stroll in the woods could be as much as your life is worth!'"

I raised one finger and noted, "Miss Hunter, your description of the Copper Beeches has been incomplete. You have told us nothing of the child you were engaged to govern, young Barghest."

Miss Hunter's look became particularly dark. "He is a monster, not a child. He describes himself as mouse-reaver, rabbit-eater and pain-bringer. These are not idle boasts. I cannot fathom why any small creature is stupid enough to wander within two miles of the Copper Beeches, but they do. Oh, they do. And when Barghest gets his paws on one… well… he makes them last for hours. Tiny little screams that echo through the hallways… He had one that lasted half a night, once, but they all fall quiet in the end."

"And Mr. Rucastle allows this?" I asked, scandalized.

"He *encourages* it. Of course, the first time it happened, I stepped in to correct Barghest. It is a governess's duty, after all. Though I had just arrived, still I raised my voice. The severity of such behavior demands at least as much. Yet Mr. Rucastle came in, placed a hand on my shoulder and made a calming gesture—by which he meant I should cease. Later, he jokingly apologized and said that Barghest must be allowed his peculiarities. After all, he claimed, there is no property so important as aggression to make a truly great statesman. He thinks his son shall grow to be a *statesman*! Never! A criminal, of course. A ravager and a strangler, I shouldn't wonder. But a statesman? Ha!"

"Hmmmm," Holmes reflected. "A most unusual lad, indeed."

"And there's more," said Violet. "He has strange absences. Though my duties would be light in any case, I have long periods of inactivity when Barghest is… well… just gone. Mr. Rucastle says he's off playing in the woods, or visiting his friends. Barghest has no friends. Only victims, I am certain. On perhaps the third day I was there, I protested that it was most irregular for a governess not to know where her charge was, especially at nine o'clock at night. But the Copper said he was not concerned and that I must become used to such interruptions. He opened up a disused old room full of dusty novels of no great quality and said that in Barghest's absence I might indulge myself to anything I found in 'the library'.""

"It sounds as if Jephro Rucastle hardly expects you to spend any time with the boy he claims you will be shaping," I noted. "Indeed, he's blocked your chief attempt to correct his behavior. I suspect he may have other reasons for wanting you in residence."

"It seems I might have been called there to fill a vacancy, Dr. Watson."

"What do you mean?"

"When I got to the Copper Beeches, there was already a bedroom made up for me. It's pleasant and feminine, but the items were clearly not purchased for me, for they are old and several of the drawers in the dresser are locked. Mrs. Rucastle has several times mentioned how much she misses her daughter, Alice, who has wed and moved to Philadelphia. I think some of the clothing and effects repurposed for me used to belong to this Alice, but here's the strange thing: the house contains no picture of her. None. Plenty of Barghest, several of Mr. and Mrs. Rucastle and even one with the Tollers, too. But none of Alice.

"Now I strongly suspected that some truth of her might be found in the chest of drawers in my room. I kept my clothes and the braid of hair that I'd had to cut off in the top drawers, but the bottom drawer was locked, and thus a mystery to me. Luckily, I am the sister of a troublemaker and had come to the Copper Beeches prepared to do a little mischief of my own. My brother's old lock-pick saw me quickly into the lower drawer. Look what I found.""

From her handbag, Miss Hunter withdrew a long braid of copper hair.

"They… they moved your hair from the top drawer to the bottom? But why would they do such a thing?" I spluttered.

"I wondered the same," said Violet. "But it turns out they hadn't. This is what I found when I examined the upper."

She reached into her bag a second time and drew out a second plait, laying it beside the first. The color match was practically exact. Even the length could not have differed by more than a quarter of an inch.

"Oooooooooooooooooooh," said Holmes. "I don't like this at all!"

"It gets worse," Violet assured him. "Mrs. Rucastle spends entirely too much time at the dining-room table. She's got a permanent mess of old crosswords, calendars, dice and odd-shaped little bones. She will spend hours poring over the crosswords and calendars. She rolls the dice and bones over them, then whispers to herself about the results. Early on Tuesday morning, she was engaged in this strange practice when she suddenly leapt up with a yell, circled Tuesday on the calendar and ran to find her husband. I was in the library so I saw her go and—from just down the hall, I heard Mr. Rucastle's voice answer her panicked mutterings. He said, 'You are certain? This very afternoon? Oh, dear me. Oh dear.'

"Now, do you remember when we first met, I told you Mr. Rucastle said he might wish for me to sit with him for a time, wearing a certain electric blue dress?"

"Nope," said Holmes.

"I recall it," I said.

"An hour later, as I emerged from the library, I found Mr. Rucastle waiting for me in the hall. He smiled and said, 'I see you like to read, eh? I happen to be a bit of a novelist myself. Only an amateur, but perhaps you might read some of my works to my wife and me this evening? Oh, it does a world of good for a writer to hear his scribblings out loud, you know. So much easier to hear where you've been obtuse than to spot it on a page. Tell you what, I'll have that electric blue dress I mentioned laid out for you. Later you must wear it—as you agreed you would, when you came here—and you can sit with us and read to Mallory and me! Won't that be nice?' He then wandered off and left me to my own devices until afternoon.

"Just after luncheon, I went up to my room and found the dress in question. Mr. Rucastle had been a bit vague in describing it—on purpose, I am certain. He'd used a quirk of our language to his advantage."

"What do you mean?" I asked.

"The dress is actually periwinkle blue."

"Eh? Then why would he—"

"And it's *electric*."

"Oh!" shouted Holmes and I, together.

Holmes wiped a tear from the corner of one eye and noted, "I don't like her stories, Watson. They're scary!"

"There are wires and electrodes all through it, with special underclothes so the copper plates can touch bare skin—"

"Make her stop, Watson!"

"Two long cords which end in naked copper cables trail from the back. Oh, and there's a little hat to match, with electrodes that rest against both temples and the base of the neck."

"Unless the wearer has a full head of hair," I observed dolefully.

"I fear so," said Violet, with a nod. "Well, once I put it on—"

"You did *what*?" cried Holmes.

"The only way to know what was happening was to play along—"

"Oh, no, no, no, no!"

"Downstairs, Mr. Rucastle had me sit with my back to the window and gave me a sheaf of papers he described as his manuscript. He asked Mrs. Rucastle to open the window to give us a little air, but the whole thing was the crudest of blinds for her to drop the two wires on the back of my dress out of the window. They then had me read. The work was presented to me as a love story between a woman named Alice and a gentleman named Ampere."

"Ampere?" I noted, raising an eyebrow.

"Yes, which Mr. Rucastle insists is a common French name and *not* a unit of electrical current. His manuscript is rather dialogue-heavy and he made me read certain lines over and over again. Notably, 'Come to me, Ampere, I await your touch. Now, at last, we can be one.' As I read it, I became conscious of a subtle shift in the light behind me—as if it were moving, uncertainly. I could just feel the hairs on my back and neck, between the electrodes, begin to prick up. Every time I tried to look around, out the window, Mr. Rucastle demanded my attention for some reason or other. Yet his and his wife's attention was fixed outside the window. They seemed greatly frustrated and Mr. Rucastle had me switch to another section of dialogue which featured the lines, 'Why do you shy from me? It is I, Alice, who was promised to you. Come to me, Ampere!' But after a time, the light faded and the feeling on my skin went away. The Rucastles wilted in disappointment. Jephro took back his 'manuscript', said he clearly needed to work on the dialogue and dismissed me to my room."

"You said Alice was the name of their missing daughter?" I asked.

"Indeed."

"Well, I think we've heard enough," I declared. "The situation is absolutely monstrous, but I believe we have enough information to draw some useful conclusions. Now, in the interest of your detective training, what do you make of it, Holmes?"

"Hmmmm…" My companion tapped his teeth with one finger for a few moments then decided, "Real-daughter-offered-to-an-electricity-demon-in-exchange-for-favors-but-parents-hide-her-away-in-the-disused-portion-of-the-house-then-hire-Violet-to-be-a-substitute-sacrifice-because-she's-the-same-size-same-age-and-has-the-same-color-hair?"

"Bravo, Holmes! Now describe the process by which you deduced it."

"Oh, there was none. I just asked myself how a wicked turkey-man would manage his affairs and that's the first thing that came to mind."

"Well, whatever the acumen, I am forced to concur with the result."

Violet gave a nod. "It is strange," she said. "I had begun to think the same. Of course, such things are new to me—my brother's tales being the only contact I've had with your strange and magical world. Yet, if you gentlemen agree with my conclusions... I think I know how to proceed."

"Proceed? No, no, no!" I cried. "You must come back with us! The danger, Violet, think of the danger!"

"Oh, I do," she said. "Yet, remember the danger that awaits me in the city? I am embracing this new and strange world. Yes, I am happy to have your assistance in my first outing. Yet, that is why you are here, sir: to help me. Not to undermine my resolve. And recall, it is not only *my* safety that is in question."

"Alice Rucastle," I sighed.

"I think I may know a path to helping her," said Violet. "Next month, the Rucastles leave on a brief journey; that is when I shall strike. On Wednesday, when I wired you, I'd asked Mr. Rucastle for permission to come to town to order a new hat. Today, he thinks I'm here to pick it up. Which I did..."

She indicated an elegant little number, beaded, netted, with a tasteful sprig of feathers on one side.

"...but I hesitate to think of the damage my reputation

would suffer if the rest of my shopping came to light."

Opening her bag, she showed us a pair of heavy gardening shears, a roll of black cloth tape, four bottles of strong whisky and a little silver derringer.

"Well, I'm relieved that at least you've made some preparation," Holmes said.

I was less convinced. "That is a .19 caliber 'glove' derringer. It would take both shots to stop a rampaging mouse. What use it might be against an electrical demon is quite beyond the scope of my imagination."

Violet shrugged. "It's hard for a lady to get much more in Winchester without raising attention. Besides which, it is easily concealable upon my person and might help me convince any of my more mundane antagonists to see things my way, if matters do not go to plan. Now, Mr. Holmes, if I should require your assistance further, how might I inquire after it?"

"The same way you just did would be ideal: a telegram and advance notice."

"And if I cannot?"

"Speak my name? Think of me? Scream for me, if you must. Really, I don't quite know. This is my first time having a contracted thrall."

"Very well," Violet said. "I suppose I'd best be getting back. How long does it take to pick up a hat, after all? I shall try to keep you gentlemen informed of my plans."

* * *

Sadly, that luxury eluded us. Holmes and I returned to London and a frustrating lack of news concerning Violet Hunter's progress.

Or, more likely, her demise.

To complicate matters further, Holmes got us embroiled in a new adventure. He brought that red-headed ninny Jabez Wilson to Baker Street and led us on a whole new meaningless campaign of self-endangerment. I will say little of the matter right now, but will make sure it is the next adventure this volume details. Suffice to say, it quite drove concerns over Violet Hunter to the back of my mind. In fact, she was hardly mentioned at all until Holmes and I found ourselves trapped in an underground vault, surrounded on all sides by hideous monsters, bound, bested and nearly helpless. Suddenly, as our attackers closed in for the final assault, Holmes shouted, "Oh no! Violet is in danger!"

"What?" I shouted at him. "*What?*"

"We've got to help her! But how?"

"Yes. Exactly. How, indeed?"

Holmes spluttered and fretted, lost for ideas. I think I became quite furious with him for I knew—deep in my momentarily doomed little heart—that he was spending zero thought or effort on our present situation. Then, in an instant, an idea came to him. His face broke into an expression of relief, he elbowed one of the monsters that held him slightly back then lunged for me and...

It was the first time I'd kissed a man.

And it was everything I'd dreaded.

To start with: it wasn't particularly well aimed. The first sensation was of Holmes's lips all over my cheek and chin, filling my stubble up with slobber. I had just enough time to scream in distress (and sadly not quite enough to punch him in the head) before his lips found mine.

The next instant, I was falling through a swirling void. All around me, I could sense the presence of demons. I had the distinct impression they were pointing at me and laughing. (Little bastards.) Even worse than the sensation of falling to an unknown fate was the realization that I no longer had control of my body. I could tell, because my repeated attempts to wipe my mouth were met by no sensation of touch, either from my arms or the spit-drenched, recently betrayed unwanted-kiss-reception-facility I called a face. Falling. Spinning. Screaming with no voice, until…

With a jolt, I found myself standing in a shabby little bedroom, staring at a periwinkle dress with wires all up and down it, laid out on a clean white bedcover. I think I tried to cry out or to throw my hands to either side to steady myself. But the hands did not move. The voice made no cry. Instead, I heard myself say, "Yes, of course, Mr. Rucastle. But a lady needs some time to prepare, you know."

The voice was not my own. As I digested the strangeness of it, my head swiveled to one side and my gaze fell, for the first time, on the horrible avianesque abomination that was Jephro Rucastle. He looked sweaty and distraught. He held a pocket watch in his hand and protested, "Yes, but we've got to leave, you see… Mallory and I do not wish to miss our boat."

"Then perhaps we might do the reading another day?" my own, strange voice suggested.

"No! Er… no, I'm sure there will be time, my dear. Only, do hurry, won't you? There's my girl."

No sooner had the door closed than the body I inhabited reeled and stumbled. It shot one hand to the bedpost to steady itself and whispered, "What is happening? Is someone there? Is it you, Mr. Holmes?"

"Violet?" I tried to ask, but no voice emerged.

Yet despite the lack of sound, she heard me. The voice whispered back, "Dr. *Watson?*"

I could feel her surprise. And mine as well. It was sickening and disorienting. Like watching two plays at the same time. No. Worse. I remember a fellow named Remmer, who had nearly lost his eye in Afghanistan. It had been hanging out of his head by the nerve for a few moments, before I replaced it. It's not a difficult procedure, you just shove it back in. But I was repelled by his description of those few moments it was out. It wasn't particularly painful, apparently. He remembered looking straight ahead, as always, feeling his feet on the ground and knowing he was steady. But at the same time, he was looking down at the ground, watching it sway back and forth as his left eyeball swung at the end of the nerve. He tried to close his eyes to stop the unwanted input, but as the eyelid whose services he required was now significantly *behind* the eye in question, he had no power to make the interruption cease.

That's what it was like, finding myself in the sudden

possession of Violet Hunter's thoughts and feelings, as well as my own. Apparently, it was no better for her, as I could clearly hear her thinking, *Ugh, this is just the worst!*

I know! I'm sorry!

I felt the body I was in retch, and very nearly vomit.

"What happened?"

I think Holmes sent me here to help you.

"He calls this *help*?"

I tried to shrug, then concentrated my thoughts on stilling the swirl of our mutual stomach. After only a few moments—before I was ready—Violet thought, *Come on, we've no time to lose.*

What are we—?

The body I was in lurched down and heaved the mattress over to one side. Concealed beneath it were the gardening shears I'd seen the week before, the roll of tape and two bottles of whisky. My hands reached down and scooped up the shears. We then went to the dress, flipped it over, and cut the long wires that protruded from the back.

They'll see they're gone! I protested.

No they won't. My body went to the dresser and withdrew a pair of stockings from the top drawer. These had already been twisted into strange knotted braids. As I watched, my hands laid one between the severed halves of the first wire, then reached down for the black tape. In an instant, I realized the genius of it. As the entire length was nothing more than copper cable wrapped in the same kind of black cloth tape…

I don't know much on the subject of electricity, Violet

thought, *but if a few inches of each wire is composed of cotton, rather than copper…*

Yes! Brilliant! That ought to stop it conducting!

My hands wound tape around the end of the old wire, the new cotton section, and the disembodied length of wire on the other side. A careful examination would reveal the deception, but a casual observer would be indeed unlikely to discover Violet's modification.

Well done! I thought. *A sound plan, indeed. Where are the other two bottles of whisky?*

Already placed in Mr. Toller's way. In a few hours, he'll be useless.

And the gun?

Secreted on my person.

To my horror, Violet thought of where she'd put it—an area she knew was unlikely to be searched, but not one in which I personally had ever had the opportunity to conceal things. The remembrance caused me to reflect on the suddenly unfamiliar shape of the body I inhabited. My mind drifted… well… exactly where one might expect. And of course, that mind was not only my own. I could feel Violet's wave of indignation and anger.

Dr. Watson!

I'm sorry! I am, but this is my first time owning… Madam, I apologize, but can you imagine what you would think if you suddenly found yourself in possession of a male body?

It turns out she *could*. A wave of mumbled, half-swallowed thoughts intruded over my own.

Ha! You're no better than I am!

Do try to contain yourself, won't you? It's about to get a lot worse.

What do you mean?

"Dr. Watson..." she said out loud, "I am expected to *change my dress.*" I watched my hand point towards the periwinkle execution dress.

What? No! No, for two reasons, at least!

I thought you said you were here to help. You are not allowed to falter, sir. The plan goes forward. With the wires cut, we're much safer, don't you think?

Well, yes, but... do it with your eyes closed, at least!

With my eyes closed? Clearly you have never struggled into an unfamiliar dress before.

Do you know something, I actually haven't.

By God... For a doctor, you're surprisingly squeamish...

To her credit, Violet did manage the operation with her eyes closed for the bulk of it. Still, it didn't matter. Just the sensation of cloth sliding into place over divots and bulges I'd never had before was enough to... well... If Violet Hunter ever elects to slap my face, she is forgiven in advance. In fact, even if she elects to light me on fire...

In less than five minutes' time, we descended the stairs to the sitting room. Mr. and Mrs. Rucastle were waiting, expectation and worry on their faces.

"Ah, yes, my dear, yes! You look perfect!" Rucastle gobbled. "Now have a seat near the window, won't you? Here is the new manuscript and I have the humble hope of an amateur fabulist that it is better than the last, hey? Ha! Oh, I say, it's a bit stifling, isn't it?"

Really? Stifling? Violet and I thought, together. *In England, in February?*

Yet Mrs. Rucastle shuffled around behind us for a few moments. I heard the window slide open, felt the cold blast of air and the ill-concealed tug as both wires were dropped through the open window.

"Yes. There. We're all ready, aren't we?" Mr. Rucastle decided. "Well, why don't we begin at the top of page eighteen, eh?"

So we did. After a few sentences of exposition and dreck, we got to the lines I'm sure were the true order of the day.

"Oh, Ampere, why will you not come to me? Do you forsake your word? Your Alice is waiting, will you not join me so we can finally…"

And here Violet faltered. The same uncomfortable thought flitted across both our minds.

"…finally *be one*?"

From the garden behind me, a slight buzz began to intrude itself on my notice. Nearly inaudible, but certainly present. I could just detect a change in the light that filtered through the window, over our shared shoulder, and onto the page.

"Here now! Here! Read this bit, won't you?" Mr. Rucastle suggested, lunging forward to turn to another page. "It's where Ampere's father explains business contracts to him. Oh, but you can read it in a female voice. I… I want it to sound as natural as it may, you know."

"A contract in good faith must be honored," Violet

read. But I read ahead of her on the page and… well… I may have lost my nerve a bit.

No! Do not say that out loud! Run! Get us out of here!

Dr. Watson! Violet thought, leaning forward and placing fingers against her brow. *We have already spoken about this! I am here to unravel this mystery, not to run from it. Now please, cease this distraction!*

No! Run!

I will not, but if you persist in this behavior, I shall… I shall… Ah! I shall touch my thigh, in a most improper manner.

It's a good thing my mind had no control over Violet Hunter's mouth, or it would have been left hanging open in terrified incredulity.

You wouldn't.

Why not? It's mine.

Jephro Rucastle, frustrated by the delay at what he perceived to be his moment of triumph, shout-gobbled, "What is wrong, my dear? Why do you not read? Are you not well?"

"Not too well, I think," Violet said. "Pardon me, Mr. Rucastle. The story continues: the service provided, the payment rendered, it must be accepted. The rules and laws we do business by mean nothing if the covenant is broken."

Behind us, the buzz increased. The light grew and shifted. As Violet read, I felt one of the wires on the back of our dress tug. It was as if someone had picked it up to regard it, wondering what it might be. For three to five minutes of pure horror, Mr. Rucastle picked passages—begging, urging, cajoling, demanding—trying to get that demon behind Violet and myself to end our mutual life.

But Ampere would not be fooled. The light became flickering and uncertain. The buzzing subsided. Mr. and Mrs. Rucastle sank down in their chairs, dejected and defeated.

"Oh well. We shall have to try again, when we return," Rucastle sighed. "For now, my dear, we must hasten for our boat. Good day, Miss Hunter. Get some rest and do feel better."

Which we did. As the Rucastles bustled about, Violet retired to her room and threw us onto her bed. Our head spun. I don't know if it was proximity to such a powerful electric force, the excitement of a near-death escape, or merely the disorientation of sharing a body and mind, but the both of us felt sick and drained.

What must we do? I asked, after a time.

Nothing, now, she replied. *Mr. Toller is not likely to drink himself all the way into a stupor with the Rucastles present. Once they are gone, he'll waste no time. So we may rest, but we must not sleep. The Rucastles won't be gone long.*

Eh? It sounded as if they were bound on a journey.

They think they are. Last night, when Mrs. Rucastle circled today on her calendar, I might have seen fit to forge a note, informing them the schedule for their ship had been modified.

Well done!

Thank you, Doctor. Of course, we are hardly more than ten miles from Southampton Docks and the Rucastles will be hurrying. It probably won't take them long to determine they've been had, but then… what will they do? Rush back? Dither? I've no idea.

Hopefully it will be long enough for Holmes to get here. Well… assuming he isn't dead. Good Lord! I might be dead! I hadn't even thought of it, but… how would I even tell? What would I do? If my body is dead, could I… could I stay here?

I really wouldn't know, Violet thought, shrugging our shoulders.

So, there we lay for quite some time, trying to collect our thoughts, to steady our stomach and to pass the time until Toller fell over drunk. We felt really terrible, but were careful to remember we must not sleep. Slowly the fading light of day gave way to twilight, then moon-drenched night. Of course, with no action to preoccupy us, my mind kept drifting back to certain facts… *I was a girl!* Every time I thought of it, Violet knew. But, she could also feel the many times I tried to distract myself from that thought with any other concern I could muster.

Just think about baseball, Violet thought-suggested. *I hear that helps.*

Baseball? What is that?

An American game, a bit similar to cricket. From what I hear it is even more boring.

What? Is that possible? Yet it did help to distract my thoughts. It was an interesting mental challenge, trying to devise a game even more boring than cricket. It would have to be mostly just standing about, obviously. But, as standing is not a game… Better to give at least one fellow a ball. Tell him to throw it, or something, but only once every five minutes. But then what would the other fellows do? Oh! One of them could swing at the ball, I suppose. But in the interest of keeping it boring, we should make it so it is often judicious for him to elect not to. Yes, yes. It was all coming together. Simply wretched.

Finally, from downstairs, we heard Mrs. Toller's raised voice and her husband's murky replies. We heard the muffled slamming of a door.

Well, I'm new at this, of course, Violet thought, *but I do believe that is our signal.*

Madam, I concur.

Down the stairs we went, to find Mrs. Toller bustling about in the kitchen, red-faced and angry. When she saw us, she snipped, "Oh, it's you. Feeling better?"

I'll take care of this, Violet thought.

"No," she said, sinking down on one of the chairs. "I feel awful. But I thought… something sweet might help."

"Well, you're out of luck. I got nuffin'."

"Last week, in Winchester, I bought a jar of peach preserves. It's down in the cellar. Would you mind fetching it for me? I'll happily share it with you, if…"

Violet had chosen her bait well. Though I did not know Mrs. Toller, the alacrity with which she turned and sped through the cellar door did seem to suggest she might be an insatiable sweet tooth. No sooner had she bustled down the stairs than Violet twisted our mutual mouth up into a satisfied smile, rose, went to the door, closed it and turned the key.

"That's one Toller down," she said. "Though I strongly suspect…"

She opened the door to the sitting room. There, sprawled on the couch, snoring into the crook of his arm, lay Mr. Toller.

"Ah, yes. *Two*."

She unclipped the ring of keys from his belt and walked us back to the unused portion of the house. Up a flight of stairs, down a hall, to an old whitewash-smeared door. This yielded to the first key she tried and we slipped inside.

I must say, Miss Hunter, you seem to have quite a high aptitude for this sort of work, I thought.

Thank you, Doctor. I could feel us smile. *Though we must not congratulate ourselves yet. There are many rooms; it may take us quite some time to try them all.*

No need. If they are trying to conceal her, they must likewise conceal her noise. She will be in the room farthest from the used portion of the house. Let us remember: Toller has been bringing Alice food every day, through an area that's been shut down to all other traffic. Find the path that isn't dusty and it shall lead straight to her, I would think.

And, indeed, it did. We came to a door at the far end of the hall. The handle looked polished from regular use, but a better clue was the wadded-up curtains stuck into the crack under the door, to stop extra noise. Violet tried key after key until, at last, the door swung open. There, tied to the far wall, with innumerable leather straps, stood Alice Rucastle. Chains would have rattled, I suppose. She wore a mask over the lower part of her face, designed, I think, to allow breathing but to stop her calling out. As we entered, she stared at us with a strange mixture of surprise, hope and… something else. Just *madness*, it seemed to me.

Something was wrong.

If the Rucastles were truly contriving to save their daughter from a demon by using Violet as a replacement sacrifice, why did they require this extraordinarily cruel amount of security? Wouldn't Alice be more likely to work with, rather than against them? Why was she restrained so? Why muted? Yet even as I began to think-ask Violet, I felt a sudden wave of dizziness. The world went black. I was falling again—falling in reverse through that same demonic void I'd encountered only a handful of hours before. And then…

I was in a carriage.

I was propped up in one corner of a carriage, with a strange red haze partially obscuring my vision and Holmes leaning expectantly towards me. As soon as he saw me move, he piped up, "Hi-ho, Watson! Welcome back! How was your trip to… er… Violet?"

"I think she's in danger, Holmes! We've got to…" But I trailed off, confused and compelled by the bright red fibrous haze before my eyes. It seemed to move with me—it seemed a solid thing. "Good lord, Holmes! Is that my hair?"

"Well… it may have—"

"Agh! What happened to my hair?" I raised my arm to grab at my horrifying red fringe, but a wave of pain assailed me and the arm flopped helplessly down…

"Agh! What happened to my arm?"

…Flopped down onto my leg, in fact—an act that

rewarded me with a second, altogether different flash of agony.

"Agh! What happened to my leg?"

"One thing at a time, Watson, please," Holmes harrumphed. "Honestly… yes. That is your hair. It is red. Why? Magic. What is the result? Our previous adventure is resolved in our favor. Plus, you have a grand new world of cosmetic possibility open to you and only a fool fears new experiences. You are welcome."

I gave him a warning glare.

"Second, the arm… Yes… I am not a doctor, you know, but I believe it may be broken. I don't remember it ever bending in the middle like that before. What else…? Ah! The leg. It's been stabbed with a screwdriver. Oh, and before you ask, there may be a few crowbar marks on your face. Don't be surprised when you find them."

"What did you do to me?"

"I? Nothing. You were the one who was trying to fight off a pack of monsters with a screwdriver, if you'll recall. This is merely the natural consequence of your choices. The only thing I am guilty of is helping. Look, I bound the wound for you."

"Ah! By God! What is this? Why does it look like that?"

"At the risk of repeating myself: you were stabbed with a screwdriver."

"And you bandaged *over* it? You didn't pull it out? That's not how you… Ow! Holmes! Why?"

"As I believe I mentioned: I am not actually a doctor."

"What happened?"

"You left in the middle of an adventure—"

"I didn't just *leave*. You kissed me into Violet!"

"Whatever the reason for your absence, you can hardly expect the world to cease operation simply because you've gone. Events moved on, Watson. I'll tell you all about it later, if you wish."

The carriage gave a sudden, violent lurch, flooding me with pain. Holmes merely tutted at the interruption and said, "But enough about you, Watson. You believe Violet to be in danger?"

"Yes! We found Alice Rucastle! But something's wrong, she's—"

The carriage shook with a second violent impact.

"Ow! Argh! She's tied up. And her eyes, Holmes! She's crazy, I'll swear to it! I think Violet's going to let her go, but I don't know what will happen when she does. We've got to get to the Copper Beeches, Holmes. We've got to help her!"

"That, of course, was my intention," Holmes said, with as much patience as he could muster. "Sadly, it seems we are not the only party interested in the goings-on at that particular domicile."

He reached across me and tugged back the curtain covering the carriage window. There, not six feet from my face, was Jephro Rucastle. His eponymous copper locks shook with wild abandon as his carriage veered towards me and smashed, for a third time, into our own.

"Upon reaching the neighborhood, I waved down the first carriage I encountered and asked how I might find the

Copper Beeches," said Holmes. "I explained I was trying to help a governess unravel a demonic plot."

"Ah. I don't suppose it occurred to you to check whether the occupant of that carriage might be Jephro Rucastle?"

"Hindsight is 20/20, Watson; try not to boast of it."

I was about to ask how Rucastle had motivated the driver of his carriage to do battle, when I heard the fellow call, "Sorry I keep rammin' yeh, Brady. But he's payin' me extra, you know?"

From above, our driver shouted, "Well, a fare's a fare, eh, Sam?"

"Heh! Too right! Too right!"

The next impact knocked me against the far wall and I think I nearly fainted. The proper treatment for a complete humeral fracture is setting and immobilization. It is emphatically *not* to load the sufferer into a carriage, set it galloping down a pitted country lane, then bounce another carriage off it, over and over.

"I don't know how much more of this I can take, Holmes!"

"Well it needn't be much, Watson. Look, we're nearly there."

By this time our carriage was so badly holed that the windows had become academic. The Copper's vehicle was in even worse shape. Half the roof and one wall was gone and the tattered curtains flapped loosely past where the Copper stood.

"Wait a moment!" I cried. "Where is Mrs. Rucastle? She was traveling with him!"

"Oh, she fell out *miles* ago," said Holmes, with a dismissive wave. "Now hang on, Watson; we're turning up the drive."

Even as Holmes spoke, our carriage swerved to the right, up the long drive to the Copper Beeches. I heard Jephro Rucastle cry out in dismay as we pulled away from him, but in only a moment his carriage swerved back in and smashed into us once more. It was too much. The front wheel of our carriage splintered and buckled. The two smashed halves of it came flying past the shattered window as our naked axle tipped down and tore into the drive. When it dug in, our belabored vehicle broke apart. The horses broke free and ran off dragging a rattling trail of broken harnesses. As the body of the carriage tumbled end over end, I could just hear Rucastle's driver shout, "Sorry 'bout that, Brady! But you had her insured, right?"

"Course I did! What do you take me for?" our driver replied jovially, as he bounced off into the woods.

I might well have been killed in the crash. Certainly, my already impressive collection of wounds would have become intolerable. Yet Holmes took mercy on me. Hardly had our carriage upended before he spread his hands to either side. A barely visible bubble of gummy air surrounded us and bulged outwards. The much-abused walls of our carriage could take no more; they separated at the corners and blew apart into so much bouncing kindling. There was a sudden, stomach-turning sensation of deceleration— though what mechanism might be slowing us, I could not guess. Once down to walking speed, our bubble descended lightly to earth, touched the surface of the lane and gently popped, leaving me lying and Holmes standing halfway down the long drive to the Copper Beeches. Holmes cleared his throat guiltily and asked, "What do you think, Watson? Did anybody see that?"

Normally, I'd say they must have. However, in that particular moment, three distinct dangers that might command more attention were emerging.

First: Alice Rucastle. It seems I had been correct in guessing that the imperturbable Violet Hunter was going to go ahead with her plan to free Alice. The evidence? Miss Hunter leaned out of a second-story window, shouting in dismay at the figure of Alice Rucastle, who dangled from the window just below her. It seems she'd torn away half the leather straps and half her clothing and was engaged in a desperate bid to flee her house. Apparently nobody had notified her there was a front door. Not that she'd have cared. A look at her face was enough to show the woman was unwell. The mask still dangled from one ear but as it flopped to the side, one could observe the expression of frantic joy that she wore as she gazed at the second attention-demanding development.

Which was: the sky. It was fair to say, we were having a spot of weather. Though the moon was still visible, it shone through a swirling cauldron of clouds. These formed a suspiciously perfect circle and moved with a furious motion quite at odds with the wind. As they spun, they occasionally fired a burst of lightning down onto the grounds of the Copper Beeches. These bolts did not always strike the same spot of ground, but they did always pass through the same space in the air, some hundred feet or so above the grass. Whenever they did, the bolts would splay out into a luminous haze for a moment, before continuing their plunge to earth. The haze was of human shape and size, slowly descending.

Ampere, I assumed.

And finally: a dog. Juuuuuuuust a bit of a scary dog. The only reason I didn't assume him to be a hell-hound is that I'd seen one before. Yet, if I had been called upon to spend one night braving the company of Foofy the hell-hound or two minutes in the company of the beast that burst from the edge of the woods... well... Foofy and I would have had a fine time, I am sure. The beast was not luminous, as a proper hell-hound would be. Not composed of smoke and shadow, but of regular flesh and blood. Well, I say regular... The thing must have weighed as much as two horses and half a yak. It had muscular, oversized front legs and comically small back ones, like a bulldog. In fact, it had the snubby face, powerful jaw and slobbery jowls of a bulldog, too, but there the similarities ended. It wore an expression of hatred and intelligence—more human than canine. It seems that—to our great misfortune—Mr. Toller's final, sober act of the evening had been to perform his regular nightly duty. He'd opened the kennel. The beast took a minute to gaze out over the scene, carefully selecting the weakest target, before it charged.

And what was the weakest target? I would have

said "me" except for a new development in the tactical situation. It seems Violet had Alice grasped firmly by the straps, and was trying to haul her back in the window. Alice, though weak from months of captivity, struggled with the desperate strength of the mad. This, combined with the assistance of gravity, proved sufficient to win the day. With a shriek of alarm from Violet, the two of them fell from the second-story window, out into the garden. At least the flower bed looked soft and loamy, but now they had the problem of the terrible hound, which turned to charge them.

"Hmmm…" said Holmes, appraisingly. "What do you say, Watson? I get the demon; you get the dog?"

"But… But…" I stammered, indicating first my broken arm, then the oblong, bandaged bulge where the screwdriver protruded from my leg.

"Well, someone's got to do it," said Holmes with a shrug and set off over the lawn. As he went, I heard him mumble, "Oh! Better not give him any metal to key in on, eh?" So, Holmes began patting himself down for metal, checking each pocket in turn and casually discarding coins, keys, his handcuffs and his magnifying glass into the grass. With a grunt of resolution and pain, I set off up the drive, towards Violet.

Now, the fellow who would seem to have the best chance of reaching her in time was not me, but Jephro "The Copper" Rucastle. After all, his carriage still rolled (slightly) and he was farther up the drive. Yet this advantage was lessened by the streetwise experience of his coachman,

Sam. Though propriety and custom demanded that Mr. Rucastle be dropped off as close to his door as possible, Sam took careful note of the monstrous hound, the descending electrical demon and the general air of desperation and decided, "Here we are, sir: the Copper Beeches!"

"But," the Copper protested, "I want to go—"

"No. Here we are, sir: the Copper Beeches," Sam repeated, firmly, then added, "I believe your fare's up to an even four pounds six. All those extra rammings is what did it, you know. All those extra times you shouted, 'Two shillings if you can catch that warlock!' eh? Four pounds six, please."

Mr. Rucastle threw a handful of coins at Sam, and climbed down from the wrecked carriage. He ran towards—well, no... He gobble-charged ponderously towards the fallen figure of his daughter, shouting, "Alice! You fool! Get back in the house!"

She didn't. Instead she picked up one of the decorative garden rocks, fetched Violet a savage blow to the head with it, ignored the charging dog and ran off towards the open lawn, tearing off whatever articles of clothing and leather strappery she could reach and crying, "Ampere! Here I am! Can you hear me? They tried to keep me dull, my love! Touch me! Touch me, my promised one, and make me bright like you!"

The hound tore past the reeling form of Violet Hunter, hot on the heels of Alice Rucastle. As it passed, Violet shouted, "No!", yanked the derringer from the folds of her vest and fired twice. From where I stood, dragging myself up the drive, I could just hear the feeble *pop! pop!* as Violet sent two tiny lumps of lead into (but probably not through) the hair over the dog's flank. This did about as much as one might expect to slow the beast's charge. Yet if this show of force was insufficient, the next one was better. As the dog closed to within a dozen feet of Alice, a prolonged flash of lightning streaked down out of the sky and spent a luxuriously long period of time for something that's supposed to be instantaneous scorching the grass at the dog's paws into a smoking, smoldering waste. This seemed sufficient to convince the blighter that Alice Rucastle was off limits. The monster looked about for new prey. Alice was closest. I was weakest. Yet, as the dog's eyes fell on Jephro Rucastle, its expression resolved into one of particular hatred. It took off towards him at a run.

Behind the charging hound, Alice Rucastle met her love. And her end.

"I am here, Ampere! I'm ready to glow with you! Please! Oh, please! Take me and together we can glo— Aaagh! Aigh! AAAAAAAAAAAAIIIIIGH!"

The night was lit by a cavalcade of flashes and strikes of lightning. When they subsided, there was naught left of Alice Rucastle but a sad little pile of ash. Or… I don't know… maybe a happy one.

"Hey!" said Holmes, from out on the lawn. His tone was hurt and angry. "I told you to turn and face me, demon! Don't pretend you didn't hear me."

I don't think any of us had, to be honest.

"The price is paid," said Ampere, with a crackling

voice as wide as the sky. Though he must have used a tremendous amount of energy in killing Alice, his glow had not diminished. Indeed, it had nearly redoubled and the human form at its center seemed better defined— more real.

"And now what?" asked Holmes. "Now you intend to wander the earth, incinerating whatever innocent person you happen across next? No! I won't have it! Come here, you little whelp!"

Ampere turned to Holmes with... well, what I can only assume was a look of annoyance. After all, that is by far and away the most common look one gives when turning to Holmes. As they closed on each other, bolt after bolt of searing white heat lashed from the demon towards my friend. But they didn't strike him. Holmes reached first one way and then the next, grabbing at empty air and pulling. As he did, reality tore and bent. Yes, the projectiles would have struck him if they could have continued straight, but now straight wasn't straight anymore. There were disturbing gaps in reality. The good news was that they seemed to spring closed again whenever Holmes let go of his fistful of empty air, but... well... it was mind-numbing to watch. The two combatants drew close.

Yet, neither Holmes nor Ampere was to be the next to fall. As I hobbled towards Violet and she ran towards me, the hound reached its target. It tore in with gleeful abandon. And *surprising* cruelty. A real dog—indeed any realistic predator—does its best to efficiently kill its prey. The important thing is victory—to find oneself as uninjured as possible and in possession of a meal. This beast did nothing of the kind. After throwing Jephro Rucastle to the ground, it started on his legs. Not only did it maul and scrape them with its teeth, but it seemed to take particular pleasure in twisting them in directions they ought not to bend, celebrating with happy barks and yowls whenever a bone would snap. The Copper's screeches reached a pinnacle of pain and desperation, echoing off into a sky charged with both electric and diabolic potential. By God, that haunting sound is a thing I shall remember always. As the beast toyed with him, Rucastle turned from screaming to pleading. "No! Please! Oh, by God, please! I know you've never liked me! But I am your family now! I am your master! Please!"

The beast, unmoved by his words, elected to end them. It stomped one massive forefoot down onto his chest, pinning him to the ground, then closed its jaws about Rucastle's horrible chin-wattle and pulled. The throat came away and Rucastle's head rolled back. The Copper's final, gobbling, gurgling screech drifted off into the swirling clouds.

The only bit of happy news to report was this: at last Violet and I reached each other. As we neared, I cried out, "Violet! Oh, thank God! Violet, are you all right?"

She gave me a queer look, as if this were a rather stupid question, and replied, "Better than average, it would seem. What happened to you?"

"Oh… I don't quite know. But my arm's broken and

there's a screwdriver in my leg."

"And… er… your hair?"

"I don't know about that, either. Apparently, I missed quite the adventure while I was projected into your body."

"*Apparently*," Violet agreed. "But look here, Watson, are you armed?"

"I think my Webley's in my left, inside coat pocket, but it's difficult to tell. Only my left arm works, so—"

I was interrupted by two sensations. Both were intrusive, but the first was not unpleasant. Violet threw open my coat and began rummaging about in my clothing. The second was significantly worse. It seems that, yes, my previous assessment of the situation had been correct. I *was* the weakest available target. Rucastle's hound hit me square in the chest, knocking me away from Violet and sending me sprawling. I felt two of my ribs snap with the shock. He was on me in an instant. His teeth tore into my already damaged leg and he flipped me face up, so I could see what he was doing to me. He let go of my leg, stepped on my hip to pin me and loomed over me with an evil smile. I had just an instant to spare before he snapped his jaws at my face. I got my good arm up to protect me, which it… sort of did. His fangs sunk into the flesh of my forearm. I could feel muscle and tendon tearing beneath his powerful grip. In desperation, I flung my broken right arm to my chest, grasping about to see if I still had the Webley. I did not.

Violet did.

I heard a loud report. The beast yowled in pain and

released my shredded arm. The giant dog turned to face its attacker.

Now, understand, the Webley-Pryse .455 was about the largest, most impressive, most expensive service revolver available. I'd bought mine—just as most of its other patrons had—to avoid the wretched Enfield the army would have provided. That said, my Webley was preposterous. An unnecessarily big, heavy thing, it fired a round better suited to knocking down rhinos than repeated precision target shooting. The grip was made for a larger hand than mine. Certainly larger than Violet's.

She didn't care.

She ran at my assailant with her arms outstretched, clutching the Webley in both hands. As she neared she pulled back the hammer and fired again. The bullet caught the gigantic dog in the side of the head and he reeled back. As soon as Violet recovered from the recoil, she pulled back the hammer and fired again. The bullet struck the beastly dog on its back, just near the spine. Her final shot struck him to the heart. With a complaining sort of wail, as if it meant to say, "Hey, it's not fair when people hurt *me*!" the beast collapsed, writhing on the ground a few feet from me. Much to my surprise, it began to issue thick curtains of swirling smoke. The body within began to shift and change.

From above me, a luminous, man-shaped being descended. Random tendrils of energy arched from him and traced scorching trails along the ground as he spluttered, "Hey! What have you two done to young Barghest?"

"*Holmes?*" I wondered.

"Of course, Watson."

"What's happened to you?"

"Hmmm? Oh, this... I had to drink that entire demon. Far too much power. Really, I can't imagine how so strong a thing made its way here. The barriers around our world must be in a right state. Oh, and you'd best keep your distance for a while. I seem to be rather electrical at the moment. Gads, it's all over me..."

Violet stepped forward, pale-faced and shaking. "Um... Mr. Holmes... Did you say 'Barghest'?"

"Yes, of course. Barghest." Holmes pointed one glowing finger at the dying creature by my side. A wayward bolt of electricity arched out and singed some of the fallen beast's hair off. Sure enough, within the swirling fog, the form of the monster continued to change: now like a huge hound, now disturbingly bipedal.

"Er..." I said. "Oh dear."

"What?" said Holmes. "You mean, you *didn't know*? I thought when Miss Hunter told us, 'He is a monster, not a child,' we were all on the same page. No?"

Violet and I looked at each other, aghast.

"What have I done?" she asked.

"Nothing about 28,000 field mice and rabbits won't thank you for," Holmes laughed. "Oh, come now... The boy's strange absences? The fact that the dog was only patrolling the grounds *some* nights? Rucastle's fear of his own supposed pet and how quickly he stepped in to make sure Violet did not try to get between young Barghest and

I had to drink that entire demon!

his monstrous instincts? For heaven's sake, his name was Barghest! Did you not know what a barghest was?"

Violet and I stared at each other, in helpless confusion.

"Well really, now," Holmes snorted. "I must say: when it comes to figures from myths and legends, the British school system leaves much to be desired. You ought to look it up sometime."

"So… what's going to happen, Holmes?" I asked.

"If those wounds are mortal—"

"Yes. I should certainly think."

"Well then, the beast's body will eventually come to rest in whichever of its two states is its most natural one."

Violet made a sour face and reasoned, "So, I am either going to have to explain why I have shot someone's dog…"

"…Or someone's *child*," I finished. "Yes, that might be a bit problematic."

"I should say so," Holmes agreed. "In fact, for a newly out-of-work governess with gunpowder residue all over her hands, I'd think it's pretty much top of the list. Allow me to suggest that perhaps we should not be discovered here."

I shook my head. "I'm not fit to travel. You two get out of here. Violet, leave the pistol. I'll tell them nothing."

"And you think that would stop them hanging you?" said Holmes. "No, no. Good thing for you two I've got rather an amazing amount of power to burn off, so…"

There was a crackling flash of light.

And then, there was 221B.

I was back in the comfort of home. Well… that's not to say I was particularly *comfortable*…

"Miss Hunter, why don't you see if you can get Watson up on the couch without grinding his wounds about too much," Holmes suggested. "I'm afraid I must go out. Still too much electricity, I fear. Oh well. Perhaps I'll take a stroll in the park and electrocute a few dozen benches, or something. Ta-ta."

And so the matter came to rest.

Of my many wounds, well, we shall come to that in a later tale. Suffice to say, I wasn't having very much fun with them.

As to what had truly happened at the Copper Beeches, I had no compelling explanation. Holmes seemed to feel he did.

"Ah, the sad tale of a lonely woman, Watson! The widow Rucastle, alone in that home with only her daughter—and her poor company, since she was rather crazy. Imagine Mrs. Rucastle's relief to discover a powerful demon in the woods behind her home. She struck a bargain, promising her only daughter in payment of the demon's services. Her prized turkey was transformed into a man—or something like it— to be the husband she knew she could never find on her own. The local barghest, magically bound to her, became the precious little boy she'd never had. What a happy little family it must have been, until the payment came due!"

"That is utterly preposterous, Holmes."

"Hmpf! I'd like to see you do better, Watson."

I couldn't.

Oh, and we seem to have ruined Hampshire a bit. Terribly sorry. Holmes was once again responsible for a minor but permanent magical change to our world. You can only encounter it within an eight- or nine-mile radius of the Copper Beeches, on stormy nights. As the electric potential gathers, the Copper's death-screeches become audible. The storm the night of our final confrontation seems to have preserved them, somehow. As the lightning gathers, Jephro Rucastle's terrible screams will echo out over the hills and forests until the threshold of tolerance is reached. Then, a flash of lightning and the rolling thunder ushers silence back to the land.

You know, until just before the *next* strike. On nights with multiple discharges, well... I'm informed the Copper's screeches have made Hampshire's springtime squalls near-intolerable.

I'd rather hoped the trauma of her first adventure might quench Violet's taste to pursue more. But no, her resolve held. Not to mention the fact that—since the Tollers and Mrs. Rucastle knew her name—it seemed judicious for Violet to pursue her next adventure as far away as possible. Holmes knew of a little problem in Egypt that needed looking into, so that is where she went.

She visited England some months later and reported her success to us. By then I was recovered enough to make her an odd little gift. Clearly, if she was going to lead a life of danger, that derringer had to go. I went to the local gunsmith and purchased her a Webley, like the one she'd used to save my life. That night, I removed the handles and shaved them down so a smaller hand might fit around and a shorter finger might reach the trigger. Then I cut the barrel so short, it was barely a quarter-inch past the revolving pin. By the time I was done, it was an ugly little bugger. I hadn't realized how much the shortness of the thing and the slim little handle must contrast with a revolving chamber fat enough to hold six .455 rounds. Not only that, but it lacked a forward sight; Violet's chance of hitting anything at a range of over fifteen feet was greatly diminished.

So I bought another one and gave it the same treatment. Now, if it were only half as likely she could hit something, at least she'd have twice as many tries.

I was rather sheepish when I showed them to Holmes. I thought he might make sport of me and I could hardly have blamed him if he had. But no, I woke the next morning to find he'd copper-plated the pair of them and somehow bleached the wooden handles a perfect white.

"I hope you don't mind, Watson," he said.

"Not at all, Holmes. They seem greatly improved."

"More than you know, I would deem. I have chosen copper because it has special significance to Violet. I have infused charms of protection into the plating. I stayed up half the night thinking which traits were most valuable to an adventuress—"

"Don't call her an adventuress, Holmes."

"But she's—"

"I know, but say 'adventurer', won't you?"

"As you like, Watson. Well, each of them is dedicated

260

to an important trait she will need and charmed to make sure that, to the best of my ability, they shall never abandon her."

Looking down at the gleaming pistols I saw the word "Wit" had been blazoned on the side of one of the barrels. The other one said "Fortune".

"Very good, Holmes. This is a fitting gift, indeed."

"You've certainly done your part, too," Holmes said, beaming at the compliment. "For now, if ever wit and fortune should fail her…"

"Ah, yes. She can then pull out *Wit* and *Fortune* and blaze away."

"Just so. We've done our best, Watson. The rest is up to Miss Hunter. Woe to whatever demon she sets her sights upon."

"I cut the sights off, I'm afraid."

"You know what I mean, John."

Violet Hunter went on to have many adventures, without Holmes and me. I recall that she was mentioned in connection with the demise of the False Skeleton Gang and the strange case of the Silken Sword of Zacsh-I-Khor. But really, I have heard so little of them that if they are ever put to paper it must be by some other hand than mine. I think of her often. In my sadder moments, I sometimes reflect on that "silly little thing" of a kiss and wonder if she ever remembers it, too. I was sure it couldn't have meant as much to her as it did to me, but… No, let me cease my remembrance of her before it becomes too self-piteous and give her the farewell she better deserves.

In my time with Holmes, I often relied on my innate cowardice to protect me. Holmes was no better. In fact, to that point in our adventures, I had encountered only three individuals who staunchly refused to let fear dictate even a single one of their actions.

One, of course, was Grogsson.

Two were named Violet.

THE ADVENTURE OF THE RED HEADS' LEAGUE

FROM THE CRAYON-SCRAWLED JOURNALS
OF MR. WARLOCK HOLMES

HULLO, EVERYONE! WATSON WANTED ME TO TELL YOU this story, because it's fairly important and he was knocked out for the best bits.

Anyway, I can't quite recall what year it was, or what season (but I'm sure it was one of the normal four). What I do remember is that Watson was quite dangerously enthralled with the Woman—which should come as no surprise as Watson was rather easily enthralled by just about every woman he ever met.

But this woman was *bad*. And there was this ever-increasing chance that Watson would be killed. And then where would I be?

Sad, that's where.

I was desperate to distract him, if I could only figure out how. For a time, it seemed as if Violet Hunter's peculiar adventure would be sufficient but, though it certainly provided a few chances to turn Watson's mind from the Woman, it evolved at such a slow pace as to allow him ample time to turn it back. Even though we were right in the middle of Violet's adventure, I knew I needed a second case.

You can imagine how happy I was when the bell rang and Mrs. Hudson announced Mr. Jabez Wilson, whom Watson now refers to as "that red-headed ninny". Mr. Wilson was big and slow, with dim little eyes that always seemed to be looking at nothing in particular and a pendulous lower lip that just hung there as if it were constantly ready to say, "I'm sorry, I don't understand." He had the most magnificent head of red hair and a story to match it. In fact, he hadn't got very far into his tale before I realized it was just what I needed and made him stop.

"I'm sorry, Mr. Wilson, but I would prefer to have my colleague Watson here for this discussion. Won't you be kind enough to have a seat over there and wait for him? He'll be along any moment, I am sure."

He frowned at me and said, "But... uhhhh... I've got to get back to m' shop."

"No you don't," I told him. "You need to sit quietly in the corner until Watson comes home, then you need to tell him exactly what you just told me."

"But... uhhhh..."

"Shut your fat gob and sit in that corner or I'll blow you up with magic!"

Which he was good enough to do.

Two or three hours later, Watson turned up.

"Watson! Watson! Watson! Watson! Look what I found! He's perfect! He's called Jabez Wilson and he's got a story for you. Go on, Mr. Wilson: tell Watson your story."

"You won't blow me up with magic?" he asked.

"Of course not! What an extraordinary thing to assume.

266

Now come on, tell Watson what you told me."

But Watson wouldn't let him. He insisted on doing that good-hosting thing he does, where he makes tea for our guest and lets them leave their corner and use the bathroom because they're starting to get all pouty, as if something terrible is going to happen if they don't. Then Watson did his deduction-demonstration thing where he asked me to observe our guest and tell him what I could discern of the man's history. Well, I'd been observing him for hours and purposely trying not to, but to humor Watson I fixed Mr. Wilson with my gaze and idly wondered about him. Instantly, my head was flooded with answers.

His hair is red! Don't trust him! Kill him! Kill him with fire! X'smex urged. But then again, when doesn't he?

The man is weak. Give him to us, said Covfefe (whom I had several times enjoined to refer to himself as "me" not "us" but some demons' egos know no boundaries, I fear).

Rak! Rak! I eat the dead! said Eirg. Helpful as ever, Eirg. Thank you.

But then I got a good one: *This man has wandered the world on a horse of wood. Swell-rider. Wave-strider. One time, a worker with his hands, until his body failed him. Now he works with wits, which failed the day he began. Bargainer in cast-offs. Collector of lost and stolen things. Purveyor of others' failure. This man, who has seen the farthest kingdoms of his kind, now ransoms trinkets from the hopeless.*

Who said it? Some remnant of Moriarty, still lodged within me? Or maybe it's just what I *thought* Moriarty would say if he were still there. Honestly, it's hard to tell sometimes.

Listening to the little buggers, I nearly failed to notice that Watson was doing his trick. See how the man had a coin with a square piercing on his watchband and a pink-scaled fish tattooed on his arm? That meant he'd been to China. His large right hand indicated he had been a manual laborer, but the softness of his callouses indicated he no longer was. And—yes—Mr. Wilson confirmed he had been a ship's carpenter. He must also be a freemason, Watson said, as—against that organization's wishes—he wore their compass insignia on his tie. He did a good deal of writing, because of his sleeves... Blah, blah, blah.

"And he is a pawnbroker," I added.

Mr. Wilson recoiled in surprise and confirmed that I was correct. Watson turned to me with an impressed expression and said, "Very good! However did you deduce it, Warlock?"

"Oh, I've no idea really. It doesn't matter. Tell him your story, Jabez! Tell him your story!"

"Oh... uhhh... very well..." our stupid guest replied. Stupidly. Because he was stupid. "It is just as Mr. Holmes says. I have a little pawnshop down on Saxe-Coburg Square. It does well enough to keep a roof over my head, but little better. I'm a widower, with no family to support. Nobody but my assistant Mr. Spaulding. Good thing Spaulding comes at half-wages, for I'm scarcely able to afford that much."

Here Watson interrupted—a horrible habit of his, for

I felt it was a really interesting story. Nevertheless, Watson archly arched an eyebrow and said, "Your assistant works for half-wages? In this market? Your story is remarkable already, Mr. Wilson. Tell me, how long have you had Mr. Spaulding and how did he come?"

"Oh… nearly three months now. He came in response to an advertisement I placed. Had six or seven fellows show up for the job, but Vincent… uhhhh… that's his name, Vincent Spaulding… he said he'd do the job for half-wages so I picked him."

"Has the man some infirmity?" Watson pressed. "Some deficiency that enables him to claim only a half-share for his labors?"

"No, he's wonderful." Wilson shrugged, very stupidly. "Clever as they come. So clever I sometimes don't know *what* he's talking about. Hard worker. No trouble with women or the bottle. Of course, he spends too much time on photography. Always snapping away. Had to give him my cellar for a darkroom. But then, he's a good lad. Well… lad… he's at least thirty, I should think. Funny-looking short little chap. White splash of acid on the forehead. Well one day, about two months ago, he comes running downstairs with the paper in his hands, crying, 'Oh to be a red-haired man! I wish to God I was a red-haired man, Mr. Wilson.'

"'But why?' said I. I know a thing like red hair is more apt to make one the subject of fun than to work any great benefit. I don't know if you gentlemen noticed, but I've got red hair myself!"

269

"Yes," said Watson. "We'd noticed."

"But Vincent was in earnest. 'Look here,' he says, waving this paper at me, 'there's another vacancy in the League of Red-Headed Men! Oh, that's easy money, sir. If only my hair were red!'

"Well I was rather interested, as you can well imagine. So I asked Vincent to tell me what this strange league was. It seems there was this Londoner—Mr. Ezekiah Hopkins—who moved to America and became a billionaire—"

"A *billionaire*? Billion with a 'b'?" Watson interrupted, interruptfully. "There's no such thing."

"Ezekiah Hopkins was one," Mr. Wilson protested, "and when he died, he laid aside his fortune for the preservation and furtherment of red-headed men. Very sensible of him, I thought. Turns out this League of Red-Headed Men is some sort of money-distribution club. You've got to be a grown man, an Englishman, and have really the reddest shade of hair. Not orange, not chestnut, not ginger, but real, vivid red! Which, I do! Well, I pointed that out to Spaulding and he jumped up and said, 'By Jove! That's right! I hadn't thought of it, but you *do*! But then… maybe it's not worth it for you to put yourself out of your way, sir. It's only a couple of hundred a year.'

"Well, the shop's near enough in its death throes that a couple of hundred a year would be most welcome. So I asked Vincent to show me the article and he laid down this."

Mr. Wilson reached into his hat, pulled forth a wrinkled newspaper clipping and laid it on the table before us. It read:

Be it known that the late Mr. Ezekiah Hopkins announces
one vacancy on the League of Red-Headed Men. Wage:
£4 a week. Duties: nominal. Only the most red-headed,
full-grown Englishmen need present themselves. Reply
11 a.m., today. 7 Pope's Court, Fleet Street.

Watson read the article once. Then he read it again.
Then his lip began to quiver. In no time at all, he was
hunched forward with his hands on his knees, laughing
with all his might. I started too. We laughed. We laughed
and laughed. Mr. Wilson harrumphed at us, but we
laughed and laughed and laughed.

"Really," Watson said. "This is too much!"

"I know!" I agreed. "Pope's *Court*? Why, a thing ought
to be either religious or judicial, not both! What an obvious
conflict of interest! Right? Ha, ha, ha!"

"What? No, Holmes. The *situation*. Think of it: a
mysterious worker shows up, agrees to work for half-wages
and then only a few weeks later, he just *happens* to mention
this ridiculous opportunity. It has every indication of a
confidence trick. If you've any doubt of it, Holmes, consider:
Vincent Spaulding has a photography habit. Film is made
with silver halides. Silver isn't cheap, Holmes. It's hardly
the sort of thing a half-waged pawnbroker's assistant can
go snap, snap, snapping away with. No, I will promise you
there is more to Mr. Spaulding than first meets the eye."

"Oh? Well, perhaps there is," I conceded. "But Pope's
Court is still funny."

"I am not convinced that any of this is humorous!"

Mr. Wilson blurged. ("Blurged" is a word I just made up. It means "screamed out in a high-pitched, unmanly sort of indignation that left little doubt that the speaker was stupid".) "My new livelihood hangs in the balance and if you gentlemen can find nothing better to do than laugh at me, I will bid you good day!"

Watson's eyes twinkled with eagerness. "Am I to understand that you answered this advertisement, Mr. Wilson?"

"Well, I wasn't the only one. By God, you should have seen Pope's Court! So many red-heads standing about that when the wind blew, it looked like Fleet Street was on fire! There were not a few red-headed gentlemen who had showed up in the misguided hope that maybe Scotland was English enough to qualify. Oh, and one or two freckle-faced red-head '*lads*' who had borrowed work-shirts and bracers and rather hoped that nobody would notice an extra curve or two beneath. But Spaulding got me through. He shoved. He kicked. He cajoled. He got me to the front of that line, marched me into Number 7 and announced, 'This is Mr. Jabez Wilson and he has agreed to fill your vacancy.'

"Behind a desk was a man with hair very nearly as red as mine. As soon as he saw me, he rose to his feet, shoved aside the rather cinnamon-headed fellow he'd been talking to and said, 'It is a pleasure to know you, Mr. Wilson. I am Duncan Ross and you must forgive me an obvious precaution.'

"With that, he sprang upon me, laid both hands to my hair and pulled with all his might. Well, I cried out at the treatment, and… if I am honest… there may have been a few tears in my eyes. Of indignation, I am sure."

"Of course. Indignation," I agreed. I like to help people think well of themselves.

"At last he was satisfied. He came away, shook my hand and said, 'You will pardon me, I'm sure. We have twice been deceived by wigs and once by paint. I could tell you tales of cobbler's wax which would disgust you with human nature. By the Lord above, though, what a head you've got! Magnificent! *Magnificent!* I'm sorry, everybody, but the vacancy is filled!' He ran to the window and shouted as much to all the hopefuls below. The entire street gave a moan of disappointment and the orange flood receded.

"'Well, here now,' I protested, 'I don't know the work yet, do I? I don't know the hours or the conditions or what you folks call nominal duties. What's it all about?'

"But Mr. Ross waved my concerns aside and said, 'Ha! When you hear how easy it truly is, I think there shall be no difficulty. Why, there's never been a red-head yet that left us! You must present yourself at ten a.m. every day. Here you shall stay until two in the afternoon. As for the nominal duties: you shall copy out the *Encyclopedia Britannica*. At the end of each week, I shall present you with four pounds. Now, the only difficult part, Mr. Wilson, is the rigidity of the hours. You must not, under any circumstance, leave this office during your regular hours. To do so is to forsake the founder—the late, lamented Ezekiah Hopkins—and to forfeit your position here, forever! There! How's that?'

"I needn't tell you gentlemen, it suited me quite well.

The… uhhhh… the money was welcome. The duty suited me—I've always been proud of my penmanship—and since a pawnbroker's trade is mostly of an evening, I lost little by spending my time so. Spaulding has been good enough to look after the shop in the hours of my absence and he does just a fine job… uhhhh… I assume."

Here Watson asked, "Are we to believe, Mr. Wilson, that you have been spending four hours a day for the last eight weeks, copying the *Encyclopedia Britannica*?"

"It's not a very good encyclopedia," Mr. Wilson replied.

I could see Watson getting all I'm-upset-because-I-am-British-and-it-is-British-and-everything-British-is-the-best, but he contained himself and commented only, "And Mr. Duncan Ross has been paying you for this service? Four pounds per week?"

"Regular as you like," Mr. Wilson said. "That first day he got me settled in the office with the letter 'A' volume. I had a little desk, in a little room, with a picture of Ezekiah Hopkins on the wall and a window that lets in enough light for me to copy by. Mr. Ross came in a few times that first day, to see how I was getting on and remind me I must not leave. But as the days went on, he came less and less. Now he only comes by on Saturdays to give me my four pounds. But I still don't dare leave, you know. Uhhhh… No, no, no, I wouldn't do a thing to endanger my position in the league. But now—oh, now—I fear it is gone! I went in this morning to fulfill my duty, and what should I find? The door was locked. And see what was tacked upon it?"

Mr. Wilson reached into his hat a second time and came up with a sheet of plain paper with the handwritten message:

THE LEAGUE OF RED-HEADED MEN IS HEREBY SUSPENDED, BY ORDER OF THE LATE, LAMENTED EZEKIAH HOPKINS.

MR. WILSON MAY REPORT TO HIS OWN CELLAR THIS SATURDAY NIGHT AT 8 P.M. TO RECEIVE THE FINAL PAYMENT FOR ALL HIS VALUED LABORS.

DO NOT ENTER THE CELLAR BEFORE 8 P.M.!

"What do you gentlemen make of it? Whatever shall I do?" Jabez Wilson wondered, stupidly.

"Isn't it wonderful, Watson? Isn't it distracting?" I urged.

Watson raised his eyebrows at both of us and said, "One thing you must clearly *not* do, Mr. Wilson, is accept this rather suspicious invitation to your own cellar!"

"But… but… uhhhh… I don't want to lose my connection with the league! They can't leave me like this! They've no right! That's two hundred a year I'll lose!"

"I think you stand to lose a great deal more than that, Mr. Wilson," Watson scolded. "I can see no great injury that's been done to you, thus far. Indeed, if all ties were severed between yourself and the League of Red-Headed Men, you are thirty-two pounds to the good, have had ample opportunity to polish that penmanship you're so proud of, and have gained a literally *encyclopedic* knowledge of several subjects beginning with the letter 'A'. Now again, I repeat: do not report to your cellar this Saturday at eight o'clock! I can think of no other motivation behind the strange actions of this League of Red-Headed Men save that of ensuring your shop is unguarded between the hours of ten and two. What have they been up to? What project have they been at that has required such an extraordinarily long time? And at such expense! You may trust to it, Mr. Wilson: this league is up to some mischief!"

"But... uhhh... *what* exactly?"

Watson sighed heavily, gave me a little squished-brow look that meant he knew he'd just been outmaneuvered and muttered, "Don't worry. Holmes and I shall investigate."

"Good idea, Watson! Where shall we go? The league's office? Jabez's cellar? Should we go now? Let's go now!"

"I'm afraid I have another engagement this afternoon," Watson said.

"But... Watsoooooooooon! We should go now!"

"Why don't you go, Holmes? Have Mr. Wilson take you around to the league's office and see if you can learn anything there, eh?"

"But... uhhhh... it's locked up," Mr. Wilson reminded us.

"I assume there is a landlord, is there not? Do you suppose he might have a key? Do you suppose he might have seen you once or twice in your hundred-or-so trips up and down his stairs, Mr. Wilson? Perhaps he might be persuaded that you have left your pen up there and need to collect it. That's a good enough course for this afternoon's adventure, isn't it?"

I will now pause to admit—and it hurts my feelings, dear reader, to write it—that Watson did not hold my investigative acumen in very high regard. As I set out with Mr. Jabez Wilson that afternoon, I had the distinct feeling that the only reason Watson had trusted me to go without him was that he was already certain we would find nothing of interest.

Which proved to be the case.

Once the landlord had admitted us to the office, I found nothing out of the ordinary except an illustrated calendar hanging on one wall. It featured a picture of a lady in her bloomers, chasing a little dog up the street. He had a hairbrush in his mouth. I assumed it belonged to the bloomer-lady, but couldn't be certain.

Also, there was this portrait of Ezekiah Hopkins on the wall behind the desk. He had a top hat, a bush of red hair sticking out from under it, a monocle and a severe expression as if he were watching the man who sat at that desk with a judgmental eye. Speaking of eyes, both of the portrait's eyes were burning embers that perpetually oozed an oily purple smoke up towards the ceiling. Jabez said it had always done that. On his first day, Mr. Ross had assured him it was some sort of trick, done with cigarettes.

Which was very clever, I thought.

Oh, and I saw the encyclopedia Mr. Wilson had been made to copy. And do you know something? Every entry was the same!

A.   I the red-headed man pledge to the red-headed master: we shall be parted no longer. Apart, we are lonely. Together, we are whole. We *shall* be whole. Together. Always. Always together. This I scribe. This I pledge.

AACHEN.   I the red-headed man pledge to the red-headed master: we shall be parted no longer. Apart, we are lonely. Together, we are whole. We *shall* be whole. Together. Always. Always together. This I scribe. This I pledge.

AARDVARK.   I the red-headed man pledge to the red-headed master: we shall be parted no longer. Apart, we are lonely. Together, we are whole. We *shall* be whole. Together. Always. Always together. This I scribe. This I pledge.

"Hmm…" I said, leafing through the first several pages. "You are quite correct, Mr. Wilson: I find the *Encyclopedia Britannica* to be remarkably substandard."

"And it's got *such* a reputation!" he cried.

"I know! I've never heard a word against it. And yet, now I get down into the nitty-gritty of the thing I find myself rather unimpressed. Let me just turn to a random page… 'Abbot: I the red-headed…' Yes. There you are, you see? *Indistinguishable* from 'Aardvark'. Any book of learning that cannot tell an abbot from an aardvark is unworthy to shape the minds of generations yet to come!"

"I weep for the future, Mr. Holmes."

"Heh. Try convincing Watson of it, though. I bet if we showed him this, he'd talk himself blue defending it. 'Britain is the best! Empire, empire! Blah, blah, blah!' I think I'll save myself the trouble, to be honest."

"So there is nothing here that might... uhhhh... help you to discover the... uhhhh..."

"No. Nothing, I'm afraid. I suppose we ought to speak to the landlord about what became of Mr. Duncan Ross."

Yet even that yielded nothing. The landlord knew nobody by that name. When we asked him who had rented the office, he said it was a very red-headed gent named John Su-do Nimh—which he supposed must be an oriental name of some sort—but the fellow had settled up accounts yesterday.

In the end, there was nothing for it but to bid Mr. Wilson good day and wander home to Baker Street. When I got there, Watson was sitting in his favorite chair, wearing his I've-just-done-something-rather-clever expression. He asked me if my investigation had borne any fruit. I told him all that had transpired. Well... I might not have mentioned the portrait, because it was only a portrait. Oh, and I may have omitted the encyclopedia, because I did not wish to argue. But, I *know* I told him about the bloomer-lady calendar because it was a seemingly innocuous detail. And Watson always says the outcome of such cases often hangs from a seemingly innocuous detail.

"Other than that," I confessed, "I'm afraid I have accomplished nothing."

"On the contrary, your labors were indispensable," Watson beamed. "I must apologize to you, Holmes: I am guilty of a falsehood. I never did have a second engagement. I only wished for you to go somewhere with Mr. Wilson, other than Mr. Wilson's pawnshop, down on Saxe-Coburg Square."

"Why?"

"Because I wanted to knock on that door myself, sure that Mr. Wilson would not answer."

"Er… again, why?"

"Reason it out, Holmes! Who else might answer in his stead?"

"The assistant, Vincent Spaulding?"

"And so he did! The knees of his trousers were dirty and worn! Why, if I were a betting man, I'd say they'd received some rather rough treatment these last eight weeks."

"So?"

"By God, Holmes, do you still not see it? Here, I'll give you another clue: I took that particularly heavy walking stick of yours along with me—"

"Watson! You didn't hold it to the sun at its zenith and cry, 'Mergh-Rhagh-Hazzan,' did you?"

"Er… no…"

"Well then, everything's probably all right. What happened next?"

"Upon meeting Mr. Spaulding and his trouser knees I concocted some excuse for my intrusion. I asked him the way to the Strand; he pointed down the street and said, 'Third right, fourth left.' He was very quick about it, hardly pausing to recall the information. I think Mr. Wilson's inadvertent admission that the assistant is smarter than the master was correct. But now for that clue I promised you: as I took my leave, I paused on the street in feigned indecision and struck the ground a few times very roughly with your heavy stick. Can you guess why?"

"To dent the stick! No! To dent the street? No! Er… to build your shoulder muscles?"

"To determine, Warlock, whether Mr. Wilson's cellar stretches out in front of his shop or behind. The street was quite solid; the cellar does not stretch to the front. Can you guess what I did next?"

"Ran round to another doctor, confessed that you have become fascinated with underground architecture and inquired if there was, perhaps, some pill that could rid you of this unwanted compulsion?"

"*No*. I walked around to see what might lie behind Mr. Wilson's humble little shop. And do you know what I found, right there between a tobacconist and a vegetarian restaurant? A branch of the City and Suburban Bank! Now, Holmes, you have all the clues. See if you can thread them all together and tell me what they mean."

I took a moment to collect my thoughts, to clear my mind as best I could and let the answer come to me.

The red-heads unite against us! Kill them all! X'smex howled.

Probably a red-headed soul-sucker, if I had to venture a guess, said either my own internal thoughts, or UUrduk, the Murder-God of the Six Ashen Wastes. Honestly, the two of them sound so alike and are so often in agreement, it can be quite the chore to tell which is which. I've rather stopped trying.

Then Covfefe said, *You're too stupid to solve it. Stupid is a good word. I have the best words. I'm gonna take human form and solve it for you, okay? No problem. I'm great.*

I wanted to tell Covfefe that he'll never pass himself off as human—he's bright orange with white circles around his eyes—but Watson was staring at me, expecting an answer. So I said, "Probably a red-headed soul-sucker, if I had to venture a guess."

"No. *What?* Holmes, why would you think that?"

"I've no idea, really."

"Have you ever heard of such a thing? A red-headed soul-sucker?"

"Er… no."

"Then why would you assume such a thing exists?"

"Again, I've no idea."

"Do you imagine that this would be a red-headed beast that sucks souls, or a regular-looking one that sucks the souls of only red-headed victims?"

"I suppose… well… hmmm… no idea."

"And why would you blame it with our present—"

"Honestly, Watson, I sometimes think your primary goal in any conversation is to force me to say 'no idea' as often as you can. It is twisted and unkind!"

Watson threw one hand up against his brow, as if he were the victim of a sudden headache. "Holmes… focus now, and think. What does it mean that the bank is so close to the pawnshop?"

"Well, let's see... er... When Jabez Wilson needs to make a deposit, he doesn't have far to go?"

"I think the point would be better stated that Mr. Spaulding won't have far to go to make a rather significant *withdrawal*. Don't you see? He's tunneling into the bank! There is no such thing as the League of Red-Headed Men! There never was! Mr. Spaulding shows up out of the blue at a humble little place of work whose cellar is in suspicious proximity to a bank's vault, agrees to work for half-wages, and immediately displays an interest in his employer's cellar. Remember? He got Mr. Wilson to let him have it for a darkroom. Well, he's now situated in a safe, unobserved spot, only twenty yards from his target. But he's still got a problem: he can't very well dig up Mr. Wilson's cellar with the old fellow around. No problem. Spaulding is far smarter than his employer. It's not long until he realizes Mr. Wilson is rather conscious of his red hair and also somewhat proud of his penmanship. Spaulding gets a red-headed confederate and formulates a plan which is as ingenious as it is farcical. Suddenly, Mr. Wilson is informed of the bequest of a previously unheard-of billionaire whose legacy will furnish him with two hundred a year and allow him to feel good about both his unusual coloration and his penmanship. *Voila!* Now Spaulding and his confederate have four hours per day to dig, uninterrupted—hence the state of his trousers."

"But if the league was such a brilliant invention,

Watson, why would Spaulding close it?"

"Because his tunnel is finished. This also explains the darkest development of this whole story: the invitation to Mr. Wilson to go to his own cellar this Saturday night."

"Why is that dark, Watson? May not a man visit his own cellar if he wishes?"

"Not if he's very wise. Remember, Holmes, it's now connected by tunnel to a bank vault. A fact that—in an investigation following the robbery of said bank—is likely to be of interest to any number of Scotland Yard's finest. I'm sure they might have more than a few pointed questions for Mr. Wilson, but it probably wouldn't take him long to spill the whole strange story of the League of Red-Headed Men and fix the Yard's attention exactly where it has fixed mine: on Vincent Spaulding. Better for Spaulding to silence his employer's tongue."

"They're going to murder him?"

"So the facts suggest. Think, Holmes, if you've got a tunnel in place, when is the best time to stage a robbery? The bank closes early of a Saturday. All Spaulding has to do is wait until the pawnshop closes at five or six, rob the bank, murder Wilson in the privacy of his own cellar, and make his getaway knowing neither crime is likely to be discovered until the bank opens on Monday morning."

"Fiendish! Brilliant!" I declared. "But... er... we're *sure* it isn't simply a red-headed soul-sucker?"

"No! Why would you think so?"

"Oh, I don't know. But I seem to be rather convinced, all of a sudden. It all just seems so... so very normal, the way you describe it. So very dull. Is there no aspect of this case that seems peculiar? Nothing to keep it a case for us, rather than for the Yard? I was so certain when I met Mr. Wilson."

Watson got rather uncomfortable-looking and admitted, "There was one small thing. Do you remember when Mr. Wilson told us Mr. Spaulding had a white splash of acid on his brow?"

"No."

"Well, he did. It's a common enough term for a dermatological condition, known as vitiligo—a localized loss of skin pigmentation. But the discolored spot on Mr. Spaulding's head gives every indication that it might be actual acid. I could smell it when I met him. I could see where it had dripped down and scalded little holes in his jacket."

I think I got very excited. "Watson! I know him! Did he have a great row of earrings in each ear?"

"Really, Holmes? *Earrings* are the identifying characteristic you require? Not a face partially constructed of a self-renewing well of acid?"

"Stomachs make acid, don't they? Maybe he just keeps a part of his stomach on his face. Anybody might. But earrings, Watson: did he have them?"

"Yes," Watson sighed.

"John Clay! I promise you, Watson. That man is John Clay."

"Who is he, Holmes? How do you know him?"

"He's a thief! Often employed by Moriarty's band. Oh, he's a smart one! Be wary of him, Watson."

"Moriarty? Capital! I've been most interested to interview members of Moriarty's old gang. Has this John Clay any magical abilities, Holmes?"

"He never needed them. Really, Watson, the man is *that* clever. Moriarty used to send him out after this magic bit or that one, and John Clay would disappear, sometimes for months on end, then it would come out he'd been living as an archbishop in Rome and had just conned the Swiss Guard out of the very item Moriarty had named, straight from the Vatican vault."

"Well," said Watson, cagily, "I'm afraid he's about to meet his match!"

"And probably a red-headed soul-sucker."

"No. Why do you persist in thinking so?"

"Who knows? Something to do with my brain, I suspect."

"Get your coat, Holmes."

"Where are we going?"

"The bank, Warlock! The bank!"

The bank manager's name was Mr. Merryweather. He wasn't all that merry, I thought. But he did remind one of weather. London's weather, specifically. Cold, foggy, grim and unwelcome. I had a very comfortable chair to sit on while Watson detailed the dastardly plan he was sure he'd unveiled. There was only one problem.

"Preposterous, sir," Mr. Merryweather thundered. "That vault is not in use."

"But…" Watson spluttered, splutterfully, "whoever heard of a bank with no vault? Or even worse: a bank *with* a vault that didn't use it?"

"This is merely a neighborhood branch of a larger bank," Merryweather blustered. "The small safe on the main floor more than suffices to hold the modest reserves we require. On the rare occasion we find ourselves in possession of sufficient funds to represent a sizable loss, they are conducted under guard to our head office that very night!"

"The vault is empty, then?" Watson wondered.

"Nobody knows what's down there. Nobody goes there since—" Mr. Merryweather made one of those faces people make when they've just said something they oughtn't.

"Since?" Watson prompted.

"I regret I cannot say. The instructions of this bank's founder are quite clear and it is as much as my job is worth to speak this institution's secrets. I thank you gentlemen for your efforts. You have come because you deemed that we were in danger and you have done your civic duty by informing us. Nevertheless, I can assure you there is no threat. Good day, sirs."

On the way out, I saw a picture of the founder. I knew him! It was Ezekiah Hopkins! Same fellow as in the other picture, but this one didn't have smoking eyes, so it was boring and I didn't mention it. Besides, I had other things to think of. Watson was fuming. As we stepped out, I asked him, "Do you need to get into that vault, Watson?"

"It would certainly be felicitous," he growled. "I had hoped to await the criminals in the darkness of that vault on Saturday afternoon. With Grogsson or Lestrade by the pawnshop to ensure our men did not back up through the tunnel and escape, we could have them trapped. It would be the perfect pinch!"

"See here, Watson, never let it be said that I consider myself above a little vault-breaking. Not when there's a friend in need! And a red-headed ninny, too! What do you think? Should we waylay Mr. Merryweather and make off with his keys?"

"No!"

"A bit of magic, then? I could melt the front wall right off the whole bank! Then we could walk in, clear as—"

"We will certainly *not* be employing any magic, Holmes."

"Well… an elephant, perhaps? He could pull the front wall off, I should think."

"Holmes, there is no need for such extraordinary measures. Although, you have given me an idea. Perhaps we might enlist the aid of a certain animal…"

"Do you need me to start looking up elephant dealers, Watson?"

"I had something quite a bit smaller in mind."

At three o'clock on Saturday afternoon, a grubby little urchin rushed through the front door of Jabez Wilson's pawnshop, grabbed a display box of pocket watches and shouted, "Yah! Yah! Bugger the toffs! Smash the state! Oh, and by the way: the Queen looks like a horse's arse!" This is exactly the primary fear of all pawnshop owners. They understand, with perfect clarity, that the underclasses are planning to betray and topple the entire British social order, sinking us into an age of darkness and anarchy which begins exactly the way everybody with a lick of sense knows it will: with petty theft from pawnshops.

The thief turned to rush out the door, but found it already blocked by Vincent Spaulding/John Clay. He had his arms folded across his chest and a little sneer that said, "Nobody around here knows it, but I'm a bit of a criminal mastermind myself and I've just got to ask: *that* was your whole plan?"

The horrified waif turned and bounded into the shop, nearly into the arms of the portly idiot who ran the place. Wilson gave a leisurely sort of lunge, but this was easily avoided and the lad made it to the shop's back room— notable for its possession of the shop's back door.

"He'll make the alley!" Wilson shouted. "Get around, Vincent! Get around and he'll have nowhere to go!"

Wilson lurched out the back door, leaving his assistant to bolt through the front and out around the side of the building, to cut off the suspect's escape. No sooner had John Clay made it around the corner to the alley than the urchin's confederates made their move. Watson and I hustled across the street and down into the shop's cellar. We had only a few minutes. We expected it should take no time at all for Wilson to find his discarded box of watches but—though he had come out on the thief's heels and Spaulding had blocked the only route of escape—we knew he would find the alleyway deserted. It would take more than a confused head-scratcher like Jabez Wilson to look down at the innocuous little rodent nibbling garbage on one side of the alley way and say, "Ah! That's probably my thief, right there."

Good old Wiggles! Even Watson was growing fond of him, I'm sure of it.

Of course, we were still left with the problem of the tunnel. If we could not find it, or if Watson was wrong and there was none, we should soon be explaining to Wilson and Clay why we had elected to raid their cellar. Look as I might, I could see no trace of the damn thing.

"Watson, where is it?"

He smiled at me and said, "You see those tubs of chemicals over there? The developing agent and the fixer?"

"Yes."

"A darkroom needs those. You see those wires strung up with the pins on them, to suspend the prints as they dry?"

"I see them."

"A darkroom needs those as well. What it does not *need*, strictly speaking, is an oversized framed poster of Trevelyan's Aerial Ballet that covers one entire side of the room and which seems to be… oh yes… look over here… this side is hinged to the wall. Come on, Holmes."

Watson swung back the poster, and so we made our way through John Clay's tunnel into the vault of the City

& Suburban Bank. We popped up through a loosened flagstone and—by the light of Watson's bull's-eye lantern—discovered a dark and dusty room. One wall was composed of aged iron bars, beyond which lay a narrow corridor and stairs up towards the main floor of the bank. There were a few large wooden crates scattered about, dusty and forgotten. Watson threw his bag down on one of these and whispered, "Come on, Holmes, let's get set up, eh?"

What a thorough fellow Watson is! He had everything. The lantern to see by, his pistol to waylay John Clay, handcuffs to secure him and his red-headed cohort. He'd brought break-in tools in case we should need them—even though we didn't—and to pass the time until John Clay's appearance, sandwiches and cards. I was just about to protest that that was all well and good for Watson, when he produced a little pot of soup and a couple of cold slices of toast. And yes, I understand that there may be some debate about whether cold toast is toast at all or if it's just bread that's been cooked two different ways. But I can tell you this: when your good friend takes the trouble to smuggle some into a crime scene for you, it is toast.

We settled in to wait. Watson said we needn't quench the lantern until at least five o'clock when the pawnshop closed. So we played cards. I was having a grand old time, but as the minutes slipped by, Watson became ever more distracted and nervous.

"Holmes, something is wrong. I think… I think *I* was wrong."

"You aren't usually. That's rather my job, Watson."

"Thank you for saying so, but... no... look at all the dust. Merryweather wasn't lying; this vault is clearly not in use."

"So?"

"John Clay's tunnel is complete. Now, if he were tunneling into a regular bank vault, he'd need to make his move on Saturday night, so he had a day and a half to escape before his crime was noticed. Yet, if the vault is disused, why would he wait? He might have already taken what he wanted. He might even have done it while the bank was *open* and nobody would be any the wiser, perhaps for years. And what does one even steal from a disused vault? Can there be anything here of sufficient value to justify such effort, time and expense on Clay's part?"

"Well, there are plenty of boxes lying about. Shall we see what's in them?"

"Good idea, Holmes. Hand me that crowbar. Quiet as you can, now. We don't want them to hear us down the tunnel..."

Do you know how decades-old wooden crates don't open? Quietly. Nevertheless, in a few moments, Watson and I had the top off the box that stood closest to the center of the room. A sheet of dull metal lay inside.

"Lead," I observed.

Watson pulled back a corner of it and said, "Lead *foil*. And look beneath it, Holmes."

As my friend peeled back the dull gray sheeting, the gleam of treasure struck my eye.

"What?" I cried. "*Gold?* Why would anybody do that?

Has somebody said to themselves, 'Well, gold is nice, but it just isn't heavy enough. Ah! I know! I'll pack it in lead!'"

"Lead is soft, Holmes. Coins can be packed in it to prevent them rubbing against each other and wearing. Look, these coins are new-minted. By God, there must be two thousand coins in this crate. French, by the look of them. Made in 1851. Judging by the date and the dust, it would seem someone has left a fresh-minted fortune abandoned down here for thirty years. Why? And why on earth has John Clay tunneled in here and neglected to steal it? The case grows in strangeness, Holmes, and I fear I have passed my depth. Something is wrong."

And as Watson paced back and forth, audibly debating whether this was a clever lure for me, or whether John Clay had no interest in money but a desire to embarrass the bank, or whether he had intended some kind of mischief that could only be carried out in a vault that was not currently in use, I began to realize he was right.

Something *was* wrong.

As Watson passed one of the crates at the edge of the room, it gave an eager little *bump*.

Bump. Bump, answered one of its confederates, from across the room.

"Er… Watson," I noted, "something is wrong."

He paused his current conspiracy supposition long enough to huff, "Yes, Holmes. That is what I've been trying to tell you for the last five minutes."

"No, Watson. Something is *wrong*. Very wrong. Right-now wrong. Look out!"

With a sudden shriek, the crate behind Watson wrenched its own top off and emitted a twisting coil of hair.

Rather reddish hair, it must be said.

This crimson flood surged towards Watson and wrapped itself around his arms and neck. As the crate fell apart, it revealed a trio of grinning skulls. Some veneer of mummified flesh still clung to them, but for the most part, bones and hair were all that remained. Quite an astonishing amount of hair for only three fellows, I thought. It flowed from the domes of each skull like the tentacles of a squid, allowing the little blighters to scrabble this way and that like oversized spiders.

"Disgusting!" I cried. (By which I meant that they were wonderful.)

Even as I said it, the other crates began to crack and fail. From each of them erupted another duo, or trio, or... er... quado of red-headed heads. They burst forth from every corner of the room, grinning with a silent sort of undead glee. Cute little buggers! They looked quite pleased with themselves, as if they had fooled us completely, which—to give credit where it is due—they had. They swarmed at me, sending tendrils of red curls to bind my arms and legs.

And I let them.

Why not?

They only seemed to want to tie me up, so where was the harm? I knew I could free myself with a word— indeed, with a *thought*—the very moment I needed to. And it would be such a shame to disappoint them. I know they were only empty-eyed skulls, but really, there was such a sense of accomplishment in their demeanor... and they were so darling, in their way... I made up my mind not to harm the little fellows or dampen their fun unless I absolutely must.

Watson, I regret to say, was devoid of such considerations. He screamed and thrashed about in a most unseemly way as the little monsters herded us together into the center of the room. He even grabbed a screwdriver from his bag as he passed and flailed about pointlessly at his attackers with it. He's a dear friend of mine, so it pains me to say so, but he can at times be utterly graceless.

"Calm yourself, Watson," I said, as they bumped me up against him. But then, from deep down within me, came a terrible feeling. Just terrible. A wrenching sort of fear that I'd let somebody down, or was about to. Amongst the voices in my head, one grew louder, more distinct.

"You said you would come to me, Mr. Holmes, in my hour of need. You promised you would honor our bargain. I fear the hour is nearing. I need you!"

Violet!

"Agh! Wait! No! *Un*calm yourself, Watson! We've got to do something!"

"That's what I've been screaming!"

"No, no! For Violet! We have to help her!"

"What? Holmes... *What?*"

"She needs us, Watson. And we promised."

Hmm... How shall I describe the progress of my thoughts, as they occurred to me and drove me to the action

I chose? I knew Violet needed us; that much was clear. Yet I knew not the exact source of her troubles—and who was better at figuring out the underlying nature of mysteries, Watson or myself? Watson, of course. I also didn't feel I could leave at the present moment. I might have projected my physical form to Violet's side, easily, but would it have been the act of a true friend to leave Watson alone in this vault? Oh dear me, no. So should I take him with me? But then what would happen with all these interesting skulls and the red-headed ninny who had asked for our help? It didn't seem right to run out on them at a moment like this, did it? Besides, I knew if I did I'd be of little use to Violet—distracted by the thought of the charming skull-pocalypse I'd left behind. Was there no way to solve all these problems? Why, if I could send Watson to help her in my stead, I could deal with the present situation, while still putting our best investigative foot forward for Violet. Yes. But then, of course, Watson was not bound to Violet Hunter by any promise or contact, as I was. All that bound them was that kiss. Ah! So if I could intrude myself into their kiss-bond, could I not also intrude my contractual bond between the two of them?

Of course! That seemed to make sense. And how does one intrude upon a kiss-bond? It's obvious, isn't it? And the little hair monsters had left Watson and me bound side by side in their feeble grasp, so, with a final lunge I threw myself onto Watson and…

Well…

A gentleman does not say.

It should suffice for you to know that Watson's soul was ripped from his body and sent spinning through the nether abysses to lodge within another body, very like his and not far away. As his physical form collapsed in my arms, powerless and angry-looking, I congratulated myself on a job well done. My only regret, I suppose, is that I should have waited six seconds longer. If I had, Watson would have gotten to see the red-headed soul-sucker.

The crate in the center of the room—that first one we'd opened—gave a leisurely creak. One side of it bowed out, then fell off altogether, emitting a flood of gold coins, wadded leaden foil and one desiccated corpse. It seems only the first few layers of the crate had contained orderly rows of packed coins; the lower part was messy, indeed. As I watched, the corpse picked itself up off the floor, groped for its monocle, dusted this on the mildewed remains of its waistcoat and screwed it in place over one eye. Well… where one eye should have been. All he had were empty sockets with little burning embers in them, which oozed oily purple smoke up into the curls of his rather magnificent head of red hair. All the skull minions that weren't tying up Watson and me bounded joyfully over to him. Several leapt up and wove their own red locks into his, dangling from his prodigious mane like ornaments on a wrong-colored Christmas tree.

"Demon," I said, "you must be master of this…"

But I trailed off. I suppose it was Watson's influence that did it. It's just… if this were a demon, where did he get a garish 1850s waistcoat? Why the monocle? Why the gold–crowned walking stick he picked up from the clutter of spilled coins? Why the fascination with red–headed gentlemen? And why the post–mortem resemblance to one or two pictures I'd seen of late?

"Oh dear, Mr. Hopkins, whatever has happened to you?"

The ghoulish banker turned to me, tendrils of hair seeking towards me in the darkness like wayward and boneless arms. "Do I know you, sir?" he asked.

"My name is Warlock Holmes."

He stared appraisingly at me for a few moments, then jabbed his stick in my direction and announced, "You're here to steal my gold!"

"Oh, no. No, I've no interest in gold. I'm here to listen to your story and learn the fate of the red–headed men."

This gave him some pause. He hesitated, as if torn between the natural violence the walking dead display towards the living and the desire to air his woes to a willing ear. After a time, he uttered, "You are an intruder."

"There, I have no grounds to refute you," I admitted. "But look on the bright side: I'm an intruder who thought he'd have a bit of a wait. I therefore have a couple of pipes sitting over there and probably about a pound of the good stuff. Care to join me in a smoke?"

"Are you joking?" the animated corpse demanded. "Of course I would! By God, it's been ages! I'm gasping!"

The skulls unwrapped their hair from me with such rapidity that I'm afraid I lost my grip on Watson, who tumbled from my grasp. Fortunately, I think his arm broke the fall. Unfortunately, I think his arm… broke. Oh, and that screwdriver he was holding? Straight into the leg. Handle-deep, I'm afraid.

Then again, I had other matters to worry about. "Come on then, Mr. Hopkins. We'll see if we can't find a couple of crates that might still serve as chairs, eh? This is my usual pipe, so I hope you don't mind if I…"

"Oh, no. Of course."

"Thank you. You may use Watson's. He's a man of fastidious habits, so I think you'll find it's quite clean. He won't mind if you borrow it. He's rather indisposed at the moment."

Soon I had us both settled with smoking bowls. I watched Ezekiah Hopkins enjoy his first few puffs and asked, "How do you find it?"

"Oh, magnificent! Just magnificent! What is it?"

"Well it certainly is not shredded Persian sorcerer, so let's not have any wild accusations!"

"Eh? No, I only meant… I used to take Tennessee Jackdaw, myself. My favorite brand. Had it shipped in from America. Long ago, you know. Before your time, I am certain."

"Well, I wouldn't be *too* certain. But tell me, Mr. Hopkins, how do you come to be so transformed?"

He gave a few, thoughtful puffs, then a great sigh. "This is what loss does to a man, Mr. Holmes."

"With all due respect, Mr. Hopkins, no, it isn't. I've lost a great deal myself and look at me. I never died from it."

"Died?" cried my host, visibly incensed. "I never *died*! Perhaps I have wasted a bit, in all the years, but I am a living, breathing man, sir, just like you!"

"Living?"

"Yes!"

"In a crate of coins?"

"Well, I mean… perhaps I have *modified* my lifestyle in order to prolong it, but what else could I do? I cannot die, Mr. Holmes—not until what I've lost has been restored to me!"

"That's no excuse not to die," I said, shaking the stem of my pipe at him sternly. "We've all lost things, Mr. Hopkins."

"Not like I have!" he thundered, rising to his feet. He raged for a few moments—not at me, I deem, but in frustration at his ancient loss. He paced back and forth, fuming. His pipe, his eyes and his mood: all fuming. Finally, he stopped right in front of me and said, "Now, look here! I went off to America, didn't I? Made all that money? Came back home to the old town to settle down. That's all I wanted. And yes, I always was a funny-looking one, I'll admit that. Big nose. Reddest hair you ever saw. Bit round. Bit *old*, by the time I'd come home. But I never wanted much. The wife I'd missed in my youth! A sweet, pretty thing to stay with me and love me; move this old blood, warm my heart. Children, you know! Someone to enjoy the fruits of my labor. To grow and play in the comfort I could provide them. I'd have denied them nothing. Nothing! But what did I get?"

"Well clearly not that, or you wouldn't be so angry, would you?"

"They laughed at me! They tittered! Nobody wanted to marry the funny old man, not even if he was rich! So clueless, he was! And that hair? The kind of girl I wanted wanted nothing to do with me. So what do you think I did?"

"Probably what all of the world's ultra-wealthy do when they are disappointed: spend lavish amounts on mystics and charlatans, trying to find a solution to their problem."

"I spent *lavish amounts* on… oh… yes… exactly as you say. But I got luckier than most, you see. I found a method that works! It was all down to Charlemagne. Or, to be more precise, one of his advisors: a man of unfathomable origin, Montevbello Goosh!"

"I don't know about 'unfathomable'. Montevbello sounds rather Italian, doesn't it?"

"And Goosh?"

"Rather made-up. Oh… yes, I see…"

"Nobody knows what the man's real name was, but it matters naught. The point is: he was fascinated about the underlying powers that made our world work."

"Demons, you mean?" I asked.

"No, no, no! That's just the thing. That is the very distinction! He wanted to identify forces that are native to *this world*. And he did! He discovered nine agencies by which the will of men can be controlled—and on any scale—individual men or entire nations. We are all puppets to them. He made it his life's work to understand and control them. He built nine trinkets, one for each power, to present to Charlemagne to help him take over the world!"

"I always thought Charlemagne was doing rather a fine job of that by himself."

"Well exactly. And a good thing too, for Goosh made two critical errors which ensured his work could never be of service to Charlemagne."

"The first?"

"He took too long. Charlemagne died."

"Well, that will do it. The second?"

"The Nine were just terrible. Awful! Yes, he had distilled the ideas and created foci that gave the holder some power over the idea they represented, but his work also so focused these powerful ideas as to grant them physical form—he granted them life!"

"Never a good idea," I observed.

"Certainly not in this case. The Nine are good for only one thing: unspeakable slaughter. They look like men, or… a bit like men. And they are easiest to control when one has the proper trinket. But they are dangerous in the extreme. One small error, the tiniest transgression against the power they represent and they will lay unstoppable waste to the perpetrator and all around him. There has never in the history of our world been a mystical power to match even one of the Nine."

"Well…" I said, with as much humility as I could muster, "*perhaps* not."

"Yet I was in luck, you see. The Nine had been recently

bound—enslaved to the will of a great American sorcerer. But—and this is the important bit—he'd managed to do it without possessing all nine trinkets!"

"How?"

"Nobody knows, but it presented a unique opportunity. He who could lay his hands upon one of those mystic foci had a brief period where he could experiment with the underlying power without invoking the wrath of that power's guardian. And I knew the one I wanted, Mr. Holmes! Everybody assumes Fear to be the greatest motivator of men, but it isn't. Not Secular Power. Not Religious Power. Not Pain. *Hope*. Hope is the greatest of the Nine. I spent two-thirds of my fortune for it, but at last—at last—I made it mine."

"And what does hope look like, Mr. Ezekiah Hopkins, when you hold it in your hand?"

His burning eyes softened, somehow. His cadaverous shoulders slumped. He gave a sad but fond little sigh. "Funny little thing, really. Just a medallion made of dark metal. The background is a house. You can see in through the door. There's a hearth. A table, laden with food. Not much, but enough to give the impression that here is a place of warmth and plenty. In the foreground stand the figure of a man and a woman, leaning together, shoulder to shoulder and holding a child up above their heads. It's crude workmanship, really, but there's just the impression that the child is laughing... It's enough that if you think of yourself as that man, or that woman, you couldn't help but reflect how lucky you'd been to have found the other.

Think of yourself as that child and… well… who wouldn't want to be hoisted, laughing, into the air by two parents who loved you, with a place of safety to grow up in? I tell you, Mr. Holmes, there is no promise of great wealth in that tableau. No power. No long life. Yet, Mr. Goosh had it exact. The truest hope of our kind is to spend our days safe, happy and provided for, giving our love and feeling love in return. And then—when we pass from this world—to know that the children we have loved will accomplish the same. And will miss us. That's all. That is all…"

Well, I will admit I was rather taken aback. I knew exactly what he was speaking of. I'd been doodling it all over my walls, my books and myself during my most recent period of recovery from grievous wounds. (I get those a lot.) It had been much on my mind, but I could never say why. Had it been an idea of my own, or something one of the voices had said to me, or an old idea that—just upon the cusp of your forgetting it—struggles to make itself remembered once more? It was an uncomfortable remembrance and I chided myself for not knowing more about it.

"Um… but you lost the medallion?" I asked.

"No! It was stolen from me!"

"By whom?"

"A thief!"

"You don't know which one?"

"No! And I can't die until I do! I need to have that back, Mr. Holmes. To have held it, to have begun working with its powers… and then to lose it? No! Intolerable!

Owning it, Mr. Holmes, does not assuage the need for it. It *feeds* that need. How can I have come so close? How can I have held the answer to all my problems in my very hands and yet have been robbed of the opportunity to unlock all its secrets and apply them? But I had learned enough! Enough to find other objects, other skills and use them to chase my dream!"

"Ah! So that's how you became—" I waved my pipe stem at his mummified body and his mighty boosh of skull-decked hair "—whatever this is."

"I learned to take souls, Mr. Holmes, to extend my own life. Now, the cost of doing it is this: the taken soul is ever with me. A part of me, in a way. But what was that to me, whose chief complaint had been loneliness? Here, at last, was a way to make a family! To gather to me the others who shared my burden: the unwanted, teased, forgotten and cast-off red-headed men!"

"Not the women?"

"No! They don't suffer as we do! I don't know why, Mr. Holmes, but people seem to think of red-headed women as… somehow… *cute*! But we! The men with the same affliction! Oh, how they hate us!"

"Hmm… I've just realized… the answer to Watson's earlier question is: *both*! You are the red-headed sucker of red-headed souls. Well played, Mr. Hopkins! Double points."

As I watched him work his way to a fever pitch, I began to realize our discussion was drawing to a close. It had been a nice time. A fine pipe. But I can't say the turn was unexpected. It's how these things usually go. We are lonely creatures, we users of magic. Each of our paths is unique and sets us aside from the body of common men. How few are our chances of explaining our labors and ourselves to someone who could understand. Thus, we often say more to each other than might be advisable. Yet, how must these things always end? I was an intruder, as Mr. Hopkins had pointed out. Moreover, I was not a red-headed gentleman and therefore unworthy of inclusion in his gestalt. I was a threat to his plan to ease his pain and one need only look at his choice of hair adornment to realize he was certainly capable of murder. Grateful as I was for his knowledge, sympathetic as I might be to his plight, I knew what was coming. I needed a plan.

Oh! And I had one! As it turned out, I had accidentally been rather clever. I began, as subtly as I could, sneakily and magic-o-quietly, concentrating on Watson.

"I will feast this very night!" Mr. Hopkins cried, eyes alight with eagerness, hands bent like claws beneath his billowing hair. "I've still got my money, Mr. Holmes! I've still got my agents! I've hired a brilliant young man named Clay to bring me a red-headed gentleman to feed upon!"

"Oh? You mean Jabez Wilson? He's not coming."

"Eh?"

"Watson and I... we warned him off."

"You did *what?*"

"Well, he was a client of ours. We were bound to protect him."

The color I held in my mind was not orange, as most

red-heads truly are. It was not that whitish pink that sometimes comes with age. No, this was *red*! Red like living blood. Red like that fish I forget the name of… you know the one I mean.

"And really, Mr. Hopkins… all this murder? Tut, sir! Tut!"

He turned on me with pure vengeance in those burning eyes.

"And Watson, especially. He's got a vested interest in bringing you down. It's no good to a man like him, letting a red-headed soul-sucker run around loose."

"What do you mean? Wait, is he…?"

"Eventually, he might find himself in your little family, so you can see why he might wish to—"

"Clear off him! Clear off!" Hopkins yelled to his skull/hair/spiders, a few of whom were walking on Watson's face and body. As they skittered aside, he approached and declared, "We shall see if he is worthy of inclusion! I am the judge and master of the League of Red-Headed Men, and I shall… Oh… oh, by God… he's wonderful!"

Ezekiah lifted Watson tenderly into his arms (and hair tendrils…) and caressed the newly magic-reddened head of hair I'd given him. I saw Hopkins tug at it a few times, staring closely to determine if this were merely dye or the finest, reddest hair he'd ever seen. To help him make up his mind, I mentioned, "We used to make terrible fun of him."

"Shame on you, sir! Shame!" Ezekiah snapped, then threw his ear to Watson's chest to ensure he was yet breathing. A smile of satisfaction spread across his

"Hey. Don't eat Watson."

ghoulish face. "Alive! Alive and wondrous! Oh, you may have deprived me of one meal, Mr. Holmes, but you have provided me with a finer!"

"Hey. Don't eat Watson," I protested.

"You mustn't think of it like that. He shall endure. Here, in his right place with his right brothers. Oh, lost one, come home to the family that understands you! Join with me now!"

With that, Ezekiah Hopkins unhinged his jaw, much like those long snakey things… What are their names…? Ah! Snakes! He stretched his awful, dead-looking mouth to a truly disturbing proportion. Just as I was beginning to reflect, "You know, I think that would fit over Watson's entire face," he… well… suffice to say that if Watson thought his first kiss from another gentleman was unsavory, it is perhaps fortunate that he was unconscious for his second. As Ezekiah Hopkins's lips sealed about Watson's forehead and chin, his burning eyes narrowed to radiant sparks and a horrible slurping noise filled the room.

Then a second one.

Then a rather desperate-sounding third.

Around me, the skull-spiders reeled and stumbled as if drunk. Hopkins threw his gaze about the room in dazed panic, wondering what might be the source of his sudden displeasure.

"I told you not to eat Watson," I said, striding up to him, straightening my cuffs. "The source of your present difficulty, Mr. Hopkins, is this: there simply isn't a soul in that body. It's off visiting a friend of ours."

Hopkins gave another desperate, soul-suck slurp, then began feebly trying to pry Watson out of his mouth with weak, uncertain fingers. Though I knew Watson to be in no danger of losing his soul, I realized he might have another problem. His body still needed to breathe.

"And as for you, Mr. Hopkins, as I said before, all this murder is really unacceptable. You are a predator of men, sir. But I am their defender—a predator of predators—and if you think I am about to let you devour my best friend…"

I held my hand out towards the crates behind us and thought of Watson's Webley-Pryse. The pistol heard me, turned its handle and sped to my grasp. I laid the barrel against Hopkins's brow, pulled back the hammer, yanked the trigger and told him (perhaps a bit later than I ought), "…you are drastically mistaken."

As he slumped down dead—*properly* dead—his little skull minions reeled about in surprise and dismay. I thought they'd die too, but the magic he'd used to animate them did not fail. And who knew how long it would take to wear off? I leaned down to extricate my friend's face from my most recent enemy's face, but… I had simply possessed no idea how hard a red-headed soul-sucker could suck! In the end, I had to use the crowbar. Once I had him free, I laid Watson's body near the flagstone that covered the secret tunnel and went back to gather our gear. I knew I must hasten to Violet's side, yet the vault had one more encounter in store for me.

As I threw everything back into Watson's big bag, the flagstone bumped open and a figure emerged. Jabez

Wilson stood sheepishly up out of the tunnel, with both hands raised above his head and a pistol pressed against the back of his skull by the exposed forearm of some hidden antagonist, farther down the tunnel.

"Uhhhh… I have been directed to inquire: who is here and what is happening? Oh! Mr. Holmes, is that you?" he stupidly asked, stupidly.

"Jabez! Did you… Did you accept the invitation to your cellar? After Watson told you not to?"

"Uhhhh…"

"You must always listen to Watson! Always! I hate to say it, sir, but Watson is right about you: you *are* a red-headed ninny! Oh, and it's not even eight o'clock yet! Double-ninny! Well, I suppose I shall have to save you. John Clay? I know it is you down in that tunnel, John Clay! Your name is known to me, and mine, I think, is known to you!"

Then I gathered all the voices that speak in my head and bound them to my own tongue so that, with all voices, in all languages, I could proclaim myself.

"I am Warlock Holmes—revenger and destroyer!
Wicked one, your plans have come to naught.
I will strike the armor from your shoulders, the
      weapon from your hand.
Now: stand and face me!"

He didn't.

From within the tunnel came a slightly muffled, "Aw,

bollocks!" Then another voice cried out in pain and protest. Mr. Clay must have brought the red-headed confederate who had posed as Duncan Ross, too, for I heard Clay shout, "Out of my way, Archie! Jump, man! Jump! Back down the tunnel or we're done for!"

I listened as the two of them scuttled back down the tunnel; then came a few moments' silence, followed by a few screams, a few thuds and silence once more.

"Uhhhh… what was that?" Jabez wondered.

"Oh, Watson took the precaution of having Grogsson and Lestrade standing by outside your pawnshop. I imagine John Clay's days of mischief-making are at an end. He's a very smart man, my friend Watson; had the whole thing figured from the very beginning.

"Well…" I added, gazing about at all the floppy, disoriented skull-hair-spiders, "…*most* of it. There are one or two details he might have missed. But those will soon come to light. Er… as long as John Clay doesn't try to fight Grogsson. But enough of such distractions! Watson and I have another adventure to get to. An important one! Not this waddle-rot you've got us mixed up in!"

"Uhhhh…"

"Yes, I made that word up. But I don't care. It seems apt. This is waddle-rot, sir! Utter waddle-rot! Watson and I have got to save Violet, so I'm going to bandage him up a bit and then you're going to help me drag him back through that tunnel."

"Uhhhh…"

"Oh, very well! You just bring the bag, then."

As we made our final preparations, the skull-spiders swarmed all over their fallen master in desperate confusion. And who can blame them? Dead, they might be. Brainless. Thoughtless. Lifeless. Pointless. But this was the first time they'd been alone.

Poor cute little skull-buggers...

It was probably my job to destroy them, but I just couldn't bring myself to do it. Instead, I cleared my throat and said, "Attention, all hair-monsters! I hereby declare this disused vault to be the clubhouse and headquarters of the Red Heads' League! All of you are charter members, with full use of the premises, all rights and privileges, blah, blah, blah! Just don't go wandering up into the bank and everything ought to be all right."

And that is where I left them.

I've been back to visit, a few times. In my later adventures, I recovered the trinket for which Ezekiah Hopkins had done so much and slain so many. And what better place to keep it? I laid it in his dead little hand, though I think he gained no joy by it.

The skull-monsters always liked to stay in a pile, all clustered up on the fallen back of Ezekiah Hopkins. The first couple of times I went, some of them would pad over to greet me, looking up eagerly to see if I'd brought them their old bodies back—or whatever other treat it is that skull minions yearn for. Yet with each visit, there would be fewer who came to see me and ever slower they would move. The last time, none of them stirred at all. There was nothing there but broken boxes and a crusty lump of lustrous hair, with about a dozen skulls in it and one complete skeleton lying at the base of it all.

I don't go back there now. It is a lonely place.

But there. I've done it. A silly little adventure from years ago. I'm sure I told Watson most of it before. The important bits, anyway. The stuff I could remember. But now he's given me a duty and I've taken it to heart. I've made this ancient and intractable mind of mine dredge up every detail and laid it all down for Watson's benefit. And for yours, dear Anyone-Watson-Cares-To-Show-This-To. Yes. A job well done, I must say.

Watson's note: I include Holmes's account of the Adventure of the Red Heads' League in this volume for two reasons. One: so that the chronological adventures of Holmes and myself might make some sense to the reader.

Two: blame.

And I do take a fair bit of it on myself, surely. But Holmes... God damn it, Holmes... Those things Ezekiah Hopkins told you in that dusty vault were the very pieces of the grand puzzle I'd been missing. If you had told me all this the moment I woke up, I could have...

Maybe we could have...

But no.

It's too late now.

THE ADVENTURE OF THE
THREE APPRENTICES

ONCE AGAIN, FROM THE JOURNALS
OF DR. JOHN WATSON

AS WELL AS I KNOW HIM, I AM AT TIMES UNCERTAIN HOW much guile I should attribute to Warlock Holmes. I know he was trying to distract me from my pursuit of the Woman, but I don't know the true extent of his efforts. "Let's find a case to keep Watson distracted" was a plan he'd not only accidentally admitted on a few occasions, but actually managed to effect. When that plan failed to distract me as long as he'd hoped, it is possible—just possible—that he elected instead for a plan of "let's find a case to get Watson horribly wounded, so he can't do anything".

Which, he also effected. Perhaps by design. Perhaps by *happy* accident.

I returned from my adventure with Violet Hunter sure that it would be my last for some time. My right arm was badly broken. The left had been mangled by a barghest. I had two cracked ribs. My leg was wounded to the bone, with no small amount of attendant tendon damage and I had crowbar marks all over my face.

Plus, my screwdriver was bent.

Oh, and my hair! It was a total loss. Holmes could have

put it back to rights, but that would have required the use of magic and—on his advice—I thought it better to just shave it all off and begin again. Holmes was convinced it would grow back normally. I explained to him that this was not the way hair follicles worked, but he explained to me that it was the way magic did, so I let myself be overruled. To my great relief, it grew back its accustomed, unremarkable brown.

I hesitate to think of what I'd have done to Holmes if it hadn't.

To fix the rest, I summoned the best trauma surgeon I knew: James Mortimer of Dartmoor. By which I mean: I sent him a letter and he agreed to come. Holmes was prepared to properly *summon* him—out of his bath, or wherever he might happen to be at that exact moment— but I insisted on normalcy. Even though it hurt. Solid fellow: James hastened down by train and performed just hideously painful surgery all over me. Nevertheless, I was confident that the worst was behind me; that so long as I was diligent in my efforts to recover, I should be whole again.

The process was a long one. I was soon able to leave my bed, but by then my atrophied arm didn't allow me to grip anything heavier than a pencil. I could make it from my bed to the lavatory and back before my leg gave out on me, but the front door was simply beyond me. My great nemesis was the stairs. The day I finally conquered them, I had my first taste of fresh air in weeks and began a series of laughably short walks around the neighborhood.

I slowly lengthened them, day by day, teaching my injured limbs their old strength (such as it was). As I labored, the last days of winter and the entirety of spring fled by. And so did something else: my sense of immediacy. I should have hastened back to the game, to face the Woman. Instead, I allowed myself to settle into domesticity and inaction. I do not know that I would ever have deemed it was time to go forth and test myself against magic and strangeness again, but—as was often the case—adventure came and found us at 221B.

Holmes and I were seated at our dining table, each absorbed in a separate discipline. By that time, I had returned to medical practice. Well… no… let us say that some of the neighborhood vagrants had discovered that there was an under-employed medical man living near them, who had no great concern over money. Thus, it had become common for me to find some ragged specimen or other, collapsed in the street—always with suspicious proximity to 221B—moaning to nobody in particular that they were unable to work in their current state and that their six idyllic, churchgoing children might starve if not for the timely medical intervention of a beneficent savior who would surely find his reward in heaven. Though— just as surely—said savior must be a bit of a dimwit if he thought he was going to be paid for his efforts.

Thus it was that I found myself laboring to concoct a tincture for a local knife-grinder's horrid foot-blight. I was hoping to find a way to apply it from across the room, with some sort of twelve-foot daubing swab. It was a difficult recipe to get right and I would have been struggling, even if it were not for the interference of Holmes.

He was at that damned jigsaw puzzle again.

He sat opposite me, staring at the splayed pieces with a frustration that was rapidly mounting to outright rage. He'd been at it for the last week and a half. Day after day—and night after night as well—he sat at our table, staring at the diverse pieces, insisting that I take my meals in some other location. Though I was glad to see him occupied, it nevertheless irked me to see him thus. I suppose I was embarrassed for him, because...

"Holmes, that is a *child's twenty-four-piece puzzle*. How many days do you intend to waste upon it?"

"Not now, Watson! I've almost cracked it!"

I was inclined to be less optimistic.

He'd yet to connect any of the pieces. Instead, they lay spread all over my table, attached to little notes which said things like, "Green. *Suspiciously* green," and, "Rectangle? Poorly executed! Two edges are somewhat irregular..."

The image was of a child leading a billy goat. By the whim of chance, one piece of the puzzle featured a complete goat eye, along with one of its nostrils and just the corner of its upturned grin. This, Holmes was sure, was the ringleader to them all and possessed of a special infamy. It always had pride of place, next to a note that read, "Egad! Who would paint such a thing?"

I was about to offer my help for what must have been the two-hundredth time, but just as I opened my mouth, the bell rang. This, I presumed, would be my rotten-toed knife-grinder, so I prepared my most professional disgust-masking face and rose to answer.

It wasn't him.

Just as I reached the door, Mrs. Hudson's voice came from outside, stuporously reciting, "Nobody is here. Nobody needs to see Mr. Holmes. And I wouldn't remember if anyone was here. I fell asleep drinking my tea and slept all afternoon, didn't I? Answer the door, Warlock Holmes. Nobody needs you."

My outstretched hand stopped, hovering a few inches from the handle and my eyes sought Holmes's. I found him utterly transformed, his gaze steely, his jaw set. Outside, I could hear Mrs. Hudson taking a few clumsy steps down the stairs. *Skree-er-ka-reeek*, went the third step from the top. I heard Mrs. Hudson stumble twice on her own, well-known steps. Whoever "Nobody" might be, he presumably stood alone, just on the other side of our door.

"Careful, Watson," Holmes whispered.

"Er… maybe you should answer it?" I suggested.

He shook his head.

"Better if you do, Watson. I'll just be over here."

He took up position in the center of the room, staring at the door as if expecting a mortal challenge to issue through it at any moment. His weight was on the balls of his feet and he had the unwavering focus of a gunfighter. I turned back to the door with an even more reluctant heart than I would have gathered for Old Stink-Foot.

"No! Wait!" hissed Holmes. "Over here. I'll be over here."

"Soames? Hilton Soames?"

My friend threw himself behind our sofa. For a moment, he disappeared entirely, but then his eyes peeped up over the edge, like those of a five-year-old lad with particularly poor hide-and-seek skills.

"All right. Open it."

I stepped to the side and craned my hand out towards the handle, mindful of the pumpcrow-strangling I'd received the last time this had happened. I wordlessly mouthed, "One... two... *three!*" then yanked the door open and flung myself away, towards the corner.

There, in our doorway, stood a gaunt gentleman, with an aristocratic grandeur. He was tall, but not as tall as Holmes. He wore a black silk hat and a theatrical cape. He was pale. Age had dusted his black hair gray at the temples. He wore a moustache and goatee so sharp, it looked as if the tips might double as glass-cutters. A tarnished silver pentagram hung around his neck on a rough leather cord and the buttons of his shirt were expertly wrought onyx skulls. If one walked up to one's local music-hall costumer and said, "Please make me look like an evil stage magician," one could not have hoped to achieve any result superior to our guest's own appearance.

Warlock's eyes widened as he popped up over the edge of the couch to exclaim, "Soames? Hilton Soames?"

"Greetings, Warlock," our guest said in a rich, severe baritone. "May I come in?"

"Well, I... I suppose... just this once."

Hilton Soames spared me a look of distaste and distrust as he breezed across our threshold, then turned his attention to our lodgings, gazing this way and that before he declared, "Cozy little hovel you've built for yourself, Holmes. I should have expected something of the sort."

"Hey," Holmes muttered.

I rose from the safety of my chosen corner, reclaimed my position by the fire (as well as some of my dignity, I hoped) and noted, "It seems the two of you are acquainted."

Our guest's lively black eyes flicked in my direction. "We are."

"And you must be a practitioner of magic?" I continued.

He snorted derisively. "Magic? Bah! A child's word for phenomena he fails to understand. I am Professor of Occult Studies at the College of St. Luke's."

"And you must be… well… evil," I said.

"Evil? How dare you? Why would you think so?"

Holmes tried not to laugh. He really did make every effort. He didn't *want* to mock our guest, but he could not quite choke back a half-swallowed, half-spat, "Phffft!"

I looked at him, with a mind to chide, but in a moment I, too, was giggling. There we stood laughing until our eyes ran, while Hilton Soames fumed.

"Evil? Oh! Oh! How dare you?" Holmes mocked.

"Why *ever* would you think so?" I asked, indicating my clothes with feigned incredulity.

We laughed a moment longer, then finally Holmes went to our guest, laid a comforting hand on Soames's shoulder, and said, "Really, Hilton, you must pardon my friend and me but… you see… some men hide their intentions well and some do not."

"Your buttons are *skulls*," I chortled.

"And as I have told you before," giggled Holmes, "if I met a kitten with that goatee, I could not trust him. Now, I know you better than to assume this is a social call. Was there something you wanted?"

"Perhaps," said Soames. His eyes found me again and searched me up and down. "Who is this?"

"Oh, it's only Watson," said Holmes. "Anything you can say to me, you can say before him."

"You trust him so perfectly, do you?"

"Well… perhaps I'd better say: anything you say to me, I might forget is secret and mention to Watson over breakfast. Plus, he's a rather clever fellow. Really, Soames, if you've got a problem, Watson is a most useful gentleman to have about."

"I do have a problem. We may *all* have a problem," Soames growled. "My carriage is just outside. Will you come to St. Luke's?"

"Could you, Watson?" Holmes asked.

"Well, I do have one appointment, but I can hardly express how glad I'd be to skip it, so… yes."

"Capital. Just let us gather our coats, Soames."

Five minutes later, the three of us were seated in a cab, bound for the College of St. Luke's. As we drove, Soames began his tale.

"Have you ever heard of Fortescue's Binding?"

"Not that I recall," said Holmes. "What happened?

325

Some fellow called Fortescue got himself tied up?"

"No. Penton Fortescue—a lord and preeminent occult scholar—discovered a method to summon and bind demons. Potentially quite powerful ones. The ritual was performed only once, to summon three lesser demon 'brothers', who took the names Bannister, Railing and Low-Rising-Safety-Wall."

I gave Holmes a quizzical look.

"Demons are weird," he told me.

"The summoning was permanent," Soames continued. "Two of the demons are dead, but Bannister has continued to serve a number of England's more prominent magical families—passed from one to another, over the generations, at no small expense. He has been in my service for almost eight years, now."

"So… Wait! Are we about to meet a demon?" I cried.

Holmes sniffed. "I'd try to manage my excitement if I were you, Watson. He can't be a very frightful fellow, or we'd have known about him before now."

"Quite so," Soames agreed. "He is almost as disappointing as a demon as he is in his capacity as butler. The three were not native to this plane and survival here did not come easy. I'm sure Bannister would be gone by now, if he had not preserved himself by eating his weakening brothers."

"Ew," I noted.

"I believe Lord Fortescue summoned these three weaklings to test the underlying tenets of his ritual. The binding was utterly successful. Bannister was not only bound to Fortescue, but able to be passed, like any other piece of property, from person to person. After his initial success, Fortescue retired to refine his formulas, codify what he had learned, and perfect his ritual. Unfortunately, the doddering old codger then suffered a change of heart. It seems he came to regard his own work as dangerous and unsavory. For years, it has been assumed that he destroyed all copies of his notes—the Fortescue Binding has been fragmentary and incomplete."

"Oh no," moaned Holmes.

"However, recently…"

"Oh. Yes. I see what's going on," I said.

"…I have, through diligent searching, reconstructed the entire ritual."

"Well, of *course* you have," said Holmes, rolling his eyes, "and aren't you just *so pleased* with yourself?"

"He can't be all that chuffed about it," I noted, "or else he wouldn't have come to us, would he?"

Soames shifted in his seat, sniffed with wounded pride and muttered, "I am afraid its secrecy has been compromised."

"Surprise!" Holmes said to me. We had another giggle.

"It is no subject for merriment," Soames insisted. "I had, for some time, been instructing my three apprentices in sections of Fortescue's ritual. I had been preparing them to aid me in the summoning. But I had been careful— most careful, Holmes—that no one student should possess knowledge of the entire ritual. In fact, their knowledge was so fragmentary—so confined to that which I needed them to know—that the lads presented no threat. I myself intended to be nothing more than a responsible steward of this knowledge."

"Riiiiiiight," said Holmes.

"I am a simple scholar!"

"Oh, of course you are."

"I am on the side of the angels, sir! I am at the head of a small but important school of human knowledge. I was tasked by Her Majesty Queen Victoria to extend and protect Britain's unique magical knowledge and heritage at the honored institution of St. Luke's."

"Yes. I know," said Holmes. "And I'm sure that the very instant he sees it, Watson will agree that there is *simply no possibility* that St. Luke's might be Britain's foremost haven for evil wizards, or those who might wish to become one."

"I am beginning to gather that impression," I said.

Soames continued. "Earlier this morning, the proofs of the Fortescue Binding arrived from the local printer—"

"Wait, wait, wait!" I interjected. "You gave them to a *regular printer?*"

"As I think I have said before, I am a humble university professor, of limited means."

"On the contrary, I think you boasted that you could afford a rather expensive demon butler," I reminded him.

"Well… I suppose I may have forgotten to mention that Bannister was donated to the college. I never stated that I purchased him. And why not send the ritual to a simple printer? What harm could the man do with it? To him, it is just three sheaves of utter nonsense. To me, a treasure beyond accounting."

"He's probably right about that, Watson," said Holmes. "So, having finished the day's advertisements about lost doggies and bicycles for sale, the local printer dashes off a copy of a lost demon-summoning ritual, delivers it to you and… then what happened?"

"I was so pleased at the state of the complete documents, I decided to take tea with a colleague of mine."

"Decided to have a gloat, you mean," Holmes chuckled.

Soames shut his eyes and drew a deep, calming breath. "Upon my return just over an hour later, I was dismayed to find a key protruding from the door of my office. I had, of course, locked the room tight, knowing the value of the document that sat upon my desk. There are only two keys to that door, Holmes. One remained in my possession. The other was Bannister's."

"And did the one in the door prove to be your demon butler's?" I asked.

"Yes. The little blighter admitted it the moment I confronted him. The reason may have been harmless enough—he says he checked in to see if I required any refreshment and forgot the key in the door."

"Poorly done, Soames," said Warlock.

"Even then, it should have been safe! Nobody knew it was there!"

"The printer knew," I pointed out. "Bannister knew."

"Bannister? Ha! Do you suppose I am in the habit of telling every demon I know that I am in possession of a demon-binding ritual? Bannister knows where the tea is kept and that's all he needs to know. Nevertheless, this cannot change the fact that, for over an hour, the Fortescue Binding sat unguarded in a room that anybody might have walked into."

"And you have reason to suspect somebody did," I deduced, "or you would not have come to seek our aid."

Soames gave a grim nod. "When I stepped back into my chambers, I realized the manuscript had been disturbed and a token of fell intent had been left for me to discover."

"Oh, I can't wait to see it!" said Holmes. "I love a good token of fell intent."

"You'll not have long to wait," said Soames.

He was right. St. Luke's turned out to be the smallest constituent college of the University of London. That is to say: it was so small as to be forgettable. It currently had only one teacher and three students, and its reputation was so slight that—though it lay less than a mile and a half from my home—I had never heard of the thing.

Really, we might have walked there.

It was a pleasant day—a bit hot, perhaps, but sunny and cheerful. Hilton Soames took some care to impress us, as we neared his section of the grand old school, crying, "Behold! The proving grounds of Trakken Feeld, the leathern steeds of Pom-Ehl, and the black pit of shattered hopes!"

By these, he meant, respectively: the track field, two dusty old gymnastics pommel horses and the long-jump pit (which, I have to admit, was formed of an unusually dark and ill-seeming clay).

From this, the reader may deduce two facts. First, that we were passing the athletics field. Second, that Hilton Soames was trying much too hard.

In truth, I think he was compensating in advance. The College of St. Luke's was composed of a single, gray, stumpy building. It must have been very old—certainly medieval. It consisted of a lower floor with Soames's quarters, his office and one lecture hall. Upstairs were rooms to accommodate eight or nine students, but most were disused. Soames pointed out which rooms were which with the butt of his walking stick as we approached. When he indicated the window to his office, Holmes cried out, "Oh! Your desk! It's magnificent!"

There seemed to be no hint of irony in his voice, so I could only assume he meant the compliment earnestly. The reason I could only assume was that Holmes was a great deal taller than I. Maybe he could see the desk in question, but I would have had to hop up on Soames's shoulders to see in through that window. As this is not the act of a gentleman, I elected to wait.

Soames led us around the corner and into the College of St. Luke's. A demon took our coats.

But not a very good one.

To my secret disappointment, Bannister was a patently unimpressive fellow. He might easily be mistaken for a human, but not a very happy one. His face was slightly too round, too shiningly white, too doughy. His deep-sunk eyes were surrounded by bags of extreme weariness that I think no true human could match. His arms were just a few inches too long and bent with such saggy alacrity that they must either be prehensile tentacles or possessed of a few extra elbows—none of them with any strength. He had the look of a being so worn down by life that his death could not be far away. Nor did it seem as if it would be particularly unwelcome.

The reappearance of his master did nothing to improve the day he was having. As Soames swept off his hat and cloak, he told Bannister, "This is Warlock Holmes and his colleague John Watson. Bring tea."

Bannister gave a subservient wobble and sloshed off towards the kitchen.

"Useless creature," Soames declared, before Bannister was out of earshot.

I watched him go and wondered aloud, "Is it usual for him to leave the key to your study in the door?"

"No. I cannot recall that he has ever erred so badly. Yet, his entire life is one of persistent domestic deficiencies. He leaves milk out. Forgets little errands. He let the cat out one September and didn't think to look for him again until March. His memory has grown as feeble as the rest of him. If you are wondering if he could have purposely opened the door for the intruder, Dr. Watson, I assure you he could not. He is bound to my will. He must do as I bid. He answers to no other man, nor can he betray the interests of his sworn master. I think it is merely the wretched contrivance of coincidence that he should miscarry his duty on the very day of the proofs' arrival. Damn it all! If I believed luck to be a living thing—a god or a demon—I would believe he hates me."

"She," Holmes corrected him. "*She* hates you."

"Show us the office, won't you?" I asked.

Do you know, it *was* a nice desk. Soames had one of those huge, lovingly polished numbers all professors seem to have, for the purpose of glaring archly at students from behind it. He also had a little writing table to do actual work at. It was topped in tasteful red leather and sat near the front window, with a little chair drawn up beside it. At this table, Hilton Soames leveled one finger—shaking with theatrical dread—and intoned, "Behold! The token of fell intent!"

Upon the table lay a bizarre little pyramid of dark, oily earth, its surface mottled by a sprinkle of what appeared to be sawdust. Holmes was utterly charmed by it. He turned it over and about, sniffed it, shook it and demanded that it yield all its secrets to him.

It didn't.

The three rolls of Fortescue's Binding were scattered about the room. One lay upon Soames's monolithic desk, where he said he'd left it. Another lay on the small writing table, next to a broken nib of pencil and a few shavings. The last was face down on the windowsill.

"Is that the regular position of the writing table, Mr. Soames?" I asked.

"No, it is usually there, near the hearth. I sometimes move it to the window if I need the light, but I will swear it was not there when I left this morning."

"I think you are correct," I said. "You have been

burgled. I would further suppose that this must be the first page of the binding ritual…"

I indicated the face-down sheet by the window.

"…that is the second…"

The page upon the writing table.

"…and this must be the last."

The page on his desk.

Soames's eyes narrowed. "You cannot possibly be able to read that text, Dr. Watson," he growled. "How did you know?"

"Of course not. One of them is face down, so I certainly could not have read that. But I can read the situation, I think. See? Your window looks down towards the entrance to this building. Your thief must have known you had gone, but dreaded your return. He took the writing desk to the window, so he could watch for you while he copied it."

"He copied it?" Soames cried. "Why, this is disastrous! How do you know he was not merely reading it?"

"He broke his pencil and paused to resharpen it," I said, indicating the nib and shavings. "Yet, it may be fortunate for us that he attempted a copy. If he had only read it, he might have finished the whole thing. Instead, he was interrupted before his knowledge was complete. He finished copying the first page and turned it face down, then went back for the second, leaving the third still on your desk. At some point, he must have seen you returning, abandoned his task and retreated."

Warlock smiled and mumbled, "Watson's getting very

good at this sort of thing, isn't he?" to the tiny tetrahedral lump he held in his hand.

But Soames disagreed.

"Wrong! He could not have seen me returning from that window, for I came in through the side door! If it were my return that surprised him, it could only come as I opened the door to this very room! If that were the case, I must have seen him. There is no other exit from these chambers."

"Except that one," I said, indicating the office's *perfectly obvious other door*.

"Oh, but that's just my bedroom," said Soames.

"May I see it?"

Soames looked annoyed, but allowed the intrusion. He had a humble room, with only two pieces of furniture, though the fault of that lay squarely on Soames. Apparently the man took such pride in his wicked sorcerer's attire that he'd felt he needed to fill the better half of his living quarters with the largest, most magnificent, most preposterous wardrobe I'd ever seen. His bed lay scrunched in a corner, in the little remaining space.

I had thought that perhaps the thief might have made his way in here and escaped through a window, but that thought was foiled. There was a window, but its latch looked to be as old as the building. It was so corroded, so crusted shut by age and oxidation that the amount of force necessary to open it must have far exceeded the amount that would have shattered it. No thief had gone that way. I squeezed my brows together with one hand and thought.

There were still so many pieces I was missing.

"Want me to just call up a demon and ask what happened?" Holmes offered.

"No! I forbid it! Look here, I will solve this problem, Holmes, and no sorcery will be required."

"Oh? So confident, Watson?" he chided.

"Holmes, there are only three students. Only three real suspects."

"Oh… right…"

"It significantly limits the complexity of this case, I would think. Besides which, we have hardly begun to explore the available clues. Mr. Soames, where were you when you first suspected you'd been robbed?"

"In the front hall. I'd come in the side door and was approaching my office when I saw Bannister's key in the lock. I cried out in surprise, then yelled for Bannister and we went in to see what had happened."

"You waited for Bannister to arrive before you went in?" I asked.

"Well, I was furious with him. And I knew he could be no more than one or two rooms away."

"And you say you cried out? So, the thief did have warning you were returning. He must have been terrified. To hear you right outside the only reasonable exit… He'd have panicked. Hmm… Tell me, when you entered and discovered your proofs had been disturbed, what did you do?"

"I think I yelled at Bannister a fair bit. Oh! And I ran about to see if I could see who might have done it."

"But you saw nobody?"

"No."

"Did you look in this bedroom?"

"Yes, but no one was here."

"Did you happen to look in that wardrobe?" I asked.

"I had no chance. Bannister had some sort of fit and collapsed on the chair out there. The old fool would not get up, no matter what I did, no matter how I kicked him."

Even Holmes, who had a tendency not to care for the clues that were given him, had to raise his eyebrows at that one. He looked up from his fell-token friend and asked Soames, "So… Bannister disobeyed your order? He shouldn't be able to do that."

"Yes, well…" Soames waved his hand about dismissively. "You've seen the beast. He's somewhat deficient. I think he was simply overcome. He knew he was in trouble."

"I rather suspect Bannister might have been putting on a show to distract you from that wardrobe," I said. "Now, Soames, you left to fetch us right after that?"

"Yes. I had to get my own hat and cloak because Bannister was so overcome. But by the time I had them, he was on his feet and just leaving the office. I told him to lock the door and admit no one until I returned."

"Well, I don't suppose he *admitted* anyone," I chuckled. "In fact, I suspect just the opposite."

I went to the wardrobe and opened the door. In just a moment, I gave a cry of triumph.

"Ha! I've got a present for you, Holmes!"

The second black pyramid was identical to the first. Holmes wasted no time snatching it from my hand and reintroducing it to its lost friend. "Look who we've found! He was hiding in the wardrobe! Oh, you must've been worried sick…"

Soames went white. "So… the entire time I was in the office…"

"The thief was hiding here," I confirmed. "He must have been trapped until you left. As soon as you were gone, Bannister was free to release him. But we've got an even bigger problem."

"What is that?"

"Is the room the same as it was when you left to fetch us?"

Soames ran back into his office and searched it over. "Yes, I think so."

"It must be at least an hour and a half since you left. How has the thief spent that time? He did not steal the manuscript, for there it lies. Either he must have thought he would not be caught, or he has been laying other plans."

"What plans?" Soames asked.

I shrugged. "I have no way of knowing. The two most basic choices are either to fight us, or to flee. If flight, I think he might have elected to take that manuscript with him. He may be laying an ambush for us, even now. I can't be certain. But I'll tell you this: no guilty man suspects he will escape discovery when there are only two other suspects."

Holmes gave a grim nod.

Soames spluttered, "What do we do?"

"Well, since we've cornered ourselves in here very nicely, I'd suggest we begin by locking the door. After that, let's hear about the suspects, eh?"

Soames practically tripped over himself, running to lock the office door. As soon as it was accomplished he turned to us and crowed, "There! Safe!"

"Well… not too safe, I should think," I told him. "We know Bannister's got a key."

"But he is bound to serve me!"

Warlock and I exchanged a look. He nodded.

"Tell me, Mr. Soames," I said, "when we walked into this building, did you or did you not tell Bannister to bring tea?"

"I did."

"And has he?"

Hilton Soames's hands were shaking, visibly.

"Perhaps he is receiving other orders from his true master," I said. "Speaking of which, tell us about your students."

"Er… well… there's Miles McLaren…"

"What sort of fellow is he?"

"Bookish and weedy," said Soames. "A very dedicated student of magic, but a bit of an eccentric. He says he wants to make it his life's work to revolutionize personal transportation, using occult study."

"Hmm… Let's consider his potential motives," I suggested. "If he had full access to that ritual, if he could summon any demon he wished, what do you think he would do?"

"Ha! I can tell you exactly," said Soames. "He'd bind the demon into a steam engine. He's certain he could make a coach-sized personal conveyance move two hundred miles in a single hour, without the benefit of a horse, if only he could muster the power. Mad, I tell you. He's got exactly the same delusions as that daffy Italian, Ferrari."

"So McLaren would happily steal the ritual to get an advantage on Ferrari," I reasoned, "but he's not athletic?"

"I should say not," Soames harrumphed.

"Then let us move on. Are either of the others?"

"They both are," said Soames. "You should see Daulat Ras—he's quite the specimen."

"Unusual name," Holmes noted.

"He was sent to us from India. He's in a Kali suicide cult. They believe that a paltry gift to their god is an insult. They therefore work to perfect their own bodies and their knowledge before destroying themselves in her name. His athletic prowess is formidable. His academic resolve is dauntless. His love of slaughter—even self-slaughter—knows no limit. His dedication is unquestionable."

"Hmm. I disagree," said Holmes. "Any member of a suicide cult who survives more than a week... well... I can't help but question their dedication. Still, it's easy to see that he might like to get his grubby little murder-claws on those proofs, eh?"

"Absolutely," said Soames. "He'd use it in a second—and in the worst way he could. It's hard to get a truly powerful being through to our realm without a willing vessel. Daulat Ras would not hesitate to sacrifice himself for such an exchange—to give up his life to let a great force of destruction loose upon the world, for the glory of his god."

"Never mind that," I said. "How tall is he?"

"What? Why does that…?"

"We haven't much time, Mr. Soames," I urged. "How tall? Compared to me?"

"Oh, a bit shorter than you, I would think, Dr. Watson."

"It isn't him," I said.

Holmes cocked his head to one side and wondered, "Are you sure, Watson? I really think he seems like the sort of fellow—"

"Oh, I don't doubt it," I agreed. "I wouldn't be surprised if he gives us a bit of trouble in the future. Yet, he does not match the particulars of this crime. The last student is both tall and athletic, I presume?"

"He is," said Soames, with a doubtful grimace, "but I almost hesitate to call him a student. Douglas Gilchrist is only here because he's a legacy. He's from one of England's preeminent magical families."

Holmes gave a snort of disdain.

Soames bristled and declared, "England has several great houses with hundreds of years of—"

"Being dimwits, dodderers and dabblers," Holmes interrupted. "Really, Watson, there are so few fellows worth fearing. It's an overrated field, I must say. Still, I've high hopes for young Daulat."

"Be that as it may, we must disregard him, for the moment," I said. "Now, Mr. Soames, what would Gilchrist do with those proofs?"

Soames shrugged, "Loaf about with them? Try to impress girls? Really, he is the *worst* magus. He's flirted with dismissal from this school any number of times. He cares about his cricket and rugby teams a great deal more than the arcane. He's so proud he got his Blue for long jump and hurdles, but it was all I could do to get him to study his part of the ritual. His father and grandfather were foremost in the field—indeed, his father gave me no end of trouble, in my youth—but the great line has ended. Douglas Gilchrist is hopeless."

"Nevertheless, he is our man."

Warlock fixed me with a stern but curious look. "You are sure, Watson?"

"I am," I said. "It all comes down to those little earthen lumps you're holding in your hand, Holmes, and to what they are *really* tokens of."

"Fell intent," said Holmes, as if this should be plain to everybody.

Hilton Soames rolled his eyes at Holmes's amateurish lack of theatricality, then leaned in with the tips of his moustache quivering and hissed, "Misfortune! Calamity!"

Holmes gave a hurt look for having been upstaged so cruelly, but rallied. He crooked his left hand into a claw and declared, "Doom!"

Hilton Soames grasped the corners of his long silk cape in both hands, threw his hands out to either side, so he looked like some sort of goateed humanoid bat and shrieked, "The death of all hopes!"

Warlock drew a breath for his next rebuttal and—as the expression of annoyance on his face gave me to understand it was likely to be an impressive one—I decided I must intercede before anybody started hovering or bending shadows. I stepped between the two men, raised one finger and said, "Long jump, actually."

"Eh?"

"*What?*"

"Good lord! It's plain to see neither of you was ever a sportsman. Have neither of you ever worn track shoes? They've got spikes all over the bottom and, let me tell you, you can bang them together again and again, but you never manage to get all the dirt out of them. Therefore, if you've been flinging yourself into a black clay jumping pit all day, you just can't stop your shoes from leaving those, wherever you lay them."

"Awww! But that's hardly doom-y at all," said Holmes, with a deep sigh. "Are you sure about Gilchrist, Watson?"

"Quite sure. Remember, Soames said none of the students knew he'd printed the entire ritual. Even Bannister didn't know. So—discounting the printer—the thief must have been someone who was capable of seeing the documents through that window and also someone capable of realizing their importance. Yet, let us remember that as we approached Soames's office—an approach that passes the athletics field—only Holmes was tall enough to see the desk. The thief was therefore likely to be someone both athletic and tall. When I saw the first 'token', I knew I'd guessed it right."

"But how?" asked Soames.

"Well, think about it: someone walks past the athletics field, sees a giant roll of parchment on your desk and wants it. He orders Bannister to open your office—"

"Why do you continue to presume that someone else may command Bannister?" Soames demanded.

"We shall come to it," I said, "but first let us see if the rest of the narrative suits. Having gained entrance, the thief moved the writing desk to the window, placed his spiked shoes down on it—leaving the fell token—and began to copy the manuscript, thinking he could spot your return. You took the side door and—if you had not cried out at seeing Bannister's key in the lock—you might have surprised him. Instead, your warning gave him just enough time to snatch his shoes off the desk and run to the bedroom, to hide in your wardrobe, where we found the second clay pyramid. There he remained—trapped—until you left to fetch Holmes and me."

"And you suppose Bannister let him out?" Soames asked.

"I do. It is a tenuous connection, but you mentioned that Bannister was donated by a notable magic family. I don't suppose it was the Gilchrists?"

"Oh! Thornton Gilchrist, I shall destroy you!" Soames howled, shaking one fist at the ceiling.

Holmes rolled his eyes. "That's a 'yes', I should think, Watson."

"He said Bannister was a peace offering," said Soames. "Proof that our years of antagonism were at an end. Of course, at the time I assumed it was nothing more than a bribe to assure I would admit his useless son to this school."

I had to agree. "It could well have been. If Gilchrist Senior could get a still-loyal Bannister and his son into your school, he'd have two spies. It would also explain why Douglas Gilchrist would attempt to copy the binding ritual, even though his own interest in magic is small."

"Would it?" wondered Holmes.

"Of course. Never underestimate the lengths a loaf-about son will go to, making sure his father's money keeps flowing in to allow him to waste his days attending university. Er… but don't ask me how I know."

"Well then… what should we do?" Soames asked.

"Confront Gilchrist, if he is still here. The problem is, we've no idea what he's up to. He could have run, in which case he's got a nearly two-hour start on us. Or he may be planning an ambush."

"He might even be trying the ritual," Holmes noted.

"Do you think he's capable?" I asked.

Soames nodded. "The ritual is remarkably simple. A competent mage could prepare for it in less than an hour. He is not competent, but he's had some time now."

"What do you think, Holmes? Are we in any danger?"

"Hard to say, Watson. I imagine, if he's got low ability, he's not going to be picky about particulars. He's likely to lock onto the most powerful arcane being he can find and just—"

But Holmes did not finish. Instead, he blinked out of existence.

"Oh…" I said. "*Bollocks.*"

Soames recoiled. "Did he just…? Did Holmes just…? You don't think…?"

"Gilchrist summoned him and bound him to his will?" I asked.

"Could he?" Soames wondered.

"I really would be the last of us to know," I told him. "If he has, though, we've got a bit of a problem. Holmes is a most dangerous fellow."

"Bah," laughed Soames.

"I am telling you: I've lived with that man for almost two years and I've no idea what his limits might be. Perhaps he has none."

"I'm sure you exaggerate," said Soames.

"Good. Then you may go first," I replied, cracking open the office door. I wasn't sure what to expect—an attack by Holmes, Bannister, Gilchrist or perhaps only an empty school—but I certainly could never have guessed the scene that would present itself.

Just opposite the door of Soames's office were the ancient stone stairs that led up to the students' quarters. At the top of these stood a flushed youth, with sandy-blonde hair and the easy confidence of the young and handsome. In one fist, he held a candle; in the other, an irregular bundle of papers—his notes on the Fortescue Binding. Just behind his right shoulder stood Bannister, looking sheepish and unhappy. Behind his left stood Warlock Holmes.

Holmes was laughing so hard I thought he might faint.

"He summoned me, Watson! *Me!* I must say, I'm flattered by the attention."

"Silence!" Douglas Gilchrist cried. "I had hoped it might not go this way, Professor. I had hoped you might never know my father had gained your secrets. But now there's nothing else for it. Minion, destroy these men!"

Holmes gave an apologetic shrug. "I'd rather not, you know. I quite like one of them. But if the master commands it… well… what else is there to do?"

Yet, Holmes did think of something else—something as efficacious as it was childish. He placed one foot to the small of Douglas Gilchrist's back and shoved him down the stairs.

I suppose most of us have fallen down a flight of stairs before, but how many have fallen down a set of steep, stone, medieval stairs? After seeing it happen to Gilchrist, I am not eager to ever perform the feat myself. At the top landing, Douglas Gilchrist had been a handsome, energetic man, rife with youthful vigor. By the time he arrived at the bottom, he was another fellow altogether. He had a great cut on one leg and one on his scalp. His face was bruised and puffy. Two of his fingers faced the wrong way and the fight had gone out of him entirely.

"You betrayed the master!" Bannister cried, and flung himself at Holmes.

"I say! Get off! Really, Bannister, this is not a fight you can win, you know."

Yet, the pudgy demon would not relent. He wrapped

both hands around Holmes's neck and tried to throttle him. Even from my limited vantage point, I could see there was no strength in his grip. He gave a horrible, high shriek and his doughy face contorted into a hideous battle-visage.

Holmes looked more pitying than scared. He reached up and gave Bannister a little back-handed slap on the cheek. No sooner had Holmes's skin touched him than Bannister broke into a great cloud of white dust. He spattered all across the opposite wall. Holmes was left coughing and brushing Bannister bits all off the front of his shirt.

"Can't fault his devotion, can you?" Holmes wheezed.

"Holmes? What have you done to him?" I cried.

My friend gave me a quizzical look, as if it were the oddest question he'd ever heard and indicated the white smear on the opposite wall.

"But... is he dead?" I wondered.

"Watson, in our future adventures together, here is a good rule of thumb: whenever you see anybody explode into bits and spatter all over a wall, yes, they are dead."

"But how?" moaned the ill-shaped pile of Douglas Gilchrist. "You were bound to my will!"

"Don't be silly," Holmes chided. "I am not a demon, sir; I am a man. All right, I may be slightly *full of demons*, so I can pardon the mistake, but my will is quite my own. And let me say: even if I were a demon, I'm not sure you'd have caught me that easily. Really, Gilchrist, a little less time on the cricket pitch and a little more with your nose in the books would do you no harm, I think. Poor marks."

Straightening his sleeves and shirt front, Holmes descended the stairs, stepped over the figure of young Gilchrist, then reached down and plucked the wad of papers from his grip.

"I'll just be taking these, shall I?" Holmes said, then turned to me and asked, "All right, Watson?"

"Fine, thank you."

"I say, that was a refreshing little mystery," said Holmes. "Just what was needed to ease us back into the swing of things, eh? You got a fun little puzzle to wrap your brain around, with only three suspects. I got to test my mystic mettle against a self-important teacher, his worst student, and an enfeebled butler demon. They won't always be such larks, you know."

"Oh, I know. Our easiest case so far. By a margin, I'd say."

Holmes nodded. "I suppose the only true threat was this binding ritual. Dangerous business. I'm afraid we really can't let you remember it, Gilchrist. Can we get him on his feet, Watson?"

He was unsteady, but he managed to rise and slump numbly against the wall.

"Any medical attention needed?" Holmes asked.

"Just this, really," I said, then reached down, grabbed his two wayward fingers and yanked them back into place. Gilchrist let out a howl of pain. "Very sorry, but it's for the best, you know."

"Good," said Holmes. "Now, Gilchrist, I want you to look at me and pay attention to my words…"

Holmes placed one finger against Gilchrist's bruised forehead and pushed hard.

"Ow!" the youth complained.

"Cats are all carnivores, but one never ate me," Holmes said.

"What?" said Gilchrist.

"Trees can't be trusted, yet they're the tallest fellows I know."

"What's he doing?" asked Soames.

"I've no idea," I admitted.

"Verbs aren't like herbs, for they grow on the tongue. Up is a lie, but down is just the state of things. You're only feeling down because nobody's feeling you up. Had you ever never not have neglected to think of that?"

I think I was about to take up Gilchrist's cause and ask Holmes if he'd gone completely off his nut, but I never got the chance. Holmes's nonsensical observations gained in speed, blurring together into an uninterrupted curtain of noise until suddenly there was a loud bang. Holmes and Gilchrist were gone. Soames leapt back with a cry, staring at the empty stairwell, then rounded on me and demanded, "What has he done? Where are they?"

I shrugged. "No idea whatsoever."

Then, with a second bang, Holmes was back.

"Well," he said, "that's done."

"Where is Gilchrist?" Soames stammered. "What have you done with him? Is he dead?"

"Don't be silly; I would never. He was an all right fellow, really. Sounds like his father is a bit of a pest, yet young Douglas is nothing but a long-jump enthusiast who found himself in a bit of a bad spot."

"So… what did you…?" Soames said.

"Oh, I merely scrambled his memory up with a bit of good old babblemancy and sent him somewhere out of the way. You said yourself, Soames, he did not belong in a school like this. Well, I am happy to report young Gilchrist has begun anew. He is a promising young police cadet in Rhodesia."

"Where?" asked Soames.

"It is a country in southern Africa."

"No it isn't," I said.

Holmes began to look very troubled. "Well… it was. Twenty years ago."

"Nope."

"Well then, it *will be* within the next twenty years, certainly."

I shrugged. "We have no way of knowing that, Holmes."

"No, we do! Because I tried to step straight across, you see? And I can't possibly have gotten more than two decades off on either side, because my legs aren't that long. So if Rhodesia isn't a place and wasn't a place then it *will be* and that is where you will find Douglas Gilchrist! Oh… though from the sound of things, when we do find him, he may be somewhat younger than he ought… Sorry about that."

Soames—who had grown quite pale during this exchange—gasped, "Impossible!"

"I detest the word," Holmes sniffed.

"Poorly done, Holmes," I said, shaking my head.

"Well, I had to do something, didn't I? Anyway, there's no sense worrying about it now. I say, Watson, it's a fine day. Fancy a walk home?"

"I'd love a breath of air. It's a bit too Bannister-y, in here."

"Quite," Holmes agreed.

"Who knows, you may have time to finish putting together that jigsaw puzzle."

Holmes's face went pale. "Finish... *what*?"

"Your puzzle. You may finally get it put together."

"Oh! Oh, that's so much... *That's* all you do?"

"Holmes! Had you not realized? Yes, you merely fit the pieces together, until they make the picture on the box."

"But that's so *easy*! That's all it takes to release its trove of secrets?"

"What? No! There are no secrets. No trove. It's just a picture of a boy and a goat."

"..."

"..."

"That's a bit of a disappointment," said Holmes. "Nevertheless, I shall have it completed in a day!" He tilted his head to one side and conceded, "Well... two days, at most. There's only one thing left to do. We have Gilchrist's copies, but not the originals. Hilton Soames, I will thank you to hand over the Fortescue's Binding manuscript, if you please."

Soames drew himself up to his full height, stuck out

his chin and said, "You've no right to demand it."

"And yet, I do demand it," Holmes said. "You've seen what I can do, Soames. Do you suppose you have the power to keep it from me?"

Soames bristled for a moment, then turned on his heel and marched into his office. He returned a moment later, holding several sheaves of paper. He brusquely deposited these in Holmes's hand, pouting. "It matters not a whit, really. I gathered the information once, it won't take me long to put it together again."

"I suppose not," said Holmes. He took a moment to spare me a gleeful smile, then turned back to Soames with his eyes twinkling and said, "But I don't suppose anybody's told you: cats are all carnivores, but one never ate me…"

Two minutes later, we stepped out into the welcoming summer breeze.

"You're sure you've taken care of it, Holmes? You're sure Hilton Soames is no threat?"

"Tut, Watson! I gave him a stiffer dose than young Gilchrist got. Hilton Soames has no idea there's even such a thing as magic, now. He's living a cheerful new life in France as an aeroplane mechanic."

"A *what* mechanic?"

"Oh, best not to worry about it," Holmes said. "But do remind me to take good care of our timeline, won't you? If I've stranded those two in a future that doesn't end up happening… well… that would be poor form on my part."

I shrugged. "I'm not sure I can help with such things, Holmes. Indeed, what most concerns me is that people are bound to notice the disappearance of two men and one demon butler."

"Agh! I hadn't thought of that! How shall we explain it, Watson?"

"By happy chance, the disappeared parties are the only men who can place us at St. Luke's, so… might it not be better to simply return home and make no attempt to explain anything to anybody?"

"An excellent solution, Watson," said Holmes, smiling. "Oh! Do you know what I've just realized? Technically, I engaged a demon in single combat today, and slew him with my bare hands."

"Holmes… it would be equally true to say you won a one-shot slappy-fight with an aging butler."

"Yes, but, since it would be *equally* true…"

"Oh, very well! Single combat. Bare hands."

"You are a gentleman, Watson."

"I am a *charity*."

We drew deep drafts of healing summer air and turned our steps, once more, towards Baker Street.

A SCANDAL IN
BOH-GRAH-GRAH-GRAH

AS I STEPPED IN THROUGH THE DOOR OF 221B AND BEGAN the business of setting my coat and hat upon their proper hooks, Holmes greeted me with, "I say! Watson! It is well that you should choose today to drop by."

"Er… I live here."

"Well, whatever the reason for your visit, the hour is a propitious one. I am about to receive royalty." He beamed broadly and waved a single-sheet letter in my direction. The paper was thick, strong, a pleasant shade of light pink, and *clearly* alive. It waved its corners lazily back and forth.

"Royalty?" I asked, stepping forward to examine Holmes's highly suspicious note. "From where?"

"Bohemia, wherever that is."

"It's a small half-German, half-Czech state, ruled by Emperor Franz Joseph. Which means… this letter, Holmes… it's all wrong!"

He recoiled from the accusation that his newfound royal connection might be tinged with any trace of disrepute. Breathlessly, he demanded, "What? How dare you, Watson!"

"This note is false. Why, I would in no way expect it to herald the arrival of a Bohemian king. In fact, I would be little surprised if it heralds the arrival of an assassin."

"Why on earth would you think such a thing?" Holmes asked.

"Because the last line tells you so."

For the sake of the public record, here is the note in its entirety:

Hello.

I am a Germish king from Bohemia, which is a real place. I have come to consult with you on a matter of extreme delicacy. You are the only one who can help me. You are the best person of all the people; we have this report of you received from all a bunch of other people, who are all real. I shall call at a quarter to eight o'clock tonight. Try to be alone and not have too many witnesses about. Do not take it amiss if your visitor wears a mask and tries to kill you.

Warm regards,
Wilhelm Gottsreich Sigismond von Ormstein,
Grand Duke of Cassel–Felstein,
and hereditary king of Bohemia

"I see no problem with this letter, Watson. Or anyway, none which your xenophobia has not invented."

"Holmes, he says he is going to try to kill you. Right here. Last line."

"No. He says he *may* try to kill me. It is by no means assured. And besides, why would he? He needs my help. Unless you choose to arbitrarily believe the end of the letter and not the beginning, you must admit the truth of this."

"Holmes…"

"Or, who knows, it may be a Bohemian social convention we are unaware of."

"I can't think so, Holmes, or else I would have heard before now what a dangerous place Bohemia is. And this language, it's positively atrocious. 'We have this report of you received'? Who speaks that way?"

"The Bohemians. Obviously." He rose and petulantly snatched his precious letter from my hand.

Yet, I could not let myself be dissuaded. I was certain Holmes's safety stood in great jeopardy.

"Holmes, if the content of the letter is not enough to warn you, I urge you to look at the paper itself."

"What of it?"

"It's *alive*. See how it moves and twists?"

"In the finest Germish tradition!" Holmes insisted.

"Oh yes, that's another thing: that is not a word. Have you ever heard any German describe himself as Germish?"

"Ha!" Holmes scoffed. "I make it a point never to listen to a German describe himself at all. It is a tedious process. In fact, I think all your protestations spring from the same source. You are upset that the king should seek my aid and not your own. You are merely jealous, Watson."

"Jealous?" I cried.

"Yes and it does not suit you. It is the ugliest of man's baser emotions."

"Jealous?" I howled again.

Holmes gave the tiniest nod of confirmation. Oh, how I hated that trite, condescending manner he could conjure. How dense he could be! How infuriatingly superior!

"Well at least I, sir, am not about to be murdered by a *fake Bohemian*!"

I stormed into my room and began digging out my service revolver. Peeved as I was, I had no intention of allowing Holmes to be killed. It is well that I hurried, for I could hear the rattle of a fine little brougham coming to a halt beneath my very window. The carriage's occupant had no patience for waiting. He did not ring the bell at the street door, but admitted himself, stomped up the stairs to our landing and knocked upon our chambers' door. Even as I leapt back towards the sitting room, Holmes swung the door wide and said, "Ah, Your Majesty. Do—"

"No! Do not! Do not admit that person. Look at him!"

There was simply no way our guest could have been human. Yes, he shared basically our same form, but his was a race bred for battle. His shoulders were broad and muscular. He hunched towards our sitting room in a ready crouch. His gloved right hand curled around the hilt of a sheathed sword, which he wore at his belt. He did, indeed, have a mask—a black vizard affair which widened at the bottom, into an altogether inhuman shape. Through the mask, his eyes were visible—aquiline things with neither white nor iris; only the liquid blackness of a sea creature's soft, fleshy orbs. He wore a military uniform, strung with altogether too much golden tasselry and braiding.

Holmes, incensed at my behavior, spun from the door to declare, "How rude! His Majesty is—"

"His Majesty is an impostor and an assassin!" I said. "Do not invite him in!"

"You must admit me," our visitor gurgled, in a deep, foreign tone. His voice sounded like two impertinent fish, arguing at the bottom of a bucket of brine.

"Does that sound like a human to you, Holmes?" I asked.

Holmes shrugged. "Well… he *is* German."

"Is he?" I laughed. If England is not the world's preeminent seat of medical science, then that honor must surely go to Germany. Thus, I'd had enough contact with German physicians to pick up a few words of that language.

"*Wäre Ihre Majestät, diese Konversation auf Deutsch fortzusetzen wollen?*" I asked.

Which means: "Would Your Majesty care to continue this conversation in German?"

Our guest tilted his head to one side, as if trying to determine my meaning, then replied, "*Roglrughrusssmrurgle? Serfngir, Grrres?*"

"There you are, Watson," said Holmes, "German."

"Those are not German words, Holmes."

"Well then, it must be Czech."

"But… but…"

"Do you speak Czech, Watson?"

"Well, no… but…"

"German and Czech are the two languages of Bohemia, are they not? Well then, process of elimination dictates that it must be Czech. The rules of deduction, which you love so well, prove it. Now please, Your Majesty, do come in."

Four things happened, almost at once.

First, Von Ormstein ripped the sword from its scabbard and lunged into the room. I gasped at the sight of it. The weapon had the most evil countenance I had ever seen. Its curved blade was composed of a matte black metal and bathed in an angry green flame, so liquid in its composition that little burning drips of it scorched our floor.

Second, Holmes beheld the blade that was, no doubt, meant to end his life and declared, "Hey! That's mine!"

Third, I shot a king. As Von Ormstein lunged through the door, I blasted him right through the hip.

Finally—and I'm ashamed to admit this—I murdered some stationery. Even as Von Ormstein fell, I spun and sent a second shot right into the middle of his letter. I don't know why I did it, except that it was a moment of action and I was scared of the thing. It died with a thin, papery scream, spilling blueish stationery blood all over our table.

Von Ormstein collapsed forward into the room, mewling piteously. As he hit the floor, his ebon mask slid to one side, revealing a row of writhing tentacles where I had rather expected a chin and mouth. To put it bluntly, our guest had an octopus where his head ought to have been. Oh, and also: he had no sense of decorum, whatsoever.

"Ow. Oh. Owwie. Why would you do that to me?" he whined.

Let me just say that, for a big muscly battle-monster, I found his conduct *most* unbattle-monsterly.

The sounds of our skirmish had not gone unnoticed by Mrs. Hudson. How could they? Shouts. Two pistol shots. A 250lb octopus monster falling to the floor and bawling about it. Luckily our landlady confined her comments to her usual, which is to say that she banged three times against her ceiling with the broom handle she kept nearby for that purpose and shouted, "Oi! Noise!"

Holmes stepped to where the burning blade had clattered to rest, scooped it up and regarded it joyously.

"I say, Watson, look!"

"What the devil is it, Holmes?"

"It is me," he said. "Or, a part of me, I suppose. It is my self-blade. The weapon of my innermost soul."

"Well, it looks positively evil."

"Excuse me? What a thing to say, Watson! This is a piece of me. Do you think me evil?"

I did not mean to insult him, but it did look nefarious in the extreme. So unsettling was it that I could think of no response, but to huff, "Well… you called me jealous."

"I suppose I did," Holmes admitted, "and it was small of me. We are even, I think. But ye gads, I'm glad to have this thing back! I've felt a bit incomplete without it, if truth be told."

He gave it a few experimental swings. I have since heard a few unnatural fellows speak of how much they feared Holmes as a swordsman. Nevertheless, there was little of the master fencer in his current actions and much of the excited-schoolboy-with-a-stick. One of his overzealous backswings chopped our armchair nearly in half and I found myself shying back from him.

"But what is it, exactly?" I asked.

"Everything that lives has an aspect of its self which is violent, which has the capacity to do harm. If one learns the true name of that part of oneself, one can conjure it into physical being. You could do it too, if you knew the right word. This is Melfrizoth. And he's happy to meet you. Say hello. '*Hello.*'"

He swung it joyously about his head and sliced off one corner of our bookshelf.

"So… this entire time I've known you, Holmes, a part of you has been missing?"

"In a sense. It still existed, of course. I just didn't have access to the physical manifestation of it. Ah, it's nice to have it back."

"But, how did you lose it?"

"Killed Moriarty with it," he said, raising his eyebrows as if to say, "Yes. I did that. Me. Pretty impressive, eh?"

But a moment later, he demurred and added, "Well… if 'killed' is the right word. Turns out I wound up with his personality stuck in me and my sword stuck through him, while his body plummeted down a mineshaft."

"And you made no attempt to recover it?" I asked.

"Well, Watson, you're assuming I could. You have not considered that I may have been somewhat slashed up and half-unconscious and… you know… not at my best."

I stared at the vile blade, considering what he'd told

me. "What's it made of?" I wondered.

"Oh, I don't know," Holmes shrugged. "This bit is the handle; that is the blade. Most of it's done out of this black stuff. Don't know quite what it is, but let me tell you, Watson, it drinks life and magic in much the same way I do. Oh, and it's got this green fire stuff all over it, which is how you can tell it's mine. See? It's the same as in my eyes."

The blade did indeed share the same otherworldly light as Holmes's eyes displayed when he was angry or about to do something magical and inadvisable.

"But the real question is," said Holmes, pointing the tip of his newly reclaimed blade at our visitor's face, "how did *you* get it?"

"I will not speak of it," Von Ormstein said. "Not while the blade is bare. If you wish to know, sheath it first in this."

He struggled to remove his sword belt, then slid it across the floor to Holmes. Warlock scooped it up, slid his wicked blade inside and said, "Well?"

"Ha!" Von Ormstein cried. "You fool! It is mine again!"

"What do you mean? It is a part of myself and no thing of yours," protested Holmes. As he spoke he gave the handle a jerk, as if to pull his weapon free and display it as proof. Only, he could not. The blade stuck fast, within the strange white scabbard.

"Huh…" said Holmes, then thrust his hand theatrically towards his sword and cried, "Ves, Melfrizoth!"

Nothing happened.

"Why isn't it disappearing, Watson?" he asked me.

"I'm sure I'm not the fellow to ask, Holmes."

But if I could not answer him, our guest could. He struggled to his knees and triumphantly declared, "It is bound! Bound to me, as it has been these many years! Fool! Binding magic is the particular specialty of the Von Ormsteins! Everybody knows it!"

"Hey! What? Give it back!" spluttered Holmes.

"No."

"You'd better!"

"Or what? What would you do?"

Holmes's green eyes lit with angry flame. The cheerily burning log within our hearth suddenly heaved itself on end and issued forth a gout of black and stinking smoke. From this miasmic ball, several tendrils of inky black vapor flowed forth, into our room. In a trice, they converged upon the frightened Von Ormstein, wrapped around him and began to tighten. They yanked his arms and legs flat against his torso then pulled him—bound and struggling—into an upright position, his face a few inches from Holmes's.

"I'm not sure what I'll do," Holmes growled, "but I'll bet you won't like it."

"Wait! Wait! Please!" His Majesty begged. "We can work this through together! Let us be friends!"

I gave a polite little cough and reminded him, "You did come here to kill Holmes, did you not?"

"I didn't want to," the cowardly, invertebrate-faced aristocrat wailed. "I had to! I am in her power, don't you see? I wished to appease her, by removing an enemy. And if that enemy had been Holmes, how could she refuse me? She would give me back the picture—I know she would."

I had no idea which woman he might be speaking of. Or which picture he meant. Or why he was so anxious to recover it. But his tone of desperation was unmistakable. Here was a creature caught in the grip of a terrible dilemma. With a defeated sigh, I realized that he was more than just an assassin. He was a client. Holmes and I traded looks.

"I'll make the tea," I said.

We trussed Von Ormstein's arms and legs with rope and got him settled on the couch. I sat near the imprisoned beast and fed him sips of tea while he told his tale and intermittently complained of his wound. I gave it a cursory examination, of course, but his flesh was stringy and filled with unfamiliar structures.

"Er… yes… let's just leave this for someone else, shall we," I decided.

Still, I thought he was in no immediate danger— in fact, he was barely bleeding. His powers of cellular regeneration were remarkable and the blackish glop that oozed from the wound seemed to be binding the tissues back together, even as I watched.

Regarding his identity, our guest would not budge from the stance that he was Wilhelm Gottsreich Sigismond von Ormstein, Grand Duke of Cassel-Felstein, and hereditary king of Bohemia—a Germish nobleman. As to what type of creature he was, he insisted that he was a Bohemian.

I had my doubts.

"You see, I am about to be married," Von Ormstein told us. "My bride is Clotilde Lothman von Saxe-Meiningen, second daughter of the king of Scandinavia. It is a strictly principled family, you know. If it were to come to light that I had been… improprietous… in my youth, the match would be broken and the balance of European power might suffer for it."

I rolled my eyes at this feeble deception, but listened on.

"But you see, to my shame, I had become entangled, some years ago, with Irene Adler, a well-known—"

"Human?" I volunteered.

"Adventuress," he said. "Holmes knows of her."

Holmes gave a helpless shrug, to indicate that he'd been overestimated again. Yet, the name stuck in my mind as important. It took me a moment to recall the connection. Adler! Last year, Alexander Holder had told me the names of three of Moriarty's trusted lieutenants: Moran, McCloe and Adler!

"Adler?" I said. "Moriarty's accomplice?"

This was enough to jar Holmes's memory too. He gasped and said, "The toymaker?"

I was just about to protest that James Moriarty hardly seemed the sort of fellow who would employ a toymaker, but Von Ormstein nodded and said, "No, no! His granddaughter."

"What? But she was merely a child, twenty or thirty years ago."

"Which would make her a grown woman now, Holmes," I reminded him.

"Oh, she is wonderful. *Wonderful!*" Von Ormstein enthused. "And despite the way she used me, I confess I love her still. Unfortunately, our time together has not left her without certain artifacts. She is in possession of a picture of me that—if it were to come to light—might be just cause for the Von Saxe-Meiningens to cross the match and bar me forever from their house and lands."

"Merely a photograph?" I reflected. "Just how is '*Your Majesty*' implicated in any wrongdoing?"

"It bears an inscription, in my own handwriting…"

"Which you could easily dismiss as forged," I reasoned.

"And my royal seal…"

"Faked."

"Plus, Miss Adler and I are both in the photograph."

"Well, you know, you might have just started with that."

Von Ormstein wrung his face tentacles and sighed, "We've tried stealing it. I've sent men to waylay her. Burgled her homes. Raided her banks. We have had no luck. She has bested us at every turn."

"Bet you I could get it," said Holmes, grinning.

Von Ormstein's face brightened. And by that, I mean that—in the manner of other octopuses—he could change his color to match his surroundings or his mood. He turned a vibrant orange and looked hopefully up at Holmes.

"No!" I said, leaping to my feet. "Holmes, this man has begun his plea by trying to cut you in half and furthered it by stealing a weapon which you claim is a part of your own self. We have no reason to trust him or to help him!"

"Hey! Yeah! That's right!" Holmes remembered.

"The blade!" Von Ormstein cried. "I will happily pay you your weapon, if only you will retrieve the photograph."

"You propose to buy my services by giving me a piece of my *self*?" Holmes roared.

"And money!" Von Ormstein quailed. "Or... I don't know... a shiny ring? I have a shiny ring."

He racked his squishy little mind for a moment and decided, "Information! My family holds undisputed mastery of binding magic, Mr. Holmes. Who else could steal your blade from you and hold it? Who else can tell you about the bonds that hold Moriarty's spirit within you? I can teach you."

Holmes tapped his lips a few times with his slender finger and mused, "Milverton. The soul-binder, Milverton. Did you know him?"

"I knew *of* him," our visitor said.

"Could you tell me how he did it?" Holmes asked. "How he bound and unbound fates—even while he was far away from the subjects of his mischief? Could you tell me that?"

"Yes! Yes! In a few words!"

"Then Your Majesty has engaged my services," said Holmes, with a smile.

"Ah, thank the gods!" Von Ormstein sighed.

"Now, tell me all you know of this Irene Adler," said Holmes. "Where might I find her?"

"She is here, in London; that's why I came. She is

currently residing at Briony Lodge, Serpentine Avenue, St. John's Wood."

"How shall I know her?" asked Holmes.

"I have a photograph of her, here in my breast pocket," Von Ormstein replied, gesturing with his horrid face tentacles.

Holmes nodded at me and I bent forward to retrieve the photo. As I drew it forth, I gave a gasp of dismay. I nearly dropped the thing.

It was her.

Her.

Even in the faded black-and-white facsimile, her piercing green gaze was unmistakable. She'd fooled me before, but this time I knew her in an instant. My murderess. My nemesis.

Irene Adler.

The Woman.

Holmes must have seen my look of incredulity, for he asked, "What is it, Watson?"

By way of answer, I turned the photo towards him. It took him a few moments to recognize her. At first he just squinted at it and then at me as if I were insane. His gaze wandered back and forth a few times, then suddenly his eyes widened. He sprang up and yelled, "Oh, hey! No, no, no! We don't want this one! We don't want this case!"

"Holmes!" I hissed. "Yes we do. This may be our chance, don't you see?"

"The only thing I see, Watson, is the most dangerous girl I've ever encountered. She's beaten my magical defenses. She utterly embarrassed your powers of reason. She melted Eduardo Lucas to brown stink-sauce! Really, we don't want this one."

I turned to Von Ormstein and said, "Pray, give us a moment, won't you? I just need to consult with my partner."

I grabbed Holmes and dragged him down the hallway towards the bathroom. Keeping my voice low, I hissed, "She is in possession of the Moriarty Rune. She's killed two people. She's struck us here at home and now we have her name and a chance to move against her. How could we pass that up?"

"Because she's scary?"

"Holmes, cowardice must not cost us the initiative."

"Initiative? What do you mean? We are not at war with Irene Adler, Watson. She took nothing from us in that burglary that we did not want gone. I'm rather pleased to see the back of Moriarty, let me tell you. And did you love Milverton so well? The spy Lucas? Who cares if she killed them?"

"It's murder, Holmes."

"Well, what if it is? There are plenty of murderers in London, John. What disturbs me is your fascination with this particular one!"

"*Fascination?* What a thing to say, Holmes. Do you pretend we should let her embarrass us and then walk away?"

"Yes. That sounds wonderful. Can we please do that?"

His look of pleading desperation touched my heart.

There was something in Holmes, when he begged, that could make me feel like a doting father. I reached out to touch his shoulder and said, "Holmes, she is the most effective agent we have so far encountered. As yet, we have no idea who she is working for or what her goals might be."

"I don't care!"

"What if she's working for Moriarty, eh? What if she— even now—is planning to put that foul person back into a human body? What if she's going to get him into the prime minister, the queen or the head of the Bank of England? What if she's planning to get him back into *you*? She's too dangerous to leave unchallenged, Holmes."

"But…"

"We must act."

He gave me a pained look. "I just don't like the amount of attention you pay to her, John. I would swear that every time you think of her or speak of her, you get just a little more doomed. I can see it growing on you. That woman is likely to be your destruction."

"Well, if she is, she will not find herself unopposed," I replied.

Holmes sighed and asked, "How should we proceed?"

"With utmost caution. She has laid traps for us before, and I don't trust the ease with which this opportunity has fallen to us. What if she sent Von Ormstein, eh? Or even if she did not, what if he runs off and warns her, in an attempt to ingratiate himself and reclaim his indiscreet photo? We must lay a plan to engage her as carefully as we can."

Holmes nodded. The two of us moved back to the

sitting room, where Holmes told Von Ormstein, "Good news, Your Majesty. Watson and I have decided to take your case. In exchange for the return of Melfrizoth and information on binding magics, we will undertake to reclaim your portrait from Irene Adler."

Von Ormstein's relief was visible. "Excellent. *Excellent.* I shall return to my quarters and await news. I shall be staying at the Langham Hotel, under the name of Count Von Kramm."

"Oh no," said Holmes, the hint of a smile playing at the corners of his lips. "You will be staying in Watson's wardrobe, under the name 'Hey, Squidface'."

As we situated Von Ormstein in my wardrobe, his true nature became clear to us. One might be forgiven for assuming he was a monster. Or an assassin. Or even a nobleman. But no, the chief occupation of our guest was this: he was a whiner.

"…It's dark in here.

"…It's dusty.

"…Am I to be alone?"

As we closed the door on him, I remembered, "Holmes, he's got that carriage waiting. It's been quite some time now."

"Ah. I'd best head down and deal with it, Watson."

"But what will you say? What story will you concoct?"

"Hmmm… None at all, I think."

Holmes gave me a sly wink, went to the doorway, pulled

on his greatcoat and went down to see the driver with naught but slippers on his feet. I could hear the muffled sounds of voices. Then raised voices. Then a sudden, shuddering boom echoed through the neighborhood, followed by the screaming of horses, the screaming of the driver, and the clatter of hooves. A few moments later, Holmes came back in and said, "Done."

The matter thus resolved, I settled in to slumber.

Only, I couldn't.

For I knew on the morrow, I would see *her*. Would I surprise her? Had Von Ormstein been sent as a lure? Had she missed me at all? How should I make my approach? A thousand half-considered plans intruded themselves on my repose, damning my hopes of slumber.

And they weren't the only things. Holmes elected to noisily pace the hallway, betwixt the bathroom and sitting room, mumbling to himself.

Von Ormstein kept asking, "…Are you out there?

"…Hello?

"…Is anybody there?

"…Hello?"

"Yes! *God!* I'm here! What do you want?"

"…I need a pillow."

Rising from my bed, I snatched one of the pillows up, threw open my wardrobe door and declared, "You're lucky I have two!" I flung the pillow on Von Ormstein's lap and stormed back to bed.

"…Wait… um… are you still there?

"…Hello?

"…Anybody?"

"*What?*" I howled.

"…Well, I'm still tied up so I can't get it under my head."

Even when I had helped Von Ormstein to get more comfortable, I still could not sleep. Holmes hovered in my doorway, staring intently at my face, as if trying to read some great secret writ upon it.

"What do you want, Holmes?"

"Nothing, nothing. Disregard me."

"Well, that's a bit difficult. I am not accustomed to being leered at as a part of my bedtime routine."

"Nevertheless, disregard me."

And then, faintly, from my wardrobe, "…I need a blanket."

I have no idea how long it took me to fall asleep. Holmes made an attempt to obfuscate his sudden fascination with me, ducking behind the doorway and only looking in every minute or so, to see if I was sleeping. Eventually, he retreated to his room, but stood in the darkness behind his open doorway, staring across the hall at my bed.

Oh, and Von Ormstein needed at least nine glasses of water.

Nevertheless, I must have eventually drifted off. I know, because I was wakened in the pre-dawn hours by a sudden cry of triumph from Holmes. I jerked to wakefulness, to find him sitting beside me. He'd pulled up a chair and apparently spent some hours leaning in over me, staring at my face as I slept.

"Watson, try 'Ossifer'," Holmes suggested, eagerly.

"What? Eh?"

"Say, 'Ossifer'."

"Ossifer?"

No sooner had the word left my mouth than a terrible pain wracked my right arm deep, ragged and hot. I could perfectly feel the shape of the long bones of my forearm, outlined in pain. I cried out and sat up, thrashing the bedclothes away from my wounded limb to see what was amiss. Yet, by the time I had a clear view of the situation, the pain had gone. There in my hand was a three-inch-long irregular-shaped white rod, sharp at one end.

"Bravo, Watson! Bravo!" Holmes cried, clapping his hands.

"What has happened? What is this?" I stammered.

"Your soul blade, Watson! I told you it would come, if only you knew its name. I have helped you find it!"

"Soul blade?"

"Yes. Your inner weapon. All the anger and danger and murder that is in you, given shape."

"But… it's barely a toothpick!"

"I suppose it's because you are not a very murderous fellow." Holmes shrugged. "Congratulations on your gentility of character."

"But why did it hurt so much to call it?"

"I don't know. That is odd," said Holmes. He reached down and pulled the little thing from the palm of my hand. He turned it this way and that, examining it. In a moment, he gave a gasp and said, "Watson! This is *bone*!"

"Wait… *My* bone? Did… Did I just strip some bone out of my arm?"

"Very impressive. I don't know if you realize it, but there is nothing in this world so magically reactive as rigid biological materials."

I had, on a few occasions, seen the facility—the practically joyful abandon—of wood when exposed to magical force. I'd seen it twist and shriek and liquefy at the merest gesture from Holmes. I had less experience with the effect of magic on bone, always excepting the agonizing moment when Hugo Baskerville had attempted to bend all of mine into exciting new shapes. Still, this equation made a certain level of sense—at least as far as Holmes's bizarre world went. After all, what is wood but plant-bone?

Holmes deposited the little thing back in my palm and said, "This could be a formidable weapon, one day. I wonder how large it might grow."

"Not too large, I hope, or there shall be no bone left in my arm. I don't want it. How do I get rid of it?"

"You simply tell it to go," said Holmes. "Use the word for 'go away'. Say, 'Ves, Ossifer.'"

"'Ves'? What language is that?"

"The universal one, Watson. The purest. Trust me, you could sit in that bed making random noises all night long, but you would never find a better sound for 'go away' than 'ves'."

Experimentally, I uttered, "Ves, Ossifer."

Immediately, the burning pain returned to my arm and

hand. It lasted only a moment and, as it subsided, I saw the tiny weapon had gone.

"Well done again," cried Holmes. "Now, if you ever wish for it, you know how to get it. Nurture it well, for it may grow to be deadly indeed."

"How would I nurture a blade made of hatred and bone?" I wondered.

Holmes shrugged. "Hate things? Drink milk?"

I sat quietly, considering. If the whole experience had not been so painful, I would have thought it only a dream. What did it mean that a thoroughly unmagical fellow like myself could summon such a thing? In short, how much of magic was perfectly natural, but not understood? Where was the boundary of what was—or should be—normal? The silence of my contemplation was interrupted only by:

"…Um…

"…Hello?

"…Can I have the other pillow, too?"

One of the dangers of adventuring in a realm of magic and monsters is that you tend to sleep late. By the time I awoke, Holmes had already completed a morning's worth of misguided work. I stepped out my bedroom door only to find him coming out of his own, across from me. To my horror, he wore his garish "disguise" jacket, his ridiculous uneven-legged trousers and had once again knocked out three of his teeth. He sported a foot-and-a-half-wide false moustache.

"Holmes… Oh, no…"

"Watson! I have a plan!"

"A terrible, *terrible* plan."

"Disguised as a common Irish working man—"

"You aren't."

"—I shall infiltrate the household of Irene Adler—"

"You won't."

"—and recover His Majesty's photograph. Who knows, I shall perhaps even learn the fate of the Moriarty Rune."

"This plan is doomed to failure, Holmes! Please, think for a moment. Do you remember how poorly this worked last time? And that was only against Milverton. Granted, he knew you better than Adler does, but let me remind you that our current foe is a master of disguise."

"As am I, Watson. As. Am. I."

"No, Holmes, you are not. I'm sorry, my friend, but you are simply nowhere near her level."

He bristled at the insult, yet controlled himself and harrumphed, "If so, that only proves my point. A master of disguise would be on the lookout for excellent disguises, but perhaps a more casual effort might slip below her notice."

I squeezed the bridge of my nose, intent on stopping off the frustration-nosebleed I knew must be coming. "By that argument, Holmes, if I wished to defeat the fastest racehorse in London, what I'd need would be a really slow horse?"

"I don't know. Possibly. I'll tell you what, Watson, why don't you attempt it and tell me how it goes? I myself have other plans for the day."

"Holmes, no! I forbid it!"

"Ha! *Escape gas!*"

He thrust his hand down towards the floor—just as he had that fateful day he'd tried to infiltrate Milverton's—and the air gave a sudden boom and filled with black and purple smoke. Yet, that had been a year and a half ago. Not only did I have a better familiarity with my friend's habits, but also the floor plan of 221B. Thus, by the time he reached the door to begin his ill-advised infiltration attempt, he found me blocking it.

"I *said* I forbid it!"

"Hmph. Well played, Watson. You have thought of everything, it seems. Oh, except perhaps: *Watson-take-a-nap gas!*"

This time, I didn't even hear the boom. I awoke some time later to the sound of someone kicking the inside of my wardrobe door.

"…Um…

"…Hello?

"…I'm hungry! Does anybody have some fish?"

Holmes was so late in returning that I had ample time to go to the market, buy a bucket of fish, return and unceremoniously dump them all over Wilhelm Gottsreich Sigismond von Ormstein, Grand Duke of Cassel-Felstein, and hereditary king of Bohemia (fake). His only complaint was that someone had already eaten the good bits. By this, he meant that they had been cleaned and gutted. He also wanted an impressive quantity of water. Yet, once this was delivered, his complaints started afresh. He didn't like our water. It was yucky and unregal—not fit for the distinguished palate of a king. On a hunch, I took the fish bucket, filled it with water, dumped in all the salt we had to hand and delivered it to His Majesty. He gulped it down joyously. I offered to partially untie him and escort him to the lavatory, but he said this was unnecessary, as he excreted all unneeded materials through his skin—in the manner of all Germans. Indeed, this seemed to be the case. My wardrobe was beginning to smell like some sort of seafood processing plant.

As Holmes had yet to return, I spent the afternoon seeing to the long-term needs of our royal guest. I bought a huge bag of salt to make more "drinking water", then went back to the docks and purchased His Majesty's next meal. The foreman seemed surprised that a well-dressed gentleman such as myself was in the market for two buckets of fish offal, but his price was quite reasonable.

Von Ormstein was so pleased by the increased level of service that he seemed to lose all desire to ever leave my wardrobe. And why would he? He had all the lavatory facilities he required, one human pawn bringing him cuisine fit for a king, a second one out addressing the problems he'd made for himself in his youth and—to top it all off—he'd got *both* pillows. His Majesty's joy loosened his tongue somewhat and I began to learn more about his unique heritage.

As it turned out, I owed him an apology. Wilhelm

Gottsreich Sigismond von Ormstein actually *did* have some claim to Bohemia. Not that he'd ever been there. He'd spent most of his days in a submerged castle named Boh-grah-grah-grah, seven miles off the western coast of Jutland. It seems, at the height of the Hapsburg family's hey-let's-marry-into-every-royal-house-of-Europe-and-then-only-agree-to-wed-other-royals-who-are-at-least-half-Hapsburg-until-we-are-hideously-inbred-and-in-charge-of-everything phase, the heads of Hapsburg had run out of royal houses in which to insinuate themselves. At least, they'd run out of royal houses *on land*. Yet, in a distinct upturn in land–sea diplomacy, they had encountered a grotesque race of underwater monster-men.

A few marriages were arranged between the mer-folk and some of the more creatively inbred monster children who lurked in the darker corners of every Hapsburg castle. What a relief it must have been, eh? How much easier it must have become for every Hapsburg mother and father to tie weights to the ankles of their little one and chuck them over the side of a boat, if there was a chance that this was an act of matrimony, rather than simple infanticide. Traditionally, it seems, these weights were made of gold and referred to as "dowry".

At last, after the full history of European royalty had been made clear to me, Holmes stumbled in through our front door.

"Dare I ask?" I dared to ask.

"Ah, yes! An unqualified success!" Holmes declared.

"By which you mean you have brought Adler to

justice, reclaimed His Majesty's photo and recovered the Moriarty Rune?"

"Ah... *no*."

"Well at least tell me you didn't wind up accidentally engaged this time."

"Ha! I am not engaged and—more to the point—neither is Irene Adler!"

"Er... how is that 'to the point'?"

"Because she was when I encountered her this afternoon."

"*What?*" Strange the wave of jealousy that swept through me when I heard it.

"Hmmm. Yes. To some American named Godfrey Norton," said Holmes. "A lawyer, from what I understand, and very popular with the ladies in that I'm-young-rich-and-handsome-and-we-both-know-I'll-have-your-clothes-off-you-in-less-than-an-hour sort of way."

"But you say she is no longer engaged? You spent the day crossing her match?"

"I would never! She may be an enemy of mine, but who am I to meddle in *affaires de cœur*?"

"So then, you..."

"Served as witness at her wedding."

I reeled back and collapsed into one of our chairs. "How did this...? What possible chain of events...?"

"Oh, it's all very simple, Watson," said Holmes, flinging himself into the opposite chair. "I went round to Serpentine Avenue and asked which house was Briony Lodge. Once I knew, I mucked about the neighborhood, until I found a place workmen might… you know… *work*. I fell in with a handful of local grooms and began trading manual labor for stories and gossip."

"A grand improvement on your previous attempt, actually," I admitted. "Allow me to congratulate you, Holmes."

"Thank you, Watson. The local workmen were happy to speak of Miss Adler. Ha! It might have been hard to get them to speak of anything else—she has quite turned the heads of all the men thereabouts. Apparently, she is a famous adventuress—whatever that means."

"It means she seduces men in order to get what she wants from them."

"Well that would explain it," said Holmes. "Amongst the grooms there seemed to be an abject fascination with her, combined with an abiding sadness none of them had anything she wants. To top her list of distinctions, she is a vaunted contralto. She trained at the Imperial Opera of Warsaw and seems to be equally at home singing *Tancredi* at La Scala or bawdy little numbers at London music halls. Wherever she goes, she is universally admired."

"I can well believe it," I said, "and yet we know her true nature is much different."

"Hmm," said Holmes, gravely. "A worthy adversary is one thing. One who can routinely best you and still have enough spare time to pursue a career in the top tier of European opera… well…"

I wilted slightly. "That is daunting."

"Ye gods, she's wonderful, Watson! I'm *so* afraid of her!"

"But this is good news! She has a public persona. She shan't be able to hide from us again. But, back to the story, Holmes."

"Indeed. I had fooled the local grooms entirely—"

"Oh, had you now?"

"Yes. All of them. Entirely. Well… there was this one fellow…"

"Ah."

"And he kept wondering why I always steered the conversation back to Miss Adler. And why, if I was an Irish working man, I sounded more Scottish, or at times, Italian. And then, when my moustache fell off, he pointed it out to everybody."

"How rude."

"I thought so. Of course, nobody else cared. By then we were all smoking pipes and laughing and drinking cups of half and half—which is something grooms do, apparently—and nobody was doing much work and a grand time was had by all. We all shouted at the man that if he didn't want to join in, perhaps he'd better go see to a horse, or something. So he left."

"To report you to Miss Adler, do you think?"

"Now that you mention it, that would make a certain degree of sense…"

"Of course it would."

"…for in half an hour or so, he came back. And he said, 'Oi, anybody who's been wasting our entire day because he's here to spy on Miss Adler might want to know: she's escapin' right now, on a secret errand of great import!'

"Well, sure enough, as I peeped from the stable door, I saw Miss Adler not twenty yards from me, wearing a wedding dress and hailing a cab. She climbed in and I despaired that I had no way of following her for I had no cab of my own ready and no idea of her destination. Fortunately for me, she told her driver in a loud, clear voice, 'Church of St. Monica on the Edgware Road, please.'"

"Rather a suspiciously good turn of fortune that a woman on a secret errand announces it loud enough for half the street to hear, don't you think?" I asked.

But he waved away my concerns and said, "Well, I've always been lucky, you know. When the next cab came along, I jumped in to follow her. The only thing I didn't have was a convincing method of infiltrating the church once we got there. I decided that—posing as a common Irish working priest—I would offer my services. 'Allo, allo!' I would say. 'I talk with God all the time and I know all about him and what he wants. You chaps are doing it all wrong. So come on and hire me and I'll fix your church up right.'"

I think my mouth was actually hanging open. "But you clearly didn't carry the plan out because nobody wound up burning you at the stake."

"Well, I was in trouble you see, because I thought they'd probably ask *which* god. And for the life of me, I couldn't remember its name. Luckily, I didn't need to, because who should be waiting for me as my cab pulled up?"

"Irene Adler."

"*Irene Adler!* And she said thank God I'd come, because she was getting married and needed at least one witness, or the wedding was not legal."

"Not quite true," I noted. "In fact, two witnesses are required."

"What? No. She said only one!"

"A fact which throws even more doubt over this already very shady situation, I would think."

Holmes threw his hands to his hips and pouted. "Well, it's your word against hers, I suppose. But she seemed quite convinced. Now, do you want me to finish my story or not?"

"I do."

"Miss Adler asked me if I knew anything about marriage ceremonies and the laws surrounding them. And I said no. And she said that was all right—in fact, that was probably for the best—and all I needed to do was follow along and promise whatever the priest asked me to promise. And that it would be really helpful to her if I did, and didn't I want to help her? And do you know what, Watson, I rather *did*, because she was so very nice to me. So, in no time whatsoever, I found myself witnessing the exchange of trinkets."

"Er… rings, you mean?"

"No, no. She had this little silver pendant of a heart, on a chain. Well, that's not quite right. You know that shape that looks nothing like a heart but we all agree to call it that, even though it looks more like someone's bottom? It looked like that. But on the back, it wasn't silver, it was black iron and looked like a proper heart, with all the gristly little tubes coming out of it and everything."

"Interesting," I said.

"Yes and just *incredibly* magical. Gads, I could feel magic just dripping off the thing. And the groom had one, too. Nothing like as pleasant, though. His was this little device with a bunch of screws and spikes on it that pretty much screamed, 'Hey, put your finger in here and let me tighten this and twist that and in no time at all I'll have ruined your life and you'll do exactly as I say.'"

"So instead of a ring, Godfrey Norton was presenting his new wife with an instrument of torture?"

"Yes. The Cruciator: that's what they called it. And the priest seemed very impressed that two of the nine somethings-or-other were being brought together. And now, neither bride nor groom could claim the right to be the owner of their own trinket, but they would be held in common—the Heart and the Cruciator—the perfect union of love and pain. And I was supposed to promise to use all of my magical force to make such a transference of ownership true—that so long as bride and groom should live, neither one would have more sway over the trinkets than the other, but would hold them in equal measure and that such bonds would be in effect from the moment of the wedding kiss."

"A promise you refused, I certainly hope!"

"Well, I did feel some reluctance," Holmes agreed. "I raised my finger and coughed a bit, until the priest called on me. And I asked if the standard English marriage ritual had quite so much talk of contractual magic in it."

"It doesn't!"

"Ah, but you are a doctor, Watson, not a priest. And he assured me that it did. And everybody was waving so much magic about, I began to think that maybe weddings are a time when one need not be so shy about magic— just as they are a time when even the bride and groom's stodgy old grandparents are not too shy about anybody's plans to make babies. It seemed strange that I'd never heard anything about it before. Then again, I don't go to many weddings. And everybody was looking at me as if I was a perfect monster if I refused to help Miss Adler on her special day. So I promised to do that, and a number of other things."

"Such as?"

"Well, I can't remember them all, but… Oh, I recall that if ever anybody tries to take ownership of the tokens of their marriage, I am to strike them down with all the forces at my command."

"Holmes!"

"What?"

"What if I should ever find it necessary to try to divest Mrs. Irene Norton, née Adler, of her dangerous magical artifact?"

"Well then, I would have to… oh… *oh*. Please don't ever decide that, Watson, or I would have to…"

"Murder me?"

"Oh, just murder and murder and *murder* you. I doubt we'd even have ashes left."

"Right. So, you made a number of damning—and I can only assume, binding—magical promises. Then what?"

"Then they kissed and the priest said they were married and they let me know that now was the time of the ceremony where the witness was supposed to leave and if I didn't it would look very suspicious. So I thanked them for the warning and went."

"And then?"

"I came right back here to report my success."

"Success? Holmes! You have been outmaneuvered terribly! How can you not realize it? So it seems we cannot attempt to take the wedding trinkets from the happy couple, but what of the Moriarty Rune? What of Von Ormstein's photograph? Did you make any promises regarding those?"

"Erm… no, I can't say they came up."

"Then there is still some ray of hope. We must find a way to reclaim them."

"Are you sure, Watson? Sometimes the wisest thing a man can do is acknowledge when he's bested."

A self-piteous voice from my wardrobe mentioned, "I always know when I'm bested."

"Shut up!"

"Oh! I am your guest, sir, and the dignity of my station requires—"

"Shut up, *Your Majesty*!"

"Well… all right."

"The concern is academic, in any case," said Holmes. "It seems the newlyweds are bound for America."

391

"What?"

"Yes, they were off to gather their things, then meet for the overnight train to Liverpool, traveling first class, then on to the SS *Britannic*, for New York."

"Did she tell you this?" I demanded. "If she did, we cannot trust it."

"She did," Holmes reflected. "But I'd also heard earlier from the groom who was to drive her to the station. They were all rather sorry she'd be going."

"Damn! Damn, damn, *damn*!"

"We're likely out of time already. Best to let them go, eh? But look on the bright side: there are so many dangerous artifacts and enemies leaving the country, we ought to throw a party!"

My mind reeled. St. John's Wood was only a mile and a half away. I could easily get there, but what would I do when I arrived? My adversary's true abilities were unknown to me. The lie of the land, unfamiliar. No time to plan. No time to prepare. And, yet, no time to spare. My thoughts rebounded from idea to idea, but nowhere saw much hope.

"Probably best to just give up," Holmes suggested.

"No! I shall never surrender!" I howled and, in that moment, committed myself—body and soul—to the best strategy my two moments' reflection had provided. "Get me Wiggles, two pints of red paint, two medical stretchers, a plumber's smoke rocket and a sliced ham!"

* * *

I've always liked ham. Savory. Hardy. Reasonably priced. Really, just a solid all-round meat choice. Nevertheless, it has its time and place. My current position—face down in a paint-smeared pile of it in the middle of Serpentine Avenue—was not the ideal situation for optimal ham-enjoyment.

My plan had only three elements: the ham-lie, the smoke-lie and the twist. As I lay with the stink of paint mingling with the salty pong of pork, I began to reflect dolefully on the structure of my strategy. The ham-lie and smoke-lie were all but transparent. Only the twist had any real chance of bringing me victory. And yet, defeat could come at any step. Had I inadvertently stacked the deck against myself, before I even began? If only I'd had more time to plan… But no, that time was gone. Now was the moment for action. Time to stand by my gun.

Well, no… time to lie in my ham, I suppose. From beside me a muffled voice complained, "Ugh. It's even worse with paint."

"Hush, Holmes. Wiggles is on the move!"

And so he was. Though I dared not look up, I could hear his footsteps as he charged up the steps of Briony Lodge and began pounding on the door, shouting, "Halp! Halp! Oh, it's 'orrible!"

A moment later I heard the door click open and a voice wonder, "Oh, dear! What has happened?"

I think my blood nearly froze in my veins. I'd expected a butler or servant. But no. There was no mistaking it: it was *her*.

"A terrible accident, marm!" Wiggles piped up. "Just 'orrible! Two men struck down in the street by a runaway carriage! Took their faces off, it did!"

"Their faces, you say?"

"Yep. Both faces, right off. So there's no point tryin' to identify 'em that way."

"Oh I wouldn't dream of it," the Woman assured him. "Now, what must be done, unfamiliar street urchin?"

"Well, we can't just leave 'em lyin' in the street, can we? Maybe we'd better carry 'em in?"

"Just you and I? How would we manage it?"

"Oh, I've got 'em on stretchers already," said Wiggles, brightly. "And there's a few of the local grooms standin' round to help."

"How resourceful of you," the murderess remarked. "Wherever did you find the stretchers?"

"Er… over by that house, I guess."

"*Very* lucky. Bring them in, lads! Just into the sitting room, I should think. You may place them on the couches."

"Right you are, marm," said one of the grooms. A moment later, my stretcher was hoisted up and I felt myself being carried up the steps to Briony Lodge. Stage one: the ham-lie was complete and successful. Well… sort of. In that we had gained admittance to the house, it had fulfilled its only function. Perhaps if I'd had more time I would have dreamed up a way to gain entrance *undetected*. There was a bump as I was placed down upon a couch.

"There, what should we do now?" Irene asked Wiggles, as the grooms filed out.

"Well... wouldn't you like to leave them unattended and go find 'elp?"

"Oh, I don't think I'll require any help to deal with these two. But how about you? Do you have more to do, in the plan?"

I could hear Wiggles shift his feet uncomfortably. "I'm not supposed to say, marm."

"No, of course not. Well, I won't pry. Off you pop and perhaps we'll meet again soon."

I heard Wiggles shuffle out, but try as I might, I could not hear Irene's tread upon the carpet. What was she doing?

There was a sudden shift in the couch as she sat down beside me, her hip pressed against my own. With a playful little snort, she began toying with the shreds of ham that made up my damaged "face". She wiggled one right into my ear, but I held my ground and did not cry out. Finally, she selected a little scrap and pulled it free. I could feel gentle pressure on my shoulder as she wiped one side and then the other clean, against the fabric of my jacket. Then came the sound of dainty chewing.

"Mmm, you have a delicious face, Dr. Watson."

So, it was to be a direct confrontation, eh? I sprang up to a sitting position and glared at her.

"Oh, look! It's grown back!" she said. "A pity that moustache regenerated as well."

From the other couch came a muffled laugh.

"And hello again, Mr. Holmes. I didn't expect to see you so soon. I rather thought you might warn your friend off, as well."

"You have a delicious face, Dr. Watson."

"I tried to, Miss Adler. I did try," said Holmes, sitting up and shaking slices of painty ham from his brow.

"It's Mrs. Norton, now," I said, glumly.

"No, no. Miss Adler will do. I haven't had time to put on proper blacks, but due to the brevity of my wedlock, I intend to revert to my maiden name."

Holmes and I were both aghast. "You killed him *already*?"

She gave me an arch look. "He had quite the same in mind for me, I assure you. As a contract lawyer, it could not have escaped his notice that the legal ownership of both tokens must revert to the surviving spouse, in the event of the other's death. Nor could he have failed to recognize that—with control of our artifacts dually held—I could not call upon my token's powers to protect myself from him. He must have thought me quite helpless. Poor little fool… His mistake was in thinking there would be no opportunity for foul play before we reached the train. Did you know he'd rented out an entire car for us? I'm sure by this time tomorrow I'd be spread out all over it in chunks, if he'd had his way."

"So, if I were to examine the vestry in the Church of St. Monica…" I began.

"You might want to make sure you didn't trip over anything," Miss Adler confirmed.

Holmes was scandalized. "He was your husband!"

"Briefly. But he was so much more, you know. He was an alluring little lothario who'd devoted his life to the study of torture—of getting women to do what he wanted, through the application of pain. Do you suppose for a moment I'd allow myself to fall into his power? Please. I'd never let him near me."

"Yet another murder," I growled.

She shrugged. "I believe this is only the second that you know of, for certain. Neither man shall cost the world much by their absence. And from what I hear of you, Dr. Watson, you've racked up about the same score yourself. Oh, and that one? Over there?" Here she paused to indicate Holmes. "Oh tut, sir, tut! A little discretion, don't you think? If not, I fear we'll reach the triple–digits in no time."

Holmes stared guiltily down and fiddled with a bit of ham.

"Besides," she said, "Godfrey was no innocent lamb, but a willing player in our game. He knew the stakes."

I grunted out a little laugh. "However did you get him to take the risk, I wonder?"

"Well…" Her hand went to the silver heart pendant that hung around her neck. "Love makes us all do foolish things. But I'm allowing myself to wander from the topic. Here you are, successfully infiltrated. I'm assuming there's more to your plan, no?"

"Er… well… yes?" Holmes admitted.

"What comes next?" Irene asked, leaning forward with kindly interest.

"Watson thought we'd be brought in by a butler," said Holmes.

"I'm about to vacate the premises. I'm afraid the

staff have all been dismissed. But why was the butler important?"

"When he went to get you, we hoped I'd have time to make my way into your house unobserved," Holmes admitted.

Irene was scandalized. "You certainly wouldn't have had time to accomplish much!" She turned a harsh glance on me and said, "I'll confess I'm rather disappointed. Imagine my curiosity when your little urchin knocked. It's not every day a girl gets the chance to match herself against one of the foremost minds in criminal investigation."

"Thank you, madam," said Holmes.

Adler shot him a look of annoyance and pity.

"Purely out of curiosity, why don't we continue?" she suggested. "Let's pretend you've fooled me entirely. Mr. Holmes, feel free to sneak out and rifle my home. Oh, and do let me know if there's anything you can't find."

With a sheepish glance, Holmes rose and shuffled through the sitting-room door. And there I was. With her. Alone.

Not feeling great about the situation, if I'm honest.

"I trust there's more to come," she said. Her green eyes twinkled with strange merriment—almost as if she were glad of my company. Then again, it was also the sort of look a tiger might give a calf. (*"So glad you've come over—I'm rather hungry and I didn't want to go to the bother of chasing any worthwhile prey, so..."*)

And of course, there was more to come. I'd made only one of my moves. The smoke-lie and twist still remained.

I knew the second move to be the weakest, the third my only hope.

All this time I had been surveying my surroundings: a lovely little sitting room, done all in white. White curtains flanked white-framed windows set in white walls. The white couches were impeccable (not withstanding a few smears of ham paint). The only item of color in the room was a portrait of Irene, depicted mid-recital, that hung above the mantel. The quality was staggering. If he'd still been alive, I'd have said she'd got Rembrandt to do it. And yet, despite the magnificence of it, it was hard to focus my attention on the portrait. Not when its subject sat so very close to me.

My opponent: she sat just two feet from me on the other side of the couch, dressed in a light, airy sundress as white as the curtains. Her real hair—for this was the first time I'd seen it—was dark, the color of good chocolate. It was cut shorter than most women's, but why not? When one reflected on how often it must be concealed beneath a wig, did this not make sense? One piece of good news: there was no way she'd secreted a weapon on her person. That dress would not have concealed it. Yet, did she need one? The look in her eye was utterly confident.

By God, she looked incredible. That strong jaw, that soft skin, the slope of her neck… Despite Holmes's repeated warnings, I had not allowed myself to realize just how fascinated I'd become with her. Now, with her sitting so close, I began to realize how much I'd yearned for this moment. Even that slightest look of amusement—the *hint* she was glad I was with her—was enough to fill me with exhilaration. Those green eyes of hers were locked right on mine, which was exactly what I'd always wanted. I had to remind myself—forcibly—the context of the moment. She was my enemy. The stakes of our game were high—perhaps our lives. I decided to feign strength.

"I'm not sure I need any more," I said, with a shrug. "You say the servants are gone. And I have heard no sound of another person in this house, so far. It would seem you are alone with Holmes and me."

"Only you, at the moment," she said, then laid one hand to her chest in faux-shock and added, "Oh dear! Did you just threaten me? Are you *armed*?"

"Why wouldn't I be?"

"Basic propriety? Good manners? Consideration? Really, Doctor, I've stared down that pistol of yours before. Did I seem much affrighted?"

"Would I even need it?" I countered. "You are easily within my reach."

Strange, the way she rose to that challenge. How the twinkle in her eyes redoubled in fierceness as well as joy. She laughed out loud. "Are you going to lay hands on me, John? Ha! In such a moment, I fancy you wouldn't even know *what* you were trying to accomplish. I, on the other hand... oh, I'd know just what to do, don't you think? Here, shall we even the odds a bit? Here..."

She closed her eyes. She stretched up her chin and craned that perfect neck. I don't know if I was thinking more like a doctor or like a predator, but there were the jugulars and the carotids, utterly undefended. Her mortality and my victory were placed—no, *flaunted*—just before me, in easy reach. She hovered still for a moment, then leaned in towards me until her cheek was almost against my own. "Here…" she said again and I could feel her breath against my ear. Her perfume was intoxicating. I froze.

And the moment was gone. She leaned back, opened her eyes and regarded me with playful curiosity. "Well," she said, "I don't know if it was discretion or cowardice that stayed your hand. But in either case, you have acquitted yourself as a gentleman. You always do, you know. Are there any other weapons I should fear?"

"There's Holmes."

"Ah, the *real* weapon," she agreed. "But whose? Certainly not his own. Would he come to your aid, if you asked it?"

"Why wouldn't he?"

"Why, indeed? He does love you, John. Do you know that? I've watched you for quite some time. And Holmes, longer. Did you know I grew up in Moriarty's empire? As a child, I watched that man take us apart, piece by piece, until at last he took our master. I *admired* him for it. But, for all his strength, Warlock Holmes has his weaknesses, too. Did he tell you about his day? Did he tell you all the promises he made me? If you and I were to come to blows, Holmes would certainly rush in here and destroy one of us. If it seems I've been overplaying a losing hand, it is perhaps because *I* know *who*."

Damn.

My position was crumbling. What did I have left? I grasped at a straw. "Nevertheless, madam, you have led me closer to my goal. Your willingness to let Holmes search the rest of the house indicates either that the items I want have been moved already, or that they are hidden within this very room!"

"Oh? And what is it you want, Dr. Watson?"

"The Moriarty Rune and Von Ormstein's portrait."

Without warning, her façade cracked. For the first time, I got a glimpse of the real Irene Adler—not the face she was presenting, not the game she was playing—her true heart. She leapt up off the couch, clapped her hands and cried, "Yes! *Yes!* I knew it was that squiddy little blighter that put you on to me! I knew it! Oh, I've been so smart! Wait until you see! Oh, Irene, you clever, clever girl!"

I was stunned. This sudden outpouring of joy took me completely by surprise. "Wait until I see what?" I asked.

"Patience, John. It won't be long. Gods, but it's masterly, though! Oh, if only I could see your face…"

As I stared up at her, wonderstruck, it occurred to me that I had no idea what she wanted. I knew why I was here. But why had she agreed to play this little game with me? Why had she let the ham-lie fool her? Rather than attempt a stratagem, I simply asked her.

"Miss Adler, what is it you want?"

"Well, to start with, I want you to call me Irene. And I shall call you John."

"Yes," I complained. "I noticed you keep doing that, as if we were—"

"As if we were what? Familiar?" she chided. "It is now within the scope of your knowledge, John, that I have been *married* to someone I wasn't as familiar with as you. And why do you suppose I invited you in here, if not to know each other better? We ought to be friends, you and I."

"Friends!" I howled. "*Friends?*"

"Why not?"

"Because you lie and seduce and cheat and steal!"

She harrumphed. "If you knew how badly the deck was stacked against me from the moment of my birth, I think you could not begrudge me the cards I play."

"And you just keep *murdering* people!"

"You've killed demons, haven't you? Monsters? Well, the men I've slain are no better! How dare you take that tone with me? If you were anything other than what you are, you'd find it hard. I bet you grew up in a nice house, didn't you? Had a mother and father? Had enough money to get you that fancy education and no doors were closed to you! The world was yours to enjoy and nothing was out of your reach but that which you would not allow yourself!"

"What do you mean 'not allow myself'? What are you speaking of?"

"It's rather revealing of a man's character, how he treats women. And, oh, John... what a mess you are... It's almost sweet! Any fool can see what you want, but you won't allow yourself to ask for it, will you? Tell me, John Watson, can you even conceive of a world where one indulges their desires and yet remains a good person?"

"If I'm honest, no. I cannot."

"A shame, since that's the only world you could be happy in. But that's you in a nutshell, isn't it? Long-suffering John Watson: the sole architect of all his misfortune."

"You pretend to know me, madam, but you don't. I was shot, did you know that? In the army—"

But she cut me off. "Were you conscripted?" she asked. "Or did you enlist voluntarily?"

"Well, I… I enlisted, but… you have no idea the things I've seen and done on my adventures with Holmes!"

"And tell me, Doctor, did he force you to come? Holmes—gentle and kind—how did he inflict his fate on you?"

"He didn't, I suppose…"

"No. Those are all misfortunes you brought upon yourself. Some people are born with worse, you know. That urchin you had announce your 'accident' could probably tell you something of what it feels like to lead a life bereft of choices. So could I. Perhaps before you sit in judgment of me, John Watson, you ought to learn something of the challenges arrayed against me, from the moment I came into this world. And yet, with only my mind, I have conquered them all!"

I must have rolled my eyes, for she laughed and conceded, "Very well. *And my looks*. But really, those almost spoil the fun. The table is tilted. The game's too easy. Nevertheless, I intend to win. That is what we are here to discuss. Are you ready?"

From the other room came a rattling clatter as Holmes accidentally pulled down a shelf.

"By God, he's taking forever," I muttered.

"Oh, let him have his fun. Besides, Holmes is already neutralized. We're here for you today, John. I'm going to tell you what I'm doing. Then you are going to walk out of here, alive, which is better than you deserve. The price you'll pay is this: you are not going to interfere with my plans."

"You think so?"

"I do. Now, what do you know of Moriarty's great quest?"

"Immortality, according to Holmes."

"Partly. More than that, though. He wants to exist at every point in history, in every dimension. He's seen enough of the worlds to know just how much a person misses out on. He can't bear to not know a thing. He can't stand that he'll only die once. If by cancer, then he'll never know what it's like to be impaled by a spear. If a spear, then what is it like to be eaten away by acid? What did it feel like to kiss Cleopatra? What did it feel like to *be* Cleopatra? And those are only some of the things he wants to know of *this* world. There are thousands of other worlds, it would seem, and he wishes to know everything that has ever occurred in any of them. He wants omniscience, more than immortality. He is a creature of great knowledge, who wishes to know *all*."

"Admirable, in its way," I admitted.

But Irene shook her head. "*Foolish*. When I was young, he took me into his confidence—just as I am taking you into mine. I learned from Moriarty. I let myself be almost his daughter. For years, I thought him the wisest, strongest, most unstoppable force in the universe. Yet, as I grew, I came to realize he was wrong."

"How?"

"What if he didn't like it? What if he knew everything, everywhere, ever, and there was no joy in it? That was his flaw: to assume that everything was enough. Perhaps what he ought to be looking for was a thing that did not exist at all: the answer to the human question. How can we make ourselves happy? Fulfilled? How can we win this strange game we find ourselves thrust into? That is my quest, John. It's not such a bad thing, is it? I'll confess, if the answer turns out to be a thing only one person can enjoy, then that one person shall be me. But if it's a thing I can share with all mankind, I happily will. You should not be opposing me, John. You should be cheering me with every fiber of your being. We should be friends."

I shook my head. "You keep killing people."

"Oh, *so what*? Honestly, you're so frustrating! I could kill *you*, you know! I could even make Holmes do it."

"Then why don't you?"

She gave me a funny little smile. "Because he likes you too well. I can't have him getting sad and accidentally destroying the world before I've solved my riddle. Luckily for you, John, I need you right where you are: by Holmes's side, keeping him happy and docile. So, despite your multiple defeats, you get to live. Isn't that nice?"

My look must have been defiant, for the merry gamester look returned to her face and she teased, "Or perhaps your brilliant plan will thwart me and I'll be in your power. I must say, though, it isn't seeming likely. How long is that second move supposed to take?"

"Not nearly this long," I admitted. "Honestly, I'm a bit horrified. If things had gone differently…"

"Oh, you'd have been in terrible danger," Irene agreed.

From the other room came another crash and a frightened yelp. What was Holmes doing in there?

"Would you care for tea, while we wait?" Irene asked.

"You know, for the first time I can remember, I'm not actually in the mood for tea."

"No? What *are* you in the mood for?"

I could tell she was teasing me—picking at my inexperience in the ways of the heart. But it mattered not. As I stumbled over my reply, my second card turned. The smoke-lie. From outside a voice shouted, "Halp! Oh, halp! Fire! Briony Lodge is on fire!"

"That sounds like your wonderful little urchin," Irene noted. "I'm glad he had more to do. A friend like that should never go underused."

Behind me, the sitting-room door burst open. There stood Holmes, amidst billowing white clouds of smoke.

"Hello," he said. "Well… mixed news. I'm afraid I was unable to locate the items we were looking for, Watson. I'm sorry. Yet, I am even more sorry for you, Miss Adler. In my search it seems I have clumsily set fire to your home. Really, just… a thousand apologies."

"No, that's all right. It's rented, you know."

Holmes blinked, surprised at her lack of concern.

"Besides," Irene noted, "I can't help but notice the distinct odor of potassium chlorate. That's what smoke bombs are made of, isn't it? It seems as if I'm being duped."

"Oh. Well, it certainly doesn't *feel* like you're being duped," said Holmes.

I couldn't help but agree. "I really had only five—perhaps ten—seconds to plan, so…"

Irene smiled at us and suggested, "Now, Mr. Holmes, why don't you take a seat next to Watson, there? We must discuss the terms of your surrender, mustn't we?"

I shifted over a bit to make room and Holmes sat sheepishly down beside me. He stared down at his lap and mumbled, "I'm sorry, Watson. But… er… you know, there is—"

"Hush, Holmes."

"Well, I will, but—"

"There's no use."

The first billows of smoke wrapped around my ankles. I coughed once or twice, but smoke had no power to make me any more miserable than I already was.

"Now, are you sure you gentlemen wouldn't care for some tea?" Irene asked.

"No, thank you," I said.

"I don't really… er… *drink*," said Holmes.

"Very well, then we shall begin," Irene said, pleasantly. "Now, my present plans take me far from England. Nonetheless I may, in the future, find myself in need of a powerful sorcerer or a resourceful agent…"

"Er… Hey, Watson, do you have a moment?" said Holmes.

"Holmes! We must pay attention! We must seek every opportunity to turn this situation to our advantage, or at least ameliorate the damage."

"I see that, but—"

"But what, Holmes?"

"You know how I was supposed to sneak out, set off the smoke rocket and pretend the house was on fire?"

"Yes! Everybody knows that, Holmes. *Everybody!*"

"Right, but… would you be angry if… if I really, accidentally *did* set the house on fire?"

And there it was: my third move. My only real chance. The twist.

Irene thought she knew Holmes, did she? Then wouldn't she know that was exactly the sort of mistake he was likely to make? How deeply did she trust her own intellect? How deeply did she disdain Holmes's? How certain was she that she'd predicted every aspect of my plan? I had to keep my eyes on Holmes. I had to keep my expression incredulous and angry. I must give her no clue. Just in the corner of my eye, I saw Irene Adler experience a moment of doubt. Her eyes flew to—was it the window? No… The painting over the mantel!

Yet, in an instant, my hope was gone. Even as she dropped into that ready-to-run crouch, she caught herself. A moment of realization spread over her face and she turned slowly towards me.

"Oh, well played, John," she said. She seemed

genuinely pleased. "A twist. You've acquitted yourself very well, I must say. By God, it's fun to play against somebody who can challenge me, from time to time. Oh, you gave me a fright. Look at me, my heart's pounding!"

I wilted. Until that moment… I don't know… there'd still been hope. Remote? Absolutely. A hope only a fool could cling to? Well, yes. Yet even that was enough to cheer me. Just having a card still left to turn meant that I'd still been in the game. But now, my game was up. Except…

Holmes cleared his throat. "Right, well… We all know I was supposed to set off the rocket. Then I was supposed to come in here and pretend the house was on fire. Then, when that didn't work, I was supposed to pretend I didn't just *pretend* to light the house on fire. But… um… what if I *really did* really did light the house on fire?"

"No!" cried Irene and I, together. "What?"

"I couldn't get it lit!" Holmes explained.

I threw a furious glance at Holmes and Irene Adler threw one at me, as we both wondered, "*Double* twist?"

"So I used a little demon-fire. But then it turns out it was rather a lot of demon-fire, so…"

Any doubt that remained was extinguished by that first whiff of *definitely-not-potassium-chlorate-smoke-but-actual-wood-and-plaster-smoke* smoke. Over the sound of distant crackling—just becoming audible—we heard a voice cry, "Oh, bugger! It really is! Halp! Actual fire! Briony Lodge is on not-pretend fire! Aw, criminy! I'm out of here!"

"Damn it!" Irene and I howled. I glanced about for the best escape route, but Irene had other concerns. She rushed to the mantel, grabbed her own portrait with both hands and yanked. She threw the excellent painting in the corner and reached for what lay behind: a built-in wall safe.

"Holmes! Get the safe!" I cried, beginning to choke on the first clouds of black, very-actual smoke.

"What do you mean?"

"Magic! Grab it!"

Holmes raised both hands towards the safe and bent his fingers. The plaster around the safe crumbled. Irene gave a cry as the safe tipped forward and fell out of the wall. It would have crushed her foot if she hadn't yanked it clear at the last second. Even worse, the wall deformed all the way to the ceiling. With a groan, the ceiling bowed down for a moment, then collapsed, showering the far corners of the room with burning floorboards and bedclothes. For a moment, all was chaos, the room filled with swirling dust and smoke.

"The fire is upstairs, too?" I howled.

"By now?" said Holmes, with a shrug. "I'd bet it's practically everywhere."

"Damn it, Holmes!"

"What? I tried to tell you!"

"Where's Irene?"

Sure enough, she was gone. She must have made her move the very instant the ceiling fell in. There wasn't enough wreckage to have buried her. At least we had the safe. And I'd been right, her treasures had been concealed in this very room the whole time. I ran to the safe, grabbed it, and pulled. No good. The thing was so heavy it had gone halfway through the floor. There was no hope I'd be able to carry it out on my own.

"Leave it, Watson! You're in danger!"

"I don't care! Get the safe!"

"Oh, very well," said Holmes, with an exasperated sigh. Suddenly the safe rose and floated, hovering in the air before me.

"Not like *that*!"

"Well how then, Mr. Choosy?"

Over the sound of the dying house, I could just hear the first constable's whistle as the alarm was raised.

"You don't think two men leaving the scene of a burning house with a levitating safe might command a bit of attention?"

"I've no time to debate the point, Watson. I'm afraid it's time to go."

With that, Holmes flicked his hand sideways and the safe flew through the front window and bounced out into the garden. Disappointed as I was with his lack of subtlety, I had to admit Holmes had a point. The house was becoming truly dangerous and this sudden route of egress was not unwelcome. I cut my hand on a windowpane on the way out, but overall our exit was pleasantly expedient. As soon as we were out on the lawn the safe bobbed helpfully up into the air again.

"Damn it, Holmes!"

"Well, you want it, don't you?"

Cursing, I removed my jacket and threw it over the hovering steel box. Yes. That was better. Now I would just… er… pretend that I had bought a large square bag of groceries and was carrying it home with my jacket over it, in case it should rain. Was I muddied, bloodied and coughing from smoke inhalation? What of it? It had been a lively day at the grocer's—that was all—and it had nothing to do with the burning building just behind me. That was certainly what we'd try to convince the constables of when they arrived. Which, by the sound of things, could not be more than one or two minutes hence. So…

Back streets and all haste—always a fine way to get to 221B. I was winded and sweaty as I followed the hovering safe up the stairs, through the sitting room and into my chamber. When Holmes lowered it to the floor, the heavy clunk drew a gasp of surprise from my wardrobe. Apparently, His Majesty had been sleeping. But he pushed the door open with his foot and asked, "Have you got it? My picture?"

"We're not sure," I told him. "We certainly have divested Miss Adler of some of her treasures, but it will take time to determine the full scope of our victory. I must examine the—"

I was about to say "locking mechanism" but before I could, the safe gave out a terrible shriek, then a little pop, and the main dial ripped out, sailed just past my head, rebounded off the ceiling and clattered across the floor.

"Damn it, Holmes!"

"Oh come now, Watson," Warlock scoffed. "We both know you'd have been at that thing for months. Besides, compared to the amount of magic it took to levitate the thing here, the transgression is minor. Now, hurry and open it up! What did we get? What did we get?"

The door swung open to reveal a brown paper parcel that clearly contained a cabinet-sized photograph and—my heart caught in my throat—the battered leaden case Irene Adler had stolen from us. Moriarty's prison. Yet, even as I lifted it free, I could tell something was wrong. There was no gentle flutter as there had been before, no vibration of life from within the box. Hopefully, and yet ruefully, I slid the catch and bent up one corner of the lid.

There was nothing.

Well… I mean there was no disembodied spirit of Holmes's great nemesis. Only a slip of paper. Drawing it out, I found a picture of an elderly wizard—Merlin, I fancied—lifting up his robes to me and proudly displaying his droopy old buttocks. Apparently, to Irene Adler's list of artistic accomplishments, I would need to add "lewd sketch artist". I staggered back and sat heavily down upon the corner of my bed.

Outmaneuvered, again.

And I was not to be the only one. As soon as Holmes untied him, Von Ormstein pounced upon the parcel and tore away the paper. As soon as his eyes fell on the portrait within, he gave a cry of alarm and flung it away, crying, "Ugh! By God! She flaunts it in my face: the only drawback to a match with a human! Not a single tentacle, anywhere."

A solitary piece of paper fluttered to the ground—a parting note from Von Ormstein's old flame:

Your Majesty is foolish to presume I would use the items at my disposal to thwart your match to House von Saxe-Meiningen. Did you imagine I would choose to expend my leverage upon you <u>before</u> you had a claim to the throne of Scandinavia? Really, Willie, think these things through. Perhaps one day you will have something I want badly enough that our paths may meet again. Until then, I wish you joy in your upcoming nuptials.

Give Clotilde my regards.
And my sympathy.
Irene Adler

I reached for the photo Miss Adler had included and—much like Von Ormstein—recoiled when I saw it, yet for quite a different reason. The picture was of Irene, dressed in… well… I suppose "a slightly undersized doily" would be the best description. Though it had been presented to Wilhelm, it was clearly intended for me. I could tell, because she'd signed it:

With fond memories of my doctor, who will, I trust, be able to identify the pertinent anatomy.

Really, just…

What a woman! I remembered her joy when I let Von Ormstein's involvement slip out. She'd said she wished she could see our faces, because she had been so very clever. And yes, she certainly had. To read the clarity of thought in her note to Von Ormstein, one could easily be forgiven for assuming her to be only a mind—a creature of disembodied ideas, always scheming, always three steps ahead. Yet then, in the next instant—gazing salaciously at that picture—it was easy to think of her as nothing but a body, an object of temptation. Indeed, hundreds before me had made exactly that mistake, granting Irene Adler a deadly advantage.

I think that was the moment Holmes proved correct— the moment my fascination became irreversible. Before then, if someone had asked me to describe my ideal match, I'd have spoken of upbringing, of an ideal living companion or a mother for my children. But no. I'd never known what my heart truly needed, until that day. Indeed, it would take years of reflection to finally come to admit what I truly desire…

To be *bested*.

Who could I ever respect more? No matter how I threw myself against her, no matter the stratagem I devised, I was never her equal. I strived to be, again and again, but… How frustrating! And yet, how exhilarating! I didn't want to admit her brilliance, yet she forced me to at every turn. From that moment forth, there was no other girl who could command my attention for long. Only *the Woman*. Only Irene Adler.

Behind me, Holmes cleared his throat. "Though I have failed to deliver the desired photograph, I nevertheless claim my fee. The immediate danger to His Majesty is ended—the wedding can proceed. I therefore demand the return of my soul-blade and all the knowledge of binding magics I have been promised."

Von Ormstein spluttered and protested, "By what right do you claim your full price, sir, when the full service has not been rendered?"

"Because I am yet in possession of an item His Majesty might wish returned to him."

"Oh? And what might this item be?"

"*His Majesty.*"

"Ah… so you are."

And that is where matters may have rested, if I'd been wise. Holmes and Von Ormstein both seemed happy to accept defeat and move forward. I could not say the same. Shaking the cobwebs from my mind, I sprang to my feet and cried, "No! Get up! Get your coat, Holmes!"

"I've still got my coat."

"Good! We've got to… got to move!"

"Where? Why? Sit down, Watson."

"No! She's still in our grasp, don't you see? Her every barb seems to be a parting shot, does it not? I believe she truly is leaving. What if she really does intend to take the steamer to New York? What if she intends to use that train car Norton hired?"

"By the twelve gods!" Holmes yelled, springing to his feet. "What is wrong with you, Watson? Exactly how many times do you need to be defeated in a single day?"

"I will not surrender! Not while there is still a chance for victory! Come on!"

"No! I'll not be party to this," said Holmes, crossing

his arms over his chest. "Think of how easily she always bests you, Watson. Think of all you could have lost today. At least you're alive, eh? Look, you've even still got all your arms and legs. Really, if I'd been betting on today's outcome, I could never have been so optimistic. So leave off, won't you?"

"No!" I shouted and started for the door. I charged down the steps to Baker Street and out into the gathering night. Twilight, already? What time did I have? Not much, to be sure. How would I find out which train, which car? I needed a moment to plan. Yet, it could wait. I must go back to St. John's Wood. I could plan in the cab. I needed a cab. As I stepped to the curb to hail one, I bumped into a young fellow dressed in an ulster. Though the night was mild, he had the collar turned up and his hat pulled low, as if he expected a sudden deluge.

"Oh! Pardon me," I mumbled.

"I just wanted to wish you a most imprudent 'good night'," he replied.

"Er… what?"

And he did. He reached up, grabbed my face, pulled me low and kissed me. I had only a fleeting instant to catch the flash of those mischievous green eyes, the slope of that perfect jaw, covered in painted-on stubble.

Kissing Irene Adler was nothing like kissing Violet Hunter. With Violet it had been, at worst, a transaction. At best, kissing for kissing's sake. With Irene, it was kissing to a purpose. Oh, there was certainly the presence of unknown delights yet to come. But there was more than that. This was kissing as maneuvering. Kissing as a move in a game she was playing, the nature of which I could not guess.

But I didn't care.

Even as I began to accept it—even as I began to pour myself into that kiss—she thrust me away and laughed in triumph. I stumbled back. My thoughts were confused, my whole body tingling. I was unsteady on my feet. The many romantic poems I'd been forced to read at school had informed me that these were signs of love, but I'd never expected to actually *feel* them. I stared down at her, in wonderment. She gazed back with winsome amusement, then reached into her pocket, withdrew a cloth and wiped away her lip-rouge.

Which was odd…

A master of disguise. A beautiful woman. Standing with a near-perfect approximation of male appearance.

And she'd chosen to wear *lip-rouge*?

Something wasn't right. I blinked away my confusion and tried to focus my thoughts. But it was hard.

"Oh, John, you're just too tenacious," she said. "I gave you two chances to beg off. *Two!*"

What was she talking about? The wave of love symptoms I was currently suffering made it difficult to tell. And then, foggily, as if from a distance deep inside me, the doctor in me stepped forth to remind me that these were symptoms of more than only love.

Dizziness.

Numbness.

Confusion.

Loss of motor control.

"Oh! I've got it!" I cried, flush with victorious revelation. "*Poison lip-rouge!*"

She smiled at me with a strange mix of fondness, pity and regret, then confirmed, "Poison lip-rouge."

I tumbled forward into the street. Through the haze of drug stupor, I could just hear the residents of Baker Street gathering round to express concern and rifle my pockets. I could not hear the Woman. I didn't know if she had stayed to watch, or merely went upon her way. But there was nothing to stop her now. Nothing to prevent the most worthy nemesis I'd ever encountered from fading back into the shadows in possession of two of nine foci that could control this planet's most powerful magical creatures and the disembodied rune of the man who would prove humanity's destroyer. As the blackness closed over me, I think—*I think*—I managed to mumble:

"Miss Adler?

"Are you still there, Miss Adler?

"I am afraid I'm in love with you."

ACKNOWLEDGEMENTS

THANKS TO MY SUPPORT STAFF: MIRANDA AND THE NEW baby! Stalwart Sam Morgan, who's been with me through it all. Sam Matthews, who has stepped in to fill the baby-gap and edit this volume. Ah, everyone should have a couple of Sams.

Thanks to Sean Patella-Buckley, who's getting so damn good I'm beginning to feel my words are just illustration-supporters.

Thanks to that bastion of Victorian dog-murder, Sir Arthur Conan Doyle. Seriously, that dude had a problem. And yes, I know I've killed three dogs in three books, but it's not my fault! They were all in the originals. I guess ol' Artie was a cat guy.

ABOUT THE AUTHOR

GABRIEL DENNING LIVES IN LAS VEGAS WITH HIS WIFE and two daughters. Oh, and a dog. And millions of micro-organisms. He's a twenty-year veteran of Orlando Theatersports, Seattle Theatersports, Jet City Improv and has finally figured out to write some of that stuff down. His first novel, *Warlock Holmes: A Study in Brimstone*, was published in 2016, and the *Booklist* review said "Mashup fans will be eagerly awaiting more," which is why he wrote the sequels.

WARLOCK HOLMES

A STUDY IN BRIMSTONE

G.S. DENNING

Sherlock Holmes is an unparalleled genius who uses the gift of deduction and reason to solve the most vexing of crimes. Warlock Holmes, however, is not. He may be a font of arcane power, but frankly he couldn't deduce his way out of a paper bag. The only things he's got going for him are the might of a thousand demons, the spirit of Moriarty trapped in his head, and his stalwart companion Dr. John Watson, who is always there to guide him through the treacherous shoals of Victorian propriety… and save him from a gruesome death every now and again.

Praise for the series:

"I laughed like a loon"
James Lovegrove

"Irreverent, hilarious and a ripping good yarn to boot"
George Mann

WARLOCK HOLMES

THE HELL-HOUND OF THE BASKERVILLES

G.S. DENNING

The game's afoot once more as the long-suffering Dr. John Watson and a bedridden and somewhat pungent Warlock Holmes (though he's getting better) face off against Moriarty's gang, the Pinkertons, flesh-eating horses, a parliament of imps, boredom, Surrey, a succubus, an overly Canadian aristocrat, a tricycle fight to the death and the dreaded Pumpcrow. Oh, and a hell-hound, one assumes.

Praise for the series:

"A rich seam of black comedy"
SFX

"Funny, clever, and entertaining"
Kirkus

WRITTEN IN DEAD WAX

A VINYL DETECTIVE NOVEL

ANDREW CARTMEL

He is a record collector – a connoisseur of vinyl, hunting out rare and elusive LPs. His business card describes him as the "Vinyl Detective" and some people take this more literally than others. Like the beautiful, mysterious woman who wants to pay him a large sum of money to find a priceless lost recording – on behalf of an extremely wealthy (and rather sinister) shadowy client. Given that he's just about to run out of cat biscuits, this gets our hero's full attention. So begins a painful and dangerous odyssey in search of the rarest jazz record of them all…

"An irresistible blend of murder, mystery and music… our protagonist seeks to find the rarest of records – and incidentally solve a murder, right a great historical injustice and, if he's very lucky, avoid dying in the process."
Ben Aaronovitch, bestselling author of *Rivers of London*

"The Vinyl Detective is one of the sharpest and most original characters I've seen for a long time."
David Quantick

For more fantastic fiction, author events, competitions,
limited editions and more

VISIT OUR WEBSITE
titanbooks.com

LIKE US ON FACEBOOK
facebook.com/titanbooks

FOLLOW US ON TWITTER
@TitanBooks

EMAIL US
readerfeedback@titanemail.com